Dragons'
Inferno

Dragons' Inferno

BOOK 2 IN THE DRAGON UNCHAINED TRILOGY

Susan Tietjen

Sunbright Press   Crescent City, CA

DEDICATION

This book is dedicated to those faithful few who are willing to sacrifice all, even themselves, for the good of others.

Susan

*"This above all; to thine own self be true,
And it must follow as the night the day;
Thou canst not then be false to any man."*

William Shakespeare

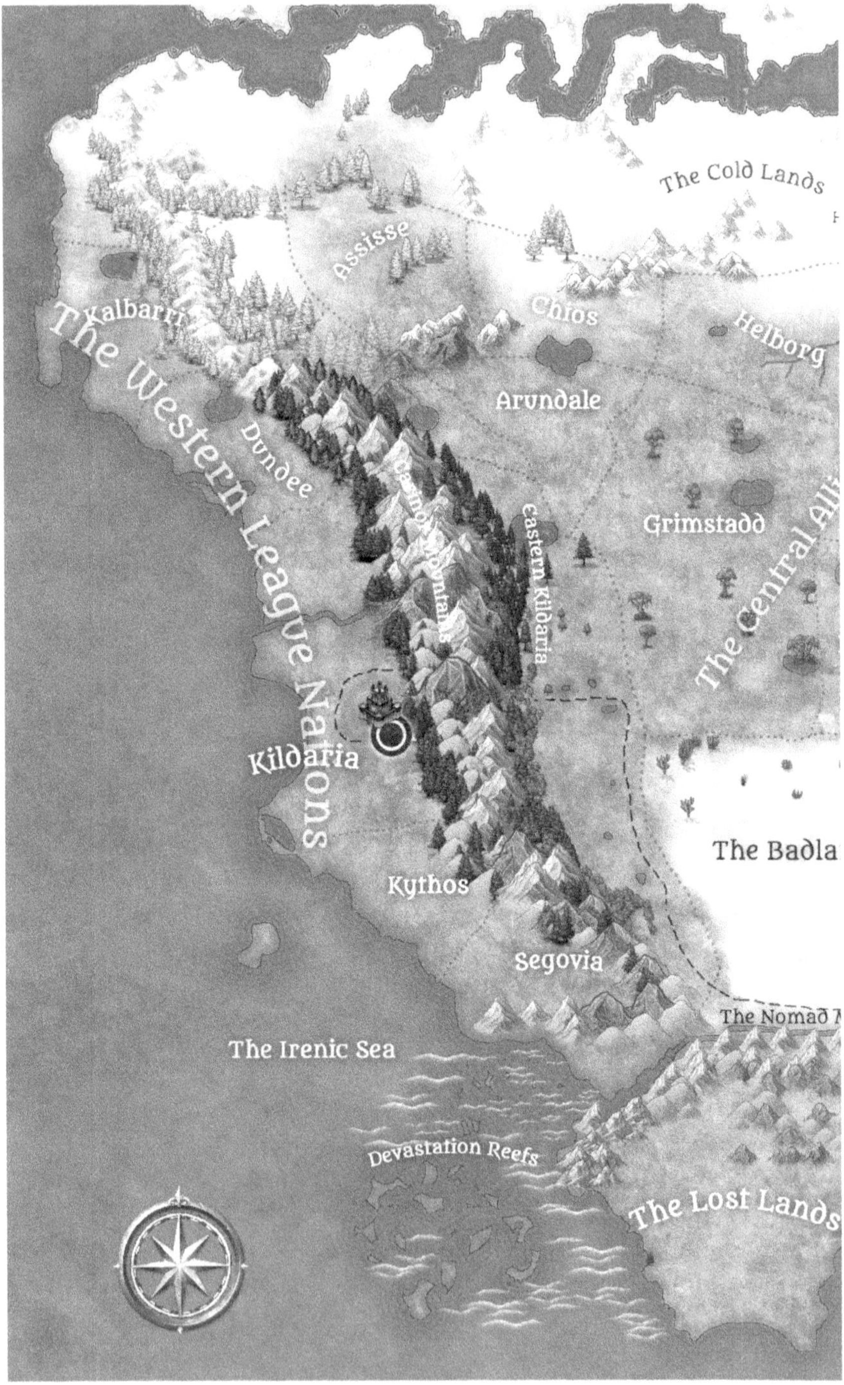
The Cold Lands
Assisse
Chios
Helborg
Kalbarri
The Western League Nations
Arundale
Dundee
Grimstadd
Eastern Kildaria
The Central Alli
Kildaria
The Badla
Kythos
Segovia
The Nomad
The Irenic Sea
Devastation Reefs
The Lost Lands

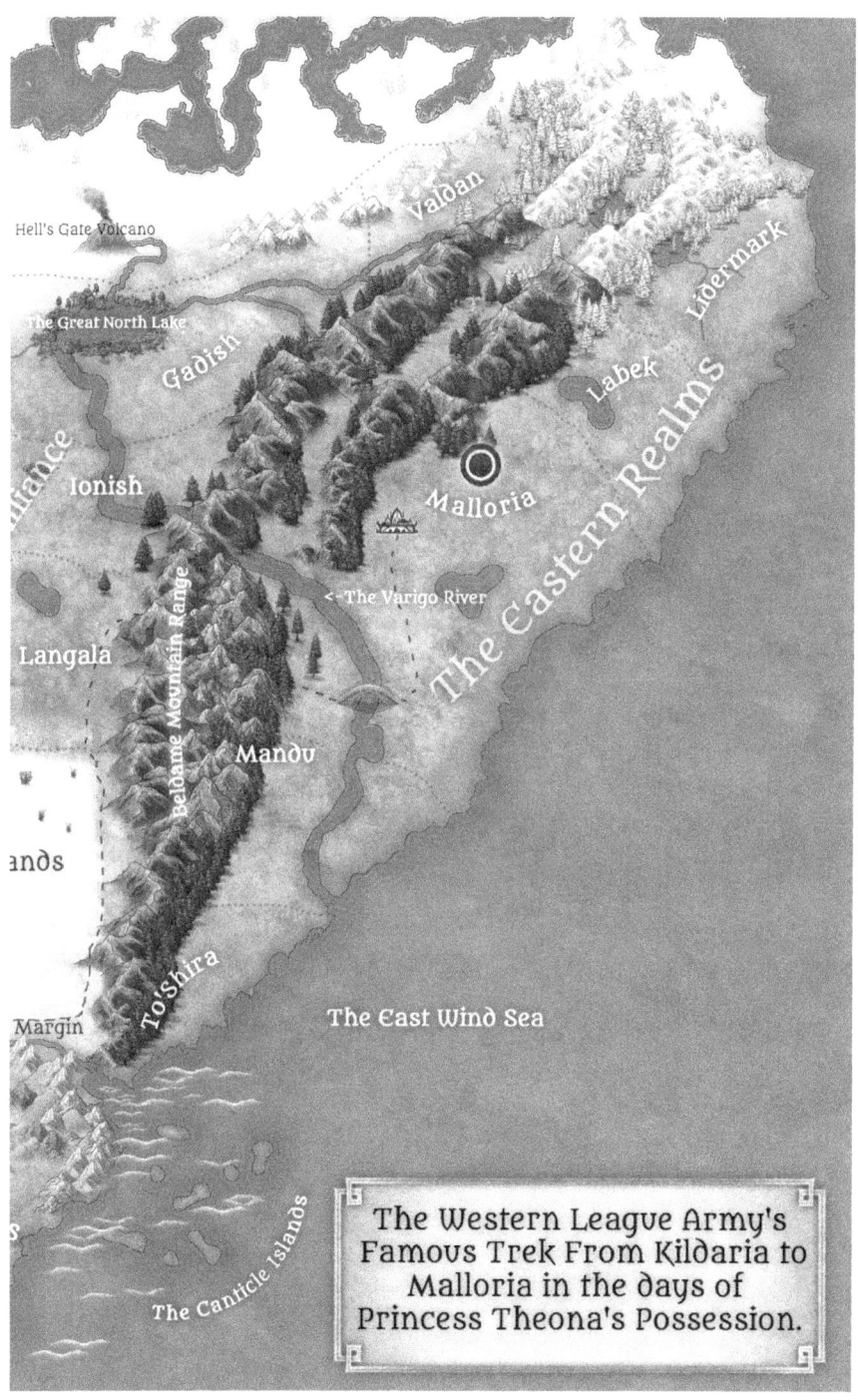

The Western League Army's Famous Trek From Kildaria to Malloria in the days of Princess Theona's Possession.

ACKNOWLEDGEMENTS

Ever valiant is my husband, Richard, who faithfully nags me to get to work when way too many things drag me off into the real world; who defends me, shares my story and my books with anyone and everyone he meets; and who still, after all these years, believes in me. Thank you, handsome.

Helen Keller once said, "Alone we can do so little; together we can do so much." That is as true about writing a book as it is about building a village. Writers provide the building blocks, but our readers apply the mortar. Without them, our little village might end up a pile of rubble.

Thank you to my loyalist readers for sticking with me despite it taking a very long time to get this book released. I'd like to say it's because it *is* a work of art and needed to be chiseled out of marble, but in truth, life throws us roadblocks (like COVID) and no matter how hard it is, we have to either go over, under, around or through them, and as Mike Berry said, "hard work ain't so easy."

Loving thanks goes to: Jessica Cole; Lori Standring, Paul Felix, Ryan Herle; and to Nick Svolos, Michael Caldwell, Catherine Andrews, and the rest of the gang at the Redwood Writers Group. And as always, my appreciation and my love to my husband, Richard, who continues to be my knight in shining armor.

Dear readers, new or seasoned, writers survive on reviews, word of mouth, and those who share. Please do.

Book 3 is in the making. I can hardly wait to find out what happens next!

From *The Confessions of Theona Seville*

I am Theona McArthur Seville, the daughter of a duke, a descendent of Cleary the Brave, and if I am successful, the future Queen of Malloria.

On my sixteenth birthday, I broke a sacred Kildarian law. I opened The Keeper, an ancient artifact carved out of Dreamwood and enchanted by the Elds of Kildaria more than five hundred years ago. They fashioned it as a prison for unspeakable evil.

I allowed that evil to entice me, to convince me The Keeper could help me find the boy I'd dreamed about and loved for years. After all, I'd dreamwalked with him inside The Keeper, in a magical village called Draakheda, since we were small children.

Instead, my opening The Keeper undid everything for which Cleary and my people had fought and for which too many of them had died. I set the monsters within it free, and they possessed me. Kildaria's King Desmond cared nothing about why I'd broken the law. He only knew I'd jeopardized the world with my disobedience and sentenced me to death.

My father's Elden counselor and personal advisor, Eld York, comforted me as I awaited execution. Magic had long been feared, but he admitted Kildaria had lost sight of the truth: magic was neither good nor bad, it was a higher power granted by our deity, Elam, and could be used for either. Cleary the Brave had chosen good, as did the Elds, who were healers and comforters. The evil sorcerers possessing me had chosen wickedness. Thus, York cautioned me to be wary of the draw of magic even in the short time I had left, because if I lost control, it could turn me into a monster.

In prison, I pondered my brief life. Every school child learned the origin of The Keeper, designed to trap the three sorcerers who conjured the first dragon ages ago, a blend of horse, serpent, and eagle. That Mother Dragon, unknowingly pregnant at the time of the conjuring, soon gave birth to bigger and more ferocious dragons, which the sorcerers enslaved and rode to terrorize the world for more than a century.

The sorcerer-dragon duos were nearly invincible so long as they remained in contact with each other. Even Cleary couldn't kill them. Pythius, the sorcerer of serpents, proved it when he stepped off his dragon, Murcod, to fight Cleary hand-to-hand. Cleary killed both with Slayer, his Elden-forged sword, but when he struck the two remaining sorcerers' dragons, the best the enchanted sword could do was lock their souls inside The Keeper.

Tales designed to make children fear magic included the story of Cleary's own granddaughter, Moriana McArthur, who did what I had done ten years after that last battle. She opened The Keeper and became possessed—as I was now—and the evil spirits turned her into one of them, as I struggled not to do.

Cleary thwarted the sorcerers' plot against the world by using Slayer on Moriana and sending her soul along with those of the two sorcerers and their pair of magic-born dragons back inside The Keeper.

Soon after I became possessed, the sorcerers awakened magical abilities I didn't know I had, and I learned why Kildaria feared both sorcerers and magic. The spirits spoke to me in my mind and then began to appear to me, along with their dragons. They promised to save me from execution…in exchange for learning to use magic to return them to mortality.

The dragons were also magical, even if they couldn't wield magic, and they could change into any of the forms from which they were created and combinations of them. They taught me to do the same. I could shape-change into creatures from any of the equine, bird, and serpent families—even into a winged horse, a leviathan…or a dragon.

I had no desire to die, which meant I had to comply with the sorcerers, but my deepest hope was to learn how to free myself and destroy them.

When a foreign prince arrived in Kildaria to solicit help in fighting a war soon to be launched by the Central Alliance, it shocked me to recognize him. Gideon Seville, the Crown Prince and Heir Apparent of the Kingdom of Malloria, was the boy with whom I'd dreamwalked inside The Keeper—now grown into a man.

In a chance meeting, Prince Gideon also recognized me and offered to marry me—thus staying my execution—so that he could take me back to his kingdom, where he believed his Elden leaders might be able to exorcise these evil spirits.

King Desmond gave us small advance groups of warriors from each of the five Western League nations as a token offering to Gideon. They weren't enough, but as we celebrated our wedding day, Gideon felt certain the king would soon grant the rest of the troops we needed. After that, all that remained to be seen was whether we'd survive the arduous trip through the Badlands to a secret pass in the Beldame Mountains on our trek to Malloria, a journey promising both hope and unparalleled danger.

And so began our adventure, filled with traitors, murderers, and thieves; with ever-demanding sorcerers determined I learn how to wield magic; with people who hated me enough to try to poison me and my family. Nothing they did stopped my marriage to the prince, and we were determined—if King Desmond granted his support—to prepare an army of mounted troops the likes of which our small continent had never seen, to march to the shores of the East Wind Sea, and to join with the forces of the Eastern Realms.

CHAPTER 1

Prince Gideon, my new husband of a mere two nights and two days, brushed a curled finger across my cheek, his face worried and his eyes sad.

"Are you sure you're alright, Theona?" he asked with concern.

I breathed deep to steady my nerves, to force a smile and ignore the dismay from the lie I was about to tell. I'd hoped never to tell another lie, but the reasons justified the means, or so I hoped. First, I couldn't get in the way of my prince's responsibilities, even if they interrupted our brief honeymoon. And second.... I paused and took a deep breath.

"I'll be fine, Gideon," I insisted, pressing his hand against my face. It felt cool and comforting on my feverish skin, but it wasn't enough. Truly, what I needed at this very moment was magical and something Gideon couldn't provide. I was tortured by guilt, loathe to admit it even to myself, but I was glad he'd leave me alone.

He leaned down and murmured in my ear. "I refuse to abandon you if you're not feeling well."

I shook my head. "You must take care of your duties, my love. If I need anything, your guards are just outside the door."

He sighed, his gorgeous violet eyes searching my face. He glanced toward the open door, where his most trusted colleagues, General Warren Bellamy, and Sir Lance Arnoe, stood talking with two generals from Kalbarri and Dundee. Talking and waiting.

Unlike some of the Western League leaders, these two had befriended my prince and believed in his message that the Central Alliance was plotting war on a massive scale. They were ready to work with both Kildaria and Malloria in striking it down before it became something no one could stop.

Despite the doubters, Kildaria's king, my king, King Desmond Fitzpatrick, had ordered armies to be sent to County Leeds from all five of the League kingdoms: Kythos, Segovia, Kalbarri, Dundee, and, of course, Kildaria. He'd selected his own troops almost immediately, but the other four kingdoms barely placated King Desmond eight days ago by sending small advance troops instead.

Thankfully, word had just come today that the remaining troops, all of them, would arrive in the capital some time tomorrow! The news ought to have heartened everyone, but instead, fights had broken out and damage had been found throughout every camp: broken wagon wheels, cut reins and saddle girths, drinking water spoiled with salt, bags of grain slashed and spilled on the ground. Warriors had also suffered injuries, some serious, as had some horses.

Three men had been arrested tonight, but no doubt there were others, and Gideon's absence had his people bad-tempered. He needed to be with them, to reassure them, although he promised it wouldn't take long.

I knew he was wrong. King Desmond had just ordered all the army's leaders to join him in the War Room within the hour, where they'd likely spend the night in debate. Beyond that, the magical gift I bore of foretelling, the dark-orange-colored *parhelia* of prophecy, told me that my prince wouldn't—couldn't—keep his promise.

I blinked teary eyes against the sadness of it, wishing I had better control over the gift—over any of the *parhelia* with which I'd been born, but I didn't. For that matter, I wished I didn't have any of the gifts at all. Knowing too much was dangerous; and having magic was what had caused me to break Kildarian law.

"Please go," I insisted, pressing his arm. "You're needed. You mustn't worry about me."

"Why won't you let Kendal stay with you? She is your maid, after all."

"Not anymore. Father cannot announce her engagement to Ian until she has severed her ties with me." Ian was my eldest brother and heir to my father's duchy. "Besides, it's late and I'm already prepared for bed. I've no need to disturb her."

He kissed my brow with tenderness. "I'll see you in a few hours," he insisted. "We deserve the last night of our honeymoon together."

I gave him a weary smile. He had enough on his mind without knowing what I knew about his immediate future.

I loved that he kissed me soundly, not caring the others watched us. Then they whisked my prince away. The door locked and silence fell. Painful, delightful, amazing silence. As close to alone as I could come, considering I'd become possessed by five evil shades just twelve days ago.

I tightened my shields as the monsters escalated their struggle inside me. They wanted out and would cut me down if I didn't do it soon, but I couldn't do it here.

In fact, I couldn't do it all until I'd addressed the malady raging within me that was even worse than the sorcerers. The desire for magic had rooted itself deep in my very soul, and I knew refusing it would annihilate me.

Fever now trailing perspiration down my forehead and making me shake, I hurried to the bedside table where I'd tossed the dreaded magical ring Moriana the Sorceress had insisted I wear. After I slid it onto my right hand, I fastened my Dreamwood bracelet on the same wrist, supposedly a modicum of protection from the sorcerers. Then I blew out the lamp on the bedside table, slipped onto the outside balcony, and in the darkness, transformed into an owl.

The thrill of that moment eclipsed the crushing pain of shape-changing. The power of magic took my breath away! Breaking free of my earthbound chains, I soared into the night!

The air smelled of freedom to my combined human-owl senses, and I relished the view below me of the courtyard's evening busyness. Torches along the battlements and on the walls of the two guest buildings, which faced each other across the courtyard and at each end of the castle, cast flickering streaks of light and shadow over the grounds. Two men in the courtyard pointed at me as I flew by.

Laughing inside, I raced away, thrilling in the use of my magical talents. I ached to assume the other forms I could take, to run through the meadows as a horse, my mane and tail flying behind me; to slide through the shadows as a serpent, in search of prey.

But for now, safely away from spectators, I changed into a dragon!

I roared with exhilaration. I was free of chains, free of brick walls and courtly demands! Free of the limitations of my own body. Not for long, but at least for the next several minutes.

The stars winked at me, as if applauding my passing. I doubled my speed and rose, higher and higher, until my lungs strained against the thinning air, then leveled off. Finally, the fever departed and the hunger for magic raging in my gut calmed, telling me that for now, the magic wouldn't destroy me.

How beautiful it was here. I'd forgotten the serenity of Kildaria at night. I swung toward the sea, loving the scent and the cool wisps of fog that hung in the eddies, the crash of the surf below me. Turning south, I continued to ignore the wrestling of the sorcerers inside me. My magic felt calmer, but I wanted to appease my curiosity.

I passed the outskirts of Leeds and overflew my home in County Mithradell. Lamp and candlelight gleamed in township windows along the way. Across the open fields I flew, fields that went on for what seemed forever between Mithradell and Thistleshire. Before I reached County Thistleshire, however, the scent of burning wood assailed my dragon nostrils. Far more of it than an ordinary household fireplace, I surmised. I slowed in amazement when I saw a collection of campfires and bright torches ahead. The truth left me breathless. An army! The flag above the commander's tent signified the troops of County Mithradell! Further on, I saw the camps of Kythos, the first of two nations south of Kildaria. Some miles past them flew the flags of the land of Segovia.

It was true! The armies would arrive tomorrow.

A storm of mixed feelings assailed me. It had taken so long for them to come, I'd nearly convinced myself it would never happen. Their presence meant we'd soon be on our way to Malloria; and as Gideon's bride, I'd be taken from everything I knew: my family, my home, my friends, to a new and legendary place that may or may not welcome me as their princess. Hopefully I'd be standing beside my prince as he helped his country and the people of the Eastern Realm prepare for war with the Central Alliance, and I prayed the Mallorian Elds had a cure for my possession. Once, the trek had seemed like a fairytale, but here was genuine evidence that it was about to come true—for better or for worse.

The wrestling inside me intensified. I couldn't put off releasing the sorcerers any longer. I circled to the back side of Mt. Carinor and landed in a small glade. Returned to my human self, I stood, blowing hard, mouth dry and legs shaking. I'd grown soft. Just two days and two nights of avoiding magic, and despite having been well fed and well rested—as well as I supposed any newlywed princess could be—I already felt weak and tired.

And my magic demanded nourishment.

A small stream bubbled through the glade, and I changed into a night heron and ate and drank freely. Then, dreading what came next, I again became my girl-self, removed my Dreamwood bracelet and tucked it into my sweater pocket, and braced myself as I held back the dragons and opened my shields to the sorcerers.

Some invisible force grabbed me, picked me up and tossed me, screaming, several yards away from the stream! I hit the ground, gasping and nearly blacking out when my head struck a large stone. Then I screamed again when another entity seized me and hurled me in another direction. I threw my hands to my face just before slamming gut first into a tree. Falling to the ground like a rag doll, I cried out when my right arm, and I supposed more than one rib, broke. I sobbed in pain and struggled with my shields, fearing my life depended on not letting the dragons out, too.

Then the mages appeared, Rhesalus and Terius hanging over me like gods ready to squash an ant. Moriana, dark hair draped over her shoulders and blending in with the curves of her form-fitting black leather dress, her full lips painted blood red and unsmiling, was the picture of controlled rage.

"How dare you?" she seethed.

"Fool!" Terius shouted, jerking me to my feet.

The pain in my arm and side nearly undid me and I screamed again.

Terius continued. "You cut us off and now we've no idea what schemes may have gone on behind your back! We cannot protect you if we aren't privy."

I fought to catch the wind they'd knocked out of me, moaning at the excruciating pain.

Rhesalus snarled, "You've wasted precious time playing house with your lover."

"So kill me!" I sobbed in equally excruciating anger. "I hate you! I hate all of you! I didn't ask you to possess me. You haven't protected me; you've ruined my life. If I can't have something as private as my honeymoon with my new husband, then life isn't worth living and I'd rather die."

"Would you?" Moriana intoned. She reached out with a long, dark-red fingernail and set it against my throat, just below my jaw. I felt my pulse beating against it. I gritted my teeth as she raked that sharp talon downward toward my collarbone, leaving a warm, wet ooze behind. It burned, but not as much as the fear of her threat. She would enjoy killing me, although she wouldn't. She needed me. But she would enjoy it.

She tipped her head and watched me as she licked the blood off her fingertip. That coupled with her grin made me feel ill inside. Then I gasped as she transformed into...me! Before I made full sense of it, she began to change again, warping her version of my hair and skin and the shape of my head into a creature that could only be described as a demon.

She grinned again, displaying a set of needle-fine teeth and the claws of a mountain lion, and viciously slashed my left cheek! I shrieked, wondering if a normal mortal would have seen her do this. Or had I truly gone insane and was doing it to myself?

Tears poured, but I held back the sobs as best I could.

"Enough," Rhesalus said sharply. "We *are* wasting time." Grabbing my face to get a good look at my cheek and neck, he ran a hand down my arm and sides and huffed disapproval at his findings. "This won't do," he said, miraculously easing the pain. To Moriana and Terius, he said, "You and your mage partner can treat each other any way you like, but I must put limits on what you do to mine. How long did you close us off, Theona?"

"Two night and two days," I rasped, my throat sore from screaming. I dared flex my arm and took a comfortable breath. He'd healed me!

A goblet of water appeared in Rhesalus's hand, and I flinched, but I took it and drank every drop. "And I've been in chambers with Prince Gideon every minute, so I've no idea what's happened in the world. Torture me if you like, but I can't undo it."

I felt like a small child, trying to sound brave when surrounded by bullies. In a way, I was. I was a sixteen-year-old girl, forced by magic into growth that made me look closer to twenty-two, married to the crown prince of a country on the other side of the continent, and struggling to learn to be a sorceress against my will. Add being possessed by these three evil spirits, their two magical dragons, and an impending war to the mix and my head felt ready to explode.

Rhesalus sent the goblet off into thin air. "No, but we have to fix it. And you must cooperate. You won't like the consequences if you don't."

"As if I have any choice," I muttered. I sobbed harder, and before I knew it, he'd wrapped his arms around me. He smelled of open fields and wildflowers, musk and sage. His unexpected kindness came along with a strange sensation that was…what? Seductive? I shoved away from him, horrified by the thought and blushing to my roots when he chuckled at me.

"I told you, Rhesalus. I won't be your mage partner!" I snarled. "I won't have any man in my life but my husband."

He chuckled. "What harm can a little comforting do, my dear? Look! You're much calmer—"

"Rhesalus," Terius snapped. He and Moriana stood looking toward Leeds and the castle. As long as my shields remained open, their powerful magic allowed them to discover an unlimited number of things both near and far. I sensed the three shared important thoughts, and then Rhesalus turned back to me, his expression alert.

"Your army has nearly arrived," he said.

"Yes. I just found out. Prince Gideon was summoned to a council with King Desmond."

"Not just because of the armies' arrival, however," Rhesalus noted. "There's been trouble."

"Yes, but not involving me."

"We need to fly," Terius interrupted, still searching the skyline— but now looking northward.

"Now!" Moriana barked.

Rhesalus paused, likely sharing thoughts with his magical partners, and then agreed. I pushed them behind my shields, left open enough for them to observe whatever they pleased along the way, then leaped into the air. With the castle far behind us and my "passengers" lurking in my mind, Terius directed me due north, toward County Bedfordshire, and the darkness embraced me as we left the city of Leeds behind. This time, I not only had the stars to light my way, I had the sorcerers' constant nagging to irritate me.

"Swing left," Terius would insist. Then, "Swing Right."
"You're flying too low," Rhesalus fussed.
"A chicken could fly faster," Moriana sniped.
I wished I could turn on her and eat her like a fox eats a chicken.
I flew close enough to the coastline I saw Bedford City to my left when I passed it, but before we reached the Western League armies that should be camped north of it, Terius turned me due east. I wondered whatever it was that had them so edgy.

Flying too long—and not quickly enough—as an owl, I changed into a winged horse. I could fly faster, which certainly pleased Rhesalus, but my wings ached and my coat soon became sweat-soaked.

"I need to rest," I said, blowing hard.

"Not yet, Theona," Terius said, sounding distracted. As if he were looking for or considering something far more important than my imminent loss of consciousness.

"I must at least change forms again," I insisted. A hummingbird sounded feasible at the moment.

"You're almost there." He paused, then, "Change colors!" he hissed. "Turn black! Now!"

I'd done it before I had a chance to wonder why. Only moments later, a familiar orange glow amidst the forested mountains gave me the answer. I spiraled downward, now every bit as curious as my sorcerous companions, foreboding rushing through me.

The watch fires and the tents, the tethered horses and guarded artillery spoke volumes. A flag I didn't recognize flew above the central tent: a black sickle on a blood-red background.

It was an enemy army, camped on Kildarian soil.

CHAPTER 2

"Land near the horses," Terius urged. "Back in the shadows, though, and rid yourself of the wings. You need to join the herd."

I sensed his scheme and did as instructed. The delicious scent of water immediately assailed me, along with the smells of unwashed men, dried sweat on horses and blankets, cooking fires and grease...and oats! My stomach protested as I scurried toward the tethered warhorses. They grumbled and nodded their heads, a swish of tails and a stomping of hooves telling me they weren't sure about me. I nosed my way between them and reached for the water bucket. Sucking down enough water to drown a fish, I then attacked the grain in the closest feed barrel.

I jumped when a loud voice fractured the night. I turned to look over my shoulder and saw a tall man with skin as dark as leather. He came up to slap me on the rump, speaking in another language, and I paused to think about what he'd said.

"Hey, Niklas, what's goin' on here? Who's the dumming what's gone off and left his horse hot, wet, and not tied up proper?"

Another man hurried over to take a look at me. "Don't recognize the mare, Frode. Not that I know every one of 'em, but I swear...."

He was short and squat with bandy legs and dark skin like his companion's, his black hair a halo of curls on his head. He stroked his scruffy chin and shook his head. "Think mayhap it's Thorsen's mare. He's been right lazy with the animal lately. Beast prob'ly pulled free to go lookin' for food and water. Get a halter on 'er and tether 'er. Curry 'er out and dry 'er off, and give 'er more water and hay, take away the grain. Could founder 'er. Then find that idiot Thorsen and have 'im stripped, chained, and staked out for the night in punishment."

Frode nodded and, after Niklas left, brought me delicious, sweet hay and fresh water. I stood calm and tractable as he brushed my coat, gorging myself on my odd meal, ignoring the sorcerers who urged me to leave so that I could bring them out in the woods.

Finally, the man left to find the unfortunate Thorsen. I melted into a tree snake, freeing myself of halter and horsehide. Armed with the creature's night vision, I saw the body heat of the horses and men around me shimmering in the night and quickly slithered toward the closest tent, skimming around it as I headed toward the pavilion at the center of the camp.

"Stop here," Terius warned me as I neared the warm, golden light of a bonfire. I climbed a nearby tree to take a better look. The flaps of the tent were thrown back, and a large table inside, lighted by a score of lamps and piled with maps and scrolls, was surrounded by half a dozen uniformed men. All of them had the same dark skin, some with heads shaven, others with a variety of braids or curls; some with beards, all of them intimidating. The tallest one bore a heavy nose ring, connected to his right ear lobe by a delicate chain, and a number of hideous tattoos on his left cheek. He seemed to be the leader, and, as I leaned down to hear him, horror crept up inside me.

"We're just a couple o' days outside Bedford. Our scouts say the Western League's armies are gatherin' 'round the castle, which'll leave Bedford, the county seat of Bedfordshire, poorly defended. We'll attack from three different directions at once, drive 'em into the sea if we have to. How are the troops, supplies, and animals faring, boys? Could anything foul us up?"

Men whom I supposed were generals expressed concerns and offered suggestions. Laughter and crude language told me they looked forward, after their long march, to the fruits of their mission: attack and pillage.

"Then we can do what we came to do," one man said with glee. "Take our hostages and use 'em to demand the head of that Mallorian meddler, Gideon Seville. Our spies have given us eyes all the way into Kildaria's capital, and before we're done, we'll have the entire country in our clutches. The Western League'll fall after that."

"It will fall hard," the leader said, his dark eyes glittering in the lamplight. "Less bloodshed amongst our own than the all-out warfare we've planned against the Eastern Realms and with better rewards. These lands're rich, m' brothers. Full of the resources we need, includin' slaves. Keep our troops quiet and kill anyone who even thinks of desertin'. We'll be back on the road at daybreak."

My heart took leave of my chest for a moment. These were invaders from the Central Alliance! They had spies in Kildaria. They were bent on a military assault, kidnapping, enslavement, hostage negotiations—and Gideon's death!

I was glad I was nothing but a small snake, hanging from the branch of a tree. If I'd given a human gasp or a cry of outrage, I'd have given myself away. As it was, it took everything I had not to turn into an asp, slither into the tent and bite every, last one of them.

"They'd kill you instantly," Terius said, reining me in.

"But we do need to stop this," Rhesalus agreed.

"Theona can do it. That is, if she follows our directions with care."

Terius said it with such conviction I sensed he was using his *parhelian* gift of foretelling. He couldn't promise me the future, but I had a good chance to help shape it—if I obeyed.

"We need to discuss this away from your enemies," Rhesalus demanded.

The nose-ringed man turned to the maps, and the last I saw of any of them, before I slithered deep into the forest, were the grins of anticipation on their faces. I returned to my human form and called muted light before summoning the sorcerers. I didn't like the worry on their faces. It couldn't mean good things for sorcerers to worry. They communed in silence with each other before Terius turned to me.

"Return to the campgrounds near your prince's army."

"I'm too tired to fly—"

"*What?* What are you talking about?" Rhesalus said, his gray eyes narrowed in annoyance. "Have you forgotten your bitter lessons, kidnapped and imprisoned in the bowels of your king's dungeons, dear child? You can open a portal home."

A portal! A magical opening from one place to another. "But...." I knew my mouth hung open in shock. "But there are no walls here. How do I...?" I saw the disgust on their faces and wanted to throttle them. How was I supposed to know I didn't need walls? Why hadn't they just told me to open a portal in the first place, rather than making me fly all the way here?

Then I recalled Rhesalus telling me that I could only go to a place I'd visited before. I'd never been here and therefore couldn't portal here. Going home was a different matter.

"Does it work the same when I'm so far away?"

"Yes and no." Moriana replied. "Opening a portal is the same, but portalling long distances takes more energy. With our help, however, it will cost you far less than flying for miles across Kildaria."

"Until you know everything about it, you shouldn't portal without help at all," Rhesalus grumbled. "It's dangerous. Now let's get to it."

I clenched my jaws in irritation.

Feeling the sorcerers adding their strength to mine, I touched the gift within my *illumina,* the heart of my magical powers. This *parhelia* was colored sienna brown and faintly scented like peppermint. I swung my arms in front of me and painted a picture with hands and mind of a shimmering doorway from here to there. It looked exactly like a doorway, standing wide open to the meadows outside the towering castle walls and the moat that encircled it. Between me and the moat, the armies' camps were gathered. All I had to do was walk through the doorway.

An intense tingling grabbed me when I did so, followed by a terrible gut pain and weakness that made me gasp. I nearly fell, and panic hit, an innate fear of impending death.

"Hold still, girl," Moriana said.

Gritting my teeth, I forced myself to obey and felt the sorcerers' powers infuse me. Relief slowed my racing heart. The discomfort eased.

"What happened?" I muttered.

"You portalled a long distance," Terius muttered in my mind. "Pay attention, girl."

Yes. Pay attention. To the thousands of tents and flickering watchfires, and the multitudes of sentry keeping an eye on each country's camp. It looked different from here than from the castle. I felt small and defenseless and glad to be tucked into the shadows of the trees and bushes outside the camps.

Moriana insisted I let them out. "You must get word to your prince, and you need our help," she said.

Yes! I must, even as I worried about what would happen if someone spotted me outside the castle. She began circling me, looking me up and down as if I were a lump of clay waiting for the hands of a seasoned sculptor to make me into something useful.

"Remember our discussion not long after your possession, about reshaping materials to create illusions? I told you that you could do the same to animals, but you can also do it with people—even yourself. You don't become them, you just put on a disguise that looks like them. You saw it when I became you. I'm going to slip an image into your mind, one of a Kildarian scout, and you're going to use that image to begin shaping yourself into exactly what you see."

The image was a near-perfect portrait of a young man in a typical Kildarian uniform, a scout's black armband around his left arm. The uniform wasn't a problem but...did Moriana really expect me to change into a man?

If not for my recent exercises with Enya and Ramah, their magical dragons, I would have thought it impossible. The dragons had taught me to change into a multitude of creatures of different sizes and shapes, from animal to woman, from matron to child to barmaid. I supposed it shouldn't be too much harder to change into something that at least looked like a man in a uniform.

Moriana badgered me to follow her instructions as I gathered the powers of the various *parhelia* I needed. The energy tingled along the backs of my arms to my hands as I called them. The change came slowly at first, as painfully as ever. My long, dark hair shortened to just below my ears. My jaw lengthened, and a light patch of stubble itched as it sprouted from my face. At Moriana's urging, I elongated my nose just a bit, sharpened cheeks that she said were too feminine, shortened and thinned eyelashes that Gideon often told me were elegant.

The effort had me dripping with sweat as I focused on making far too narrow shoulders broader and giving muscles to my arms that would have no difficulty wielding a sword. A woman's chest had to change into a warrior's breast, and slender hips and sturdy thighs looked anything but feminine when I finished. Of course, the entire effect was lost, stuffed inside a dress, so I altered my gown into a scout's tunic and turned my drawers into trousers. What was it Ramah, the male dragon, often said? Get the feel of the form. Adjust sinew and bone until you don't just look like what you want to imitate, you become it. I flexed my arms and stretched my shoulders, finding them heavier, broader, stronger. I lengthened leg bones and thickened my neck.

"Amazing," Rhesalus intoned. "You are amazing, Theona. We couldn't have asked for better. Move about for a minute, find your balance. And don't walk like a girl."

I stumbled at first, like I often did with a new form. All three of my mentors picked and poked at me. Terius told me to make myself taller. Moriana snapped at me to change my slippers into boots. I'd been unhorsed and injured, they said; needed to be bruised and filthy from walking for two days in the forest; needed to look hungry, thirsty, and one step away from delirious.

I felt every bit as miserable as they wanted me to look.

"The camp in front of us is your prince's," Moriana pointed out. "Make your way to his command tent. The closer you get before they catch you, the better your chances of pulling this off. Avoid too much risk, however. I'm sure you'd prefer to fly away than to have cold steel hack off your head."

I gulped and nodded, putting the sorcerers behind my shields. If only I knew where the command tent was. I wished I could fly around until I found it, retire to a place between tents to make the transformation in the dark, and then try to reach Gideon. But I feared changing one bit of my appearance now that I had it the way the sorcerers wanted it. Instead, I must try to sneak into Malloria's camp past a multitude of armed warriors without getting killed.

"We'll be with you, of course," Terius whispered in my mind.

"You'll remove my trail of magic? I can't maintain my disguise and do that too, especially considering I'm not very good at it."

"We've been doing it all along," he replied.

I moved around the camp's perimeter until I saw the Mallorian flag atop Gideon's command tent. I had to sneak past the sentry and then wind my way between dozens of warriors' tents to reach him.

I'd not made it more than a few tents' rows into camp when a cry erupted.

"Who goes there! Enemy in the camp!"

A handful of warriors, weapons drawn, charged at me. I staggered to a halt, arms raised, so frightened I had no trouble appearing to be out of breath.

"I—I," I squeaked, realizing I had no idea how to speak like a man. I floundered for a minute and coughed painfully as I lengthened and thickened my vocal cords. This time I at least didn't sound like a mouse. "I need to speak to Prince Seville. I bring news!" I insisted.

"Who are you?" One man stepped closer, his dark eyes ablaze. "How do you know Mallorian?"

My eyes widened in shock. Without thinking, I'd spoken to them in Mallorian!

"I'm a scout. We speak a variety of languages." I hoped. "I lost my way home. This was the closest camp. Haven't the strength to go much farther—not far enough to reach King Desmond—and I need to speak to your prince. Please! He's in danger."

"He's wearing a Kildarian uniform," one man said. "What if he's telling the truth?"

"What if he's not?" someone else cried. "He's a spy. Kill him!"

"No! Please!" I insisted. I wasn't too proud to beg. "I'm a scout! I bear news of a threat against both Kildaria and your prince." I prayed they at least believed that much.

"Where's your horse? Your two scout companions?"

Terius nudged ideas into my head, and I grimaced. "The scouts are dead. My horse tossed me and ran off a few days ago with my weapons and supplies."

They muttered amongst themselves, then finally the one who seemed to be in charge insisted they take me to the prince. Another soldier pushed me forward, jabbing me hard with the tip of his sheathed knife. I stumbled and swayed, so tired from the use of magic I had no trouble convincing them I was nearly done in.

"Corporal Beaumont requesting audience with His Highness the Prince!" the leader called as we approached the closed command tent, next to what I supposed was Gideon's tent and that of his guards. The guards' weapons were already drawn. The command tent flap opened, and General Bellamy stepped out. I gulped. I was so very glad to see him, but he obviously didn't have the same regard for me.

"What's this all about, Beaumont?" he growled.

"Found him sneaking through the camp. Says he's a 'scout' for the Kildarians, got lost on his way home from wherever he's been and needs audience with the prince. He speaks Mallorian."

Bellamy glared at me, his brows drawn tight. "You have one minute to explain yourself, mister. Don't waste it."

Again, I gulped. I felt my thin grasp on my magic shimmer and panicked. I couldn't let my disguise slip. They'd know what I was and kill me for sure.

"I've news for the prince," I insisted. I needed to see Gideon. I had to convince him of what I'd seen.

"You will tell me. If I deem it important, I'll present it to him."

I felt Moriana's ring warming my hand again, but I couldn't see it. I closed my eyes and shook my head as if I were near fainting. The ring grew hot, like it heard my thoughts and approved. I lowered my head so that Bellamy couldn't see my satisfied grin before I crumpled to the ground, as close to losing consciousness as I could allow myself to become without really doing so, which would lose my disguise.

———————

"Here, lad, take a drink," a voice said.

I opened my eyes and blinked, the sweet scent of water making me desperate. The man lifted my head off the ground and let me drink, then pulled the tin cup away when I began gulping it down.

"Not so fast. You'll sicken. You've been without for a while, haven't you?"

I looked up into Sir Lance Arnoe's plain face, thinking I'd never been so glad to see anyone in my life. Then, past his shoulder, I glimpsed another familiar face that changed my mind. Gideon stood watching me thoughtfully, his handsome features making my heart flutter.

He must have seen the look on my face. He frowned at me and pulled away, reminding me that looks of affection might seem peculiar coming from some strange, young, male scout.

Bellamy grabbed my arm and hauled me to my feet, where I struggled to gain my balance. Amazing that trying to play the part of a man was more difficult than becoming a dragon.

"Out with it, mister," Bellamy demanded. "What brings you here?"

I ignored him, my gaze fastened on Gideon's. I knew thousands of lives rested on these next few minutes, and I'd have only one chance to convince them.

"Your Highness, a contingent from the Central Alliance is camped east of Bedfordshire County, maybe a day or two out. I've learned of their plans and their strengths. If King Desmond acts quickly, the attack on Bedford, the county seat, can be stopped and could seriously cripple our enemies. If you do not, they'll destroy Bedford and take hostages to bargain with, against both Kildaria and Malloria."

Bellamy exchanged looks with Gideon, and Arnoe and a few others muttered in anger.

"Where's your proof?" Bellamy growled.

"Be strong, Theona," Rhesalus urged me.

I forced myself to stand my ground, as I supposed a man would do, and glared at Bellamy.

"I overheard their plans; I saw their camp; I know their strengths. Give me pen and paper and I'll draw it all out for you. Believe me or not. Then I demand to see my king. I'm a Kildarian subject on Kildarian soil, and I've threatened no one. I'm not even armed. You've no right to detain me. Sir!"

I swayed where I stood, blinking hard against the fear. My unprecedented use of magic made me desperate for food and drink, for my comfortable bed. It terrified me, for Gideon's sake, to think they wouldn't believe me.

"Bring him to the table," the prince said.

They all but dragged me into the command tent. There were two "rooms" on either side of the central area, in which sat a large table and chairs. I couldn't see what was in those rooms, but above the table in the central area hung a multitude of lamps. Why would they bring me in here? All around lay maps and piles of important-looking papers. Sir Lance rushed to move most of them out of the way, pushed me into one of those chairs, and shoved paper and ink in front of me.

"Help me," I begged Rhesalus and Terius. *"I saw what I saw, but that doesn't mean anything. How many men? How many horses? What of their armory?"*

I heard Terius growling in my mind. *"Stupid girl. Should have paid better attention."*

"You're not helping, Terius," Rhesalus scolded. *"Draw the camp first, Theona. The tents will give them an idea of the size of the army, and the rest we'll help you with as you go."*

"But I'm no artist."

"Good enough, even if you don't know it, and I'll help you," Moriana said, I felt her guiding me toward that pink *parhelian* strand of light, sustained inside my *illumina*, connected to the arts. I found myself hastily sketching an aerial view of the enemy camp. Tents, wagons, portable armory, pickets for the horses. Bellamy, Arnoe and the guards surrounding me murmured as they watched. Gideon remained silent.

I flipped to a new sheet of paper and began again, drawing the men I'd seen in the enemy tent, where the plans of war were made. The leader, with his tattoos and nose ring, stood out, a quick sketch that I thought oughtn't to have impressed anyone. Apparently, I was wrong.

"A Valdellian Warlord," Bellamy hissed, and Gideon nodded.

"The scout got close. He's either telling the truth or in league with them."

I sought a third sheet of paper. Numbers began to pour into my mind, engulfing me with information I could hardly write fast enough. I dropped the pen and pressed both hands to my face, cringing from the pain exploding inside my skull.

"Slow down!" I shouted silently. *"I can't bear it all."*

Sorcerous laughter greeted my plea, but after that, the headache abated, and it came easier. Line after line of figures appeared on the paper, but I paid little attention to them. The scratch of pen on paper, the flow of information, the intense concentration all possessed me. After I'd noted every last reasonable bit of information, I bolted out of my seat and managed to make it outside before vomiting the water they'd given me. I expected to get tackled or even stabbed in the back for running, but the grumbles of the men whose shoes I'd spattered proved they were glad I'd at least taken the stinking mess outside.

It didn't stop them from grabbing me and slamming me back into the chair. I knew this was just the way men handled such things, but the sixteen-year-old girl inside me wanted to cry.

"This is incredible," Gideon remarked, flipping back and forth between the pages. "You are incredible," he said to me. Then to Bellamy, he added, "They mean business."

"Aye, my lord," Bellamy replied. "You said they plan to take hostages, corporal. What do they want with them?"

I met Gideon's gaze squarely as I said, "They will offer them in exchange for the head of Malloria's crown prince."

The momentary pause, while these men absorbed my meaning, suddenly shattered.

"What!?" Bellamy shouted. "They're planning to use Kildarian noblemen and their families as hostages to force King Desmond to execute our prince?"

Gideon was as expressionless as granite.

"No," I said. "They will insist he be surrendered so they can torture and then kill him with their own hands."

Gideon turned to one of his guards. "Fergal, we need to get this scout and his drawings to the king. Send a messenger to warn His Majesty we're coming. Have horses ready for us in ten minutes."

The guard nodded and hurried off.

Gideon looked down at me, his normally lovely violet eyes eerie in the light of a dozen lanterns. I felt as if they could see through me. "What's your name, corporal?"

My mouth fell open as I realized the sorcerers hadn't given me that part of the scheme. What a horrid conundrum. Did King Desmond have a list of Kildarian scouts? If I gave the wrong name, I'd find myself in chains again and hanged for subterfuge. Likewise, if someone in court knew I wasn't the scout I claimed to be. Apart from that, I could stay away from my apartment for only so long before someone found me missing, but returning home required this "young man" to disappear.

"Patience, Theona," Rhesalus said to calm me. *"Trust us. We won't let them destroy everything you've worked so hard for."*

Having heard those words before, I allowed him to reassure me. And then came a name.

I swallowed the knot in my throat. "They call me Tally," I replied. "Name's Collin Talliford, but I'm good with numbers, so they call me Tally."

I saw the edge of Gideon's mouth creep up into a wry smile.

"Alright, Tally. You said the enemy camp is east of Bedford, but you also said you got lost heading back to the castle. How did you judge their location?"

Terius muttered in my head.

"I just got lost the last couple of miles, and mostly because of the campfires. The haze blocked the stars. I stumbled upon your camp first."

Gideon tipped his head at me, weighing and measuring me. Then he handed me the fourth piece of paper and asked me to sketch a map of the land between Leeds and Bedfordshire and the road the enemy camp planned to take to Bedford.

My stomach rolled in apprehension. I had no idea how to do what he'd asked.

"We do," Rhesalus insisted. *"I repeat: stop fighting us and we'll help."*

I hardly noticed drawing the map with incredible speed and accuracy. I hadn't done it, of course. Moriana had done it through me. It made me feel ill again, to think of her using my body as if she owned it.

Bellamy lifted the map to examine it, and then pulled one out of the pile on the table made by professional cartographers. I held my breath as he compared it with mine.

"You've an amazing hand, Tally," he said. "Guess that's why King Desmond employed you. Lance, if he wants it, give him some bread and more water while we wait for the horses."

CHAPTER 3

King Desmond Fitzpatrick—the king of Kildaria and the commander of the Western League—treated me no kinder than Gideon's men. Perhaps less so, because he'd been dragged from his bed to hear my tale. When the truth sank in, however, his weary face drooped in dismay.

"Incredible. The war hasn't even officially begun and already we need to fight it on two fronts." He harrumphed and turned to one of his aides. "Collect O'Brien from his quarters. It's his duchy, and he should take the forefront on this."

"Yes, m'lord," the man said, nodding before departing.

I'd never set foot in the king's private study, a place that seemed more equipped for planning war than studying: a large square table surrounded by chairs, and chairs against walls hung with maps so colorful and intricate they could pass for artwork.

Gideon, hands clasped behind his back, studied one of the maps of the outlined counties of Kildaria.

"Wonderfully detailed maps, Your Majesty. This is Bedford?" he asked, pointing at it. The king joined him and nodded. The others in the room—Bellamy, Gideon's guards, another of the king's advisors and two of Kildaria's guards—gathered around them. Somehow, I got sandwiched between Bellamy and Gideon.

With a sweep of his hand, the king made quick work of pointing out the demarcations of each county and its seat—which reminded me of my flight just hours ago. Blackburn County sat the furthest north, sharing its northern border with the country of Dundee. South of Blackburn were Bedfordshire and Leeds counties. Then below them were County Mithradell, County Thistleshire, and the nation of Kythos. On the east side of the Carinor Mountains, Kildaria's northeastern border joined with Grimstaad, the home of the Valdellian Warlords, and the southeastern with the Badlands.

"This is the road into Bedford from Grimstaad?" Gideon asked with confidence. He knew because it looked like the map he had in his command tent. A wide pass serpentined three-quarters of the way across the map and through the mountain forests before crossing the Blackwater River and heading toward the coast. "I assume this is a bridge?"

"The Bitterroot Bridge," King Desmond growled. "It's seen better days, but O'Brien's people haven't taken seriously the need to either reinforce or rebuild it. It's their main route through the Carinors, and if anything cataclysmic ever happens, it will fall."

Gideon seemed to perk up at this information. "The main route? There are others?"

"Nothing as wide or as well-traveled, but yes." The king pointed out four of them. Only one had a bridge notably wider than a wagon's-width.

A noise at the door preceded a guard announcing Duke O'Brien's arrival. Alarmed at the summons, the nobleman stormed into the room to hear the details.

"Sire, the rest of my army is on its way to join the fourteen hundred I already have here. It's too late to send them back, but I can't dispatch them to Malloria with the Valdellians threatening us. I need to take my troops home."

The king held up his hand. "Don't be hasty, O'Brien. We need to consider every option first." He turned his wise but aging eyes on me. "Where did you say the army's situated?"

I had no idea. Then, as if Rhesalus had taken my hand in his, I placed a dirty fingernail on the road a good distance to the east of the bridge.

"Excellent," Gideon murmured.

"You've an idea," my king said.

"I do, depending upon your resources and the duke's willingness." Gideon tapped on the bridge that spanned the river. "Blast it."

"What?" O'Brien sputtered.

"Destroy the bridge. If you've enough powder to take it down, and if your people can manage without it until you can build a new one, then you defeat the Valdellians instantly, without a single confrontation. None of your smaller roads and bridges are suitable for an army as big as theirs. The Valdellians will be forced to retreat."

O'Brien and the king looked stunned for a moment and then broke out in laughter.

"I don't like it, but it's inarguably effective," the duke admitted.

"We've no time to waste," King Desmond said. "I'll send a message to Bedford by bird at dawn."

O'Brien nodded. "And I'll take my personal guards and head home. We'll enjoy wreaking havoc upon them."

King Desmond clapped a hand on O'Brien's shoulder. "And you'll get your new bridge after all. We'll send engineers from Leeds to help." He turned to grip Gideon's hand in his own, his smile softening. "Surely this will go far toward convincing the remaining doubters that this war's threat is real. Had you not come to warn us, we'd have been caught unprepared. Thank you, Your Highness."

To the rest of us, he said, "Gentlemen, we've challenges ahead of us, but praise Elam, the rest of the army will arrive tomorrow, likely around midday. Some of the various leaders and generals already here may have doubts, but as of four days ago, the Western League's kings all agreed. We must prepare for war.

"However, my friends, let us not forget that the new arrivals will need several days to a week to rest and restock. Much could go wrong in that time, especially if we fail to catch the insurrectionists. Make it a priority."

"Yes, Your Majesty," they all replied.

I stood open-mouthed and silent.

"O'Brien, do what you must to protect your lands and people, but let the warriors you've assigned to Malloria go. The Valdellians are most likely but a small part of what's coming. We need every Kildarian county to remain firm despite handing over these warriors, because if Kildaria shows uncertainty, the other nations will follow suit."

"Yes, Sire," O'Brien said with enthusiasm before leaving.

The king turned to the prince. "As we've discussed more than once, this will be one of the largest mounted armies to have ever marched across the continent, and—despite the reassurances of generations of seamen that ours is a small continent—it will be anything but child's play. We'll not tolerate good men and women dying from lack of the very best planning. It's time those who have resisted get serious about it."

The king sent one of his men to rouse the leaders of every nation, to meet in the War Room in thirty minutes. Sleep must take a back seat to danger.

My liege lord turned to face me, every inch of him a king, but I was too tired to let him frighten me.

"Good job, Talliford. We remember you. You've served Kildaria well. Rather than facing a hostage crisis, we can instead celebrate the rising of a new army." To Gideon, he said, "The festivities we ordered to be held late morning Friday shall proceed. We need to set forth and stress our support of the plans for your march. Agreed?"

"Agreed," Gideon said.

"Guards," King Desmond said to two other men. "Take this scout to the infirmary; see him fed and his wounds treated."

All I wanted was sleep. I hardly noted being shuffled out the castle doors, through the courtyard, and into the infirmary at the back of the north wing. It took monumental effort to not lose consciousness when I was coaxed onto a rock-hard cot between two other "patients." They fed me, a light soup that tasted awful, and tended my wounds. Then, after the healer, who'd healed nothing, trimmed the lamp and left me alone, I clumsily opened a portal to my bedchamber.

I never made it to the bed. I slumped to the floor, barely aware of having rid myself of Collin Talliford before passing out cold.

———†———

"Princess Theona?"

I heard the voice and recognized it but couldn't move. I wanted more sleep.

"My lady, are you alright?"

My right eye insisted on opening, and I stared up at Kendal. Confused at her presence and the bright morning light in my room, I opened both eyes and sat up, breathing deep to calm the nausea that gripped me. I'd used too much magic last night and was overwhelmed by it, but then the queasiness dissipated, and I remembered with mixed feelings that the armies would arrive today. I also remembered the Valdellian Warlords. They were terribly real, not just an awful dream. And what about my disguise as a Kildarian scout who'd escaped the infirmary?

"My disappearing last night wasn't good, was it?" I asked the sorcerers. *"What will happen?"*

"You were a fool to portal on your own, but you're also a hero, dear girl." Terius said with disapproval. *"We planted memories in the healers' minds of a brave young man determined to catch a few*

hours' sleep and then return to his duties. He'll never be seen again, of course."

I ruminated for a moment. *"This Tally was real, wasn't he?"*

"Yes," Moriana replied. *"He and his companions were caught and killed by Grimstaad's Valdellian Warlords three days ago. His memory will be honored because of you."*

A happy-awful thought. I didn't want to hear any more. I wanted even less to do with the sorcerers and closed my shields.

"My lady?" Kendal asked again, concern etched on her lovely face. Fair and green eyed, she'd been my lady's maid and best friend since early childhood.

"I'm fine, Kendal," I replied, completely recovered except for the nausea. "I didn't sleep well last night. Why are you here?" She wasn't supposed to be here. She needed to stay away from me.

Her concern deepened. "Your prince sent a message for you, but the messenger couldn't get you to open the door. When maids arrived with your breakfast and you still didn't respond, the guard sent for me. Had I not come, I fear they'd have knocked the door down and walked in on you, which didn't sound like a good idea."

A terrible idea. I was dirty from last night's caper and would have no way to explain it. The scents of sausages and eggs suddenly assailed me, and I didn't care about anything but eating.

Kendal helped me into my robe, covering up the mess, and escorted me to the table in Gideon's sitting room. She opened the door for the guards to catch a glimpse of me and explained I had just slept late, dismissed them, and then rejoined me.

The sight of an envelope, lying beside my plate and bearing a hastily written note from Gideon, overrode my hunger for a moment. I grabbed it and tore it open.

My love, please forgive me for not rejoining you last night. The problems were worse than expected. As you know, the rest of the troops I requested from King Desmond will arrive today. Thank Elam for his generosity.

The troops will need time to recover before setting out for Malloria, but the servants must begin your preparations immediately to have you ready on time. Shan't likely be more than a week. My country's intelligence expects attacks to begin against the Eastern Realms in early June or even the end of May. I fear reaching Malloria in time to help.

We'd leave in a week? Or less? The reminder made my heart sink. Forever from now to Gideon. Far too soon for my liking.

For your comfort and safety, I insist you return to your old rooms where my sentry will continue to guard you. Perhaps Miss Tavish should care for you until you have a replacement. I know you see more than the ordinary person, my darling. You also know I'll do everything I can to join you soon. You have all my love.

I adored the flourish of his signature and laid it against my chest as if I could touch him by touching the note he'd written. I couldn't help the tears filling my eyes. I knew he'd be safe, but I missed him terribly.

Kendal offered me half her food, saying she didn't want it. I knew better. She knew me, and she knew I was starving. Magic always did that to me.

"My lady, please eat up, so that I can clean you up for the day. At the same time the guards sent for me, I received a missive from your father. He needs to see you right away, asked me to bring you to him. He didn't say why."

The hunger consumed me, and the food barely satisfied it. Afterward, Kendal worked her own magic, getting me washed up and dressed. Then she sent for servants to move my belongings back to my old rooms.

After that, with the manacles and chains I had to wear outside my chambers back in place, she and my guards escorted me to my parents' apartments. Father's and Mother's concerned expressions piqued my curiosity even further.

I caught sight of Miss Morgan, my old governess, quickly herding my younger sister and brother into her bedchamber, leaving us alone in the main sitting room. I wondered where Ian and Lon, my older brothers, had gone.

"Theona, you still look too thin," Mother commented, kissing both my cheeks and leading me to a high-backed chair and a small table near the fireplace—and a plate of luscious pastries.

"I'm fine, Mother," I said, selecting a pastry and trying hard not to drool. If I was too thin, I supposed I needn't feel guilty about indulging. "The dragons and sorcerers ...." How should I put it? "They take a lot out of me."

The fire in the grate felt wonderful and the sweets tasted of heaven. It was a cool day and windy enough to raise a dusty haze outside the window. Father claimed his seat opposite me, directing Kendal to take the chair to my left.

"You're a part of this, Miss Tavish," Father said. "I've had correspondence with Baron Tavish, and he, your mother and your siblings are on their way to Leeds. They are thrilled with the possibilities between yourself and Lord Ian. Nothing will be made public, of course, until the engagement between Lord Ian and Lady Eileen is formally broken, but we won't wait any longer than we must before posting your banns."

I stared at Kendal's blushing face. I'd missed the mainstream of castle life for less than three days, but I felt as if I'd fallen asleep and woken up a hundred years later. After I'd become possessed, Duke McDuff had chosen to renounce his daughter's engagement to my brother, an arrangement made when both were but babes-in-arms. I'd explained Ian's and Kendal's affections to my mother and paved the way for their marriage. Now, it seemed everything was falling into place for them.

Kendal's lovely emerald eyes shone with joy.

"Now." Father turned to me. "As to matters concerning you, Theona. Prince Gideon and I have diligently discussed ways to make your journey to Malloria both more comfortable and safer. To lessen some of the trouble, the king and I have thrust numerous assignments on Darby Murdock, Nevin Leath and Egan Gilroy, several outside Leeds, and you know that the prince's guards are more committed to protecting you than to confining you to your rooms."

I shivered at mention of the three men. They wanted me dead.

"Your mother has also been concerned about Miss Kendal's transition from your lady's maid to Ian's fiancée, not just for Miss Kendall but also for you. You need a new maid, a servant good enough for a princess but also one who can protect you."

My cheeks paled with dismay at remembering the warriors who broke into my apartments five days ago and kidnapped me. Kendal had been helpless to stop them.

"Beyond that, besides needing to learn to ride your horse as soldiers ride, you'll need new gear and clothing and lessons in self-defense."

"What?" I straightened, electrified by the idea. Would I be allowed to use weapons? To learn the secrets of the martial arts? My friends, the girls at least, would be horrified by the idea, but I'd always wanted to learn. I just couldn't imagine King Desmond allowing it under the circumstances.

"Your mother has found someone she thinks is the perfect lady's maid for you and hopes you'll agree. The woman is on her way to join us. Unless you have genuine objections, I insist you accept her."

As if on cue, someone knocked at the door. A guard announced the arrival of our guest, and we came to our feet as the door opened. My breath caught at the sight of the woman who entered the apartment. She looked familiar.

Likely in her mid-twenties, the woman's dark skin and black eyes signified her Kythosian descent, and she had curly black hair long enough to braid and pin around her head. Despite being stocky and rather plain, she had a delightful smile, but what fascinated me most was the odd array of *parhelia* in her *illumina!* My guard went up, however, when a tickling sensation touched my shields. Had she just tried to read my thoughts?

"My goodness, Princess Theona," she said, giving a most proper, courtly curtsy. "You've grown up. And you've married a prince. Some Kildarians are proud of that, my lady, despite…well, you know."

My possession, I thought. I grappled with her name and where I might have seen her. Her brogue came from a farming neighborhood in County Thistleshire, where a good number of people transplanted from Kythos lived—and where Eld Tully, the First Eld, or Prime Advocate of the Quorum of the Elds, was born.

She grinned at me as if she'd gotten away with stealing cookies, and I gasped as an onslaught of delightful memories flooded through me.

"Zahra Timbu!" I cried. "I cannot believe it's you. You used to steal apples for me from the orchards."

Her smile drooped as she glanced at Father, who struggled not to laugh. She cleared her throat and said, "'Tis wonderful to see you again, Princess. I remember our time together with fondness. You were full of life, determined to take on the world, and followed me everywhere, watching me care for the horses and pestering me to let you sit on them when no one was looking. It's been a long time. You couldn't have been more than six or seven—"

"Eight! I was eight years old when you left, and I was angry with you for it. I couldn't imagine why you'd want to go off and join the cavalry."

She all but laughed. "I was eighteen, plain as a picket fence, and longing for adventure. Never had the problem with the enlisted men—or men in general—the prettier girls did, and I've been a natural with a short sword and a crossbow since I was a wee thing. Got my fill of it, more's the pity, when I near lost an eye in a skirmish 'tween Dundee and that heathen country Arundale. I'm twenty-six now, been back home, keeping house for Lady Kell nigh on two years."

Lady Kell? Why would this robust, outdoorsy young woman agree to serve Thistleshire's countess? I couldn't envision anyone wanting to serve Lady Kell. Her tongue was as brutal as an icepick.

Zahra chuckled. "She won't miss me, my lady. I've short patience for people with arrogance they don't deserve. Lord Kell wouldn't let me go, even when she told him to hang me, but I'd rather serve you if you'll have me."

I barked quick laughter. "Of course, but...I'm possessed. How can you make peace with that?"

She shrugged. "Our goal is to get you to Malloria, as far away from Kildaria and those bloody—excuse me." Her face darkened again, except for a pale scar I noted on her left eyebrow. "Away from those blasted dragons' birthing place, so they'll die and take the sorcerers with them. Your prince will be so far in o'er his head with travel plans and military headaches, he'll not have time to teach you about horses and weapons, and in the meantime, I'm an excellent bodyguard."

Into my mind again rushed the horrors of those traitors barging into my apartment. They'd dragged me off to King Desmond's dungeons where they poisoned and abandoned me. It proved I had my limits, like anyone else. If I had had a defender, perhaps things would have turned out differently.

Mother chimed in to add more. "Zahra's mother was once a lady's maid to the queen, Theona, until she married Zahra's father. Then she traveled for years with the armies as a cook and laundress, to stay close to Mr. Timbu. When she died, we invited Mr. Timbu to bring his children and come to work for us. Zahra often told me that her mother taught her and her sister about state dances and ceremonial dinners and the honor of waiting on the queen. Zahra knows how to take care of you, my dear."

Zahra's voice softened with emotion as she added, "Both my parents are gone now, bless their souls. Consumption took my sister last spring, and Amari, my brother, lost his wife and two girls this winter to diphtheria. He'll march with the army, and since we're all the family we have left, we'd like to stay together."

"Of course," I said, feeling badly for her, but also dying of curiosity about the *parhelia* she bore.

"You can teach me to ride, but can you teach me to fight?" I asked.

"What?" Mother said sharply.

"Mother, I can't always hide behind other people, not in the face of war." Especially, I thought to myself, if magic failed me at a crucial moment. "I want to learn to use a sword."

"What?" My mother said again. Father failed to smother a grin.

"I can fence, and I can use a bow and arrow, but there's a big difference between competing with a lot of spoiled noblemen's daughters and standing up to someone with a sword. Zahra, you said you can use a short sword and a crossbow. Are you good at them?"

Zahra choked on laughter. "I can hold my own with a sword and can put a bolt through an enemy's eye at fifteen yards—on a galloping horse. Not many can say that, especially a woman. Upper body strength, you see. But I was trained in self-defense by the best—my own father—and my sight 'tis better at a distance than up close. Steady hands, too. Whether I can teach you depends on you, but I'll give it my best." Then she paused and looked at Father. "If I've your permission, Your Grace," she added.

Father, still fighting not to laugh, said, "No doubt, it would appall many to think of putting weapons in Theona's hands, but Prince Gideon and I believe the opposite. The nobility cares only about their own safety, and thus far, she's harmed no one. The same cannot be said about what's happened to Theona. Besides, fewer would be at risk if she can protect herself, and if I know my daughter, she'd do everything possible to defend others as well."

I blinked my eyes against tears at hearing my father's faith in me. The anxiety softened on Mother's face and Zahra smiled and nodded.

"If your father believes in you, how could I not? Let's start with your riding lessons first, my lady, and go from there."

I pressed the woman's hand, a silent pact between us that I suspected would mean a great deal in the days ahead.

Father turned to Kendal. "It appears we've found someone to replace you, Miss Tavish. You'll want to move to your parents' apartments when they arrive, but until then, please do as we suggested last night and come to ours forthwith. You can share a bedchamber with Miss Morgan. Zahra needs your room in Theona's quarters."

Kendal—Miss Tavish—looked lost, glancing between Zahra and me and then my parents. I understood her struggle with no longer belonging in the life she'd led. The last two weeks of my life had deluged me with so many changes, I had a hard time either remembering what I'd once been or understanding what I was to become.

"I'd be honored, Lord McArthur," she replied at last.

I could hear the tears at the edge of her voice and threw my arms around her and hugged her tight. Perhaps adoring one's servant wasn't considered proper, but I had no qualms about showing my feelings to my dearest friend and future sister-in-law.

"I'll love having you for a sister, Kendal," I murmured in her ear. "And maybe one day we'll be together again, and I'll be able to tell the whole world what you mean to me."

We broke down and wept, and for a long, quiet moment, we forgot there were other people in the room watching us.

CHAPTER 4

With Kendal moved quickly from my apartment and Zahra moved in, a melancholy set in that my new maid seemed determined to dispel.

"Your Highness, 'tis a good thing Miss Kendal's formal courting can begin now, but even more important, you're now able to concentrate on your goals. We'll change you into your riding clothes, collect our horses and begin your lessons. 'Twill get your mind off your worries and help me gauge your abilities."

I sighed, wiped my eyes, and thanked her. She knew exactly what I needed.

That morning seemed to herald a new life for me: two hours a day to ride in broad daylight and in the company of someone besides guards or testy sorcerers. Two hours of accomplishing something that did not involve magic.

People paused to watch four guards, two of Gideon's and two of Father's, escort us to the Royal Stables. Some faces reflected disapproval, but others just looked curious.

Zahra's lanky dark-bay mare stood a hand shorter than my gray gelding. My "maid" vaulted aboard, but my chains made it difficult to mount. One of Gideon's guards help me, but I felt ridiculous. I also felt my face pale when I caught Nevin Leath and Darby Murdock staring daggers at me from within the small crowd that gathered. What a relief to finally jog across the moat and to the open pasture Gideon and I had used before we married, as far from them as I could get for now.

Zahra immediately took charge. The guards frowned but offered no objection when she removed my chains, insisting I couldn't "manage my mount proper" with them on.

"Besides," she added. "If you're as dangerous as some seem determined to believe, I doubt chains are worth much."

Thank heavens she understood. I was no more a prisoner than a canary with the cage door standing wide open. I stayed not because I was a prisoner, but because the sorcerers insisted on it, and also because of Gideon, and for both Kildaria and Malloria, even if they didn't realize it.

The wind had died, and the hazy blue skies dotted with clouds made the day feel luxurious. Zahra admitted Father had let her ride my gelding the night before to get to know him. She reassured me that while he wasn't a true warhorse, he was near as good as one.

"The seller claimed he'll even come when you whistle for him."

I laughed. "Like a dog?" I asked.

"Yes."

She was serious. I'd never heard of such a thing.

"What's his name?" she asked.

I blinked twice. "I don't know. Father never said."

Zahra snorted laughter. "Pardon me, princess. A faithful friend needs a name. It will help you bond with him. What fits him? My mare's a frisky sort. Her name's Chipper—Chip, for short. Your prince's stallion is Valere, Mallorian for Valiant."

Valiant. Why didn't I know that? So appropriate for my prince.

The gray gelding hadn't liked me when we first met. After I hid the snake-dragon side of my magic and heightened the horse part, he seemed drawn to me instead. I felt remiss at not having shown him much affection in return. Naming him sounded perfect.

He was a handsome animal. Dark dapple-gray coat, long near-black mane and tail, and a wide blaze on his face. His dark brown eyes radiated intelligence. The stately name of an old, faithful friend of my father's, a clever, gray haired knight with dark brown eyes, came to mind. Sir Caspian.

"I think Caspian befits you," I said, patting his neck and offering him the sugar cube Zahra handed me. The animal nodded as he chomped the cube and snuffled my cheek, as if he approved, which made us laugh.

In our two hours together, Caspian and I learned to communicate in ways I never knew horse and rider could. To stop or turn, move from walk to canter instantly, to back or spin left or right with just a light touch of the rein, gentle leg pressure and a shifting of my weight. An occasional verbal cue encouraged me more than him. I felt exhilarated when we finished—despite being dripping wet and exhausted—and grateful to return to the stables, once more in chains, where a groomsman was supposed to take our horses.

We dismounted and waited, the guards calling for the groom twice. With no response, Father's guards went inside to see what was keeping him.

"Zahra," I murmured when I noted a handful of men garbed in dark clothing ambling toward us. Even worse, black baklavas covered all but their eyes. I saw no signs of weapons, but I had no doubt they had them.

"Right rear," Zahra said to one of Gideon's guards, but before either man could move an inch, one of the men put something to his mouth.

My eyes widened and I fought a scream when a dart sprouted from the neck of the guard closest to me. A split second later a second dart hit the other guard. Both dropped to the ground like rocks. Zahra jumped in front of me, demanding I stay put. When a second man raised a tube to his mouth, she roared, spreading her arms wide, and my jaw dropped when she turned into a lustrous black monolith with human proportions.

The darts held no magic, but when they hit her, they rebounded as if she'd blown them back at them. They struck the men who'd fired them, and they too fell to the ground. The other four pulled knives and short swords, but when Zahra drew her own weapons, they turned and fled.

"Typical bullies," Zahra muttered when she went to check the attackers' pulses. "Powerful in a herd, milksops when someone calls their bluff. They're fine, just sedated." She checked our guards, too, pulling out the darts and declaring them equally drugged. Running footsteps pulled me from my stupor as Father's guards arrived to pull off the attackers' baklavas and assess the situation.

"Princess. Are you alright?" one asked. I nodded, still speechless, as Zahra explained the events to them. It wasn't long before men-at-arms came to carry the two attackers to dungeon cells and the two unconscious guards to the infirmary, while Father's guards escorted us back to our rooms. There, I found myself staring numbly into the courtyard from the glass doors of our sitting room's balcony.

"The guards found the grooms bound and gagged in the stable, my lady. The rebels meant to kidnap you," Zahra said, pity in her eyes. Not the matronly type of pity, the empathetic variety. "If they'd meant to kill you, they'd have hit you first and with poison darts. It's good they underestimated me, but they won't make that mistake again."

I sat down on the sofa, opposite Zahra, and sighed as I rested my brow in my hands. Another kidnapping, another potential poisoning. Others hurt because of me. I could only pray the two men captured would give up their comrades.

But that wasn't all that troubled me.

"What did you do to them, Zahra? I was behind you and couldn't see it all, but I saw enough. So did anyone who was watching us."

She smiled a wry smile. "As to the others watching, let them tell their tales. Most were focused on the little mob coming toward us and didn't see what I did. You know I'm gifted, too, Princess. I felt your assessment of me when I arrived at your parents' quarters, just as I tried to see your talents. I think you stopped me somehow."

I looked up at her. "I closed my shields against you."

"Shields? I've never heard of such a thing. Must be a talent I don't have."

"You've several talents," I replied. "As well as Insight. If you can see my *parhelia*, then you also have Insight, as do I."

Her face brightened. "I do, yes. Glory be, my lady, your magic amazes me. So many talents and so many of them very strong. It's unusual."

The reason the sorcerers chose me as their host and enticed me to open The Keeper.

"Your lemon yellow and cyan blue I have hunches about," I said with a wry smile. The yellow was for heightened stamina, and the cyan blue was a *parhelia* that allowed her to connect with another person's mind—as she'd tried to do with me.

As to the way she'd handled the attackers in the courtyard? Her talent was connected to the coal black *parhelia* I'd noticed when she first came through the door that morning. Eld York had taught me that cankered *parhelia* turned black as they fell under the control of Eblis, the Lord of Darkness, but Zahra grinned when I told her this.

"The canker begins in the center. A faded glow from the original color remains an aura around it. True evil may turn it completely black, but the color is flat and the *parhelia's* movement is sluggish. This *parhelia's* true color is black, and it shines like polished onyx and moves like lightning. 'Tis like a mirror, collecting whatever magic someone else casts at me, and allowing me to do one of two things with it. I can reflect it back at the one who throws it, or I can hold it in check until I need it. Gives me one use of that talent whenever and however I wish. I've only used it a few times."

"But those men didn't use magic."

"No, but I can still deflect whatever someone throws at me, and it returns at the same speed. There just isn't any power to collect or store."

I contemplated the meaning. "So, if I tried to turn you into a mule, I'd turn myself into one instead; or you could hoard that spell and turn me or someone else into a mule later?"

She beamed at me. "About sums it up, although it's the energy I store, not its use. Could turn you into a rat or a snake if I wanted. I wouldn't, leastways not a snake. Hate snakes. What about your talents, my lady? You've so many."

I felt myself relax at the question. How good it felt to be able to talk freely about my gifts. Other than for Gideon and my family, I supposed that the entire world would think them but proof of the evil sorcerers who possessed me.

I admitted to my talent of shape-changing, and she begged me to show her. She clapped like a girl at a circus when I changed into a chestnut foal—better in our apartment sitting room than a full-grown horse. She was, however, far more enthralled with my becoming a hawk and demonstrating my ability to fly.

"I'd give anything to know how it feels to fly. A magnificent talent, if you ask me. What else can you become, my lady?"

"A variety of any of the three creatures used to create the first dragon as well as combinations of them. Eagle and horse combined becomes a child of Pegasus. Serpent blended with horse becomes a sea serpent." I did not tell her that combining all three created a dragon. I couldn't admit that to anyone. The sorcerers might learn of it.

"You have the talent to shape-change, too," I informed her. She sat up ramrod straight, her face infused with excitement.

"What form can I take?"

I laughed. "I have no idea. We'd have to experiment to find out. Be warned, however, that it's a difficult talent to develop and dreadfully painful. Reshaping bones, changing arms into wings or legs or getting rid of them entirely, sprouting scales or feathers or fur. It isn't easy."

"I do understand, but it would be worth it. I'd love to become a bird. I'd love to fly. We must try it some time."

I agreed, but when she urged me to demonstrate more, I thought to fascinate her by melting into a boa. She scrambled across the room, shaking uncontrollably, her face breaking into a sweat at the presence of the common-constrictor-me. I changed back to myself immediately and offered profuse apologies for frightening her.

"Told you I hate snakes! You ever become such a creature again without warning me, my lady, I'll find my crossbow, and it makes no difference to me if you are a princess!"

I tried hard not to laugh to avoid insulting her. It was an empty threat, but it certainly reflected her fear.

"I won't ever do it again, Zahra. I promise."

She nodded and wiped the dampness from her brow then gave me a weak smile. "'T'would be my misfortune I could only change into a snake."

Now I did laugh. "Then I wouldn't wish it on you, although when you've assumed a form, you feel a kinship with it and enjoy perceiving the world through both your human senses and that of the creature. Zahra, should we send missives to my father and the prince about what happened in the courtyard?"

"Your prince's guards will notify your prince and your father, and the men-at-arms are to notify the king. If nothing else, this *proves* you need to learn to protect yourself. Had all of those men fired darts, we'd all be unconscious or had our throats slit—except for you."

I nodded, believing that with me kidnapped, they would have demanded Gideon's life in return for mine.

Where was Gideon? Was he safe? Were our attackers part of the traitors I'd heard the Valdellians mention? Or another group of rebels?

Relief flowed over me when the dark orange of my gift of foretelling allowed me to see something of future events and reassured me that my beloved was safe…for the moment.

A knock at the door brought refreshments for us before we headed to the armory. I was about to be measured and fitted for armor and outfitted with the array of weapons I would need for the trip.

I wanted to laugh. The idea of armor offered a certain fascination, but I'd likely fall over in it and die.

What a sad irony to think of the princess-me, who had never wielded a wooden sword preparing to don a warrior's mail. I had no delusions about ever becoming much of a warrior, despite needing to learn how to protect myself in non-magical ways, but I had to admit the Valdellian Warlords' plot against my husband made we want to hack something to pieces.

Apparently, blacksmiths keep unfinished pieces of armor in various sizes in their shops to speed the forging process, as well as chain mail and all the appropriate garments to buffer tender skin from rough metal.

My curiosity, however, turned to flaming-hot-cheeked embarrassment when Zahra helped the chief blacksmith take my measurements in only my small clothes and chemise. She did her best to reassure me, but it was awful. When we'd finished, the man said before departing that he'd do *his* best to fit something to me quickly.

I still couldn't take any of this seriously.

Then Zahra redressed me and led me to the armory, where—despite our guards' displeasure—she fitted weapons for me out of a vast display of swords, daggers, and knives mounted on or leaning against the armory walls. Thank heavens I would not have to learn the more brutal weapons, like crossbows and war hammers, morning stars, halberds, maces and mauls. Zahra offered rudimentary teaching with each item selected for me, leaving the sword for last.

Despite my brothers' teasing, I was passably decent with a foil. Lon, my next-older and more patient brother, had taught me the correct footing and balance and how to protect myself with a foil; but a foil was not an arming sword, and even the wooden practice sword was so heavy I was nothing better than awkward and bumbling. At least I wasn't likely to decapitate myself with it.

Unable to use magic to either protect myself or fight back—at least if I wanted to learn anything, I earned dozens of scrapes, bruises, aching muscles and a proportionate amount of fatigue and non-magical hunger. Healing myself would have rendered the exercise pointless, so I had to content myself with frequently leaning against the wall to catch my breath.

"I think you're getting the feel of it, my lady," Zahra said at last, far too kindly.

"I couldn't kill a flea, but I think I figured out how to defend myself a bit."

"You did. I'm pleased that you learn so quickly."

Not far from us, another couple was fencing. When I removed my helmet, one man, his hair near-black and shoulder-length, stopped and doffed his own headgear.

Egan Gilroy. The man who would have executed me two weeks ago without a trial. My stomach turned. The glare on his face mirrored his hatred. No doubt he thought my attempts at sword-fighting were ridiculous. No doubt, my very existence disgusted him.

I also couldn't help wondering if he'd had anything to do with the men in the courtyard. Their failure might explain his anger.

"We need to return to our quarters, my lady," Zahra said, reclaiming my attention. "The maids will have a fine, hot bath ready for you when we arrive, along with our luncheon. No doubt your parents will want your attendance at supper, so I'd suggest a nap after luncheon, to restore you for tonight."

I'd lived a life of comfort as the daughter of a duke, but I'd been as likely to climb a tree as to have tea parties with my friends, especially the servants' sons. The concept of taking afternoon naps had never been pleasant for me. Until now. The upheaval in my life, the late nights being tortured by sorcerers, the long days with unending demands, had changed my attitude. "That sounds wonderful," I replied, wistful at thinking about Gideon joining us at supper. I had no idea if he could get away from his camp tonight but hoped so. Yes, a nap sounded lovely. If I could sleep.

I did. I slept better than I had in a long time.

In my dreams, I imagined flying northward to Bedford and then east to the Blackwater River. The Bitterroot was an ugly trestle bridge. Too many of the boards on the deck were warped or chipped and blackened with age. One bracing overhead was broken, although it seemed determinedly sturdy.

Warriors and local militia on both sides of the river, all armed, stood guard. If they'd known for sure when the Valdellians would arrive, they could have inflicted terrible damage by destroying the bridge as their army crossed it. Unfortunately, they had no such information and preferred not to risk their own people waiting for them.

Men began scrambling up the bridge's vertical beams, set in rock and concrete in the Blackwater's riverbed. When they reached the bridge, they ran pell-mell to the Bedford side of the river. Cries echoed around them as they turned to watch with bated breaths.

The blasts shook the earth, debris-laden spouts of water catapulting sky-high. The east end of the bridge crumpled first, then the rest snapped, tipping sideways and tottering for a moment before crashing into the water, breaking into pieces and sweeping downriver.

Exultant cries and fists raised to the heavens signified a fight won without bloodshed.

I drifted in and out of the dream, and then found myself in a tree above the Valdellian camp. They were closer to the river than I'd expected but for some reason not alerted by the blast. Perhaps the thick forest had dampened the sound. Whatever the reason, they'd soon walk into a deadly trap.

I smiled a bird smile, thanking Elam for his intervention in the fight between good and evil, and headed home.

I came awake, yawned and stretched, and then wondered about the dream. It seemed so real. Was it another of my visions of the future? I didn't remember any manifestation having offered so much detail.

Just as Zahra came to peek in on me, a ruckus erupted outside. I was out of bed and rushing out to the balcony ahead of her.

Several carriages were crossing the drawbridge into the courtyard, but that was nothing compared to the river of mounted warriors and wagons pouring through Leeds City toward the castle. Even though I'd expected it, it took me several seconds to realize the immensity of this moment. The rest of the army had arrived!

I felt badly for Duke O'Brien and his party having to forge through this throng on their way back to Bedford. I wondered if he'd break his promise and take some of his warriors with him.

"Oh, don't they look magnificent, Your Highness?" Zahra declared. "I scarce can take it in. There's so many—and so fierce looking, too."

And they were. The southern countries came first, Segovia at the front and Kythos on their flank, southern Kildaria mixed in with them. Kalbarri and Dundee, led by northern Kildaria, were a distance behind them, all with flags raised high.

Horses prancing and harnesses jingling, thousands upon thousands of Western League troops poured in. They began making camp around the edges of the moat, spreading out into the fields that surrounded the castle on both sides. Throughout the valley, shouts rang out, bugles blew, drums beat, and whistles and cries rose from the various details.

Tents sprouted on the north side of the castle, near the original vanguards' camps. The same was certainly happening on the south side, but we couldn't see it from our balcony.

Cook-fires plumed; a perfect network of parked wagons formed; and warriors unsaddled, tethered, fed and watered horses. In no time at all, it began to resemble a city of its own.

And tomorrow, the king would hold a celebration for the army, the League, their most esteemed leaders, and the delegation from Malloria.

A horrid chill raised goosebumps on my arms. A celebration! That was the perfect place for bad things to happen. I begged my *parhelia* of foretelling for enlightenment, but it ignored me. I ached to see Gideon. He was in the middle of this, and I not only wanted to know everything he knew, I feared for his life. Frustration turned into pent up energy that I needed to divert.

"Talk to me about your cyan blue *parhelia*," I asked Zahra. "I have the same gift, and if it does what I think it does, I want to learn how to use it. *Now*, if I can."

CHAPTER 5

"You haven't used it, Princess? As I told you, it's the gift of Mind-Pairing."

"Mind-Pairing?" I'd seen the dragons and the sorcerers seeming to exchange information without speaking and called it mind-reading. Was it the same? I'd give almost anything to know how to do it. "I wasn't taught from childhood how to use any of my gifts," I reminded her. "But I'm worried about Prince Gideon, and if I could Mind-Pair with him, reassure myself that he is alive and well, I'd be so grateful."

"You can, if he can't shield his mind from you, as you did from me. *That's* a fine trick, if you ask me."

"It's the only protection I have against the sorcerers and dragons."

"Ah. Likely the reason you're still sane. Haven't heard of anyone surviving possession in their right mind, although I must admit you're the first possessed person I've ever met."

"Eld York said the same," I replied, chuckling. "The Elds have an unfathomable library full of information about the strangest things, including possession, but unfortunately no cure for it."

"Well, it won't matter, if taking you to Malloria kills those bloody—uh—wretched monsters."

I didn't have the heart to tell her that the sorcerers denied the tale. "How far away can you perceive another person's thoughts?" I asked instead.

"I can Pair with my brother almost anywhere, and could with Mum, when she was alive, Elam rest her soul. Couldn't be with her when she died, so I Paired with her to say goodbye. 'Tis harder with mere acquaintances and strangers. Mind-Pairing opens my head to everything inside that person: impressions, emotions, conversations with others. Sometimes it's utter chaos and overcomes me. Haven't tried to listen to many people outside my own family for years." She gave me a kind smile. "I'd be willing to teach you, but I must give you fair warning. You'll be invading His Highness's private thoughts, and you can't take that lightly."

I understood and promised to take it very seriously.

The process, however, involved *two parhelia* if I wasn't near someone. The first, called Searching, would help me find the person with whom I wanted to Pair. The second, the cyan blue, would make the connection. Her magic fluttered into my *illumina* like a butterfly and settled on a fuchsia-colored *parhelia* that would Search for Gideon.

"Close your eyes for now. Searching can unsettle your stomach a bit."

My eyes widened instead. "Is that you?" I asked, realizing I'd "heard" her inside my mind, as I did the sorcerers and dragons, only this time I felt the stirring of my cyan blue *parhelia*. Mind-Pairing?

She nodded. *"We're already connected. Think your words, princess; 'Twill prepare you to Mind-Pair with your prince."*

"This is incredible. It's as if we're speaking, but our mouths aren't moving. But...you're right, there's more. You feel...pleased. No, you're excited."

"Come, Princess. We mustn't waste time. This may take a while and will sap your strength."

Mentally I found myself hurtled out of the castle to the camps in a dizzying sensation of speed, life diminished to darting shadows and flashes of light. Pressing my eyes shut, I struggled not to get lost in the scores of mental noises and impressions coming from the multitude of people around us.

Without warning, I suddenly felt Gideon's presence and saw the world through his eyes! His mind roiled with thoughts and emotions. He was upset with several people, arguing with a few, reassuring others who were upset. Vision and sounds sharpened. His men were livid about the Valdellians' plot to kill him. Some wanted to ride to Bedford to help blast the bridge, others to hunt down and slay the Valdellians themselves.

A Bedford leader complained. "Blowing up the bridge will cripple Bedfordshire for years. We should fight them instead."

A Mallorian insisted, "And some of you will die. Blasting the bridge guarantees the Valdellians cannot kidnap your leaders or take Prince Gideon's head, and you won't lose a single Kildarian life doing it."

"He's right," Gideon said. "You are all needed here. The best way to win this war is to fight it before it begins, and its first major thrust will be at the Eastern Realms, not in Kildaria. This is a minor skirmish, and we're defeating it before it begins. Our army of horsemen, the largest cavalry ever gathered, will thwart them in the Eastern Realms in a way an army on foot cannot."

My agitation grew when three men strolled by, stopping to watch. One I didn't know, but the others were Darby Murdock and Nevin Leath.

One warrior, a squat Segovian with a gnarled face approached, his hands fisted.

"Don't care about bridges and don't care about the Eastern Realms, *prince*. And I'm not the only one what hates you and King Desmond, and most especially that witch you married. If you haven't figured it out yet, there's more than one scheme afoot to rid the world of all of you. We're not above kidnapping or assassination to achieve our goals. And you can't catch us. We'll escape, we will, just you wait and see. As for me? Taking off your head seems more than reasonable!"

I gasped when he lunged toward Gideon, a shiv in his hand! I couldn't help the scream that erupted from my mind—Paired with Gideon's roar of anger and fear.

My prince dodged back and then grabbed the man's wrists, their arms shaking as they fought for advantage. Gideon's *parhelia* as a warlord didn't even have time to take shape before General Bellamy, Sir Lance, and two other Mallorians snatched the attacker and drove him to the ground.

The warrior snarled with hatred. "You can stop me, but you can't get all of us." Then he jerked his arm free and plunged the knife into his own heart.

I stared in shock as the blood poured out of him onto the ground and the light left his eyes.

The cacophony of voices engulfed me, but the general bellowed to the others, "Go on about your business! Leave us to sort this out."

Leath and Murdock exchanged furious looks as they walked by. Leath ignored Gideon but Murdock stopped to spit on his boot. Bellamy reached for his sword, but Gideon stopped him.

"He's nothing but a nuisance, Warren."

"Don't underestimate me, buffoon," Murdock said with scorn before walking away.

Bellamy let out a breath of frustration. "He didn't defile you, Your Highness?"

"I'm fine," Gideon said, staring at the enemy lying dead at his feet. "Our rebels and the Valdellians seem equally determined to rid themselves of me, and possibly every Mallorian here. Has anyone had any success interrogating the rebels that were caught?"

"No, Your Highness, not yet. I suspect they'd rather die than reveal their masters."

I jumped when something touched my arm, black and white images and snatches of gray fleeing away. In an instant my awareness came back to my sitting room.

"You're growing pale, my lady," Zahra said.

"He wasn't safe, Zahra," I said, trembling.

"But he is," she insisted. "He has good men 'round him and Elam watching over him."

I sat back, stunned by the nightmare I'd just witnessed. Zahra appeared equally troubled but continued to reassure me.

"You've had a lot to take in on one day," she said. "Meeting me, going riding, getting fitted at the armory, the army's arrival, and attacks against both you and your prince."

Not to mention the night I'd endured with the sorcerers and the Valdellians.

She continued. "Your emotions are high. You need time with your family. Let's ready you for supper. 'Twill get your mind off your troubles."

I looked forward to it more than anything but seeing Gideon right now. Kendal always managed my hair well, but Zahra surprised me when she accomplished turning my wild mop into a flattering collection of braids and knots. Granted mother had said Zahra learned from her mother how to care for a queen but, considering this woman had spent years as a soldier, I couldn't imagine hair fashions and elegant dresses being part of her repertoire. She did it so well, however, I wished Gideon could join our meal so that he could see it.

He couldn't, of course, but my parents greeted me with joy when I arrived—exuberance far above any I deserved—and then I realized we had company. Or rather, my parents did. Not far behind them stood not only Lon and Ian with Kendal, but four more people. Kendal beamed. Her parents, Baron and Baroness Tavish, and Kendal's younger brother and sister had arrived!

They came to offer me reserved bows and curtseys, all as fair-haired and green-eyed as Kendal. I noted the baron was more boisterous than I'd remembered him, his baroness warier. Kendal's two younger siblings eyed me with fearful awe, no doubt having heard the stories about my possession. I had no doubt they looked forward to my leaving Kildaria and Kendal behind.

"We've wonderful news," mother said, gripping my hand with excitement. "An hour after the Tavishes arrived, the Elds requested an audience with us. They've granted the dissolution of Ian's betrothal to Lady Eileen."

A thrill shot through me. It was wonderful news. "You can marry now," I said to my brother and his new fiancée.

"They can," Mother agreed. "Although Eld Tully cannot announce Lord Ian and Miss Kendal's banns sooner than three days from now, but it's already approved."

"I'm so happy for you," I said, wincing at my brother's rib-breaking hug and grinning at Kendal's gentler hug and kiss.

"You had an integral part in it, sister," Ian said. "We cannot thank you enough."

It was time to eat, but before we could sit down to table, a knock came at the door. I shrieked when Gideon entered and again when he came to scoop me up and spin me in circles, laughing with delight. No doubt Mother thought both of us ill-mannered at our outward display, especially when Gideon kissed me soundly in front of everyone. I didn't care. I was so very glad to see him. He was safe. He was here. He could stay by my side for a few hours. It was so wonderful, the food tasted a thousand times better, the air smelled sweeter, his hand in mine felt a hundred times more delightful than usual—and I hardly noticed my multitude of scrapes, bruises, and aching muscles.

I couldn't tell Gideon much about my day to avoid upsetting our guests, and our conversation never broached what had happened to him that day—which I had to pretend to knew nothing about. I felt guilty that Zahra knew more about my magic now than Gideon did, and I'd promised him I'd share more of my talents with him after we married. If only constant interruption hadn't made it nearly impossible to discuss much of anything.

"You know I can't stay with you again tonight," my prince whispered in my ear when it came time for him to depart and he held me close for a bit.

"I know, but I do need to talk to you as soon as I can."

"I heard what happened at the stable. I'm furious, but I don't want to shock your brother's future in-laws discussing it."

"Nor do I, but that isn't all I need to tell you. As soon as we can, Gideon, please."

He nodded and kissed me a gentle farewell. "As soon as we can."

Terius looked down his nose at me when he said, "Because you locked us in for two days, and your army will leave Kildaria soon, we'll have to skip some of the steps we'd planned to take you through in your training. Let the dragons out."

My heart skipped a beat. The sorcerers had been angry with me for keeping them trapped for two days and two nights. How would the dragons react at having been held back for three days and nights?

"I thought you said we'd be done by the time the army came."

"You robbed us and them of three nights. We'll be done when we're done. Do it now," Terius insisted, Rhesalus and Mariana staring at me.

I did as commanded, trying to force myself to relax, but Enya and Ramah appeared with gaping maws and eyes fiery red with fury.

"You shut us in!" the gigantic drake, Ramah, roared.

"Why?" Enya echoed him, her fangs bared.

I cowed down in paralyzing fear, my hands clapped to my ears. If the sorcerers could throw me around like a rag doll, even if they weren't mortal, what could these creatures do to me?

Terius raised a hand and spoke in the language of sorcery. The dragons pulled back, snarling but listening. For all the world, the sorcerer seemed twice as powerful as the dragons despite being only a fraction their size. The three stood rapt long enough I knew they, too, were reading each other's thoughts, talking about me, about what had happened today.

They showed little sympathy for what I'd endured, but I sensed their relief at my survival. Then something else Terius told them caused Ramah's demeanor to change in an instant. He turned to pin me with that cold, serpentine gaze that made me feel hunted. What the sorcerers wanted to do with me tonight must be particularly important.

"It's time to step up your education," Rhesalus said. "I'll guide you through it."

"I'm better at it." Terius eyed us both, his lip curled in amusement. "Not particularly."

"I insist," the eagle-mage said, his eyes unblinking as he stared at me.

"If you hurt her—"

Terius laughed. "I've no desire to damage your mage partner, Rhesalus."

My temper flared. "I'm not—"

"You will be," Moriana insisted. "We told you not to attach yourself to the Mallorian prince."

"Then why did you allow it?" I retorted, my blood boiling.

"Because you'll do anything to protect him," she said. "And we need him."

"For what?" I glared at her.

Moriana's vicious smile peeled her lips back from her teeth. "He's a powerful man, Theona. He is, after all, a prince."

An important truth, of course, but what wasn't she telling me? I knew the lie was there, hidden deep inside her.

Terius actually smiled. "Theona, tonight you'll learn to use a powerful magical talent few people possess. It's the first *real* step toward returning us to mortality. If you're successful, you've every possibility of stopping this war before it begins."

They'd promised me that before, but it hadn't happened. They often lied to me, and I supposed this was one of those lies.

But, if I could do this, maybe I could get rid of them at last! I felt half sick, half excited, and equally enticed by the privilege of learning to use this talent, even if I despised having to use any of my gifts to help them.

"First, can you Call animals?" Moriana asked.

"Call them?"

"Yes," she said, her eyes glittering. "With your mind, your magic. You cast your thoughts to them and make them come to you."

"I think I Called birds once." I'd been seated on the balcony and seen them flying by. It was a magical moment when they turned and came to me, some even feeding from my hand.

"Really?" Rhesalus's eyes danced with amusement. "Excellent. Here is the talent for doing so." He directed my thoughts to the connected *parhelia* inside me—although he didn't call it a *parhelia*. Only Eld York had done that. "Try Calling a snake. We'll need it for our experiment."

Experiment? I didn't like the sound of that. But how did I "Call" a snake?

"Do as you have with all your other talents. Coax it, stroke it, find its pulse and command it."

The *parhelia* was the softest baby blue I'd ever imagined. Mentally, I touched it and flinched as visions went hurtling through my mind of all creation being subject to it: the plants, the animals, the earth itself and everything on it. It made the power of the Elements seem tame in comparison and forewarned me with instinctive certainty that misuse of this *parhelia* could inflict untold destruction.

I was about to learn how to do something with it that involved an innocent animal. I didn't like it at all.

How could I Call a snake? Applying my owl senses, I combed the forest and detected a myriad of creatures skittering and slinking through the dark, reptilian and otherwise. Only yards away, I sensed movement and went toward it. I found a small hognose snake, the sort Ian and Lon liked to play with as boys, threading its way through the loam.

I tried Calling it the way I'd Called the birds but felt no response. Did they even communicate with each other? I didn't know if snakes could hear in the human sense, but if hearing wasn't necessary, then how would this talent work?

I couldn't help my natural tendency, even in this moment that seemed filled with evil potential, to turn to Elam when I needed help. Maybe The Greatest Teacher of All would guide me. Every element on the planet, every star in the sky belonged to him. Surely, he understood this talent he'd given me. Hopefully he also understood I had no intentions of using my talents to do harm.

I closed my eyes and prayed. Stroking the *parhelia* brought a response that snapped my eyes open again. The serpent slithered toward me, no fear, no hesitation. I picked it up and took it to the clearing.

Terius chuckled and rubbed his hands together. "Your girl *is* marvelous, Rhesalus."

Rhesalus grinned. "She is, isn't she? Now my sweet, you must understand the power you'll use tonight before you try to use it, because it is quite dangerous."

Were there any that weren't?

Terius's sorcery now drew my awareness to a somber, mulberry-colored strand of light hiding deep within my *illumina*, the place that held all of my *parhelia*, my magical talents. The strand tasted bitter.

"In mortality, creatures' souls, their *rumoria* or spirits or life force or whatever you choose to call them, are bound to their bodies by nature. Soul and body separate at death, and the normal order is for the good soul to return to Elam's Garden, while the rest go to the Underworld, the Realm of the Dead.

"We thwarted that by binding our souls to the dragons' life-force, which in life made our sorcerer-dragon pairs next to immortal. Even if death did occur, we could avoid the Underworld by taking possession of a mortal being.

"Our friends the Elds, however, thwarted that by trapping our *rumorias* inside The Keeper. You know they made the vessel of Dreamwood and enchanted it with their Elden power, which neutralized our magic. We remained 'alive' and in this world but couldn't escape to possess anyone.

"When Moriana opened The Keeper, we took possession of her, but she was unable to free us before Cleary the Brave struck her with Slayer and sent all of us back inside The Keeper. We've waited for centuries for you to be born and to grow up and rescue us. Now, by satisfying certain exacting requirements, you can set us free, which involves producing bodies for us and embedding our souls in those bodies. When we have our own bodies, you will be free of us."

I couldn't envision how any of it would happen, but I knew I'd do whatever I must to get rid of them.

Terius continued. "Learning to transfer Ramah's soul into a living being, in this case a snake, is your assignment for tonight. In essence, you'll help the dragon's soul temporarily 'possess' the snake. Practice is essential because it's difficult, and the more intelligent the recipient, the harder they resist you. You must master it before giving us our mortal frames because failure will kill us—and you."

I cringed at the thought, even as he reassured me that with a less intelligent animal like the serpent, I was in no danger and Ramah in very little.

"The discomfort will pass quickly, and the snake should be fine afterward."

Discomfort? Should be fine? I gulped, remembering too well opening The Keeper and becoming possessed by these monsters. Discomfort and being fine would not describe it.

"You don't need to bring the dragons out to do this, but for now, visualizing the process will help you make sense of it. Begin by using the mulberry-shaded *parhelia* to grasp the snake's life force. When you're sure of your control, mentally touch Ramah's *rumoria*. Your talent will take over, transferring his soul from within you to the snake. Ignore the sensations. They will trick you into thinking he's flying *through* you, but in truth he's leaping from *inside* you."

Translation? This "process" would be anything but pleasant for all three of us.

"Remember," Terius urged. "Once you've connected Ramah's *rumoria* to the snake's, you must hold on tight until the link is complete. Letting go will kill the snake."

I breathed deep to calm my nerves. Forcing Ramah's spirit inside the snake seemed wicked. I'd have refused if I'd had any choice.

Ramah's eyes twirled blue-green with excitement. I ignored him, took hold of the *parhelia,* and reached for the serpent's *rumoria.* It shuddered, as if irritated by the contact, but I held on. The instant my magic touched Ramah's *rumoria*, he shrank to the size of a mouse. Hot, hard pain tore into me as he streaked through me like a bolt of lightning—or so it felt—and drove into the snake.

My knees buckled and only Rhesalus's waiting arms kept me on my feet. I gasped, unable to speak, wanting to scream, horrified to see the dragon's essence overwhelm the snake. The creature twisted violently, as if set on fire.

Rhesalus whispered in my ear over and over, begging me to not let go. "It's only a snake, child. It's just responding to instinct."

"It's suffering," I croaked. "It's dying."

"No, it's fine, but you cannot stop now, or it will die. All will be fine. Ramah's gaining control. Watch."

The snake quieted as Ramah's *rumoria* settled into its body, flattening the serpent's life force against its inner walls like a useless piece of furniture.

Immediately, the snake's body began to swell. My magic sang to me as it followed the dragon's progress, as did Ramah's joy in finding a home, in being able to experience tangibility again.

The snake-dragon creature blossomed, growing larger and larger and sprouting four legs, two wings, and a dragon's head. Knobbed horns appeared, making Ramah into Ramah. Rearing back his head and bellowing, he rose to his hind legs and stretched his wings so wide he would have dwarfed the castle. The ground shook when he dropped to earth again.

I quailed into Rhesalus while the sorcerer laughed with glee.

"Ah, Ramah, you're fabulous. Would that we could head off into the skies as we used to do. Far too long have we been denied the joys of mortality."

Ramah did his best to strut around the clearing, his tail scraping the ground and his wings catching on tree branches and brush. He lowered his snout and smelled the earth, reached up with a huge, clawed hind foot to scratch behind his tiny ear. Deep inside, he laughed the way I'd always believed a dragon could. He touched noses with Enya, her eyes as wild and blue-green as his.

"Incredible," Terius murmured, gripping Moriana's hand.

They looked odd together, the sorcerer and the girl these creatures had possessed when she, too, was only sixteen years old. Like me, she appeared in her twenties, also having matured quickly because of the influence of the dragons.

Terius, however, despite appearing closer to forty, was more than one hundred forty years old when Cleary imprisoned him and Rhesalus inside The Keeper five hundred years ago. After Moriana joined them, Terius bonded with her as his mage partner, something I feared was far more important than just the joining of magical powers.

Ramah grew restless, crouching down and flexing his wings as if preparing to spring into the air.

"No, no, dear boy," Terius scolded. "Not yet. Theona's not strong enough to keep you and the snake together. If the snake dies and she cannot separate you, you'll die with it. Now, return your host to its normal size and shape."

Ramah glared at him but obeyed, and Terius turned to me, his golden eyes filled with a blend of unbelievable delight and respect.

"Next, you must remove the dragon from its host. Beware. The spirit has a natural affinity toward the body and will fight you. This time, fasten onto every inch of Ramah's soul, then the snake's soul. As you separate them, remember taking out any piece of the snake's *rumoria* will kill it."

Every inch? How did I know how many inches comprised either a snake's or a dragon's *rumoria*? I flinched as Ramah's chaotic thoughts and impressions raced into me. His life force permeated every cell of his host's body, while the creature's *rumoria* languished. How did I get him out?

When I realized the serpent was dying, I panicked. I tugged at Ramah, wincing when I felt both creatures' pain. Ramah loved it here! He longed for mortality! He didn't want to leave.

Silently I begged him to comply. Both would die if he didn't, and who knew what would happen to me. Ramah's plaintive wail when he conceded sounded like he was being asked to die.

Perhaps, in a way, he was.

The dragon's essence seemed to "ooze" out of those cells, pulling together and leaving the creature to itself. The excruciating flash of pain and heat came as his *rumoria* stormed back to me and then materialized beside Enya. The howl erupting from him as he leaned into his mate nearly tore my heart out. Who needed to speak a foreign language to understand how grievous losing that brief taste of life had felt?

The sorcerers held their collective breath as they observed the snake.

Mentally touching the creature's *rumoria*, I found it alive but stunned. It had forgotten how to breathe! I nudged its soul, stroked it magically, touched its lungs and commanded them to draw in air. It lay unresponsive.

I prodded it with my finger, telling it verbally to wake up, and finally its *rumoria* shimmered and twisted, filled its mortal cells, and allowed itself to gasp for breath. Confused, the serpent sped away in a crooked path, finally disappearing into the leaves and loam of the forest floor.

"Marvelous," Rhesalus murmured, his gray eyes glittering.

And then the truth dawned, and I gnashed my teeth in fury. The *real* test of my success tonight wasn't joining Ramah with the snake, it was whether the snake survived. What a despicable abuse of innocent life!

"You expected the snake to die," I accused.

"Of course. I don't know of anyone who's succeeded the first time," he said with amazement that rivaled Terius's.

More people had done this before me? What a horrible thought. Why? When? "You'd have made me do it again if I'd failed," I accused, upset by the idea.

"But you didn't fail, my dear girl."

He grinned, and Moriana hugged Terius, who laughed with joy. Even Enya seemed pleased, all of them likely convinced they were another step closer to rejoining the world from which they'd been torn half a millennium ago.

Rhesalus caressed my head, his feathery touch reminding me that he was only a spirit. I pulled back and glared at him.

"You need to take care of yourself, my dear," he said, grinning. "Hunt well and then sleep well. We'll see you again tomorrow night."

They disappeared and I locked my shields against them, for a grateful moment enjoying the delusion of being alone.

The questions I'd have liked to ask plagued me. It couldn't be this easy to return the sorcerers and dragons to mortality. If so, Moriana could have done it before she was sent into The Keeper. What more would I need to know before I could make it happen? And how soon would I learn it?

As much I wanted to rid myself of these monsters, I doubted I'd like the answers when they came.

As great a burden as these thoughts were, I now had a greater concern. I needed to see Gideon, but doing that first required a test I dared not put off.

CHAPTER 6

The test? To see if I could I take another living being through a portal with me safely.

In my owl persona, I caught a field mouse and portalled with it to my room. My heart skipped a beat when the mouse hung limply by its tail in my fingers—which flipped into heart-racing excitement when the mouse returned to its frenetic squealing and kicking. I hadn't harmed it! I could portal others with me!

Then I did eat the mouse—as an owl—and sailed to just outside Gideon's tent. Metamorphosed into a tiny thread snake, I slid inside, where I became myself, kneeling by my husband's cot. When I summoned mage light, the warrior part of my prince made him bolt upright. His jaw dropped when he saw me in the lavender glow.

"Theona!" he hissed, recoiling as if I might attack him. "For Elam's sake, what are you doing here? You near scared the tripe out of me!"

I shushed him, terrified of alerting his guards. I kissed him, just to calm and reassure both of us.

"Gideon," I whispered, my lips touching his. "We need to talk."

"In the middle of the night? And how did you—?"

"Shhh." I kissed him again. "Please trust me."

His hands gripped my arms, and I winced.

"Sorry. I had to know you were…real."

"A kiss isn't enough?"

He laughed quietly. "It should be, shouldn't it?"

"I need to take you somewhere. It's important."

"I repeat, in the middle of the night? And surrounded by guards?"

"Please trust me. Where we'll go, they cannot follow, and if we're quick and quiet they'll never know."

A hint of uncertainty flashed across his face, and those gorgeous violet eyes studied me carefully.

"No more caves and dragons."

"And no Keeper, either. But it does involve magic. You wanted to know what I can do, and I can't put off showing you."

He slipped off his cot, appearing hesitant but also curious. I rose and opened a portal to my usual glade. His head reared back, and he stepped away from it.

"What sort of darkness is this, Theona? Is this the Underworld?"

"No, of course not. It's nighttime. This is a portal, a magical door to another place, and that place is a glade on the back side of Mt. Carinor. *Please* trust me, my love. You know I'd never do anything to hurt you."

His shoulders stiffened but he nodded, although he refused to take my hand as he ventured into the glade. At least his long sniff of the fresh night air and a good look at the forest surrounding us appeared to impress him. I followed him through the portal, the headache and stomach pains proving that traveling further and taking something larger than a mouse with me exacted a higher price.

"This is the way you escaped the dungeon, isn't it?" he asked.

"Yes. And how I left my parents' apartment and returned to my own when my kidnappers poisoned me."

I remembered the horrid, bitter taste of it, their hard fists striking me, the terror of being locked up and left in the dungeon to die.

"Gideon, we also need to talk about *your* talents. Knowing your own magic will help you master it, but it will also help you better understand me." I knew he remembered the connection he'd felt with his own *parhelia,* of being a potential warlord, on our wedding night. I hoped he still wanted to know more.

Chagrin puckered his face. "I imagine your magic is an awful burden, Theona. If I hadn't seen what I've seen, if I didn't know what I know, I couldn't...." He let the rest hang.

If not, he couldn't trust me. He couldn't believe in me. I didn't blame him, but it hurt all the same. Still, he'd admitted the night before we married that he'd seen a vision of the two of us fighting side-by-side and back-to-back—a vision I'd also seen.

"We have to remain united," I reminded. He had so many talents, so many *parhelia* tucked within his *illumina,* they would make him a powerful man, and he needed to learn how to use them.

"Tell me all," he insisted. "Hold nothing back, Theona. I won't tolerate being caught off-guard by your abilities, no matter what they are."

I nodded my understanding. We would address *his* talents later. As I'd done with Zahra, I gave him a performance, changing from a tiny flycatcher to an eagle to an owl to a budgie. I landed on his finger and metamorphosed into a small king snake, winding around his arm. Reshaping into a larger python, I hung toward the ground, where he set me down. Sliding away, I became a coral snake, a sidewinder, a rattler. Then I transformed in the twinkling of an eye into a braying donkey, a zebra, which barked more than it brayed, and my white-mare self.

Gideon's eyes were wide with unconcealed wonder as he walked around me, murmuring something about this being "incredible."

Returned to myself, I took his hand in mine. "There is more, my love. Some you won't like, but you asked to know the truth."

Again, I shifted into the mare then sprouted the wings that turned me into a child of the legendary Pegasus. His jaw dropped and he again took a step back. I spun away and in a swift gallop leaped into the air and took flight, sweeping over him and around the glade, then landed again. I stayed a distance from him when I returned to myself. Would he accept what I'd shown him, or would he want to destroy me? I wouldn't blame him if he thought all of this was witchcraft and wanted to put an end to it.

"I cannot share some of what I can do tonight," I said. As with Zahra, I explained the potential blending of the three creatures that made the dragons, not only winged-horse but also leviathan. As with Zahra, I couldn't admit to becoming a dragon. I only hoped he'd forgive me if he ever found out.

"I can change sizes, too," I explained, "just as I chose to become a small bird or a large one. I can also change my own appearance, which may not please you."

I then shifted into the young scout Tally. Gideon's eyes bugged, and he took another step away from me.

"Theona, are you suggesting—?"

"Yes," I replied in that man's voice. "It was I who came to you in disguise. The sorcerers forced me, but it was the only way to stop the Valdellians. My information also helped convince many of the disbelievers in the League that the impending war is real."

Gideon threaded his fingers into his hair and blew a puff of air through rounded lips. After long thought and an even longer silence, he said, "Was this...scout...ever real?"

I shared the tale with him and saw the sadness in his eyes.

"How have you learned all this? I've accepted that 'magic' as we perceive it doesn't exist, that what the Elds maintain is the power of Elam is something incredible, something capable of shaping worlds and stars and turning mountains into seas—and if turned dark can destroy everything we know and love. I just can't imagine you learning all of this on your own, especially as a prisoner."

I gave him a wan smile. "You're right. My captivity is an illusion. I stay here for you, my love, and for the good of Kildaria and the Western League nations. My 'magic' isn't polluted—at least not yet—but I haven't learned how to use it entirely on my own, a fact I don't like any more than you do."

"Then how?" he insisted.

"It began the night I opened The Keeper, although I had no idea the things I saw and learned were inspired by the sorcerers. When I began to understand them, they started appearing to me—"

"You've seen them? Talked to them?" His eyes bugged with horror. Did he believe me, or did he imagine me talking to myself like a lunatic? Not that that thought hadn't entered my own mind more than once, of course.

I nodded. "And I've worked with them—because they force me to—but they've also taught me more about my magic than I ever could have learned on my own. Kildaria's Elds haven't encouraged anyone to openly teach our people how to wield magic in our day because magic is mistrusted and shunned by most, and most of those with it dare not admit it."

Gideon forced a resentful grunt. "As it is in Malloria. I've never been able to admit what I can do to others."

So, I told him. About my own family's abilities, about Kendal's, Zahra's, and our nemeses Leath, Murdock and Gilroy.

With solemnity, he asked, "How can you have so much power and not want to conquer the world with it?"

My hesitant smile faded. He didn't wonder why I didn't want to, he feared that I did.

"I haven't that much power, Gideon, and wouldn't want it. Besides, if I did come by it, the sorcerers would either wrest it from me or use me to get what *they* want. I'll do whatever I must—even die—to prevent that from happening. That's why we must talk. You have to be prepared to leave me if things go wrong."

I dropped to one knee before my future king, my head bowed. "My love, I can think of nothing more joyful than surviving all of this insanity, ridding myself of the sorcerers, and being your wife and Malloria's princess forever. I will support, defend, and obey you as my liege lord. I swear fealty to you to every degree humanly possible."

He touched my shoulder and urged me to my feet. For the first time since meeting Prince Gideon Seville, I felt his full sovereignty—and felt distanced from him because of it. I couldn't blame him. He had a nation to protect, but it didn't change the deeper hurt that carved its way into my heart.

"You know my talents better than do I, Theona. You know I've received visions and knowing that we need help to fight in the war against the Central Alliance is part of what brought me and my One Hundred to Kildaria. What powers do I have that you could—and are willing—to train me to use?"

My breath caught in surprise. He trusted me? He wanted to learn?

Thus began our first night of exploring the possibilities. We talked, I taught, and he made attempts to utilize some of his talents. He did well with a few of them, better with a couple of others. The talents he bore that were similar to Zahra's allowed me to confess to him Zahra's part in helping me to learn to Search and to Mind-Pair. Not that he liked what he heard about my having Paired with him without his permission, but when I helped him touch those two important *parhelia*, I felt his amazement at how they worked and the potential advantages they offered us. If only I hadn't felt him withdraw a little more. He didn't want me to invade his thoughts—in essence spy on him—or interfere with his awareness without his knowing it.

"I can see the advantage, but my thoughts and beliefs are my own, and I won't have them infringed upon."

I offered repeated reassurances that I would never do it again without permission, but I feared it would be a long time before he excused what I'd done.

"I'm exhausted," he said at last. "I can't imagine surviving more rounds of obnoxious meetings in the morning without some rest."

"And you must eat before going to sleep. Whatever do you have left to talk about?"

He cocked a wry smile. "You wouldn't believe it if I told you."

I would have preferred his taking my hand when we portalled back to his cot, but he didn't.

Despite the tension between us, it seemed strangely quiet in the tent, curiously safe against a harsh world waiting outside to pounce on us. The nausea settled when I breathed deep, but I wanted to weep when he didn't kiss me good night, he just stared at me as if he was uncertain I was still human.

I leaned toward him, whispering, "If all you do is sleep in your tent at night, why can't you sleep in our rooms with me?"

"Too many of my men don't trust you. I'm doing my best to convince them that you haven't ensorcelled me. So far, I've succeeded."

But I wasn't sure I believed that he believed it when he said good night and turned toward his cot.

Thus dismissed, I opened the portal that took me to my bed, where I cried myself to sleep.

———+———

I loved many of the fine qualities Zahra brought into my life, but one thing of which she was not adept was making a genteel morning entrance. She charged in and threw the curtains open to the morning's stark light, shocking me from sleep and feeling ridiculous, drooling out one corner of my mouth.

"Oh! Princess? Are you alright? I didn't mean to startle you."

Sleep had restored my strength, but I was far from alright. I came to my feet and barely made it to the washbasin before heaving up my guts. I hated this reminder of what happened when I used too much magic. Even worse, this was the second night in a row I'd done it.

"Heavens!" Zahra cried. "A bit under the weather, are we?"

All I could do was dry heave and nod, wishing I only had a case of the stomach flu. I'd probably survive that. I wasn't so sure about this.

Zahra gave me a cool washcloth for my face and helped me back into bed, where I curled into a ball and tried to tame my churning insides. Her hand felt warm on my forehead, proving I had no fever.

"Mercy, my lady, I know you didn't drink a drop of the hard stuff at supper last night. But you're not feverish, and you've not been married long enough to, uh, well...."

Flushing in embarrassment, I raised my wrist and showed her the Dreamwood bracelet I'd somehow managed to slip back on before falling into bed. It prevented conception.

"Ah," she said. "Well, it won't be that in the near future. Which is good, of course, because it wouldn't be right to bring a wee bairn into this situation; but there's something different about you this morning, something…unsettled…about your magic. I can feel it."

"There is?" I sat straight up in bed and then fell back down again, fighting another wave of nausea.

"You've used a bit of it, maybe more than is wise. That can play havoc with your mind."

I pressed my hands to my face and grumbled. "How do you know so much about me, Zahra? We haven't seen each other for eight years, and I was a little girl when you left."

"Before putting in for this post, I spent some hours counseling with Eld York and his Elden comrade, Eld Terris. Learned a good deal more about your possession than I like, that's for sure. The rest I've gleaned from the little time I've spent with you."

I wiped eyes still watering from the pain of trying hard not to be sick, even as Zahra's comments brought back more faded memories of our years together. She could keep me in line without spoiling my fun, and I'd trusted her with some of my biggest secrets.

"You're right. I used too much magic last night." I swallowed hard. Would she ask me to explain more?

"Right. Well, your breakfast is here, and odd as the idea sounds, you'll feel better after you eat. And you won't toss it back up if you start out slow."

I blinked away my tears, grateful for her understanding! Even better, I could see she wanted to know what I'd done with my magic, even if it wasn't her place to ask, and she didn't. She disappeared into the sitting room only to return with a plate full of food. The first few bites challenged my stomach, but after that, I ate like a starved cur.

Clamoring outside suddenly interrupted us: hammering, people calling out, things being dragged to and fro. Curiosity once again had us heading to the balcony.

Preparations were already underway for the celebration! King Desmond had scheduled it for just before the midday meal, when he would address the crowd, introduce all of the new combined army's leaders, and allow Prince Gideon to make a few remarks regarding what an historic moment this day and this event was.

Afterward, the throng would enjoy a generous banquet in the courtyard. Already the construction of two platforms was completed, where the king and other dignitaries would stand. Workers were making tables, several already set up to hold the food. Fires roasted haunches of meat that servants turned on spits, and no doubt the kitchens were equally busy with other dishes.

A forbidding feeling inside me made me swallow hard. How I dreaded that feeling. I'd had it more than once since becoming possessed and dared not ignore it. Something awful was about to happen.

"Do you think we could ride today?" I asked Zahra. I longed to get out of the castle and away from the crowds.

"Not likely, my lady. Not with all the tumult going on. Perhaps tonight, after everything settles down. I suppose we could venture to the armory, do some bladework if you like."

That sounded wonderful. I needed some way to work off the anxiety cramping my insides.

We spent a little time with every weapon I now owned: knives, daggers, my sword, a small shield, even bow and arrow. Zahra was amazing with her bow and made me want to improve. The work helped my mood, despite earning me more bruises and sore muscles.

When Egan Gilroy arrived later with his fencing companion, I was grateful that a bare-chested young man interrupted us. Well-defined biceps and chest muscles that glistened under a layer of sweat from head to waist and blackened gloves on his hands suggested he was one of the blacksmith's assistants. He asked us to follow him to one of the curtained spaces where the blacksmith had measured me for my armor. The blacksmith himself awaited us there.

"My armor," I murmured in awe, seeing it arrayed in one of the cubicles. "How did you finish it so quickly? You must have worked on it all night."

"No m'lady, don't work alone. I've two other master blacksmiths and several apprentices to help. Now, I need a fitting. Would be a miracle if it doesn't need adjustments, but I've been known to work a few miracles."

His droll smile had me grinning. He departed and left Zahra to help me trade my clothes for the layers of equipment.

"I'll name each piece as we go," she said, "so that you'll get used to them. If ever a disaster arises, you'll need to know how to apply as much of it as you can on your own. Just know that unless you were fighting on horseback, you'd likely not wear all of it. It's far too heavy to walk in very far, and if you fell, you'd never get up on your own. If you can't use but a few pieces, choose the chain mail and the chest protection."

First came the padded jerkin, a buffer between my skin and small clothes and the armor. Rather than plain gray, the handsome, red-dyed fabric, edged with white piping, reminded me of Gideon and his country's colors.

The ring-mail hauberk felt more luxurious—in its own, strange way—than a heavy necklace. It tinkled metallically as it cascaded over my head and arms and down to my thighs.

Then came the cuirass—back and front plates connected by leather straps—which molded to my torso, and pauldrons and gorgets for my shoulders and neck. Vambraces and cuisses embraced my arms. Gauntlets fit my hands perfectly. Fauld and culet would protect my belly and backside.

For my shins and calves were the greaves, poleyns for my knees, and sabotages protected my feet.

I hated tight spaces, and this was terrifying. I feared the weight alone would topple me like a felled tree. Still, Zahra wasn't done. She strapped the baldric, a leather belt for my sword, so that it would hang from my right shoulder to my left hip. Its red leather matched the jerkin. Then she opened the curtain and stepped into the short hallway between armory and blacksmith shop to call the blacksmith.

He came to examine the armor's fit, making a few adjustments on straps but otherwise expressing his own amazement that it fit so well.

"Well, I suppose miracles do still occur," he said, giving a quiet chuckle. "I've more for you, Princess." He said, stepping around the corner and returning with a sword and shield. He handed me the short sword first. He'd reworked and sharpened it for me, and the deadly, polished blade flashed in the light, its grip neatly wrapped in braided red leather that matched the baldric.

It was a handsome weapon. I swung it a few times, despite fearing it would knock me from my feet. Its near-perfect balance amazed me.

Slipping it into the sheath, I next took the shield. Kildarian warriors traditionally used round shields, but Zahra had requested a heater shield for me—five-sided, with a flat top and wedge-shaped sides and bottom, its tapered tip pointed toward the ground. It was edged in white, with a red center, and decorated with the crest of Malloria. It was beautiful. Heavy but beautiful.

Last came the helmet, and I sighed with relief when Zahra set it on my head. It was a simple conical version, designed like a small cage with vertical bars before my face. Bless Zahra. She knew the type of helm that provided narrow eye holes wouldn't work for me. The armor was bad enough. But this? My smile faded at remembering the brief vision of me fighting alongside Gideon—and the assurance that the day would come when I would need all of this. Strange that this was the armor I'd envisioned.

At both the blacksmith and Zahra's encouragement and assistance, I made a brief effort to move around in the cumbersome, clanking outfit. I felt as silly as a little girl dressed in my mother's hundred-pound evening gown.

"Come, my lady," Zahra said. "You must see yourself." She led me to a wall just outside the alcove that bore a tall strip of polished metal—as close to a mirror as I supposed most warriors had occasion to come.

The vision that stared back at me shocked me.

Only four days ago, Gideon and I had exchanged our vows as Forever-Mates. I wore a wedding gown fit for a princess. Oddly enough, today I felt every bit as elegant in a completely different way. I could imagine myself a warrior, ready to battle our enemies.

"Excellent work, sir. I thank you," I said.

The brawny, bristly-cheeked man gave me a slow, solemn bow. "Fenwick Blacksmith, my lady. 'Twas my pleasure—our pleasure. Admire Lord McArthur and consider your prince a good man. Both vouch for you, and both want the best for our countries. I pray Elam blesses all of you with vict'ry."

Zahra asked if I'd like to practice in the armor to get a feel for it, but it was as spotless today as it would ever be, and for just today I wanted to leave it so. How my old friends would laugh if they knew how I felt. They all pined for satin and silk and would wonder what I could possibly find bewitching about leather and steel.

It was time to retire to my rooms to prepare for the celebration, so Zahra helped me change clothes and turn my armor over to the blacksmith for safekeeping. The crowd of servants had grown in the courtyard as we wove our way back to our quarters. I didn't like it when three men, working on benches for the seating, blocked our way and ignored our guard's demands to make way.

One dropped a hammer on the ground too close to my toes, and I grimaced when another hawked and then spat in my face. One of our guards and Zahra whipped their knives from their scabbard and advanced on the man. He laughed and ran off. The other two parted to let us through, but the third man tried to trip me as I passed, infuriating me. I wondered how he would explain what happened next.

Without thinking, I shape-changed my right leg into a horse's rear leg—hidden beneath my clothing, of course—and kicked him as hard as any cow had ever kicked a person. His scream and the sound of cracking bone brought others to see what had happened.

Horrified, I knelt to comfort him, offering to collect a physician for him. He slapped at me with his good hand and cursed me to Hades, giving our guards the perfect opportunity to help Zahra and me escape. I'd thought I'd laugh at getting even with the man, but instead I felt terrible. I'd used my magic to hurt someone. I'd sworn I'd never do that, but I'd lost my temper.

I must never do it again.

CHAPTER 7

"You look lovely, Princess," Zahra said, stepping back to allow me to come to my feet. Having bathed and layered me in clothing fit for a princess, she'd arranged my hair in eye-catching braids and curls. I felt more ostentatious than I had in metal—even while simply wearing my favorite rose-pink gown and matching slippers. I would have allowed myself to enjoy it—if only that feeling of impending doom hadn't returned.

"Thank you, Zahra. Truth to tell, I'd rather be out in the fields, riding Caspian."

Zahra chuckled. "And I would join you. Come. It's time."

Four of Gideon's guards escorted us to the courtyard. A light fog had rolled in, although the day still felt warm, and the assembly, now allowed to enter the courtyard, throbbed with excitement. People of all ages and all walks of life came, warriors and family members, lesser dignitaries, noblemen and noblewomen, leaders and officers. The delicious aroma of the cooking food wafted around us. I felt half-starved.

Zahra and I were directed to the lower of the two platforms, facing the south wing. We joined my family, and with them were the other heads of state, the High Council, the Elds, and the assorted details that guarded us. Zahra traded places with me when Councilman Egan Gilroy went out of his way to step on my foot and gouge me in the ribs with his elbow. I could imagine that he liked to torture crickets and butterflies when he was a boy. No doubt were we alone, he'd have exchanged a knife for his elbows.

King Desmond's much taller rostrum placed the monarch's back to the castle proper, to our left, and included Queen Bernadette, Prince Gideon Seville, their guards, a few royal servants, and the chief commanders of each of the Western League's armies.

The foreboding grew stronger, standing the hair up on my neck, making me search the crowd and the grounds. What was going to happen? When was it going to happen?

I jumped when bugles blared a fanfare to the crowd. Zahra was also on edge, as aware as I that conspirators likely lurked nearby. The king had supposedly increased his sentry throughout the crowd, but it did not silence my magical alarms.

I didn't dare Mind-Pair with Gideon. He needed to concentrate on everything around him and invading his thoughts would distract him.

King Desmond Fitzpatrick greeted us all briefly then thrilled the crowd by knighting three warriors who'd served well for several years. Some of the warriors traveling with us were related to the new knights and deserved to witness it before leaving. The throng cheered.

My gaze roamed the courtyard, flitting from face to face, watching for anything out of place, especially at the back of the crowd. Armed guards patrolled the parapets, which should have reassured me. It didn't.

The king's speech was one of the shortest, most eloquent I'd ever heard him give. Again, the throng cheered. Then the king's demeanor changed. With gravity he announced, "Our dutiful commanders for the new army were drawn from the bravest of the Western League. The result is one of the finest armies ever assembled. To encourage cohesion, we're renaming the collective army. It will travel to Malloria under the title of 'The United Forces.'"

Cheers rose as four servants stepped forward to unroll a handsome stretch of material for everyone to admire, a flag made of six different colored squares, each representing the five nations of the Western League and Malloria, the sole representative of the Eastern Realms. A standard-bearer would carry it at the front of the army both on our trek and whenever we rode into battle.

More cheers, more clapping.

Still no sign of anything out of the ordinary in the courtyard.

The king praised every country for meeting his demands, the headcount from troops to wagons to horses mind-boggling, including more than thirty-five-thousand warriors.

"We shall now put to rest rumors, both right and wrong. As many of you may have heard, the army will be one entity under the command of Prince Gideon Seville. Each country will maintain a level of autonomy in that each will serve as a division, headed by their own commanders, but still answerable to the prince."

Some grumbles arose and, in the far distance, I heard a few boos. King Desmond glared at them.

"If you doubt the seriousness of this matter, consider what happened in Bedfordshire. The Valdellians would have torn Kildaria apart as a nation—and from there each of the Western League countries; and if not for the heroic efforts of a single Kildarian scout, we might not be standing here today.

"Please understand that we received a message by bird this morning that the Bitterroot Bridge was taken down, effectively stranding our enemies on the east side of the river. Using militia and a military detachment, Bedford ambushed them in the narrow pass, and although the vast majority of the enemy escaped, they lost two wagons and fifty warriors, while Kildaria did not suffer a single casualty."

A brief pause of shock was followed by wild screams and shouts of happiness, back-slapping and hugging and cheek-kissing. I no longer saw a single sour face in the group. They were convinced. The Valdellians were real, they'd planned to attack Kildaria, and they'd failed.

King Desmond also outlined what Gideon had discussed with my father and brothers regarding how the army would travel. I didn't understand much of it, but I could see my prince's ideas still didn't sit well with some of the Western League leaders. This was, however, the moment to make it plain the decision had been made and would be respected.

I tore my eyes from my king, glanced at my prince-husband, and again combed the crowd. They were intent on the speech. Even the children were quiet. A few soldiers strolled the parapets and disappeared from sight. I couldn't, of course, see any of the sentries on the wall behind me.

"Commanders," the king said, "I remind you that you will need Malloria's men to pilot you through the Badlands, and without them, you cannot cross their borders. Never forget that our mutual goal is to defend the Eastern Realms from the Central Alliance and to end the war as quickly as possible so that we never have to face it here."

A couple of those commanders around him looked sour, but the applause from the audience more than made up for it.

A few guards leaned over the wall on the far end of the courtyard, toward the drawbridge. One waved at a little girl in a brown dress, holding a young woman's hand. The little one waved back with a broad grin.

I could tell Zahra didn't see anything out of the ordinary, either. Why, then, had goosebumps grown goosebumps on my arms?

A movement on the parapet directly opposite us caught my attention. A face slipped behind one of the crenellations, a furtive movement that didn't feel right. I touched Zahra and pointed, whispering to her to take note. Again, I saw the man's secretive glance at the courtyard below.

Without warning, he and three other warriors, spread along the length of the wall, rose simultaneously, bows in their hands and arrows knocked. Time seemed to slow as they drew those bows and sighted on their target. I fought through a mind full of shock to call on my magic. Were their aims true? Would they kill my prince?

No!

They weren't aiming for Gideon!

Their target was the king!

"NO!" I shrieked, pointing at them. *"Traitors! Murderers!"*

Screams broke out and people panicked and stampeded in every direction. Time now stood still as bow strings snapped forward and launched their bolts earthward, vanes spinning along the arrows' trajectories.

In that same, timeless moment, I sought out Gideon. He stared wide-eyed at me, horror written on his face. He didn't know the arrows weren't meant for him.

Without thinking, I shed myself of my chains and whipped through a portal, trying to place myself between King Desmond and the four razor-edged projectiles flying toward him. In my mind's eye, I'd thought to shape-change myself in some impossibly insane way into a human shield.

Childish thought. I'd never know if I could have done it; I didn't have time. No time to brace my body or my soul against those deadly shafts, to deflect or destroy them.

I gasped in agony, as in what seemed a single instant, one pierced my right shoulder, another carved a channel beneath my chin, and the third skimmed my left side and fouled itself in the bodice of my dress. Then I screamed when the final arrow passed through my left hand…and into the king.

"No!" I shrieked again, the shock and pain as well as the impact twisting me to the side and dropping me to my knees.

Behind me, King Desmond's look of panic dissolved into confusion at seeing the arrow in his left arm, where the tip had gone clean through.

"Desmond!" Queen Bernadette screamed, reaching for her husband. In the midst of the chaos, warriors bellowed orders, drawing swords and pounding for the castle walls to chase down the enemies. King Desmond's personal guards steadied him, but when he tottered and turned the sickly shade of chalk, they swept him up and knocked me aside as they charged for the castle doors.

My world crumbled around me, and Gideon was too far away. My head spun and hot stickiness leaked from my chin. I couldn't open my magical shields, but I was so consumed by pain I didn't care. I couldn't brace myself with either hand. A wet gurgling in my chest terrified me, the bolt buried in my right shoulder burning with unholy fire. Blood poured from the gaping wound in my left hand in surges that marked the beat of my heart, spreading into a crimson stain that looked obscene on my favorite gown.

Why couldn't I call the sorcerers—anyone—for help? Why couldn't I grab the arrow and pull it out?

"Your Highness?" a woman's voice said at the periphery of my awareness, followed by ear-splitting demands for help. "The princess is wounded! I need help to take her to her room! Healers! Bring Healers!"

Zahra? Zahra was here, but where was Gideon? Where was my mother? People gathered round me, and someone lifted me and carried me from the scene. My rescuer smelled like Gideon. I cried out in pain with every step, wishing I could stop him, wondering why I couldn't use my magical powers to heal myself.

Wondering why I couldn't seem to find my magic.

Stray pieces of that horrible day, when I'd been kidnapped and then poisoned, drifted into my thoughts.

This was better; this was worse.

I wasn't alone, but all around me voices argued, and when my prince set me down, a multitude of hands began tormenting me as they poked, pulled at, and prodded my wounds.

"The arrow's the barbed sort, and it may be lodged in her lung." "If we pull it out, she'll bleed to death." "If we push it through, we could destroy her lung." "She's drowning in her own fluids."

"Stop! You're hurting her!" Gideon's voice roared.

Silence struck. I managed to open my eyes to see sweet Gideon's face, molded with grief, hanging over me.

"Theona, tell us how to help."

It was strange to see his cheeks damp with tears. I gasped for breath and struggled to speak.

"Pull," I whispered, sucking air in through bubbles that tasted thick with blood. Sticky hot froth dribbled from my mouth and rolled down my cheek as I said, "Pull out the arrow—"

"No!" he sobbed. "It will kill you!"

"It's the arrow…that's killing me. It's bewitched."

"The pain could destroy you. You could bleed to death."

"Then we've nothing to lose. I can't…hold on," I coughed hard, "much longer."

I looked around and realized someone had bound my left hand and torn my gown from my right shoulder. When had that happened? A wave of nausea laid hold of me at seeing the bandages soaked with blood and the arrow's nose buried deep in my flesh. Gideon looked pasty as he rested his right hand on my chest, just below the arrow, and gripped it mid-shaft with his left hand. He pulled it out quickly, leaving me arching in agony and screaming, blood gurgling at the back of my throat.

Certain that the arrowhead must have taken half my lung with it, I screamed again, then begged to sit up. Gideon slipped onto the bed behind me, bracing me against him as blood poured out of my mouth. Someone wiped my face with a rag; I was too blinded by pain to see who. If I could have dropped my shields, the sorcerers could have helped, but I couldn't. I panicked for Gideon. If I died, the sorcerers would possess him.

With the arrow gone, clarity began to return. The scene shocked me. My entire family had crammed into the room—my room—along with Kendal, Zahra, Elds York and Terris, a portion of Prince Gideon's men, and half a dozen healers. As if a dam had burst, the healers rushed to staunch the bleeding and address my wounds, telling each other what to do.

With the arrow gone, my magic now ran free. I opened my shields but…the sorcerers remained silent! How dare they? Did they want me to die? They could take over Gideon any time they wanted. Why would they wait until now? No, as they so often did, they believed I could and should do this on my own, and I loathed them for abandoning me.

I looked up and managed an agonized but perverse grin at Gideon before I closed my eyes and summoned that warm, gentle indigo *parhelia* of healing, not only my own but borrowed from every one of the healers. A flood of indigo light swept through me and flowed toward the Dreamwood bracelet hanging on my right wrist. The bracelet seemed to spring to life as that radiance wrapped itself round and round it, drawing on its power, multiplying my own, multiplying it ten-fold through theirs.

I coughed and spit again, breathing hard and fast. I pushed the power upward to the torn places inside my chest where death congregated, accelerating the process of clotting and abating the inflammation. Magic rushed nutrients to the wounds and hastened the growth of new tissue. Damaged pieces pulled together and sealed themselves in place. By degrees, the pain eased, and my breathing calmed. I relaxed into Gideon and floated on the euphoria of relief. The complexity seemed endless; it took only seconds.

"Dear Elam!" one of the healers said, jerking his hand back and stepping away from me. "What was that? Look at her! Did you feel it?"

"*Feel* it?" a young woman said. "I *saw* it. It was as if I was…inside her. How did she do that?"

I felt the fear mirrored in their eyes.

"Theona?" Gideon stroked my cheek. "Can you speak?"

My dark brown eyes met his beguiling violet ones. I'd fallen in love with those eyes before I'd fallen in love with Gideon. I coughed again and sputtered, grateful when Gideon gave me a sip of water from a glass on the bedside table. I smiled my love to him and breathed deeply, grateful I could do so. Then I turned an imploring look on those strangers who were both fearful and amazed by what I—and they—had just done.

"You know," I rasped, my throat still raw from screaming. "There's something…*different*…about you, about the way you can sense what's wrong inside a person, the way you know what to do to fix it—or know when you can't."

Breathe, I told myself again. Push away the exhaustion. All I wanted to do was sleep. And maybe eat.

"Some may struggle, others may accomplish it with ease, but you all feel there's more inside of you that you can't reach. I'm sorry for not having time to ask your permission. My situation was obviously too dire. Blended with mine, your magic made it easier and faster for me to heal myself." So that I could breathe. So that I wouldn't die. "In compensation for it, I've given you a gift." I took another precious, easier, exhausted breath.

"Now you know how to truly, completely heal, more surely than generations of healers before you. Some will call this witchcraft and dislike you for it, but it's your Elam-given talent and your duty to use it for the good of others. Ask the Elds if you do not believe me."

Every eye in the room turned to the two Elds. York shifted in discomfort but nodded.

"She speaks a truth our country has rejected for far too long. Our fear of what we call magic has come from decades of prejudice and misunderstanding. There is no magic. What we call magic is not a summoning of devils. It is Elam's powers, entrusted to mankind. Used for evil, it creates monsters like sorcerers. Used for good, it blesses living beings. Had all of you been properly trained and guided from the beginning, you could have done what Princess Theona just did. And more."

The healers grumbled and shifted, some obviously not convinced, some rosy-cheeked with excitement.

I gave Mother and Father a wan smile as they pushed through the healers and came to one side of me, my siblings crowding in with them. Zahra and Kendal slipped to the other side at Gideon's knee.

I glanced up at Gideon, whose eyes shimmered with both joy and tears. Mother took my hand, her fingers stroking the thin scar that was all that remained of the gash. A scar to add to too many others I'd garnered so recently.

Eld Terris said, "Princess Theona, I am glad you're going to survive. Prince Gideon, Duke and Duchess McArthur, I beg your leave. The healers need to return to their duties. Others may have taken wounds, perhaps people trampled in the stampede, or the sentry who chased the assassins, maybe even the perpetrators themselves."

"Thank you for everything," Gideon said to him, and to the healers added, "Princess Seville would have died without you. Princess, have you any counsel for them after so extravagant a use of magic?"

I smiled weakly. He understood at least some of its demands. "Yes. I have counsel that you dare not ignore. You'll shortly find yourselves voraciously hungry and wearier than seems normal. Ignoring the need can make you ill. Do not put off taking care of yourselves." I didn't want to frighten them by adding that it could kill them.

"We'll make sure they obey, Princess," York said, wishing me well again before he and Eld Terris herded them off.

I gripped Gideon's hand tight. "Please check on the king. I'm worried about him."

"I saw the arrow hit the king," Lon interjected. "The wound didn't seem that serious."

"Our monarch is old, Lon," I said. "Shock alone could kill him, but these weren't ordinary arrows. They were poisoned." Poisoned with magic.

Lon paled at the revelation.

Father said, "Ian, you and Lon take guards and gather news for us about the king's condition. Watch your backs. We've no idea who we can trust."

I agreed. We'd done everything we could to keep Gideon safe, even if he wasn't their target, but the assassins had still found a way onto the wall. They could have killed him or anyone else today.

My sister Keely climbed cautiously onto the bed, tears in the corners of her dark eyes, a bit of dust on one freckled cheek. "You were hurt bad, Theona," she said.

"But I'm fine now," I reassured her, smoothing away the dust. She was such a tender-hearted child.

I glanced at my parents and again at Gideon. "I'm likely in even more trouble now, aren't I?" I murmured. "How will I explain my survival to the king?"

Gideon barked incredulous laughter. "What? You're worried about explaining how you healed yourself? Theona, most of the Western League's most powerful people saw you disappear from beside your parents and appear in front of the king. That was far more shocking than healing yourself." His smile thinned. "I admit I'd like my own explanation about that. Let's just pray your feat saved His Majesty's life."

My blush of embarrassment faded as a knock at the door interrupted us. Thankfully, one of the guards opened the door to servants delivering food for all of us. Unfortunately, my brothers also arrived, bringing a note for Father. His grave expression as he read it drove my heart to my toes.

"The gossipmongers are already at it. Your survival has spread, my daughter. You, Prince Seville, and I have been summoned to the king's chambers immediately.

My caretakers protested vehemently. "It's too soon!" "She's too exhausted!" "She needs food and rest, Your Grace—"

I twitched when a brief flash of dark orange light struck me with an image of King Desmond being laid to rest. I lurched to my feet, grateful Gideon steadied me when I nearly fainted.

"I must," I insisted. "I've had..." I paused, not wanting my foretelling to frighten my little sister and brother. "I sense that the king isn't doing well. Feed me while you dress me. I'll rest later."

Keely began to cry.

"It's alright, little one," I told her. "I'll be back in just a bit. You can stay here and wait for me if you like." Mother nodded her support and hugged Keely tight.

The men retired to the sitting room with the children to eat while the women stripped me of the bloodied, tattered gown and chemise, did their best to wash me off, and tossed clean clothes over my head. Apples, cheese, and buttered bread only barely relieved my immediate hunger but would have to do for now.

Someone had somehow found my chains in the mayhem and fastened them to my wrists, while Zahra tucked a shawl around my shoulders. The prince lifted me into his arms, far gentler than needed. I was no longer wounded, just exhausted. Father and Zahra on either side of us and Father's and Gideon's guards flanking us, we headed for King Desmond's quarters.

Worry roiled inside me. Would the king die? What would happen to me if he did? To Gideon or the army? My shields were tight now, but how much had the sorcerers witnessed? They'd want an accounting from me later, but I certainly would demand one from them.

"So glad you came quickly, Lord Cedric," Sir Sweeney said as he admitted us into the Royal Bedchamber. He was the king's closest assistant and his brow puckered with grief. "He's been asking for you. You know His Majesty admires you greatly."

"How is he, Sweeney? I fear the worst."

Sweeney dared place a hand on father's shoulder and squeeze it. "His physicians have done all they can, and it isn't enough."

Surely, without realizing it, I'd swallowed hot rocks. Whole. They'd gotten stuck somewhere between my heart and my stomach and set everything on fire. This couldn't be happening. The king couldn't die. Kildaria would be lost without him. The Western League might fall apart. They might choose not to support Gideon's mission. And did I dare add I'd have suffered for nothing?

Zahra remained at the door with the other guards, but Gideon carried me to the king's bedside and Father joined us as we went to our knees.

Queen Bernadette sat on the other side of the bed, pressing her husband's arthritic fingers to her tear-stained cheek.

"Cedric," King Desmond said, his voice thin and quavering. Drawn and gray, he reached his other trembling hand out to take Father's. "It's time we spoke more seriously of things we've only danced around for years."

Father's reply was filled with dread. "There's no need, Your Majesty. You'll recover and rein over Kildaria for another decade or more."

The king laughed quietly and shook his head, the effort making him gasp for breath.

"Let's not fool ourselves, dear friend. We're old, and our physicians tell us the shock damaged our heart. We won't make it through the night. We've no legitimate heir, and I cannot in good conscience declare either of my weak-spined cousins as king-in-waiting. The League is destined to fight a long and nasty war. It cannot be left without a ruler, and you are a born leader. We've asked you many times in the past and will not take no for an answer."

Eld York told me just two weeks ago, a lifetime ago, that King Desmond favored my father as his heir. The idea had shocked me then. Now? Could my father truly become King of Kildaria?

"I'm honored, Sire, even though I'd prefer not to have the honor." Father's face grew almost as pale as the king's.

King Desmond laughed again and then pressed a hand to his chest, wheezing several times before saying, "Well said, young man. Better you than one who would conspire to take the throne from us." He turned his moist eyes toward me and frowned.

"Princess Theona. You continue to puzzle us. You've unparalleled magical power. It was our position, along with your father's, that you should have been informed and trained in its use from birth. Because you were not, you became possessed. I suppose those sorcerers could teach you to use it better than anyone alive, but you know they'll seek to bend those talents toward evil."

He paused, grappling for words. Then his eyelids drifted shut and his breathing stopped!

CHAPTER 8

"Your Majesty?" I said, terror making voice sharp.
His eyes snapped open, and he gasped. Then he huffed and calmed, determined to carry on as best he could.

"We've deep respect for Prince Seville and his judgment. He says you've done all you can to resist the sorcerers. We've also seen and heard of your decency from the beginning and have now been a recipient of it. It seems Elden fears that you might follow in Moriana's footsteps are—*relatively*—unfounded. Certainly, if you'd desired our death, you wouldn't have jeopardized your life for us."

He waved away one of the physicians who offered him a drink from a silver chalice.

"That said, my lady, we must still address the shock of seeing you, quite literally, appear out of thin air right in front of us. Your cry of warning had hardly made sense to us before you were there, standing between us and them. For a split second, we were more frightened of you."

I bowed my head in mortification. Was it I who'd caused his heart to fail?

"Now, here you are," King Desmond continued, "and I see no sign of the grave wounds I know you sustained in our behalf. How are any of these things possible?"

I cleared my throat and explained. "I'm able to move various distances through a magical doorway called a portal, Your Majesty. I couldn't have gotten to you quickly enough any other way. I also have the gift of healing, and six healers attended me as well. Elds York and Terris will bear witness to it. I'm so very sorry I couldn't stop the arrow from hitting you."

King Desmond wheezed a chuckle. "You stopped three arrows then both slowed and deflected the fourth. A simple explanation for simply unimaginable events. I believe you did everything you could, child. We'd be dead if you hadn't—although we find it ironic you sacrificed yourself for an old man who will not only die anyway but who has kept you in chains. The chains seem ironic as well, considering they didn't prevent you from...what did you call it? Portalling?"

I panicked when that wave of dark orange prescience took hold again, warning me to do something now or King Desmond's life would be lost.

"Sire, might I try healing you? I'm sure your physicians have done a remarkable job. It's just that...well...under the circumstances...."

The king's thin, bluish lips pulled up in a wry grimace. He placed his gnarled hand in mine. "What harm can it do? We're in no hurry to join Elam. Give it a try."

His tone said he didn't believe I could do it.

Exhaustion ignored, I closed my eyes and began the journey I hoped would save the future. Repairing his arm was simple, and removing the poison was easier with him than for me because it wasn't killing me. The king's heart, however, was another matter. Contracted with age, it struggled to keep its proper cadence. I bathed the tissues with indigo-colored healing, hoping for any improvement, but I was amazed when those tissues softened and stretched, and immediately, the stroke of each muscle fiber better coordinated the flow of blood to its various destinations. Today's damage faded into the lightest of scars. I couldn't, of course, cure the most difficult of his ills. He was old, and there was nothing I could do about that; but for now, my magic had given him an endowment of time.

When I opened my eyes, my surprise at the success was mirrored on His Majesty's face. He let go of my hand and touched his chest, feeling the change in his heart's rhythm and amazed at the release of the gripping pain. He looked at his physicians and Queen Bernadette and sat upright. He might still be weak and tired, but his color had vastly improved.

"Desmond?" the queen said in shock.

"Praise Elam! Princess, you do have the gift!" the king cried as he grabbed the queen and hugged her, tears of joy wetting both their cheeks.

"We could feel you doing whatever it was you did," he added, and then he frowned. "You're sure this didn't involve those blasted sorcerers?"

I grinned at him. "Positive, Sire. It's simply the talent for healing."

He wiped his cheeks with the backs of his hands and gave such a deep belly laugh it dispelled the gloom and had everyone in the room grinning.

"There's nothing simple about it," he said. "We don't know what to do with you, Princess Theona. We see no point in having you in chains. Obviously, they cannot contain you any more than they did Moriana. Not that that reassures us; it doesn't. We simply accept the fact you intend Kildaria no harm—at least for now. You understand, of course, if that changed, so would our leniency. And of course, guards must continue to accompany you whenever you leave your quarters, although I suspect they may protect you rather than protecting others.

"Prince Seville," King Desmond said. "Remove Princess Theona's chains. Princess, keep in mind no one knows who is friend or foe at the moment, and you frightened every witness in the courtyard half out of their wits. Some may recognize your loyalty, but others will be even more afraid of you than ever. Your enemies may now stop at nothing to try to destroy you."

I nodded, realizing that His Majesty would likewise order my death if he believed I'd become dangerous. I grew numb inside as Gideon unlatched the manacles and handed them to Sweeney.

"Our gratitude is yours, Princess," King Desmond said, still pale but pushing aside his bedcovers to slide to the edge of the bed. To Sir Sweeney, he said, "We need a full report of the attack: the damage, the injuries, any arrests. If any of the would-be-assassins were caught, we want them brought before us in two hours. We'll question them until they beg for beheading."

King Desmond's gray eyes twinkled at Father. "And when things have calmed a bit, we will call a court and announce to the world that you, Lord Cedric McArthur, will be my heir. Kildaria will sleep better knowing the loss of her monarch won't leave her in chaos. Understood?"

Father inhaled deeply and bowed his head in obeisance.

"Good." He eyed his physicians and the queen. "All present here are our witnesses to this matter should anything happen to us before we can put it in writing and make the announcement." "Please settle your daughter in her quarters, McArthur, and return immediately. Prince Seville and I will await you in our personal study—after we've changed out of these bloodied robes—where we can discuss the attack in greater detail. Bernadette, my love, please see to refreshments for the three of us."

Gideon gave me a disconcerted look as the queen headed off and Father took my arm and attempted to lead me away. I mouthed "good luck" to him. Absently, I rubbed my wrists, now freed of those awful chains. I nearly laughed at the joke. I wore them to assure others, not because I was the king's prisoner.

The sorcerers, of course, were a completely different matter. I was as much their prisoner as if I were in a dungeon and only they had the key. I hated that they'd remained silent when I needed their help and wanted to know why. My eyelids fluttered and I swayed on my feet, then the darkness of sleep fell over me as Father gathered me into his arms.

I learned later that my father took me to my quarters and Zahra put me too bed, frequently rousing me to ply me with food and drink throughout the day. I barely remembered taking them.

"Go back to sleep now, Princess," she whispered each time. "Mustn't come fully awake yet. All the magic you've used, it'll turn you upside down, it will."

Headache and nausea came and went, and the hours slipped away. Then came another dream.

The stench of fire draws me. Through smoke and haze appears the roof of an unfamiliar castle. Hundreds of buildings of various sizes and heights surround it, A-frame roofs with eaves that curl slightly upward. Water encircles the buildings, except for a single, seemingly endless covered bridge that spans the lake from the castle to nowhere.

I fly toward nowhere.

Land and forest. Huge trees, not Dreamwood trees, ablaze against the gray shades of dawn. I fly over it. Fire, as far as I can see. People, animals screaming in panic.

A small mountain ahead and, beyond it, a wide open plain. In it, legions upon legions of armies. Clashing, screaming, killing. Blood running everywhere.

I land on a familiar tent. Gideon's banner flutters atop it.

A neigh of terror draws my gaze. Caspian gallops through the scene, grows wings, and streaks toward me. Arrows meant for me strike him instead. I scream silently as he tumbles to the ground, wings broken, still as death.

Soldiers stream from the tent and my heart stops. Valdellian Warlords! Where is Gideon?

Aloft as a dragon, I search the camp. On the outskirts are horses hamstrung, equipment and weapons flung to the ground, wagons on fire. Another Valdellian warrior intimidates prisoners of war with a whip. I collapse when a woman looks up at me and cries out. My mother—

I came awake, bathed in darkness and sweat, the nightmare holding me by the throat. I breathed through the anxiety, trying to believe it was only a dream.

Amazingly enough, I felt fully recovered physically. The coiling tentacles of magic inside me were again ready and eager to be set free. How could that be? I'd nearly died. Again. Yet, I felt as if it had never happened.

Zahra joined me, her face tired but creased with a kindly smile. "Welcome back, Princess. If you're up to it, your family would love your singular presence at supper as usual."

Supper? It was evening already? Like a butterfly emerging from its cocoon, I sat up, swung my feet to the floor and stretched. "It oughtn't to be so, but I feel wonderful."

"Wish I could understand how that happens, my lady," she said. "Seems too far-fetched, if you ask me."

I chuckled and did my best to explain how magic rejuvenated itself—even if I didn't fully understand it myself—and added that it grew stronger and stronger as I used it, provided I had sufficient nourishment and rest when I needed it.

"Thank you for your vigilance, Zahra. I owe you a tremendous debt."

"Pish, my lady," she said, waving me to my dressing table. "'Tis my honor."

"*You* are exhausted," I insisted. "You need to rest, too."

"My consolation is that, if healing works for you and if ever I need it, it could work for me."

She arranged my hair as efficiently as ever and escorted me along with my guards to supper. The Duke of Mithradell sat at the table, quiet and pale, with Mother, equally long-faced. The rest of us were excited about Father's appointment as Kildaria's heir. Apparently, Lord Cedric McArthur was not, and Mother was worried about him.

The atmosphere thankfully brightened for all of us when Gideon arrived. Sharing the worries of sovereignty with the prince seemed to ease my father's burdens. I wondered if my prince meant to ease my worries when he said he would accompany me back to my rooms. He needed to talk to me, but he didn't say why.

As for me, I looked forward to curling up in his arms for as long as I could, but I was sad that playing with nasty sorcerers and their dragons would have to steal part of the night. If only that had been my singular challenge—or even the worst.

Gideon excused Zahra for the night, leaving my prince and me to our own devices, but I felt him holding back. When I questioned him, he rose from the sofa and paced slowly about the sitting room, chewing on his bottom lip. I'd never seen him do that before.

"I just can't wrap my head around it, Theona," he said. "The scope of your powers. The presence of the sorcerers. The thought that the shades of two mighty dragons are also locked up inside you."

"You've known that since you met me," I murmured. "What's changed?" Had Gideon decided he didn't want me? Would he abandon me after all?

He continued, "I've had dreams and other magical experiences of my own. I don't fear them or magic, and I truly believe we're supposed to be together."

He didn't *sound* like he believed it.

"I love you, Gideon. I always have. I would never hurt you."

"Or at least, you don't think you would. We've no idea how bad things are going to get. You said yourself that I need to be prepared to get far away from you if your magic turns dark."

I took a deep, settling breath and nodded. "I did and you should. But they haven't, and I don't intend that they ever will."

My thoughts fluttered to the memory of the man I'd cow-kicked in the courtyard. I hadn't told him about it. Was I afraid to admit what I'd done?

Gideon nodded. "I believe you. But what we intend to do can change in difficult circumstances."

They could.

He turned to meet my gaze. "I just need time to think about all of this. You showed me what you can do just last night. Then the attack on the king happened today, and you frightened the entire courtyard, even me. You did it for all the right reasons, but…."

I sighed. "You know I could harm others as easily for the wrong reasons."

He nodded. He combed his fingers through his hair, then lifted his jacket, which lay across the back of the sofa, and put it on. He was leaving.

"I must be fair with you, Theona. I can't pretend everything is perfect when I'm unsure." He saw the tears gathering in my eyes. The pity on his face nearly undid me. "I don't doubt *you*, Theona, it's the sorcerers. The situation. I don't know why, but for the first time since we met here in Kildaria, I understand why people are terrified of you. Please, my dear, just be patient and give me room to think and…and pray."

I nodded, wiping away my tears and squaring my shoulders. A hardness settled into my belly when he walked out the door and the guards locked it behind him. Maybe this was best after all. We could still fight the enemy together, but perhaps he was safer as far away from me as possible. Maybe it was better he didn't love me. Then he could make hard decisions unaffected by emotions.

Perhaps I needed to do the same.

CHAPTER 9

"Trouble follows you wherever you go," Moriana observed, her nose wrinkled in disgust.

"You're not referring to what happened to the king?" I replied, vexed. "All I did was try to save him, and I didn't appreciate you leaving me to either heal myself or die."

Terius replied, "The ensorcelled arrow kept you from opening your shields enough that we could help you."

"But you didn't warn me before it happened."

Rhesalus raised a hand and stopped the discussion. "You handled the situation superbly my dear. We knew you would. You do need protection, however. Both for yourself and for us. Your enemies will seek your death more earnestly now, and your prince's as well."

"You're not worried about me. If I fail you, the prince can take my place. You just enjoy making me miserable."

"Now, now, be nice. We've got work to do. You must Link Enya tonight," he said.

"Do you ever stop conniving?" I snapped.

"Do you?" Terius said, his gaze hard as steel.

"Me? When do I connive?"

"What do you do when you're alone with the dragons?"

My mouth went dry. I'd dreaded the day the sorcerers would ask that question. I dared roll my eyes at him. "You're joking. They tell you everything. What do you do with them when you're locked up behind my shields?"

"You're joking," Terius tossed back. "They do as they please. What control do you think we have over them?"

"Plenty. And I practice flying with them, something I'll never enjoy doing with you." But his question planted an idea in my head I would have to discuss with the Dragons later.

"Call a snake," Terius sneered, his eyes flashing.

"Not until you explain the purpose," I insisted. "The real purpose."

"You know the purpose," Moriana said, peering down her nose at me. "You just don't like it."

"I don't understand it *and* I don't like it," I insisted. "And I won't do it until you explain it."

Terius shoved Rhesalus aside and all but bowled me over in his fury. "You dare challenge us, girl? Who do you think you are?"

"I am Princess Theona Seville," I sneered, nose to nose with him, "the daughter of Lord Cedric McArthur, the Duke of Mithradell; and the wife of Gideon Seville, the Crown Prince of Malloria. I am your prisoner, but you are also mine, and when I become your equal in the world of sorcery, it will give me great pleasure to destroy you!"

Terius roared in anger and lunged for my neck. I supposed he'd have broken it if Rhesalus hadn't grabbed him.

"No!" the horse-mage shouted, dragging him away from me. They struggled, hissing bits of the Language of sorcerers at each other. The Language. That arcane tongue linked with sorcerous incantations and other magical spells. I wasn't very good at it. I didn't want to be good at it.

Eventually, Terius calmed, but his cheeks remained red with fury.

Rhesalus turned to me, his face carved like granite. "Do not play the fool, Theona. You know everything you love stands in jeopardy if you go too far. Don't give us the excuse to destroy you and take your prince instead."

I gnashed my teeth against the anger raging hot inside me. I despised giving in to Terius. I hated torturing innocent creatures for these hideous lessons. But I would not let these monsters touch Gideon.

Dragging in a deep, angry breath, I sought the gift of Calling, that velvety baby blue *parhelia* that could bend the will of all Elam's creatures to mine. Rather than speaking it, I mentally "shouted" it to serpent-kind, into every corner of the forest.

The air quivered, more vibrant than when I opened a portal, and I cringed. Sounds of things sliding over the matted forest grew louder, creatures rushing toward me in their hurry to obey. In the glimmer of mage light, I watched as they surrounded me, serpents of all sizes and colors, vipers that hissed or rattled at each other, ground snakes and tree snakes, constrictors and racers. Some I'd only learned about in school and oughtn't to even be here in Kildaria, perhaps not even in this part of the world. What had I done?

I should have been terrified and perhaps was, but mostly I felt fascinated. They gathered around me, some spiraling up my ankles and legs toward my hips. A colossal boa climbed to my neck, its scales cool against my skin, its loops hugging my shoulders. It perched there as if it belonged. Other snakes joined it, until they could find no further purchase. Their weight should have smothered me, but I felt buoyed by them, exhilarated by their obedience. The rest of them seemed contented to sit at my feet.

I glanced with shock at the sorcerers, who stood with mouths ajar, and then at the dragons. Enya's eyes were huge with expectancy. Ramah grumbled and shifted, his tail twitching. Enya would face the test first tonight, but Ramah longed to taste mortality again, even for just a few minutes. I felt like a traitor to the snakes that surrounded me in entwined mounds of deadly innocence.

Three sorcerers had created the dragons centuries ago. Pythius, friend and partner to Terius and Rhesalus, had been killed by Cleary the Brave, my many-times great grandfather. While Terius was mage to eagles and Rhesalus to horses, Pythius was the one who controlled serpents. How had he selected the snake for the experiment? Did it matter? I turned to the dragons.

"Enya, is one of these snakes like the one Pythius used to create the Mother Dragon?"

I ignored the sparkle in Rhesalus's eye at my request, proof I'd just discovered a piece of the puzzle that would make this disgusting business successful. He, too, looked away, perhaps hoping to hide his reaction, which proved the dragons right. The sorcerers played a relentless game, a balancing act that forced me to either master my magical talents on my own or to ask for their help when I couldn't. One made me grow stronger, but the other made me subservient. They could use either to their advantage, but every time I asked for their help, I feared I lost a piece of my soul.

Enya's long neck arched as she snuffled the collection of serpents cloaking my shoulders. The largest one, a beautifully colored constrictor, recoiled at the brush of her spirit against it.

"That one is...good, better than the others," her voice purred. "But something isn't quite right." Her eyes shone the bright red-gold of anxious anticipation flecked with green. She was uncertain.

Ramah's head joined hers, his snuffling more powerful, his eyes gleaming the purer yellow of delight.

"He'd suit me," he said, nudging Enya's neck. "He's perfect. I can feel it."

The shock of discovery hit me. The snake was male! The snake Pythius had chosen was female, as was the dragon she became.

Looking over the crowd of snakes, I found another boa on the other side of the glade, an even larger one. I pointed it out to Enya. She moved to the edge of the horde and snuffled it as well.

"Yes. She's excellent," she hissed, her eyes gleaming yellow.

I sent the other snakes away. The air rippling as it had before but not so notably, the forest floor rattled and snapped again as the creatures hurried off, leaving behind the two chosen serpents and an ominous silence—and my realization that I'd just committed to torturing them.

The instant I connected with the snake's *rumoria,* and Enya made the painful flight "through" me into the serpent, the fray turned violent. The snake twisted and writhed, fighting hard, fighting forever, bunching and twisting and finally convulsing. I hung on tight, barely able to keep my mental grasp on the snake's *rumoria.*

Then, as before, its awareness gradually dissolved as Enya took control and the metamorphosis from serpent to dragon began. Ramah's roar joined Enya's as she rose to her hind legs and spread out her wings in triumph!

"Yes!" she cried. "This is it! It feels right."

Then she disappeared!

Ramah keened, his eyes dark red with alarm, as he searched the starry night for his mate. A vicious tug on my *rumoria* followed her as she flew above us, completely invisible in the dark.

Rhesalus slammed his hand on my shoulder, snarling. "She's likely headed home. Bring her back. Now!"

Home? Where was home? How was I supposed to bring her back?

Without preamble, Rhesalus's power grabbed mine and took us both "Searching" for the dragon. If Zahra hadn't taught me, I wouldn't have known what we were doing. Finding Enya was like listening for a distant voice across a great chasm.

My knees turned to jelly, and I sat down hard, stretched as thin as I could get without being torn apart. Even worse, the poor snake suffocated inside the shell of her own body, pressed to the walls by the vastness of Enya's life force.

Enya reveled in her freedom, the thrill of this physical body, her rebellion toward the sorcerers. Above her hung stars that looked different; below her lie the vastness of the sea.

"Get hold of her!" Rhesalus hollered.

I barely had the sense to hang on to both Enya's life force and the snake's.

"You're hurting me, Enya. You've gone too far. I could die. In my soul, I know this isn't all there is to it. What if my dying kills the snake? It will kill you, too. Come back. Let's do this right, when I'm ready."

Her intolerable grief, so like Ramah's, bore down on me. How desperately she desired to be mortal again, to feel all the incredible sensations that came with a living body. How deeply she wished to be unchained from the sorcerers and live a life of her own.

She shook off my thoughts, but only moments later I felt the pulling sensation lessen and sensed her circling above us in the sky. She roared in mental anguish then landed at the far end of the glade, her frame rigid with dissatisfaction. Ramah grumbled at her, and she bowed her head in shame. She'd have chosen stolen mortality over their bond.

When she relinquished her hold on the snake, her translucent white essence swept through me and back to her place beside Ramah. Like a wounded bird, she dropped to her belly and pushed her head under her leathery wing.

The snake lay stunned, alive and unharmed as the others before her, but as with the others, she seemed to have no awareness of herself, no drive to live.

I knelt beside her and stroked her smooth skin with no response. I pressed her ribs, trying to revive her. A minute. Another minute, and then she started, pulling into a loose coil, her breaths panicked, but seemingly too exhausted to do anything but lay there. I stroked her again and urged her to find freedom, and finally, she aroused and tasted the air. I Called for her to depart, and she slipped into the waiting arms of that baby blue *parhelia* and wherever it transported her.

Whispers behind me told me the sorcerers were thrilled with my success, but I couldn't celebrate. If I'd failed, they'd have made me try it again. And again. I ignored them, distressed by all of it, and made worse by the terrible fatigue and hunger that writhed inside me like a snake bent on tearing out my insides.

"You know the routine, Theona," Rhesalus said, his voice urgent. "You must eat. Now. Then return. You'll rest a while and then work on the Language."

Of course we would. With it, I could create spells that made my magic much stronger than it already was—two or three times or even a hundred times stronger with some of my *parhelia*. If I could get the Language to work.

I glared at him before I changed into a small snake and rushed away to find food and drink. My brief nap under a bush felt even better.

Unfortunately, the Language defied my best efforts to learn it. Although each of my sorcerous companions badgered me to death about it, I made little progress, which frustrated everyone.

"Theona, your obstinance could spoil everything," said Terius. "You will need the Language to create our bodies, and you'll not be free of us until you do."

I shuddered to think of it. I'd come this far, but if I couldn't master the one set of lessons I despised, I'd never be rid of these monsters—unless they had me killed and escaped into someone else. Like Gideon.

"Enough for now," Rhesalus said. "You've at least passed the test with Linking the dragons to snakes. Now we need to make it little more challenging. Call some birds. We'll see how far you can get with linking them instead."

"What?" My heart dropped. Birds? I hated that the dragons' excitement escalated at the pronouncement.

No doubt, they'd prefer a more intelligent creature that could fly, but a bird's intelligence would make it fight me harder. It just seemed wrong. Besides, failure was more likely, and failure could be lethal—to all three of us.

Terius glared at me. "It's that or learning to defend yourself against another sorcerer." The challenge on his face suggested he would enjoy torturing me either way.

"I'm learning to defend myself with Zahra, and the blacksmith just made me a set of armor," I snapped.

All of them laughed.

"Ridiculous," Moriana said, and Terius grinned at me.

"We're not talking about mortal weaponry, girl," he said. "It's often said 'there are things in life even worse than death.' Some are so terrible that death would be the better choice. Facing a sorcerer who's bent on destroying you is certainly one of the worst."

I shivered with fear, and Rhesalus set fingertips on my cheek and stroked it. Tingles washed over me as his face hovered above mine. He lifted my chin and gazed deeply into my eyes.

"You are a most exquisite woman," he murmured. "I'm committed to doing all I can to help you reach your greatest potential."

His words threaded into my mind and found a way into my heart. How different it felt to be considered a woman…an exquisite woman, not a small, gawky tomboy. The dragons had changed me, and I looked completely different now.

Unfortunately, possession would never gain me admirers. But I didn't need them. I loved the Prince of Malloria, and he loved me despite my transgressions, despite being a little uneasy about my magic at the moment.

My mind snapped out of whatever fugue Rhesalus had cast over me. I hated that he persisted in doing this.

"Don't touch me," I said firmly, pushing away from him.

"No harm, my dear," he said, chuckling, palms turned upward in placation. "Call some birds. The quicker we get them Linked, the sooner you can catch a few hours' sleep."

"You'll need it." Terius smirked. "Tomorrow may be full of surprises."

I resented it when he tossed out bait but never admitted to what he knew about the future. Again I Called hard, wide and far. Again the air rippled, and birds of all kinds fluttered around us, shrieking in protest as I made them land at our feet.

Ramah paid attention to none but the eagles. It made perfect sense, of course. Terius had used an eagle to create the Mother Dragon. I sent the others away.

The first eagle I tried was a beautiful creature, a dark chocolate brown male with just a touch of white in his tail feathers, meaning he was young. Young and proud and strong-willed, and he fought Ramah to his own death. A part of my heart went with him. What a tragic waste.

The next specimen was a mature bald eagle.

Every bit as handsome as the first bird but more timorous, the minute Ramah flew into him, his heart stopped. I could not save him. Dispirited, I turned my back on the sorcerers and, through tears, examined the remaining candidates. Like sorting through *parhelia*, I studied their spiritual strength, far more concerned about that than their physical prowess.

Four seemed likely subjects, but two were females. I chose the male that seemed a rather "average" sort. He still resisted more than the snakes, but he wasn't self-destructive. Ramah also stayed inside him a while longer than I liked, but Terius allowed it, silently communicating—Mind-Paired?—with the dragon. I wondered what they discussed. Would Ramah tell me? Whatever happened, the effort was a success.

"Very good, my dear," Rhesalus said, patting my shoulder. "Now try it with Enya."

Enya grabbed control of her counterpart with such fervor the poor eagle went into shock. It took twenty minutes for the dragon to succeed. Terius again "talked" with the dragon, if that's what he was doing, while I grew anxious for the eagle. I felt her distress keenly when we let her go and made a firm resolve I'd never use her again, even if she were the last bird on earth.

Rhesalus pronounced my night's work a resounding success. It brought me both relief and dismay. I'd made very little progress with the Language, I'd avoided having to spar as sorcerers did with magic, but Linking eagles had gone well enough that I knew the next step. They'd make me Link with horses. I couldn't imagine doing such an awful thing to Caspian or any horse.

I was nearly numb with exhaustion when I locked away the sorcerers, but I held the dragons back for a moment. They studied me with curiosity.

"I have an idea," I put forth.

Enya's eyes narrowed. "One the sorcerers might not approve?"

I gave a nod. "You once asked me to set you free before I Linked the sorcerers with their new bodies. I suppose learning to Link you with horses is one of the last steps prior to doing that. I also suspect you'll have a greater affinity toward horses than you do to either snakes or eagles, which means it may be easier to do and harder to undo. Is that so?"

The two dragons shared a look and then Ramah nodded. "It may be. What game do you play?"

I snorted laughter. They accused me of playing a game? "If we work together to frustrate the Link, we can buy some time. Working together without the sorcerers, as we do when we fly without them, we could practice Linking without their knowledge. Provided it's safe for me."

"And when you've mastered it, you'll know what to do to set us loose first?"

"Yes. But I won't practice unless it's safe. I have no desire to kill myself attempting it."

Ramah's grumble almost sounded like laughter. "We are more capable of teaching you than they are, and it would serve all three of us well."

"You'd do it despite this being a conspiracy that borders on treachery?"

Enya bared her fangs in what almost mocked a smile. "Maybe because of it, human child."

"Then we shall try it tomorrow night."

"Not tonight?" Ramah said with sarcasm.

"You know better. I need food and rest, but we will do it tomorrow night."

I closed my shields and hurried toward the mountains. Somewhere nearby, I smelled a most unfortunate grizzly bear.

———✝———

Zahra again barged in to wake me. Thankfully, it seemed devouring grizzly bear just before dawn calmed overworked magic.

"Your breakfast is here, my lady. You must eat. The attack on the king was only yesterday, and I suspect you were too long with your sorcerers last night. You're looking fearsome thin."

I did? I was? I nodded, then drifted off to sleep for a few more minutes. Dreams haunted me, visions of sorcerers tormenting me, of killing fields full of winged horses. Of Moriana trying to force the Language down my throat.

"No! You must say it this way." "Long vowels, Theona. Short ones give that word a different meaning." "What do you mean it sounds like I'm relieving myself? You sound like you're sicking-up." "Try it again, again, again."

"My lady?"

This time my eyes snapped wide. "Yes?"

"Might I ask? What does *'Ust ert expir'* mean?"

You will die. Odd that it came to me immediately, now that I'd gotten a few hours' sleep. I made a face at her as I climbed out of bed and submitted to her ministrations.

"I think it means I was dreaming."

Zahra harrumphed. "Odd lot of dreams you have, lying there, twitching and moaning and saying the strangest things."

She frowned, then donned what I supposed was my voice as she said, *"'Appro za mein.' 'Cedra plat, cedra aste.' 'Nute! Dut arsa eka mand. Obid!'"*

I stared at her in astonishment. How could she remember—and say—all of that so easily when I'd struggled for hours with it—and for weeks before this?

Appro za mein? Come to me. *Cedra plat, cedra aste?* Go here, go there. And then, the words of the sorcerers torturing me: *Nute! Dut arsa eka mand! Obid!* Now! Do as I command! Obey!

One challenge I detested was memorizing incantations I couldn't practice, like spells that controlled peoples' minds or those that could harm or kill them. Besides having no intentions of ever using them, I hated memorizing. It bored me half to death and trying to remember them gave me another headache.

Sick of it, I pushed it all aside. I was so very, very hungry. Again. And the scent of food in the sitting room had me salivating.

I couldn't believe how quickly time had flown. It was Saturday morning. Monday was the first-week anniversary of my marriage. If only I felt as secure about my relationship with Gideon as I had then.

April played its springtime tricks on us, giving us a day of misty fog. Still, we managed to find a place to ride a good distance from the castle in a farmer's fallow field just outside the city of Leeds and far from the armies' camps. We also practiced Mind-Pairing, and because Gideon had said he'd be willing to attempt it later that morning, we safely—if only briefly—did so. We were all impressed by our success.

After Zahra and I retired the horses and took advantage of mid-morning tea and refreshments, I changed into the now-familiar attire suitable for blade-work: breeches and light boots, and my hair braided and stuffed down the back of my tunic. Once we left Kildaria, I'd not see a dress until we reached Malloria, both for ease with riding and, if need be, for fighting.

I took more scrapes and bruises, but as before, the work at least dispelled some of my frustrations, especially concerning Gideon. All round us, however, whispers from warriors likewise there to hone their skills made me uncomfortable. Only the most trusted officers were now allowed on the castle grounds and even fewer given stalls for their horses or access to the armory. No doubt, the Western League would prefer I'd died while protecting the king. What right did I have to use the armory? We did not stay long.

Tavishes joined us in my parents' apartment again for luncheon, but when Gideon joined us, along with Eld York and Eld Terris, I suspected something was afoot. I was right. Approval had been given to post Ian and Kendal's banns this Sunday!

Father offered a toast as we laughed and clapped. "To new beginnings, to victory, to long and healthy lives and happiness."

"Hear, hear," Gideon murmured, his lovely violet eyes meeting mine, his gaze softer and more thoughtful today. The others echoed him. I wondered if I dared believe he'd made peace with our situation.

Kendal, on the other hand, had the requisite tears in her eyes when she met my gaze, the two-fold reasons for them once more matching mine. A lifetime of love and joy lie ahead of her, but I would not be a part of it.

"And to the future King of Kildaria," Sir Tavish said, his face suffused with pride. "We are thrilled to be such a special part of it. Long live the king."

Who could blame him for feeling that way? Ian would likely inherit the throne from Father and make Kendal his queen.

Happy talk followed, although my attention was fastened upon Gideon. He seemed calmer this afternoon, and I prayed it meant he'd made peace with everything that had happened between us and with King Desmond.

Then a knock at the door interrupted our tranquil atmosphere, a messenger bringing summonses from the king for both Gideon and Father. They excused themselves immediately.

Gut level, I knew something was wrong, but my powers of seeing into the future revealed nothing. When they returned, our quiet time was shattered. Father looked grim, Gideon shaken.

"I fear our plans have changed," said the prince. "I know it's a shock, but I support King Desmond's decision. The army is to march at dawn tomorrow."

"What?" Mother cried, leaping to her feet.

All I could do was stare at him. The future I'd feared for weeks had just landed like an avalanche on top of me.

"Tomorrow?" Kendal asked, taking my hand. I squeezed it tight, tears burning my eyes.

"I'm afraid so, Miss Kendal," he replied. "It would be better for the army to have another week to rest, but the attempt on King Desmond's life has your monarch demanding our immediate departure." Searching my face, he added, "It's best for me as well. We'll have a better chance of reaching Malloria before our enemies invade. Theona, to make things easier on us in the morning, we must spend tonight in camp."

CHAPTER 10

I felt the color drain from my face. My prince shared my distress, but when Mother protested, he offered a consolation.

"Your Grace, the families among the nobility who have warriors in the army are invited to join us tonight, after supper, to say goodbye before we retire. Please come. Baron and Baroness, your family is also welcome."

To Zahra he said, "You have the afternoon to finish my lady's packing, as my retainers are now doing for me. Theona, I will come at the four o'clock hour to take you to the courtyard. Our horses will be waiting for us."

My warrior-maid curtsied before rushing off, and I was so very grateful Gideon took me into his arms to comfort me before departing as well. I may have opened The Keeper, but this was part of a war that none of us wanted and was none of my doing.

Gideon left and guards soon came to take me to my rooms, where Zahra had a small army of maids helping her pack my trunk. It was a monster thing but frighteningly small when I realized that everything I could take with me would soon be locked inside it. I mourned the things I had to leave behind.

Zahra had my undying gratitude when she didn't push me to make decisions. I had no doubt she knew all too well what it meant to have few personal belongings.

The hour came, and Zahra and the servants escaped with both our trunks, while Gideon and his bevy of guards greeted me in the hall. Accepting the kerchief he handed me to wipe my eyes, I waved goodbye and offered sad, silent farewells to every corridor, every wall, every window as we marched past, nodding at servants and guards who dropped curtsies or bows, people I'd come to recognize and some to even like.

Stepping into the courtyard in the bright gold of late afternoon, we met General Bellamy, Sir Lance Arnoe and Zahra with grooms and our horses. Caspian nickered at seeing me, making me smile through my tears.

"I cannot believe this," I Mind-Paired to Zahra.

"Nor I, my lady. 'Twill be good to get on with it, but 'twas not a pleasant way to go about it."

I sighed my agreement.

We rode to Malloria's camp, which had changed dramatically since I'd been there disguised as Tally the Scout. One of the requirements Gideon had made of all the troops—as he had with his One Hundred—was that there would be no camp followers. The troops did all the work, the warriors selected because they were as qualified to manage the camp skills as they were to fight. As soon as we arrived, we handed our horses over to the warrior-groomsmen who waited for them.

Gideon's One Hundred were dwarfed by the armies now surrounding them. As King Desmond had announced, five divisions each laid claim to at least seven thousand warriors, more than thirty-five thousand in total.

It more than overwhelmed me. A steady clamor engulfed the entire area, with warrior-cooks preparing supper over crackling fires for thousands of people, warrior-hostlers and warrior-groomsmen caring for the army's horses and weapons, warrior-laundresses and warrior-wagon-masters packing nearby wagons. We passed four drays filled with cages of messenger pigeons and silage. Warrior-hunters dressed game of all kinds, some to toss into brine barrels for future meals. Racks held meats in various stages of drying. The sights, the smells, the loud conversations inundated me. My stomach grumbled despite my being upset.

How could any of them truly believe they could move something the size of a shire from one side of a continent to the other? I wished I'd paid better attention when Father and my brothers had discussed this very thing with the prince more than once.

The familiar Mallorian flag hung above Gideon's tent. Above that waved the new flag of the United Forces. The command tent, where I'd been questioned as a scout, stood to the left of it, and the prince's personal servants—men I'd never met—had quarters in a tent on the right side.

Gideon made the introductions to men who received me far more civilly than when I was dragged through the camp by people ready to slit my throat. Inside the prince's tent—our tent—I felt a moment of relative calm. A separate room to the right, partitioned with a thick curtain, provided a place for Zahra and granted the three of us and our cots a modicum of privacy.

"I'm sorry, my love, but I've scores of matters to see to before I can bed down," Gideon said, kissing my hand and pressing it to his cheek. "Zahra will help you make sense of all this."

I nodded, numb from head to toe, still unable to believe this was really happening. His leaving left a hole in my heart, but thankfully Zahra dared take my hand in hers and squeeze it.

"'Tis hard, my lady, but not fatal. Come."

Apparently, porters had delivered our trunks before we'd even left the courtyard. Zahra's was in her sleeping room, while mine and Gideon's sat on either side of our cots. Zahra pulled a key from her pocket and unlocked mine.

Her voice filled with kindness, she began to pull some items from within it and placed them on my cot. Court attire was for now a thing of the past. She told me about our proceedings for tomorrow, but I caught sight of something so formidable I couldn't listen. To the right of Gideon's trunk stood a small table with The Keeper atop it, and against it leaned Slayer in its scabbard. They looked as ancient as they were, and while no eldritch menace emanated from them, their very presence unnerved me every bit as much as this day had done.

I did hear Zahra talking about what to expect of camp life, but I'd missed part of it. I didn't actually care, and again she squeezed my arm, her dark eyes searching my face.

"'Tis o'erwhelming at first, my lady, but you'll get used to it. As you'll get used to not having the luxury of fine meals and glazed chamber pots and fancy bathing rooms. In truth, you'll come to consider bathing a luxury of its own. Supper comes early," she added, "as does the call to 'lights out.' Morning begins before sunup, and I'm sure you understand no one defies military order and discipline without facing consequences. The rules provide us with protection."

She also suggested we locate the latrines, to know the path before dark. Afterward, we took supper seated on logs surrounding the blazing fire nearest Gideon's tent. I felt so very grateful when he rejoined me. I was starving and appreciated our meal despite its simplicity: dark bread with what the army apparently considered a rare indulgence of butter and honey; and stewed beans made on this night with beef, a variety of vegetables, and simple spices.

The busy conversation at campfires all around us calmed me, including Gideon's pleasure at having Sir Lance, General Bellamy, and others of his commanders join us. With the sun now spreading a coral stain across the horizon and the late spring night growing chill, the campfire's glow and its pleasant fragrance calmed my anxieties and replaced it with a special sort of homeyness with which I fell instantly in love. Perhaps this wouldn't be so bad after all.

In truth, I'd not only camped overnight with my brothers many times—against Mother's wishes—but I'd also flown through the mountains in various forms, eating everything from bear to moose, and slithering through the forest feasting on crickets and worms. This could hardly be worse—provided no one tried to poison me.

Beyond that, I now had the chance to see Gideon in his element, engaged with his warriors, and witnessed the powerful side of an extraordinary man, a future king, a commander that men trusted.

A short time later, however, a cry rippled through camp, shattering our relative calm. In the far distance, bugles rang, and then came the sounds of a large party approaching.

A few rode on horseback; the rest came on foot, but several warriors reported that those on foot had come as close as they could by carriage. People around us murmured louder, then one cried out "It's the king!" Others joined him. "Glory be, 'tis the Prime Advocates!" "The McArthurs are with them." "And all the Elds. And the High Council!" "Can't believe they're visiting us just before we leave." "'Tis good luck, I say."

My heart swelled at the thought they believed this, and even more so at seeing my father riding beside my liege lord, both in light armor. I'd rarely had the privilege of seeing King Desmond in mail. He seemed stronger and more dignified than ever, his golden cape buttoned to the shoulders of his cuirass and billowing out behind him. I smiled at the thought his healing had worked well for him.

The party stopped before us, and Eld York cast me a portentous gaze. The king's visit was no social call.

Garrett Hew of the council gifted me with a kind smile and a nod, but I earned the normal hostile glares from Darby Murdock and Nevin Leath, to my right, and Egan Gilroy across from me. What a relief to know I'd likely never see them again.

The king and Father dismounted, and like a wave in the ocean, the entire camp, as far as my eyes could see, dropped to its knees. A heartbeat later, the king bid us rise, and the Elds and High Council joined him. Guards surrounded them, reminding everyone that these were dangerous times.

Another blare of the horns sent scribes hurrying through the troops, disseminating scrolls with information that those who could read would impart to everyone out of hearing range or who could not read.

"We've no time for courtly ceremonies," King Desmond said, his voice stronger than I'd heard it in years. "More rumors have abounded, and tonight I must dispel them. For the good of Kildaria and the Western League, I have designated Lord Cedric McArthur, the Duke of Mithradell, as the heir to the throne of Kildaria and the commander of the Western League. In two days hence, his crowning as king-in-waiting will take place, but make no mistake, from this moment forward, we consider Lord McArthur as legitimate an heir as if he were our son."

The response varied, but the vast majority of the troops greeted the announcement with gladness. Many may not like me, but most admired my father.

The king continued. "In addition, the Prime advocates have given their approval to a request from two of our most venerated members of the Elden Quorum. I fully agree with their decision."

He waved forward aged Eld Reagan and his much younger Elden companion Eld Kane. Eld Reagan was the one who had identified the poison forced down my throat by traitors just before Gideon and I married. He'd saved me and my family from a terrible death.

"These two exceptional Brothers have requested passage with you, to serve the needs of the army on your journey, and to commune with the Elden brotherhood of Malloria when they arrive," the king said. "Long have the two nations been separated; long have we wished it were otherwise. Tonight, on the eve of a newly forged alliance against a common enemy, we grant you their support."

The shouts of joy from the troops rang out. Both men's Elden powers were well-known. Their accompaniment was nothing less than a godsend.

My heart ached for them, however. According to Kildarian tradition, Quorum members served for life, but if they left, replacements would be selected within the month. If they managed to return, they would never serve here again. Eld Kane was a relatively young man. He'd lost his wife and toddler son a few years ago from the pox, so he wouldn't be deserting a family who needed him here, but Eld Reagan was a different matter. He was also a widower, but he was old and going blind, and I worried about him surviving the rigors of the trip. Despite that, I suspected he wanted to continue as my protector against poisons, a formidable thought.

The king wished us Godspeed, urging us to win the day, and then excused his party and rode away, leaving the Elden Quorum to visit and family and friends to say their final farewells. The crowd of warriors streamed forward to greet them.

Eld York looked careworn and emotional when he and the Prime Advocates approached me, pressing my extended hand between his and offering me a courtly bow.

"I wish I could be the one to accompany you, Princess," York said. "I believe a part of me will never recover when you leave."

I batted my eyes against a new onslaught of tears. I wasn't sure I'd ever recover from any of this.

"Thank you, Eld York. My father will need you all the days of both of your lives. I couldn't let you desert him."

He laughed quietly. "He would not let me desert him. But you'll have my prayers day and night to find success on your journey. Rid the world of the sorcerers, Your Highness, and find the happiness you deserve."

"I'll do my best," I promised.

He and his Elden companions then offered an Elden prayer for us, bestowing blessings upon us of a safe and triumphant journey.

Eld Rin, the Second Eld, his dark, almond-shaped eyes filled with sympathy, said, "My lady, your road is long and dangerous, and temptation is inevitable. Such is the way of life. If we lean on Elam and resist that temptation, the effort will refine us. If we do not, it can lead us to destruction. You must stay alert to remain victorious over it."

Eld Tully, the Prime Advocate, added, "Stay close to Prince Seville, my lady. Together, your gifts will complement each other. Divided, you will not stand."

I knew he spoke the truth. Gideon and I had both seen it in prescient visions.

Eld Trevino, the Third Eld, spoke last, reminding me to be a blessing to everyone I encountered. "Seek to defend the defenseless at all costs, my lady, and you will find the reprieve you so deeply desire."

Eld Tully had given me the same counsel in a vision in the temple just before my wedding. It renewed my hope that I could be forgiven for having opened The Keeper.

When they'd finished, they bid us farewell and mingled with the crowd to offer encouragement to as many as they could before we turned in. Then my parents hurried toward me, and I vaulted into my father's arms. He crushed me in a bear hug, and then Mother, her blue eyes sparkling with unshed tears, smothered me with kisses.

The children came next, little Shane and Keely, then Lon, then Ian and Kendal. The Tavishes were cautious, of course, but not unkind, and even Miss Morgan, the children's nurse—my old nurse—at least gave me a tight smile and a courtly curtsy. Miss Morgan had avoided me since coming to Leeds, terrified by my possession, but perhaps she realized our parting was permanent.

We settled round the fire again, to discuss the night's events. My family also presented us with small gifts. Among them were trinkets and scented soaps for me, a new razor and a kerchief for Gideon, and a knitted shawl from Mother that she said she'd made for my birthday and forgotten to give me because of everything surrounding my possession.

"You won't likely need it until Wintertide, but it will remind you of home whenever you use it."

"Oh, Mother. It's beautiful! Thank you," I said, so full of tenderness and fear I could hardly bear it. I pulled the shawl around my shoulders and felt a mother's love knitted into it. "I'll take the best care of it, I promise."

Singing broke out in some of the camps, and behind us a thin, older warrior took up a fiddle and began to play. Gideon murmured to me that it was the tradition in Malloria's army, when it was safe, to enjoy music and sometimes dancing while traveling, especially the night before beginning a campaign. Tune after tune, some familiar to me, most not, the man played. I wished he could go on forever.

"A gift to you, princess," the man said at last, his wizened face filled with kindness. "War lies before us," he said in his soft Mallorian accent, "but Elam watches us from His Walkway Above. May the words of Cleary the Brave guide us all in the days ahead."

He spoke the words of the poem first, a sweet Kildarian prayer that my many-times-great-grandfather penned in his youth, and which became both beloved and renowned. Then he played and sang it with a voice as clear and mellow as that of his violin.

> "May your hands always have work, and never too light.
> Keep the wind at your back, your face in sunlight.
> May your purse always bear coin, no matter how little.
> Among all your friends, may one play a good fiddle.
> After rain comes the rainbow, and love wipes away tears.
> May Elam heal your heart and ease all your fears."

The quiet echoed around us for a moment—until drums interrupted the camp again. It warned our visitors it was time for them to leave and us to head for bed. Tears again seasoned our every hug and kiss, marking our last greeting and our final farewell. Ian and Kendal lagged behind, Kendal holding my hand tight.

"I love you, sister mine," she said. "Return to us. Find the answers in Malloria and come home."

I smiled and nodded, even while I knew I wouldn't likely keep that "promise". She'd forgotten that if I survived, my place was with Gideon, not in Kildaria.

Ian pulled her off into the crowd, barely close enough behind my parents to be considered proper. I shook my head and prayed in silence, *Elam, watch over them. Please, watch over all of us.*

Regret in his voice, Gideon said, "Theona, I've one last meeting with the commanders to address our divisions' orders for tomorrow. Zahra will settle you for the night. I'll turn in as soon as I can."

Zahra did so, changing me into the more practical pair of sleeping breeches and a loose tunic she'd put on my cot earlier. She also placed my new shawl near the bottom of my cedar trunk to keep it safe, and as I lay down on my cot, she slipped into her "room" for the night.

In a brief, near-whispered Mind-Pair, I felt Gideon's request to wait up for him, so that he could be sure I didn't feel neglected. I loved him for it. He knew I needed him, and it meant I could put off meeting with the sorcerers, which gave me a quiet, private moment to weep tears of grief for all that I'd lost.

————————+—

I arrived for my nightly magical lessons testy. I'd done everything the sorcerers demanded of me but had not only learned nothing that could stop the war but would now have to continue my lessons on the road to Malloria.

I came demanding we concentrate on the exercises I'd failed in the past. I was still only passable at erasing the trail of magic, and I wanted to learn how to become invisible. They laughed at me.

"What's so funny?"

"That fact that you still think you have any say in this," Terius replied. "The army's unexpected departure changes our situation drastically, and considering we've difficult work for you tonight, you'll be miserable if you do both what you want to do and what we have planned."

I insisted.

"Then I have a proposition," Rhesalus said. "I can make erasing the trail of magic easier for you, to lessen the risks." Deviltry gleamed in his eyes. For some reason, he seemed younger tonight than when I'd first "met" him, and perhaps even more attractive. Because he was often kinder than Terius, I found myself feeling safer with him.

No. I scolded myself for thinking it. I could never allow myself to believe that.

He reviewed the basics of magic with me, referring to my talents as *parhelia,* a term I'd learned from Eld York but which the sorcerers had never used before. I nodded, pretending to be enlightened by his instruction. If I told him too much, such as the colors or other essences each *parhelia* bore, I'd likewise admit to having Insight, but I suspected I couldn't hide it much longer.

He placed a hand on my cheek and looked deep into my eyes, drawing my awareness inside my mind to my *illumina,* calling it by name. Its spherical shape pulsated like the core of a great, white sun inside me. Its translucent, constantly shifting "membrane" of light encircled the *parhelia* within it. My stomach dipped at the silent maelstrom of *parhelia,* like miniature flashes of colorful, slow-moving lightning. Each bore different powers in a kaleidoscope of colors, some flavored, some scented, others that "felt" soft or hard, cold or hot. As I watched, a pale orchid *parhelia* was born, coming to replace one that had faded from age and was in the process of disintegrating.

Rhesalus's presence felt like a gray cloud in my mind as he pushed my awareness deeper inside me, toward the *parhelia* that erased the evidence I'd used magic. It bore a sweet, honey-like scent and a faint lavender glow. He told me to look down, and I saw the "evidence" I'd used magic lying like spilled milk around my feet. Using the *parhelia*, he explained, entailed mentally "wiping the spill dry," like wiping up milk with a sponge.

With his guidance, I learned to use it almost instantly, which only served to prove how cruelly these monsters had treated me. Even the strictest of tutors I'd faced as a child had never left me to flounder the way the sorcerers did, and I wasn't convinced it was because they thought it was the best way to learn. I'd begun to believe they wanted to slow my progress enough to blame me for not reaching their goals before we left Kildaria—which would in turn put off my being able to get free of them.

Becoming invisible proved far more difficult, even with the horse-mage's help. The talent, paradoxically both a shiny silver and yet somehow also transparent, had no flavor or odor and felt smooth, cold, rigid. It tingled with power.

It also alluded my attempts to "grasp" it, as the sorcerers called it. Rhesalus's directions only took me so far before the *parhelia* would seem to collapse and hide itself behind my other talents. The harder I tried, the worse it became.

I clenched my teeth when I saw both Moriana and Terius snickering at my failure. Making fun of me did *not* endear them to me.

I didn't realize I'd grown faint until Rhesalus turned my chin toward him and looked deeply into my eyes.

"You need to hunt, my dear. Now. You've used too much energy."

I had. I felt wrung out like an old rag.

I didn't even have the strength to lock the sorcerers behind my shields. I left them in the glad and traveled only a short distance as an owl to feed and rest. However, when I returned satiated, the tension between the sorcerers made me hide in a treetop to listen.

"I tell you she's ready to do more," Terius insisted.

"She is and she isn't," Rhesalus snapped. "She's new. Untested. Being forced to take in too much too quickly."

"And growing amazingly more powerful every day," Moriana said. "If only I'd learned half so quickly."

"But we've pushed her into it. That bears its own consequences." Terius said, "Magic teaches itself over time, and she's beyond the point where she's likely to do something foolish."

"I disagree. She's also headstrong and brave. She's willing to take risks that might land her in trouble."

Rhesalus's statement flattered me. He considered me brave?

Terius argued. "Removing her trail of magic and finding some success with becoming invisible would decrease some of the pressure on her. She could practice night and day. Haven't you noticed we're just one day away from a new moon? Her magic should be at its weakest, but she's stronger than ever."

Moriana said thoughtfully, "Perhaps because of the speed of her growth, her weakest point now is equal to where her strongest point once was."

"We haven't the luxury of analyzing the reason," Terius insisted. "We just need to take advantage of it."

Rhesalus's brow furrowed. "No. We risk shattering her."

"I don't think so." Terius shook his head.

"But—"

"Rhesalus, darling," Moriana said, coming to cuddle against the horse-sorcerer. "You know what's coming. She has to be ready, or all is lost anyway. We aren't in danger of dying, after all. If the worst happens, we'll move on, take her prince. But the fact is, we're running out of time."

Terius's mage partner had obviously made her point. I could see Rhesalus relenting. Pretending I hadn't eavesdropped, I glided to the ground at their feet and became myself again. All three assumed expressions of innocence. Had I not overheard them, I would never have known how little they valued my life, even to the point of destroying me to get what they wanted.

"You look much better, Theona," Rhesalus said. "Now. We haven't enough time to work on invisibility but *must* concentrate on Linking again, this time with Enya."

I was annoyed at my desires being brushed aside but also relieved when they asked me to bring an eagle, not a horse. Unfortunately, Enya was overzealous and defiant with the creature, and after she did find purchase, I couldn't remove her, despite Terius's ranting and threatening. I begged Enya and reminded her that if the eagle died, so would she. She let go soon enough to save herself, but the eagle died.

It felt so wrong I burst into tears again, earning looks of disgust from Terius and Moriana and a frown from Rhesalus.

"We tortured it," I snapped. "It's wicked. Tell me what this disgusting experiment is supposed to accomplish so I can make peace with doing it."

Smirking, he replied, "Theona, you know what it's for, and you've exceeded any of our expectations. It's typically harder to place spirits inside living creatures than it is to take them out. Why you struggle with the opposite, we don't know, but if you've accomplished the most important part already, which will prepare you to place our spirits inside the bodies you will produce for us, the other part— *removing* a spirit—is…well…both anticlimactic and immaterial."

Anticlimactic and immaterial? How disrespectful of life!

I stared deep into his steel gray eyes, even more certain he withheld some part of the truth from me. Sick of it all, I sent them away, not caring if it infuriated them. I needed more food and enough sleep to face the labors our first day of marching might entail.

CHAPTER 11

The singsong-blast of a bugle threw me out of bed and onto the floor of the tent—thankfully piled with layers of skins—and scared me half to death.

"Princess Theona?" Zahra cried, rushing from her sleeping area to help me up. "Are you hurt?" Then she gasped and stumbled back from me when I called out mage light and flung it toward the tent's ceiling. "Oh, mercy, my lady, you mustn't do things like that. Think you'll give me a heart attack."

I might have laughed had another series of bugle-blasts not echoed across Leeds from varying distances.

"W-what is that?" I cried, clutching my bed covers to me. It was cold and dark as midnight, and I imagined Valdellian Warlords coming to crucify us. I cringed when Zahra did laugh.

"Surely, you've heard reveille before, my lady. 'Tis our wakeup call."

Wakeup call? It was morning already? I vaguely remembered Gideon coming to bed and holding me for a spell before I met with the sorcerers, but when I returned from my night's lesson, I didn't even remember falling asleep.

"Nothing's amiss, Princess. Prince Seville wanted you to sleep for a bit longer, but now it's time to get ready. We must eat and collect our mounts. Warriors are coming to pack our tent."

Zahra dressed me in the loose uniform of Gideon's warriors: fawn-colored leather trousers and a beige linen tunic. Good for horseback riding, along with my knee-high brown riding boots. I shivered against the early morning cold, grateful for the light cotton vest and dark red doublet Zahra added. They'd lend me warmth until the sun rose, while providing adequate cushion under my armor if I had to don it in haste. I could also tie them on the back of my saddle if I grew too warm. I wondered if anyone would protest when they saw me with both the short sword and dagger, encased in two neatly tooled scabbards, hanging from the sword-belt around my waist.

Guards with lamps escorted us through the beehive of activity to the pits—an embarrassing experience to say the least—and then we returned to our simple breakfast of biscuits and sausage. Most of the cooks were already putting out campfires and packing their equipment.

Prince Gideon seemed more himself when he greeted me, his dark hair damp and combed back from his brow. He looked smart in his travel uniform, and I offered him a prim smile and curtsied, feeling silly without skirts. He chuckled in response.

The Elds came to offer a brief holy day invocation for us, the best they could do under the circumstances, after which General Bellamy, with many others, began bellowing orders. Then, as the barest of dawn crested the Carinors, life as I'd known it, ended.

Gideon led Zahra and me to where Elds Reagan and Kane—dressed in their own more practical riding gear that included light blue tunics and short-cloaks—stood waiting for us with our horses. Gideon lifted me onto Caspian and then leaped aboard Valere. Caspian seemed terribly proud of himself as he pranced in place, excited to leave the camp that would soon be nothing more than a memory,

With everyone now mounted, a final blow of a bugle repeated throughout the army brought silence to the host, all waiting for Gideon to make the signal for us to begin. He pumped his fist into the air and the bugles rang. Gideon to my right, Zahra to my left, and Gideon's men and the Elds surrounding us, we set forth on that clear, lovely Sunday morning, on the twenty-ninth day of April.

The meadows stretched for miles around us, westward toward Leeds and the sea, southward from the capital to Mithradell, northward from the castle to Bedfordshire, and due east to the mountains. Gideon explained that the open spaces would allow the army to spread out and travel faster toward Cleary Pass.

Pride filled me at seeing Kildaria's warriors sitting tall and gallant in the saddle and the entire United Forces moving with impressive precision. For now, all the wagons drove in a wide line to the rear, a plume of dust and chaff from the meadow billowing out behind them like smoke from a great bonfire, not at all pleasant for anyone behind it.

Gideon informed me that King Desmond had ordered both ends of the pass closed until we traveled through. Still, a throng of local citizens waited for us at its mouth to cheer us on. Another reception on the other end of the road would greet us, granting us provisions and horses to replace any that didn't fare well on this leg of the trip.

Along the way, I began to learn how the army would travel and why many of the Western League commanders opposed it. Positions drawn at Gideon's final meeting last night put Kalbarri in the vanguard position at the front of the army. Malloria's warriors and Gideon, as the chief commander, knew the way and would always maintain second position behind whichever division acted as vanguard. For now, Kalbarri's commanders would join Gideon's.

Dundee, Kythos, and Segovia followed us in that order, and Kildaria took the dubious honor of rearguard.

One glaring disagreement between the leaders had erupted over the wagons' arrangement. Each division would keep their wagons with them, and the divisions behind them would maintain a gap sufficient to avoid the dust and horse droppings as best they could. The arrangement would still create some unpleasantness but reassured the commanders that each division's weapons and supplies were nearby, which lessened the discord.

Unless otherwise instructed, riders would travel abreast in groups of four and the wagons in threes to shorten our cavalcade and speed our progress. Change would occur only in areas too narrow to support it or wide enough to allow us to spread out and travel faster *en masse* as we had through the fields.

Thus, we ventured into the wondrous beauty of Cleary Pass. Our cadence, a comfortable walk, was marked by the jingle of bridles, the clopping of horses' hooves and the rumble of wagons. The road grew narrower and climbed steadily until it reached a safe distance above but parallel to the Carinor River. From there it would rise and fall only slightly until we reached the other side of the mountain range.

My parents came this way whenever they visited the eastern side of the duchy, but I never had. The sights and smells, the grand mountain tops and rushing river below, and the final view of Kildaria before we turned the last corner fascinated me—and diverted the sadness. Wildlife abounded here: deer and elk, rabbits and squirrels, even an eagle that glided overhead.

Eventually, however, reality defeated novelty. Conversation faded, replaced by vigil, as every warrior scrutinized clifftops and clusters of trees for enemies. The sun rose higher and brought the heat with it. I quickly shed my jacket and was glad to don the wide-brimmed cap Zahra had stuffed into my tunic pocket that morning. Inevitably, the excitement faded and riding to war became, well, boring.

We paused only to rest and relieve riders and horses, especially the wagon horses. We ate lunch on horseback, taken from our rucksacks—mine already deemed safe by Eld Reagan—and although the water inside my water skin was warm and musty-tasting, it at least slaked my thirst.

I peeled myself from Caspian's back later in the day when we took a blessed respite from the saddle, ruing not having had enough time to practice. I was stiff and sore. Healing myself served no purpose, either. The more magic I used, the hungrier I became, and I had no cure for that but supper—however close or far off that was.

Thankfully, mid-afternoon offered an early bivouac on a spacious plateau. Forewarned that this was one of only two places in the Cleary Pass where the entire cavalcade could camp together, the followers continued to pour in until after dark. Only a handful of leaders would raise tents tonight, including Gideon, unless the weather changed. It would reduce the work in the morning and spare time and equipment.

Herein lay one of the biggest disagreements among those planning this trip. For most of the trek, when the vanguard reached the day's stopping point, the entire army would stop and make camp wherever it stood. Outriders and scouts would maintain communication between the divisions, and buglers spread throughout the cavalcade would use prearranged signals to direct the company. When we could, we would allow the horses to graze. When we couldn't, we'd picket them and feed them the provender brought with us.

It made good sense to me. Everyone would ride from sunrise to sunset, make simpler camps, and be ready to ride again as a group the next morning.

As for the warriors and generals themselves, I overheard a handful of them squabbling about having the sleeping army strung out in a line that could leave it open to attack. Gideon admitted the risk but pointed out that these warriors were also used to smaller armies. Structured in the ordinary way, this one would stretch out for fifty to sixty miles. That meant, it would have to be broken into two or three groups and each couldn't travel for more than half the day before it would have to make camp. The rearguards wouldn't reach the main camp until eight o'clock at night or later and would not set out again until noon the following day.

Even with riders and wagons traveling abreast as planned, the cavalcade still stretched nearly twenty miles long, but Gideon's approach at least moved the entire cavalcade together. Considering few areas existed along the road where we could collect into larger groups anyway, the argument seemed pointless. What we needed were good sentries and quick access to our weapons, and each division's wagons traveling close satisfied the need.

After supper, some warriors repeated last night's playing of instruments and singing, but others sparred with their weapons, which stretched stiff muscles and helped allay some of the bickering. If only those amusements hadn't added to my homesickness.

I dreaded meeting with the sorcerers that night and put it off until the early morning hours. When I let them out, they snarled and snapped at me like angry dogs. Terius made me Link with eagles again and Moriana drove me relentlessly with the Language. As to the latter, I somehow made good progress, enough that I felt the Language becoming a part of me—or at least my desire for it did. I still wasn't good at it, but hundreds of words fluttered inside my head, like dandelion fluff caught on the wind: *Partra undor. Plana faell. Appro za mi. Mutata flosa*…. Each gave me more dynamic control of the world around me, changing, destroying, and creating things. It became harder and harder to refuse the call to try feats the sorcerers hadn't even suggested. Once warned by Eld York of the dangers of letting my magic take over, I worked hard to do no more and, when possible, less than my unwelcome guests demanded of me, but the enticement only grew stronger. Enya would have reminded me that learning on my own lessened their control over my magic, but I feared playing with something so dangerous alone.

On Monday morning, again at barely dawn—and marking the first week's anniversary of my marriage to the Crown Prince of Malloria— Dundee took over the vanguard as planned, the rest of us fell into place behind Dundee, and Kalbarri dropped to the rear. The journey seemed a repeat of Sunday's. We could only discuss so much about the lovely terrain, and nothing more exciting happened than eating our meals, cleaning rocks out of our horses' hooves, or addressing bodily functions. And complaining about aching legs and backsides and longing for a bath.

That night, near the top of a mountain, the road came to a large meadow, not wide enough for the entire army to camp but level enough to graze many of the horses. We would bed down on the road. I felt mixed emotions when I caught sight of a herd of wild horses at the edge of the meadow. No doubt the sorcerers would want to take advantage of them that night.

I was right. After the camp slept, I flew into the meadow and released the sorcerers, and Rhesalus's grin was too full of calculation.

"Ah, my beauty, this is excellent."

"What is excellent?" I said, hoping he meant something other than the horses. How could he see anything in the light of a sliver of the moon?

"Wild horses, my dear. We need to take advantage of them. Learning to Link them is the key to the next step in setting us free."

"I don't like it," I snapped, teeth gritted.

"Oh, but when you've mastered it, you'll be ready to prepare bodies for the dragons; and it's only a small step from there to giving us ours."

Was he lying again? I had no idea, but I reminded myself that I needed to do whatever I needed to do to get rid of them. I just hoped nothing that happened tonight would harm these animals.

The herd was asleep. Beautiful horses, wild and spirited. I couldn't help the tears that flowed when I saw them.

"You must get over this childish melodrama," Rhesalus insisted. One hand on my back, he leaned in to kiss my temple and my thoughts scattered as his incredible fragrance of spring flowers and open fields engulfed me. His gentle caresses soothed away the tension deep inside me, and when he rested his cheek on top of my head, his very presence was the essence of kindness. For a split second my mind dozed, and I stood there with Gideon.

This time, when reality dawned, I forced myself not to overreact. Pulling gently away from him, I schooled myself to act the innocent sixteen-year-old girl I once was, knowing I must appear comforted, not revolted. I blinked in confusion at seeing him appear even younger than he had just the night before, without a doubt a very handsome man.

He was manipulating me again, trying to charm me to his will. Even worse, he wanted me, every bit as much as he wanted his virile male body back. He must hate it that he couldn't rid the world of Gideon and stake his claim on me.

Who knew what would happen if the situation ever changed?

"I have one condition for doing this," I said as sweetly as I could muster.

"Condition?" Terius snarled. "I remind you that you've no rights to set conditions on anything."

I slipped behind Rhesalus, pretending fear. My silent appeal for protection earned me exactly what I wanted.

"Need I remind you that my mage partner is my business, not yours, old friend?" Rhesalus said.

Terius looked ready to bite roofing nails in half, but he shut his mouth.

"What sort of condition, Theona?" Rhesalus asked, turning to slip an arm around me. "And don't think I'll give you anything you want just because you ask for it."

"Of course not, but I know you'll understand. Terius and Moriana belittle me and browbeat me, while you help when I get confused. I'm not so afraid of what I need to learn when you protect me. I want to work with you and you alone."

I saw a flicker of triumph cross his face. The triumph inside my heart mimicked it. If I could win over Rhesalus, perhaps I could pit him against the others.

"I'll teach you what I can, dear girl, but Moriana is a natural with the Language and Terius has talents you have yet to learn."

"But if you supervise *their* lessons, they'll surely treat me better."

He all but preened and nodded his agreement. Now, if I truly had the dragon's support, we were four against two.

I then reasoned with Rhesalus that I'd only Linked the dragons with eagles a few times and might not be ready for Linking them to horses. I wouldn't admit that I thought it might be the easiest of all. Rhesalus said he understood my concerns but insisted I try.

Of course, we—the dragons and I—did everything we could to frustrate the situation, failing time and again, although I no horses were harmed. If not for Rhesalus, I was certain Moriana and Terius might have beheaded me.

Seeing my fatigue and hunger, Rhesalus sent the dragons away so that I could hunt and rest. Afterward, the sorcerers again turned their focus on the Language, and then Terius had me practice opening portals with him, the "rules" I learned thankfully lessening some of the discomfort.

At last, the sorcerers bid me good night, but I brought out the dragons rather than retiring. It was time to practice on our own.

"Fly with us, human, for the joy of it," Ramah grumbled, and I did. Here, we had the space to hunt as snakes, run across meadows as horses, become behemoths and cavort a distant lake. Finally, we took wing as eagles and flew east through the mountains, arriving at a great lake in a shallow hollow draped in a gossamer veil of fog. Nearby, another herd of wild horses had bedded down.

I landed at the lake's shore and summoned the dragons, but they ignored me when I spoke to them, looking every which way with wild abandon, their eyes flickering a kaleidoscope of colors. Vaulting into the starry night, they soared toward the deepest part of the hollow. Confused, I followed and landed beside them. They shut their eyes, raised their wings, and hummed in pleasure as the mists swirled around them, ignoring my questions about their seeming nonsense. Then, when we took wing again, I'd have sworn—even in the dark— they appeared a brighter shade of jade than when we'd landed.

I would never forget the way the mare I selected for Enya staggered and bounced off, bucking and kicking when the dragon Linked with her. I felt her fear and pain, and when she fell to her knees, the guilt crushed me. She could break a leg, or her neck, or have a heart attack and die.

"She's calming," Ramah reassured me. "Don't let go of either of them, not even for an instant. Your aversion makes it that much harder for us to fasten ourselves inside them."

Finally, Enya blossomed within her host and became her fascinating jade-dragon self. She took flight but swung lazily away from the herd and settled behind us to enjoy the feel of her newfound mortal frame.

A nearby colt, on the verge of turning into a stallion, watched with fascination. He would do well for Ramah.

I'd barely taken quick scrutiny of the young chestnut's *rumoria* when Ramah flashed through me and instantly Linked with the animal. The shock of having both dragons Linked at the same time drove *me* to my knees. I couldn't hang on to all four entities at once! *"I'm secure!"* Enya shouted inside my head. *"Let go of me. Get Ramah through it!"*

The colt's thrashing and shrieking went beyond panic and scattered the herd. Then he bolted, disappearing into the inky blackness of night.

In the silence that descended, I felt Ramah gaining control. Enya bellowed and Ramah answered her. In a flash, they vaulted into the air, coiling around each other and flapping two sets of wings as they headed together toward the stars.

"You're going too far!" I insisted. *"I'm losing my hold on you. You could die!"*

"You will not lose us," Ramah said. *"And we will not die. These animals are...right. The snake is too brainless, the eagle too wild. The horses are perfect."*

Their connection tugged at me as if my own soul were being stretched too thin. My legs grew weaker and weaker.

I murmured, *"But if you go too far, I fear I will die."*

How ironic to be killed by a magical experiment intended to protect all three of us from harm in the future. Had they betrayed me just to get what they wanted? Could they live in these forms after all? My thoughts began to dim.

Dizziness overcame me and the hard ground rose up and struck my head. I blinked twice, seeing more stars than meadows, but they weren't the celestial variety.

I grew numb, and everything turned black.

I heard two voices squabbling on the periphery of my mind, one male and one female, but not human. They were panic struck, feared they'd pushed someone too hard, could have killed her.

"I couldn't help myself," the male said. "The stallion was too great a temptation, and I couldn't hold back. I never thought about her."

"Should we call the sorcerers for help?"

The sorcerers. Mentioning the familiar word caught my attention. The scent of wild grass and spring flowers brought back odd memories. A late-night chill produced goosebumps.

"She's coming 'round!" the male voice cheered.

I blinked, peering through the darkness at two very large, very frightening-looking creatures hanging over me: huge, long, almost-equine heads with serpentine snouts; knobbed horns and wide golden eyes that glowed in the night; long sinewy necks and bodies, with even longer tails, spiked along the ridge; lizard-like legs with feet equipped with razor-sharp claws; wide, membranous, bat-like wings.

The dragons! I sat up quickly. They were still inside the horses but changed into dragons! But they didn't smell like horses. More like birds but with a faint, earthy tang that reminded me of snakes.

"Are you injured, Theona?" Enya asked anxiously, resting her jaw on the ground to better see me.

"I-I think I'm…alright," I replied.

Both tripped over themselves to offer apologies, odd from a pair of overgrown reptiles.

"You can't ever Link at the same time again," I scolded them, coming unsteadily to my feet. "It felt as if you were going to jerk my soul out of my body and catapult it into the heavens."

"Agreed," Ramah said. "At least until you're better at this."

"And only if I say you can," I insisted. I'd nearly died. It was the third time in six days. The hunger that now took hold of me felt desperate.

I unLinked the dragons—one at a time—closed my shields to them with a promise we'd try again tomorrow night if we could find horses, set off in search of game before I lost the strength to do so, and then headed back to camp.

———|———

Tuesday and Wednesday echoed the previous days in their determined monotony, which heightened my homesickness. Only having Gideon and Zahra with me made it bearable, even if my prince's duties often kept him too busy for me. On Wednesday night, we camped early at the second location large enough for the army to gather, around Lake Tralee—the same lake I'd discovered on Monday night! It was one of three that emptied from the Carinor Mountains into the ocean, and in evening's light it was truly more beautiful than I'd ever imagined.

That Wednesday night marked another feigned failure with Linking horses, forcing Terius to make me practice with eagles instead; and I made enough progress with the Language, Moriana seemed at least somewhat mollified. On Thursday, our fifth day on the road and now led by Kythos, we heard the buglers announce our approach to the foothills as we descended into the farmlands of eastern Kildaria! The excitement of hundreds of cheering souls waiting to wish us well on this side of the pass chased away the doldrums and my sense of loss. I did feel Zahra and Gideon tense on either side of me, murmuring their fear that enemies could be mingled within the crowd. Such uneasiness was contagious, and I couldn't help wanting to pull back when what appeared to be groups of town leaders headed toward us, fully armed.

CHAPTER 12

Relief relaxed my arms and slowed my pounding hear when the town leadership welcomed Gideon and the army's generals with warmth. Even better, they delivered the promised provisions and traded fresh horses for a few that had proved poor travelers and for one that had gone lame. The townspeople seemed sincere, saying they prayed for our safety, and begged us to defeat the Central Alliance. To my surprise, a handful of kind people even dared wish me well in finding a remedy for my possession.

With nothing but farms on either side of the wide road and crops knee-high as far as the eye could see, we couldn't cut corners through fields. We had to stick to the road until we reached our next campsite. It was in a fallow field, blessed with a full reservoir and room to gather. Here we refilled water barrels, cooked and—yes!—bathed, and relaxed. At least I tried to relax.

"Tell me about the Badlands," I said to my tired, distracted husband at supper. "I'm guessing we're about three days out now. Surely you don't think that if you told me the truth about them, you'd scare me enough I'd refuse to go with you."

He gave a soft laugh. "It's a little late for that, but no. In truth, I suspect that because of your powers you'll fare better than the rest of us. What about you, my dear? Have your shades shown any signs of weakening?"

I sighed. "No, my lord. The sorcerers seem as powerful as ever." I still hadn't gathered the courage to admit that the sorcerers had told me the tale was only a tale. "I wish they weren't, but for now, please explain this dessert land we will soon travel through."

"I suppose I should, but where shall I begin?"

"It's a desert. I assume it's hot," I quipped.

He laughed again. "As hot as Hades, and dry. Thankfully we'll have several oases and wells to help us along the way. The weather and natural inhabitants are another matter."

"Sounds ominous," I muttered.

"It can be," he admitted. "You know Kildaria shares part of its eastern border with the Badlands. This road we're traveling turns southward and leads us along that border to the Badlands Route. The Route divides the Badlands to the north from the Nomad Margin to the south, and it's, well, almost magical in nature. You won't believe it until you've seen it. It will take us all the way to the Beldame mountains, and by treaty, it's been a neutral path for generations. If, however, we leave The Route, we forfeit our safety."

Zahra—who'd had some experience in these lands with Kildaria's army—added, "We're safe, my lady, so long as we stay on the road."

Gideon nodded. "No one seems to know why, but nothing grows on it, not even the toxic plants that thrive everywhere else in the desert. Unfortunately, poisonous animals, sandstorms and flash floods have no such boundaries."

We dared not try to outrun such threats, either. We'd risk getting lost in the desert, and if we left the road the natives would attack us. Our only defense seemed tenuous: hiding under oilskins and turning our backs to the storms.

As to the wildlife? I couldn't envision such a barren area sustaining anything, let alone a veritable encyclopedia of creatures. Among them were vicious thieves, like coyotes, desert boar, and scavenger birds; poisonous snakes; flesh-eating insects; and small reptiles with the jaws of a crocodile, which hid in the foliage around watering holes. We needed to avoid water until it was deemed safe by experienced warriors. The army's size would scare off most of them, and unless the temperature dropped, most wouldn't likely bother us at night; but still, I was grateful we'd sleep in our tents and off the ground on cots.

The creatures I feared the most? White sand spiders. They lived in black hillocks scattered across the desert floor and were creatures the size of rats who could run almost as fast as a rabbit. They had venomous fangs and a bite that could kill a horse in thirty seconds. I gulped at the thought.

Gideon continued. "We know little about the tribes of the Badlands, other than for being remarkable warriors in a barbarous way. If you venture onto their land, you're at their mercy, and they have little of it. Few have survived to tell tales about them.

"As for the Nomad Border, south of the road, cartographers believe it goes as far as that mountain range." He pointed southward, supposedly toward peaks I couldn't see in the dark. "It's belongs to three native tribes: the dark-skinned Mengeddi, the red-haired Ketelic, and the Hamars. The Mengeddi and the Ketelic drape themselves in long robes and veils for protection from sun and heat, but while the Mengeddi prefer colorful materials, the Ketelic blend into the desert with grays and browns. Unlike the Hamars, they sometimes come to trade with caravans on the road.

"The Hamars are a nasty-tempered lot that wear little clothing. They keep to themselves. Unfortunately, all three groups consider women property, like cattle, and enjoy stealing them from each other and from traveling parties—which, of course, puts every woman in our cavalcade at risk. Few kidnapped have ever escaped to tell what was done to them, and trust me, you don't want to know."

I flinched when the beat of drums sent the troops to bed. From now until we passed through the Badlands, we wouldn't use the bugles, which were more likely to draw attention, but the drums' concussions still startled me.

Gideon squeezed my hand. "As long as everyone does their part, we should be fine," he reassured me.

Or he tried to reassure me, but in some measure failed, for I had no doubt some would not do their part.

Fatigue put me to sleep right away, although the heat and ideas of huge spiders and desert savages had me tossing with restlessness.

———+—

If wishes were horses, warriors would ride.
If wishes were eagles, maidens would fly.
If wishes were serpents, wise men would hide
If wishes were dragons, sorcerers could glide.

I came awake in a cold sweat, the nightmare still crashing through my mind: a great battlefield, filled with armor-clad horses and warriors fighting to the death; overhead: a handful of female warriors, their swords clutched in their fists, riding monstrous eagles; around my feet: serpents. Horrid, poisonous, vicious things that hissed and lunged at anything that moved. And above me flew Ramah, Rhesalus astride his neck, the sorcerer's cape fluttering around his shoulders and his hands wielding his power.

The disturbing poem I'd once not understood now seemed an absurd mockery of something that was yet to happen.

I felt physically well, but a dark, ominous cloud hung over me, as if something terrible was about to happen, just like before the attack on King Desmond. Home seemed as far off as the moon; and while Gideon was my safety net, he soon fell fast sleep and left me feeling alone and vulnerable.

I gasped when something made me open my eyes and I saw faint blue-colored magic curling around The Keeper's carved mountain. What was happening? It felt as if the artifact's flickering energy was beckoning me, and Slayer, leaning against the table, lurked in the shadows beside it.

I gulped, wondering what I should do. The sculpture was beautiful, an amazing creation, but I wanted nothing to do with it. When I used to visit my father's library as a child, I swore I'd seen the intricate village that sat at Mt. Draakheda's feet come to life. Gideon and I had shared a dreamwalking state in that village twice a year for many years, and as we grew older, we fell further and further in love in that village. I had, however, been tricked by the sorcerers into opening the hidden door in the sculpture's mountain, supposedly to find clues for locating my prince in real life. That act had destroyed that life.

My heart pounding, I slid out of our tent and flew off to work with the sorcerers, where I gained a bit more control over some of my magic with the Language. We found no wild horses for Linking—for which I was grateful—and I refused to risk using any of the army's animals. Even one horse lost would weaken the army.

Of course, that meant I couldn't practice Linking with the dragons on our own, either, which frustrated our scheme a bit; but I turned my efforts instead to improving my skills with dragon warfare. At least I did until the heat and hunger turned me too cantankerous.

Thus, done for the night, I managed to prey on a stray herd of antelope and then returned to my cot, thankful the temperature fell during the night and gave me some rest after all.

The level farmlands around us seemed vibrant in Friday morning's bright sunlight, and I felt better rested than I had in some time. Segovia assumed the lead for today and tomorrow. As my prince had predicted, we would travel somewhat southeast through endless miles of Kildaria's small cities, towns of all sizes, hamlets and farmlands until we reached the Badlands Route. Seeing these lands for the first time not only made me starkly aware of the kinsfolk who labored hard to provide for our country, but also made me realize how vulnerable these families and towns were to enemy attack.

Gradually, the fields and orchards dwindled until finally the plains welcomed us. No fences, no farms, an occasional cabin or hut but mostly open spaces, which meant we could again spread out and travel faster and more comfortably.

Later in the day, one of Gideon's wagons rumbled close behind us, the one that bore our armor and weapons along with The Keeper and Slayer. I no longer considered the pull of the Elden creations my imagination. It had grown notably stronger in the last few days. Even the distance from them and the blankets covering them from curious eyes couldn't dampen their magnetism for me. I almost dreaded setting up our tent at night.

As the Carinor Mountains shrank behind us, the rivers became fewer and lakes smaller but more frequent. Stands of trees gave brief shade from the sun and heat, but wildflowers and grasses in some areas grew as high as the horses' bellies. I tried not to notice the spread-out army trampling them. It seemed indicative of the future we all faced.

The last two nights, we set up camp around lakes, taking advantage of their obvious benefits including nearby game, which relieved our austere diet of dried and salted meats and dried vegetables and beans. Snobbish princess or not, I was thrilled that it also offered us another blessed opportunity to bathe. Zahra was right. I longed for the days of hot baths and scented soaps.

These evenings left an impression on my soul: seeing our camp set up, hearing the musicians play, watching the warriors dance and the swordsmen and archers practice. I loved watching my prince spar with Sir Lance, having never seen Gideon wield a sword before. He was so good, I hoped he never witnessed how I flailed with mine.

We had no practice swords, only leather sleeves to cover our own swords. Zahra urged me to a private area behind tall shrubs or rocky places to practice with her, thus giving my bruises the opportunity without an audience to turn into deadly wounds or missing fingers. Thankfully I retired each night with all digits in their proper places.

Even better, Zahra finally dared to take the talents she didn't know well more seriously, especially shape-changing. Because she'd never used the talent as a child, it seemed as wild as an untamed colt despite being eager to be put to work. It was like watching two strangers bargaining for control.

On Monday evening, without warning, Zahra's eyes rounded in triumph, and although she gritted her teeth against the pain, she pushed onward. Shoes and clothes seemingly absorbed into her metamorphosis, scaled legs, webbed feet, and the reshaping of arms into wings blessed with glossy black feathers heralded the form she was taking. Her lengthening neck and shifting face, at first a hideous blend of human and avian features, sprouted a red bill, then finally settled into the form her magic had bequeathed her.

"Zahra," I said, dropping to my knees in front of her. "You're glorious! You're a beautiful, black swan."

Her thoughts came to me swirling with confusion. *"I'm a bird? Does that mean I can fly?"*

"Swans do fly, but even better, they swim. This type of bird makes you a creature of air, land, *and* water."

After all, if the only shape she could have assumed was a chicken, she wouldn't be able to swim or fly. When she flapped her wings in excitement, I cautioned her to wait to learn to use those wings. She needed to understand the dangers and how to avoid them first.

"Well, I might not be a splendorous form like a winged horse or an eagle, my lady, but at least I can fly. Although I'm not sure what good a swan would do either of us. Rather than guarding you, I'm just as likely to wind up Christmastide supper as any silly goose."

I laughed. "It might not be your only form, but even if it is, your ability to fly is a capital boon."

She gave a hissing sound that I supposed was swan laughter then struggled to return to herself. When she'd accomplished it, she gave me a wide grin and immediately announced she was starving.

———†———

On Saturday, one week after leaving Kildaria and our last day before facing the Badlands, that otherworldly feeling of dread returned. Trouble was at hand. I hesitated about Pairing my concerns to Gideon. He had enough to manage all day, every day. I removed my Dreamwood bracelet to eye Moriana's ring, but it ignored me. Useless thing. Even worse, The Keeper seemed to glare at me, and I now sometimes thought I heard it…whispering? Was it trying to tell me something? Slayer's embellished handle also caught my eye. It was beautiful. It begged me to wrap my hand around it, to pull it from its sheath.

I all but ran from the tent.

Zahra and I joined the female warriors at the lake before breakfast, taking advantage of our last occasion to bathe for some time to come.

I wished I could wash away that awful premonition that prickled the nape of my neck, but it intensified on our hike back to Malloria's camp. Along the way, we passed a group of Segovian troopers, handsome, swarthy men who glared at me with eyes that glittered like obsidian. Even their black trousers and khaki tunics with the emblem of their country adorning their left sleeves—a black sickle stitched onto a red background— intimidated me. They reminded me too much of the Valdellian Warlords.

My magic tugged at me, as if urging me to prepare to defend myself. I couldn't help it when I Mind-Paired with the warrior who looked the most dangerous, "listening" to what he whispered to two of his friends and feeling the depth of his emotions.

"She'll bring us misfortune for sure," he whispered to one man.

"And death," his companion said. "Unless something happens to her first."

Walking between them and me, Zahra kept her hand on her dagger, her challenge obvious. I stared back at them, feeling the magic coiling inside me, at the tip of my fingers, at the forefront of my mind. Visions of shape-changing into creatures far more dangerous than they could imagine abolished my fear. They had no idea that in many ways Zahra was protecting them from me rather than me from them. Besides, tearing them to pieces as a dragon would have monumental consequences.

The third man took a step toward me then—

"Princess Seville!"

The feeling collapsed, and I looked ahead to see Sir Lance running toward us, his face drawn with worry.

"Please come, my lady. You cannot believe what's happened."

The men pulled back and we hurried after him, me fearing something was wrong with Gideon, Zahra muttering she wanted to skin the men who'd dared consider hurting me.

We approached our campsite and saw what appeared to be a dispute. Thankfully, Gideon stood well and whole alongside General Bellamy and General Brodie, a red-headed Dundeean whom Gideon greatly respected. They, in turn, were surrounded by several warriors and wagon-masters from Kildaria, Dundee, and Kythos.

Two individuals, their backs to me, were restrained by warriors, both people dressed in rumpled, dirty, but aristocratic clothing. One was a slender blonde woman held by a broad-shouldered Kythosian, the other a dark-haired young man in the clutches of a pair of Dundeean wagon-masters. Shock made me gasp when I realized I knew them.

"No!" I hissed. "This cannot be!"

Bolting between the captives, I turned to face them and gasped at seeing Ian and Kendal staring at me! Well, at least Kendal was. Both were thin as rails and filthy from head to toe, their clothes torn, Kendal's hair in chaos, several bruises and a long scrape on her right cheek—and Ian appearing half beaten to death.

"Oh, dear heaven! Ian! Kendal! What happened?"

Kendal pulled her arms from the Kythosian and threw them around me, sobbing. Ian, however, weak as a kitten and wan as death, couldn't see me. Both of his eyes were swollen shut. The Dundeeans weren't detaining him, they were holding him up, his face bruised, nose broken, and dark hair matted against his head by dried blood.

"Theona? We were kidnapped," he managed to rasp.

My mouth went dry when I remembered the words of the squat Segovian who'd railed at Gideon before taking a knife to his own heart. He'd sworn the conspirators would do anything to rid the world of Gideon and King Desmond, even kidnapping or assassination. He'd sworn they could get away with it and then escape, and while they hadn't killed the king, no one had been arrested for the attempt. Gideon was concerned that traitors traveled among us. Perhaps they were one and the same.

"When were you kidnapped? How?" I asked them.

"On the night we said farewell, my lady," Kendal said. "Lord Ian and I were a good hundred feet behind our parents, headed back to our carriages. It was quite dark, and as our families climbed into their vehicles, three men jumped from the shadows and grabbed us. One of them hit Ian so hard on the head he dropped to the ground like a sack of bricks. I would have screamed, but another had his hand across my mouth and told me he'd kill Ian if I made any noise. Next thing I knew, someone threw a bag over my head and smothered me until I fainted. I awakened sometime later under a tarp and in the back of a wagon."

"I came awake in a wagon bed, too," my brother croaked. "Someone would punch me through the wagon's tarp if I made any noise. In the middle of the night, two dragged me away from the army to take care of my needs, give me a bit of water and food, beat me if I complained. Did it every night since we left Leeds." He pointed at his eyes. "I never saw any faces. Thought I'd suffocate under that tarp, and I've never been so thirsty or hungry in my life."

"Two women did the same to me," Kendal said, her hand pressed to what I perceived were bruised ribs. "But they hid under cowls and didn't do so much damage."

General Brodie pointed at one of the Dundeean wagon-masters and in his brogue said, "He's the one what found Lord Ian in the back of his wagon, Your Highness." He nodded toward the Kythosians and added, "They discovered your Miss Tavish in theirs. My lady, I've known my wagon-masters for decades, would trust them with my life. They had nothing to do with this."

The other commander, a dark-haired Kythosian, introduced himself. "General Jallo, Princess Seville. I'd say the same for my drivers."

Gideon and General Bellamy exchanged looks filled with sorrow.

"You know we've traveled too far to turn back now," Bellamy told my prince.

"I do," Gideon replied. "Lord Ian, we've no choice. You'll have to go with us. I'll send a message to Kildaria by bird, so at least your families know you're with us and safe. We'll do everything in our power to return you to your homeland when it's possible."

Kendal slipped from my embrace into Ian's, burying her sobs in his chest. Malloria lay before her, as it did for me, with no assurance she'd ever see Kildaria again, and unless something drastic happened, my brother would likely never fill my father's shoes as Duke of Mithradell.

"I can address their wounds in our tent," I Paired to Gideon.

He agreed. "Sir Lance, take them with Princess Theona to my tent to see to their needs. Miss Kendal, I'm sorry. We haven't a pleasure mount for you. You've your choice of a warhorse, a wagon horse, or a place on one of the laundresses' wagons."

"I'm not fond of horses, Your Highness," Kendal said, paling more. "I'll go on a wagon."

"Are you sure, Kendal?" I asked with desperation. I didn't want her out of my sight. "You can ride double with me until you get used to it."

Kendal shook her head. "No, my lady. You know I'm terrified of the beasts. I'll make the best of it."

Zahra and I escorted Kendal to our tent, while Sir Lance and one of the Kythosians all but carried Ian. After we'd seated them on my cot, Sir Lance excused the two wagon-masters, watching with both fascination and barely disguised fear as I gently laid my hands upon Ian's shoulders. Lance had heard the stories about my magic but still didn't know what to make of it.

"Don't fight me, brother," I murmured, knowing he still wasn't comfortable with magic—despite having his own talents. "It might be a little uncomfortable, but we've done this before." We had, the day of the poisoning. Ian had down his best to help rescue the family.

The seriousness of Ian's injuries sickened me. Broken bones and bruises everywhere were nothing next to the permanent damage to his left eye. Even the right was serious enough he was near-blind. I fought hard not to sob in grief and anger.

Praise Elam, healing came quickly and completely. Ian gasped in shock, blinking eyes that worked again and touching a nose returned to its rightful place. What had been grief turned into joy, and when I finished with Kendal, they again folded each other in their arms, their tears now filled with relief.

"I don't know what to say—"

"Then don't," I told Ian. "Someday you may need to return the favor." We gave them water, and Zahra provided them with waterskins and slices of jerky to see them through until better food was prepared.

Sir Lance took Ian to clean him up and get him a uniform, while Zahra took care of Kendal. Later, Ian—looking skeletal but still rather dashing in a Mallorian uniform—and Kendal, thin but graceful in one of my riding habits, needed encouragement not to wolf down their breakfasts. I had no such limitations. I wolfed at my pleasure. Sir Lance and Ian then escorted Kendal to the wagon she would share with Malloria's warrior-laundresses. Ian insisted on riding alongside her.

They looked so vastly improved, I preferred to believe no one would recognize them, which was good. Going from near-fatal injuries to restored health so quickly would remind warriors of King Desmond's healing at my hands—not a good thing for now.

At the end of what resolved into another monotonous day I met with the sorcerers. They pushed me hard with Linking with several wild horses in another herd not far from us, but Ramah and I did a phenomenal job bungling it. Terius, all but ready to chew horseshoe nails, insisted on my learning to fight as a sorcerer instead.

I botched that, too, failing at casting and deflecting important spells, which proved once again that I needed a far better grasp of the Language. They gave up on my lessons in the early morning hours, leaving me to wonder if they might someday give up on me. A chilling thought, considering I would have to die for them to get free of me.

CHAPTER 13

So, this was the Badlands.
Gideon's description of it proved far too kind. I surveyed the horizon surrounding us, wondering how people could find their way through a terrain bearing few landmarks. It looked flat and empty as far as the eye could see—apparently a dangerous assumption that courted death in more ways than one. Faced with scorching temperatures I'd never in my life experienced, I also wondered if it might spontaneously burst into flames.

The road we'd followed through the plains disappeared only hours after our march started that morning, leaving Mallorian scouts to navigate us across bare, sandy or weed-covered earth to the beginning of the Badlands Route. It seemed uncommonly wide, as hard packed as cement, and nearly straight as an arrow all the way to the eastern horizon.

It was Sunday morning, Worship Day, the beginning of the second week of our trek, and the Elds offered the requisite, simple Worship Service prior to our setting out. Only those gathered close enough had the blessings of hearing it, reminding me of the starkness of a soldier's life.

To the road's left and equally stark, along the southern border of the wedge-shaped Badlands, lay undulating white sand dunes. Somewhere north of the dunes sprawled Grimstaad, home of the Valdellian Warlords, supposedly blessed with superb grazing and farmlands. I saw no hint of them here.

To our right, just as Gideon had described them, were the lands of the Nomad Margin. At present, it was nothing but a dry lakebed with scattered tumbleweeds all the way to the distant southern horizon, edged by a row of saw-toothed mountains. The mountains shimmered in the heat waves. Were they mishappen by a mirage? Small and close or distant and towering? Supposedly the Great Chasm, which separated the Lost Lands from the continent, was somewhere on the other side of them.

No doubt dunes and lake beds came and went on either side of the road but none of it looked hospitable. Not even the weeds welcomed us: goosefoot, poisonous henbane, tumbleweeds, and woad—with its beautiful, toxic yellow flowers and inch-long thorns.

Now our metaphorical walk on a tightrope would begin. We'd gone over the rules a final time late last night: about how we would travel, how we would camp, our need for relative quiet and small, brief campfires at night. The warrior-hostlers tied the relief horses head to tail in short columns to make sure even they wouldn't leave the road. A tightrope, indeed, and we dared not fall off it.

My harridan consorts, the sorcerers, added their own last-minute warnings that last night.

"Some of the tribal shamans are powerful sorcerers, Theona," said Rhesalus, "and most of them are under the Central Alliance's influence." Which meant the Alliance roamed the Badlands at will and could attack us just as well as the natives could. Also, the shamans might sense my use of magic and be drawn to it.

"Avoid using your powers without our presence, so that we can shield you from them," he suggested.

Was he telling the truth or just finding another way to manipulate me?

Thundering drums rolled through company after company, warning us it was time to set forth. Warriors vaulted onto their horses or wagons and the columns formed. The road was wide enough we could still ride in our groups of four, almost knee-to-knee, or the wagons wheel-to-wheel in their groups of three, but we dared not spread out.

Gideon joined us. He offered reassurances, but his tense shoulders and furrowed brow spoke louder than his words. "Stay close together. Call out if you see anything that worries you," he told our small group.

"Yes, Your Highness," Zahra said, nodding. Her military background made her more comfortable in this place.

Gideon said to me in an aside. "Please tell me you feel some weakening of your dragons and sorcerers, Theona."

"I fear not, my lord," I murmured.

He sighed. "Then we've more than one issue to face, my dear. Your possession. This place. And our possible traitor—or traitors. We agree that no one would kidnap your brother and his fiancée for no purpose. If they'd wanted to get rid of them, they'd have killed them."

All of it haunted me, including the troubled look in Eld Reagan's aged eyes and on Eld Kane's paler face. No doubt they feared what lie ahead of us for the same reasons.

Kildaria would take the lead from now until we left the Badlands. Thankfully, the wedge-shaped territory reflected the contours of the entire continent, meaning that the southern border was the shortest of the routes that spanned it from west to east. Further north it might take two weeks or more to cross the Badlands. Here, it would take only six days. Six of the worst days of my life.

The level road was free of obstacles, and thankfully, I saw very few of the dreaded black spider mounds. One white sand spider did dart out of its hole and wave its grotesquely spiked front legs at us midday. I gulped at the incredible size of the creature and wished I could find another world on which to live.

Gideon reassured me that the spiders preferred to hunt in the cooler hours of early morning and evening. I couldn't say I was thankful the sun had climbed high into the sky and the heat had turned from uncomfortable to sizzling, but I could appreciate that it discouraged the hideous creatures.

The outriders, the bravest of all warriors in my opinion, kept communications open by riding back and forth along the edge of the caravan throughout the day, handing messages from one officer to another and warning of things ahead or behind.

Riding, eating while we rode, stopping rarely...over time, I worried more about being burned to death or dying from the persistent boredom than from white sand spiders. At least I could look forward to the nights bringing us a slight but blessed relief from the heat.

That night's camp consisted of only as many small tents as would fit side-by-side along the northern edge of the road. They discouraged predators, protected us from unexpected storms, and blocked the light of the cook-fires from the Badlands. Not allowed to graze—if there'd been anything to eat—the horses were snubbed to wagons on the south side, along with the relief animals, and fed the fodder we'd brought with us.

After supper, the cooks extinguished the fires and silence fell as if in a graveyard: no music, only soft voices when anyone spoke, no one but the sentry walking around. Bedtime came early.

I dozed briefly before cautiously opening my shields to the sorcerers. Guided by a gibbous moon, I followed their directions into the Nomad Margin, where the sorcerers and dragons welcomed me. I was safe here, so Rhesalus said, as long as I remained protected by them. They put me through my paces, begrudgingly saying I'd improved with everything they asked of me. Even Terius admitted I did better than average with portalling, although the furthest portal gifted me a painful twisting of my gut and a blinding headache. Terius reemphasized that distance was the key. I supposed that meant I needed to "memorize" my limitations, but I had little idea how to do that.

Hungry as usual afterward but too drained by the heat and too tired to care, I hurried "home", dropped onto my cot and fell into a restless sleep, drenched in sweat.

Relief came, a few hours before dawn, when the desert sucked the heat from the air and chilled me enough to burrow under my blankets. Falling back to sleep, I suffered haunting dreams of those blankets twisting around me and squeezing me tight. Heavy. Too heavy. Hugging me tighter and tighter, making it hard to breathe.

"Dear Elam!" Zahra hissed. "Princess Theona, you must wake up."

My eyes snapped open to our pitch-black surroundings. Gideon's soft, measured breathing continued undisturbed beside me.

"What's wrong?" I whispered.

"I can't move, my lady. Something's holding me down."

"As with me, Princess," Kendal whispered harshly. "Something's wrong."

I froze when I realized my blankets were every bit as heavy as I'd imagined in my dreams. I called mage light, letting it hover just above me, and gasped but dared not move.

My entire cot was filled with snakes! Draped over my legs, entwined around each other, lying head to tail alongside me, the creatures, all poisonous, made a living blanket that no doubt could kill me in an instant.

A handful of the creatures lay across Zahra's belly. Kendal had only three serpents with her, but one was a cobra—a cobra?—coiled above her head. Gideon, still asleep, had a rattler lounged on his chest. Zahra moaned, her tearful voice trembling.

"You know I cannot abide snakes, my lady. What do I do?"

"Do not move," I pleaded. "Please. Give me time to sort this out."

In the near distance, a sentry's outcry was followed by the screaming of horses, which woke Gideon with a start! I gripped his hand tight while trying not to dislodge any of my unwelcome bed partners. Had snakes besieged the entire camp? If so, this was no ordinary invasion.

"You mustn't move suddenly, Gideon," I insisted as I explained our predicament. "Please trust me. I'll help everyone as quickly I can."

Dousing my light, I opened my shields to the sorcerers to enlist their aid. Where were they? I needed them! Hearing nothing, I shape-changed into a snake myself and slid off the cot to the floor. Channeling the gift of Calling to the serpents in our tent, I waited for the rasping sound of their response and then led them outside.

The racket in camp became an uproar. Human screams meant people were bitten. I needed to hurry. I needed to help. I slithered to the edge of Malloria's camp, away from the scores of lanterns people were lighting, and in the shades of darkness became human. I had no desire to find my snake-self attacked with swords, spears, or arrows.

The baby blue *parhelia* of Calling drew all the serpents to me, docile, obedient, a needful thing considering the vast majority were venomous. I looked back at the camp and saw Gideon, Zahra, and Kendal step gingerly from our tent. General Bellamy tossed a large sidewinder out ahead of him as he left his own tent. Amazing that the creature didn't bite him.

More torches and lamps flamed to life, driving the night's darkness into misshapen corners and spaces between tents and under wagons. Snakes lay everywhere, slithering beside and over each other as they headed my direction.

"Stand still, man," Eld Kane demanded of a warrior who looked ready to bolt.

"The horses!" Gideon Mind-Paired. *"I hear them panicking!"*

"People first," I insisted. *"Tell them what I tell you."*

He raised his hands to calm everyone around me, shouting, "Don't move! If you step on them, they'll bite. They'll ignore you if you stay still."

Most listened, some didn't. A man went down in front of me, struck by three rattlesnakes at once. His screams made my ears ring.

"Stand firm, people!" Gideon shouted. "A rare chill last night drew the snakes to us from the desert. Princess Theona can help.

Those of you who saw her protect King Desmond know she has the power, but you must help her by staying where you are."

Rare chill? Bless my sweet prince for making excuses that both cast me in a favorable light and bought me time. I stepped into the lamplight and all eyes fastened on me, full of terror, anger, hatred...and hope. The bitten man raised his shaking hand to me. He wouldn't live five minutes without help.

Pushing away the bedlam, I took his hand and healed him. The shock vied with the relief from pain and death on his face.

"Praise you, my lady," he said, voice quivering with emotion.

In the next instant, nearby horses' screams turned into the cry of horror from their hostlers, followed by the thundering of hooves. Scores of animals had broken their tethers and fled!

"Theona!?" Gideon's Paired anguish said more than words. Without our horses....

I wanted to panic with him. The sorcerers refused to respond to my requests for help. If I didn't handle this right, how many people would die today? What if I died?

Desperate, I shut my eyes, took a deep breath, and whispered, *"Parta."* The Language felt powerful on the tip of my tongue. The snakes separated to either side of me, like a living walkway. I forged through them, heading into the Nomad lands and across the dry lakebed. I gulped at seeing the undulating masses flowing out of and from between the tents and under the wagons. Where had they all come from? Surely there couldn't be so many snakes in all the Badlands! Slithering, sliding, some striking at each other, others pausing to rattle tails or raise hooded necks and hiss, they came like dogs, their scales rasping on the dry, broken land.

"And where do they go from here, witch!" a tall Segovian woman cried, shaking a doubled fist. "Set them free and they'll just come back. And what do we do without enough horses? We'll die here. This is your fault. You did this to destroy us."

I buried my anger and, praying against white sand spiders, stepped barefoot onto the powdery sands. Legs shaking in fear, I waited while hundreds of serpents gathered round me. This was taking too long. Too many were too far away. How would I deal with all of them?

At least the night shielded me. I didn't need human witnesses to what I might need to do or to what I might need to become. My thoughts whirled, my options seeming grim. The best recourse I had would protect us; I only hoped it didn't cause greater problems. I opened a passage, tinged the baby blue of a Calling, to someplace far away. Where? I had no idea. The snakes came, undulating masses that surged across the sand into the cleft that shimmered between here and there. I closed it when they'd passed through.

The magic drained me, but more cries came for help from injured warriors. A few lazy serpents straggled toward me, unfortunate creatures in the situation. Their sacrifice gave me the food I needed to carry on.

Gideon Mind-Paired reassurances that all was under control in our section of the army, so I flew off to aid the needy. All along the cavalcade, I drew the snakes away, but the healers were flooded with the injured, and some preferred to die than to accept my help.

I returned to my prince, shock rocking me back on my heels when I saw him and his general kneeling over a writhing Sir Lance. Gideon's knight had been bitten! Perhaps I dared something irreverent but knowing how too many felt about the Princess of Malloria, I shifted into a stranger, a woman glowing with a faint, ethereal light. Flowing white hair and diaphanous white gown replaced my warrior's garb as I approached my prince.

Gideon's violet eyes reflected his own shock at seeing me, but in the next instant, he lowered his face to hide his secretive smile. Zahra, knowing me instantly, lifted Sir Lance's pant leg, where I laid my hand. In seconds it was whole again, and Sir Lance sagged in relief. Whispers became acclamations of reverence. Others were brought for me to address.

"'Tis an angel," a warrior said, helping her friend rise.

"'Tis a miracle," said a wagon-master, rubbing the ankle that no longer bore a cobra's bite. "May Elam be praised."

Mind-Paired to my prince, I said, *"I've been leading the snakes away, but too many of the wounded refused my help. This is the only way I could do it, even if it is a lie."*

He gave a subtle nod, his gaze filled with gratitude.

The wounds varied throughout the cavalcade and not just from snakes. Panic, horses striking out in fear, overturned wagons, weapons hitting people rather than serpents, all took their toll.

I fed and I healed; I healed and I fed. Then I returned to Gideon as myself, exhausted, barely able to keep my eyes open.

The unbelievers screamed. "Kill her!" "She's a witch!" "Send her to the desert." "Let the foxes and the white sand spiders have her." "Let the Mengeddi take her for their pleasures."

Gideon cast a baleful look around him and demanded their silence with an upraised hand. "If you cannot see what she's done for you, then it is you who are the monsters," he snapped. "She's not a witch! She wields the same magic the Elds do, and she did it to save your sorry hides."

"Liar!" a Segovian warrior yelled, his face red. "The Elds serve Elam. They cannot do what she just did or what she did to King Desmond."

Standing nearby, Elds Reagan and Kane pushed their way through the crowd, bringing a hush to it.

Reagan said, "You're a fool. You know nothing about Elden history. What we call magic is nothing more than Elam's powers vested in mankind. Open your stubborn brains and remember the days of Cleary the Brave. Most people could do things today's generation would find amazing."

"Like calling snakes follow you?" the warrior spat.

Eld Kane snapped, "And Calling game when people were starving, or healing the sick or injured, which is what healers do."

Warriors around us grumbled, but this one flushed in embarrassment, dropping his gaze and taking a step back.

Reagan stared each one of them down. "Did Princess Theona just save you?" he asked one. "She would have let you die if that had been her intent. Now bring the rest of the wounded so that the healers and Eld Reagan and I can help Her Highness finish this. Or don't and let them die."

Thankfully they left no one to die. I was more grateful the warriors who were healed helped change the hearts of many of those who witnessed their cures.

Reports began to arrive of more damage. Twenty wagons had toppled, scattering weapons, supplies, and provender on the ground. Some were damaged. Tents were wrecked, water barrels spilled. There was much work to be done before we could march, including the most important goal of all.

"You've saved us," Gideon murmured, gripping my shoulders in appreciation.

"Not yet. I must go for the horses," I replied. "Will you join me in our tent?"

He did, and he fed me and then kissed me and held me tight, thanking me over and over for what I'd done, especially considering my critics.

"You thank me, but I pray Elam will someday forgive me for how I had to go about it."

"What do you mean?"

"I had no choice but to use some of the serpents for food, and I disguised myself as a being that warriors mistook for an angel."

He pushed me away and searched my face. "You know I've had my own reservations about your possession, Theona, but one thing I know for sure. You're not Eblis's underling. Not when you serve as Elam's champion. None of us could have done a fraction of what you just did, and you have no idea how grateful I am to you."

I loved him for his faith, but nothing could erase the guilt. I kissed his cheek, changed into a sparrow, and as he left the tent, supposedly so that Princess Theona could rest, I flew south after the herd.

———|———

Catching horses seemed simple in comparison to rounding up snakes—even if I did have to fly for miles to find the lion's share of them and then turn them back toward the cavalcade. I was grateful I could turn them over to others to return them to their specific camps in a cavalcade nearly twenty miles long. In dawn's pink blush, I herded them as a winged horse, thanking Elam that the beasts were too tired to fight me. When I spotted Caspian walking between Chip and Valere, I dropped to the ground and joined them as a horse. We passed injured animals along the way, which I mended, except for the two that had died from snake bites, and added them to the herd.

I searched the horizon, wondering if any of the barbarian tribes' shamans were aware of me. I had no idea if the sorcerers had shielded my magic from them as I worked.

Near the cavalcade, I became myself and caught Caspian by the halter. "Hey, dear friend. Let's go back to water and food." I scrambled onboard bareback and led the herd to the army at a jog.

I felt in part vindicated when I heard the cries of joy at our arrival, but I also felt too keenly the sorrow of those warriors whose horses wouldn't return. New mounts would come from the relief herd but could never replace their equine friends.

I turned Caspian over to the hostlers, demanding they take the best care of him. Pale countenances and quick nods told me they knew who I was and wouldn't dare disappoint me.

I turned around and ran into Gideon, who swept me up and hugged me tight.

"Thank you, my princess. Again, you've saved us!" He pushed me away and searched my face. "Good heavens, Theona, you look pale as death. Does using magic always do this to you?"

I shook my head. "Just using too much magic or for too long," I said. I felt frail from the accumulation of everything I'd done since last night's magic lessons and not enough to eat. Now I realized that, even at daybreak, the scorching ground had blistered my feet.

"My lady?" Zahra trotted toward us. "I'm so glad you're back. You've my undying gratitude for returning Chip to me. Now I must take care of you. I've food and drink for you, and your cot awaits you."

And I needed my face washed and my hair re-braided and, before we marched, the strength to heal my poor feet.

"Thank you, Zahra," said Gideon. "Theona, it will take quite a while to sort things out, but we need to move on as soon as we can. We'll attract trouble if we stay in one place too long."

I nodded, my thoughts beginning to scatter as I imagined my pillow calling to me.

"You've passed a most important test, Theona," Rhesalus thrust into my mind. *"Your magical instincts performed impeccably. You fought as a sorcerer fights."*

"No thanks to you. But I didn't fight anyone. I just collected and sometimes killed snakes and healed as many warriors as I could. Why did you leave me to face the night's horrors alone?"

"A sorcerer Called *the snakes, Theona. He—or perhaps she, we don't know—is a powerful mage, here in the Badlands. Had you failed, all of you who survived the snakes would have been stranded here and attacked by the natives. Thanks to you, that won't happen."*

A sorcerer had done this? No wonder there were so many snakes. Not that that made me a hero. Not by any means.

"It's not fair that you can't warn me when you're not going to help," I said, sulking.

"Life, my dear—"

"Stop. I don't want to hear it. I know life isn't fair, but you're far worse. I'm going to sleep for a while. Don't bother me."

CHAPTER 14

I'd barely closed my eyes before it was time to open them again, the marvel of magic healing itself the only thing that made it easier to face being urged from my cot so that men could pack our tent. Gideon waited for me outside, and Zahra had just told me our horses were saddled and ready for us when I heard a voice calling from the rear of the camp.

"Make way! Hail to the prince! Make way!"

I turned see two Dundeean warriors hauling a man toward us, one who looked as bedraggled and miserable as Kendal and Ian when they'd been found. General Bellamy and Sir Lance joined Gideon, and Ian and Kendal followed, all of us wondering what had happened now.

"Your Highness!" one of the men cried. "We've another captive!"

My jaw dropped. I couldn't believe my eyes. *"Nevin Leath?"*

It was he, High Councilman Nevin Leath, Darby Murdock's chum. He stumbled along, his wrists bound, blinking his eyes against the bright sunlight. He seemed overjoyed to see Gideon, and falling to his knees, bowed his head to the ground.

One of the Dundeeans pointed at Leath and said, "Found him under one of our overturned wagons. Took a while to get him to you."

"Don't tell me you were kidnapped, too," Gideon said, frowning.

"Too?" Leath looked up, confused. "Someone else was kidnapped?"

Gideon pointed at Ian and Kendal. It was Leath's turn to gape.

"What? Why? This doesn't make any sense."

"Please tell me something I don't know," Gideon snapped. "Such as how you got here."

The man's story sounded nearly identical to Ian's, although his clothes weren't as dirty, and he had just one small bruise on his right cheek and only a few scratches on both hands.

"I want passage back home!" he demanded.

Bellamy laughed. "We're sixty leagues into the Badlands, Leath, and we haven't warriors or horses to spare to take you back." He summed up the last few days' travels, including our snake attack. "Find it odd you weren't hurt as badly as the duke's son and his fiancée," he added.

When Leath gave him a confused look, the general growled, "Hope you can handle a warhorse and consider yourself lucky to ride it. If you've any complaint, you're welcome to walk to Malloria."

The councilman paled even more, but submission softened his face. He murmured his thanks when Sir Lance cut the ropes from his wrists. Coming to his feet, his legs shaking, he gulped down water from a waterskin someone handed him.

Gideon said, "Before we head out, we'll see to your wounds and get you clean clothes and enough water to wash up a bit, and someone will bring you food." To one of his guards, he said, "Get him a horse and have him ready to go when we are."

As Leath shambled away, my prince muttered, "Something's wrong with this, Theona. I don't like it."

I nodded my agreement. All of it reeked. Was the councilman a victim or a conspirator? Was he really kidnapped? Or one of those who'd escaped and was pretending to have been kidnapped?

Not three yards away, Leath looked at me over his shoulder, his eyes glittering with hatred.

———┼———

The company set out again.

Afternoon broiled us, and we needed to rest and water the animals more often because of the toll from the snake attack—a challenge because water barrels had been tipped in the mayhem and we had to ration our supply. We had no idea when or if we'd find more water soon.

Several wells and desert pools were supposedly ahead of us, but in the desert, travelers always worried. What if they'd gone dry? Or gone bad? Or desert nomads or dangerous creatures were lying in wait for us?

Two wellsprings along the path proved brackish, but just past midafternoon an outrider came to report a safe watering hole just ahead. As if glad to hear the news, a few of Kildaria's horses became unruly. No doubt they smelled it.

One Kildarian warrior riding immediately in front of us found himself fighting to keep his stallion under control. One of Father's men whom I barely knew, General McBane, shouted at two other warriors.

"Collins! Grady! Help with O'Neal's animal. We can't risk—"

The two warriors had no time to obey. The muscular bay took the bit between his teeth, reared and spun away from the group. His rider pulled the animal's head toward his knee, but it responded by bucking and nearly unseating him.

I gasped when I saw a black hillock not far from them! One of the revolting snow-white spider-creatures rushed to the brow, its raised front legs rigid with anticipation.

"O'Neal!" the general cried. "Jump off!"

The flash of refusal on the warrior's face turned to fear when he saw the spider. The stallion bucked again and thundered off directly toward it. O'Neal leaped from the saddle, rolled across the sand, and headed for us at a dead run. The stallion veered away from the nest but too late. Like lightning, the spider streaked across the desert floor, bounding twice and, while airborne, sent out a long silken thread.

The silk stuck to the stallion's face, and the horse skidded to a halt, shaking his head at the feel of the sticky substance. The spider darted up the filament and into one of the horse's nostrils. The animal screeched in pain, evidence it had been bitten, rising to flail the air with its front feet.

Pitching over backward, the horse's cries of agony turned my stomach. O'Neal stood watching, fingers threaded into his hair, tears in his eyes. No doubt this animal had been his long-time friend, too.

The stallion's struggles lessened and stopped and finally gave way to convulsions. After it relaxed in death, the spider scurried from the horse's nostril waving eight bristly legs in a bizarre fashion, its ghostly white eyes fastened on its prey. A split second later, a half-dozen smaller spiders streaked out of the nest and leaped onto the horse, slicing open its hide and cutting out sections of meat to feast upon.

General McBane's orders brought O'Neil a relief horse. Still shaking, O'Neil backhanded moisture from his eyes and climbed aboard the sturdy gray gelding.

I wiped my own eyes and urged Caspian onward, praying I would never have to see such a terrible thing again.

Silence, like holding our breath, took us to the watering hole—amazingly large in this desiccated place. An oasis they called it.

We refilled everything that needed refilling, watered our animals and ourselves, and moved on.

"What about the spiders?" I asked Zahra, my skin crawling at the thought of them.

"They've their prey, my lady. Devils don't eat often. 'Tis the way of desert creatures. Kill and eat quickly, store what they can, then sleep for days."

I nodded, only marginally reassured. After all, this was just one sand spider mound. How many more were out there?

Fear of sand spiders fled when we later faced a rogue sandstorm. It tried to choke me to death, coated my hair with dust, and left all of us amazed it hadn't sandblasted the clothes off our backs.

Yet even that paled when we passed a smaller watering hole where a handful of strange insects, twice the size of dragonflies and wings colored a bright red, buzzed around the carcass of a small desert boar, half-buried in the mud. I knew without asking that these horrid insects had killed the beast. Word sent to the rear of the cavalcade warned everyone to give it a wide berth.

Last, came a cry forewarning us of an impending flash flood. How this could be? Were the Badlands determined to throw their worst at us all in one day?

Dark clouds from the northwest swooped over us like gargantuan bird wings, the wind bearing a driving rain that stung nearly as badly as blown sand. It departed quickly but left us dripping until time came to make camp. Soggy wood would make poor cook-fires and I wanted to help. I could dry the firewood so the cooks could prepare a warm supper, but when I sought the sorcerers' support, Terius muttered that I oughtn't to waste good magic on mundane situations. I wondered if the monster would have let his own mother suffer if her needs were too mundane.

On Tuesday, our third day in the Badlands and ten days since we'd left Kildaria, that unsettling feeling something was wrong returned.

"What is it now?" I asked Rhesalus, hoping that at least *he* would respect my concerns. Alone in our tent for a moment before breakfast, I jumped when all three sorcerers appeared.

"Surely you know by now that looking into the future can have undesirable consequences," he replied.

"But something will happen."

"Things happen every day, girl," Terius said, eyes glittering.

"But you know and just won't tell me," I replied with venom.

Moriana clicked her tongue. "If you worked as hard on honing your talents as you do on trying to dig information out of us, you'd learn it for yourself."

I narrowed my eyes at her. "Terius would help *you* if you asked. He just doesn't like me." I met Terius's gaze, daring him to deny it.

Rhesalus allowed a sad smile to tug at the corner of his mouth. "Theona, this is an enchanted place populated by powerful beings who rarely care about anything but themselves. Rather than hoping to prepare for a particular enemy, you should be prepared for any adversary at any time. The reason we're trying to teach you how to defend yourself against other mages, of course."

"Will trouble come today or tomorrow? Or the day after?"

Terius replied, "You've three more days before you reach the northeastern plains and the turn in the road that takes you northward to Malloria's Beldame Mountain Pass, girl. Anything can happen in three days."

My magical guests disappeared when Zahra came to announce breakfast was ready. If my own powers of foretelling granted me nothing worth my efforts, then I didn't know why I bothered with it. It was even more useless than the sorcerers.

I could only say, upon reflection, that at least *this* day was as ordinary as it could get.

Not two hours before making camp that night, however, General Bellamy called a halt. A buzz of alarm arose as everyone noted another cloud of dust on the horizon to the north of us. No sandstorm or rainclouds this time; it came from debris and dust thrown into the air from the largest army of riders I'd ever seen headed toward us at breakneck speed!

Warriors near the wagons jumped in to grab what they could of armor and weapons; those of us further away had to settle for what was close at hand. The tumult had Caspian prancing about and tugging at the reins, making it impossible for me to even pull out my knife, let alone my sword.

Foreshadowing slammed into me, shriveling my soul. Strange magic glimmered in the distance, one I recognized without ever having seen it before: the savages headed towards us were led by a sorcerer!

The numbers staggered me. They approached the entire length of our cavalcade, at least as far as I could see, and came to a sliding, dusty halt not twenty yards from us. The hatred radiating from them felt alive.

I sought the sorcerers and felt them nearby, as if looking over my shoulder, but they said nothing about these primitive beings. Broad-shouldered and brown-skinned, the warriors rode sturdy ponies that bore an equally wild look. Slippers of seamed snakeskin, leggings of buckskin, bushy brow-bands fashioned of foxes' tails, and necklaces sporting a variety of beads and feathers—and human teeth—were all the warriors wore—even the women. Their fierce faces seemed cast of iron, their eyes the eeriest crystalline blue I'd ever seen.

One woman, so thin she barely looked female and wearing a peculiar headdress made of braided snakeskin and feathers, nudged her horse forward and raised a feathered spear. I knew without question that she was the sorceress, but was she also some sort of shaman? I thought primitive peoples gave only men that honored title! Her voice was loud and harsh, and at first, I couldn't understand her, and then I did.

To Gideon, I murmured, "She's leading them—and she's both shaman and sorceress. She said to lay down our weapons or they'll slaughter us. They're neither Mengeddi nor Ketelic, are they, my prince?"

"You understand them," he observed, and I nodded. He calmed Valere's restlessness with a touch and a soft word. "They're Hamar warriors, and you're right. She's a shamanist. Odd she's confronting us rather than their chieftain. I don't see a chieftain among them."

He pondered a moment then turned to shout above the crowd. "Can anyone speak this warrior's language?"

No response.

The shaman's magical aura pulsated around her. I flinched when I looked into her soul and saw a myriad of *parhelia*, most dark and cankered.

Not far from me, I saw the Elds' faces petrified with fear. Zahra Mind-Paired her insistence I get behind her, while I heard Kendal weeping behind me and Ian trying to console her.

"What shall I do?" I asked Rhesalus.

"Stay out of it," Terius hissed.

Stay out of what? Nothing had happened yet.

In contrast to earlier that day, the *parhelian* talent of foretelling slammed into me hard, leaving me gasping. The images that played out in my mind seemed unrelated, an aggregate of possibilities I supposed were connected to the various decisions I made. In more than one version, I saw Gideon die, and in all of those but one, I saw the sorcerers involved. No. I couldn't stand back and do nothing to protect my prince.

Gideon's unanswered request for help made me swallow hard.

"I speak their language!" I shouted, using magic to project my voice far and wide. I felt the sorcerers twisting inside me with anger. I clamped my shields tight. Pressing Caspian forward, I stood just behind the general, where the shaman could see me.

"We have heard your demands," I replied, recounting her threat, and then said, "We have no quarrel with your people. We want nothing more than to pass through these lands in peace."

The woman's nostrils quivered with rage. I had no idea why, but I knew she considered me an inferior, only one step better than a dog. I had no right to speak to her.

She tipped her head back, raised her spear, and let out the most horrible shriek I'd ever heard in my life. It had a language all its own, a magical cant that maddened her fellow warriors and sent them barreling toward us with spears and brutal-looking knives in hand!

Something whooshed past my left ear, headed toward the Hamars. I jerked around to see Zahra had loosed an arrow, which found its mark in the right eye of the barbarian closest to us. He dropped immediately and his horse shied away, crashing into two other horses and upsetting some of the savages' ranks. It gave the warriors around us another moment to ready themselves, and then the clash began!

Sparring, stabbing, slashing, the savages attacked us. General Bellamy and his horse pushed Zahra and me behind Gideon, sandwiching our mounts between Valere and Chip, and pushing Ian and his horse behind us, against Kendal's wagon. Kendal's eyes were terror-stricken.

The warhorses screamed, rising on their hind legs, front hooves knocking the enemies from their mounts or striking their faces. The back hooves of some crashed into the ribs of Hamar ponies who'd gotten past them. Mighty leaps of others put them on top of those ponies, plunging them to their knees.

Unfortunately, the warriors they missed seemed invincible, dodging the horses more than they were caught, driving their spears into human chests and arms, hacking hands and severing fingers, stabbing equine necks and bellies.

The shaman stared hard at me, leaving no doubt in my mind that their main thrust in this part of the attack was at me. Swords slashed and slashed; people and animals screamed in fury and pain. Sweat rolled down the faces of the troopers around us, determination alive in their eyes. The din rose so loud and the cries so terrible it brought back the visions I'd had—which were forever lodged in my mind—of Cleary the Brave's battles with the armies that Rhesalus, Pythius and Terius had commanded in their day.

The Hamars were enemies to respect, but they were outnumbered and outrivaled. As good as naked, far more fell dead among them than those of the League were wounded. They had no bows, no arrows. No swords, no shields. How could this shaman expect them to best an elite army that wielded the best weapons warriors could own and protected themselves with finely crafted shields and armor?

When more than half the savages were dead, many began to flee. I stood dumbfounded as the shaman pointed her spear at one warrior and struck him with a shaft of lightning, setting him and his horse on fire and sending them shrieking across the desert. The rest of the deserters turned back.

Then she raised her spear high and hit the ground with the heel of it, crying out in her language, "Bring us the Strength of the Father and the Power of the Deep!"

The earth shook, nearly unseating all of us. Caspian reared and shied, forcing me to throw my arms around his neck to stay onboard. As if my nightmares had taken life, the sands before the shaman parted and macabre creatures scrabbled to the surface, looking around them hungrily. I'd seen these creatures before, in vision!

"Look out!" I screamed. "Changelings! The shaman has called Changelings from the Underworld!"

"Impressive," Rhesalus murmured in my mind. *"You remembered."*

"As if that matters," I retorted mentally. "Perhaps you'd like to help me now."

"I told you to stay out of it," Terius growled.

When the shaman's eyes met mine, my head spun and nausea rose up inside me. Unbidden, another faint, dark orange premonition gripped me. This woman and her people would torture me if they ever got their hands on me.

Terror flashed through me, and I nearly lost my mind. If not for Gideon and Valere coming to stand beside me, I might have turned Caspian and run. As it was, horror held me in its grip as the Changelings rushed to the dead and fell on top of them, disappearing into them like water seeping into sand. A snap, like a jolt of lightning, made my hair literally stand on end, and then the Changelings raised the dead to their feet.

The macabre scheme spun my mind upside down. Not only would they turn our own against us, but their Changeling army would also be nearly invincible, every death becoming a new Changeling warrior, until eventually, they would take us all.

The shaman chanted and again struck the ground with her spear, and suddenly the Changelings held weapons: shields, swords and sabers, bows and arrows, crossbows, and maces made of iron. They rushed us, and the true destruction began.

Blood, warm and sticky, splashed my face as one of Gideon's guards took the head off a barbarian who had most certainly been a living man. My stomach rebelled even worse at the sight of severed hands and arms, of horses going down with spears thrust into their hearts. Warriors and horses fought, blood flowed, rage and pain roared. Gideon's men continued to thrust themselves in front us, pushing us further and further back from the enemy.

What made no sense was seeing the Hamars still taking the brunt of the destruction. Did the shaman not care if we destroyed her entire tribe?

One of our guards fell to the earth, an arrow through his chest. Blood spouted from his mouth, and then a Changeling melted into him, lifted his sword, and came for Gideon!

Gideon fought like a lion, his muscles bulging like living ropes. Around him slashed both Mallorians and Kildarians. When the

Changeling lost its head, the body dropped to the ground, and the hideous shade shrieked as it disappeared into the earth.

My heart leaped. They could be destroyed!

The hiss of arrows whispered around me, a thicket of quivering shafts sprouting from another Changeling's body. It wore a sneering smile on its face as it continued to advance, unfazed. It could be killed under the right circumstances but not this one. What should I do? I certainly couldn't take off its head. I shouted at the sorcerers mentally, demanding their help.

Terius did nothing but repeat himself. *"You should have listened when I told you not to get involved."*

The shaman's gaze again met mine as she dropped her staff. In its place appeared a short javelin. I had no room for fear, only dread. I'd done this before. Only seconds to prepare, no time to imagine all the things I could have done to protect myself.

She flung the weapon, and I froze when it whistled past me...and drove its nose through Gideon's left shoulder! I screamed in terror, while my prince sat looking at it, dumbfounded. Valere pawed the air, whirling south and charging through the Nomad Margin toward the distant mountains, Gideon barely in the saddle.

Two Changelings reached for me but Caspian reared and struck with his hooves, driving one warrior to the ground and wrenching me out of another's grasp. Wheeling around, he bolted after Valere. I kicked his flanks, urging him into a dead run, and weeping at having to ignore Zahra's and Kendal's shouts behind me. In early evening, freed of the day's mirages, the mountain crags seemed larger and much closer than I'd thought. If poor Caspian could run that far, I might catch Gideon and find a place to hide with him.

"Run, Theona," Ramah whispered in my mind. *"You can't imagine what they'll do if they catch you."*

"Run with all your heart," Enya urged.

How could I desert my brother like this? How could I leave Kendal and Zahra behind to die?

How could I not catch Gideon and heal him?

I glanced back and saw Zahra on my tail, but the rest were trapped in knots of violent skirmishes.

Sobbing, I urged Caspian on, praying for those I could not help. Caspian stumbled, reminding me that our horses hadn't completely recovered from yesterday's snake attack. I begged him to hang on.

CHAPTER 15

I called out to Gideon, but when he didn't respond, I Mind-Paired with him. *"Gideon! Gideon, stop. I can help you."*

The buckskin's reins tightened, and my prince rocked in the saddle like a child taking its first ride. When I caught up, I was horrified to see Valere near-crazed with pain, trembling from a deep, bloody gash in his right shoulder and another that had torn his left nostril in half.

When I caught up, I took the reins from Gideon. "Hold, boy," I soothed Valere. "That's good. Now stand."

Panicked at the sick, gray look on Gideon's face, I reached over as best I could from one horse to the other and touched my prince's hand. It felt like ice.

Zahra caught up, her uniform splattered with blood and a long cut on her right cheek. Shock further marred her face when she saw the prince.

"Something's wrong, Theona," Gideon croaked, his other hand wrapping itself around the base of the javelin's shaft. "I think it's poisoned."

As mine had been. I could heal a simple poison or maybe even remove the magical spell, since I wasn't the injured party, but first I'd have to get the shaft out. It had gone clean through him. I dropped the horses' reins and reached for it.

A hot current blasted my hand away, making me yelp and leaving me nursing burnt fingers. This poison was different. Enchanted, yes, but imbued with magical life, and I had no doubt that as long as the javelin remained, evil would continue to seep into Gideon.

Kneeing Caspian against Valere, I begged my love to forgive me, gritted my teeth as I grabbed both ends of the sizzling shaft, and somehow managed to break the head off and yank the shaft out. Gideon screamed, and with sweat streaming down his face, leaned over his horse and vomited.

Understanding too well how he felt, I comforted him as I attempted to heal him. His color improved a bit, but the poison ignored me, moving through his body like thick, molten lead—a dark, bitter thing that I knew would take his life the minute it found its way into his brain.

I resorted to reaching out to the dragons. Maybe they would answer me. *"Enya, Ramah. What do I do?"*

My head whipped around at the pounding of hoofbeats in the far distance. A group of savages galloped toward us with a vengeance. I screamed at Zahra, grabbed Valere's reins and spun Caspian toward the mountains, praying we'd find a place there to hide.

A war cry that curdled my blood floated across the shimmering desert. I spurred Caspian into a dead run, dragging Valere behind me. Zahra helped, slapping Valere's rump with the end of her reins, urging the poor creature on. He was doing his best, but his very life's blood poured from his wounded shoulder, and the bloody gash in his nose hampered his breathing. Gideon hung on for dear life but couldn't do so much longer.

Suddenly, I yanked the reins and sat Caspian down on his heels, horrified to see what lay ahead of us. It seemed the cruelest of all jokes.

I leaped from the saddle and ran to the edge of a sheer, insurmountable cliff. Below it was a ravine so deep its bottom was shrouded in evening shadows and mist. The distant crashing of water made everything crystal clear. I knew where we were.

The Great Chasm. It separated the land of the Nomads from the Lost Lands. Everyone thought the chasm was on the other side of those mountains, but they were wrong. The ravine came first, and beyond that, the feet of the mountains sloped upward from the southern cliff's edge. Behind those peaks rose even more mountains, pointing toward the sky like dragon's teeth.

Tears of hopelessness rolled down my cheeks. The horses were spent and there was nowhere to hide.

Zahra jumped off Chip and ran to me, gasping at the sight of the ravine. "Dear Elam. This can't be."

I flinched when Moriana's ring burned my finger. I ripped off my bracelet to look at it. The image etched on its surface stunned me.

Yes! Of course!

A moment's compassion overwhelmed me, and I replaced the bracelet, laid my hands on Valere, and did the best I could to heal his wounds in the few seconds I could spare. At the same time, I urged Zahra to help remove our horses' tack and set them free. Determined, she helped me pull Gideon down before untacking Valere. Shooed away, the stallion joined the other two, heading eastward in a thunder of hooves and a spray of sand and dirt. Hopefully, they'd find safety somewhere.

Gideon could hardly stay on his feet, his face white and his eyes glazed over. The cry of the warriors drew closer.

To Zahra, I said, "Please trust me. You're about to learn to fly, just not the way you'd hoped."

We abandoned the tack, stuffed our water skins inside our rucksacks—which Zahra shouldered—and then I asked her to wrap her arms around Gideon. I folded my prince's arms around my neck, his head resting against the back of mine. He went slack as I lengthened my neck and legs and dropped to all fours, in an instant coming to look like Valere, with Gideon and Zahra now seated on my back. Great wings shot out of my shoulders, larger than any I'd ever grown. The sorcerers were virtually insubstantial, so I had to compensate for Gideon and Zahra's human weight.

The barbarians were almost on us. Panicked, I balanced on the edge of the chasm, my precious cargo perched on my back. I Mind-Paired a warning to Zahra to hold Gideon tight then leaped into the air and prayed I could make it to the other side.

Zahra cried out, thrill bound with fear. The barbaric shrieks behind me fell silent.

Greater panic rushed over me. Wings too ponderous, atmosphere too thin to grab, a load too heavy, we fell more than we flew. Gideon and Zahra interfered with my wings. The water roared as we drew closer and closer to the sea.

Heart thundering, I changed my proportions and finally managed to slow our descent. Grabbing an updraft, I sailed halfway across the chasm, fighting for breath. Sweat dripped from my shoulders and flanks.

More adjustments to my size, proportions, and wing length finally granted me full control. It wasn't so difficult when I did it right, and I couldn't resist circling back to see the savages perched at the edge of the escarpment, thunderstruck. A horse with or without wings couldn't laugh, but if it could, I'd have done so. I wished I could hear the stories they'd carry back to their shaman when they returned.

I headed toward a ledge on the far side of the chasm. It was barely wide enough to stand on but allowed me a place to catch my breath. Like it or not, I'd have to fly over the first row of mountains to find safe shelter.

Row after row of mountaintops, each higher than the one before it, opposed me. Snow-draped summits had their feet buried in light vegetation, but their shoulders lay bare. The scarlet of approaching sunset urged me to hurry, but I was exhausted and grief-stricken. What would happen to my brother and Kendal? The army? Our friends? The Elds….

No. I must leave all of them to the care of Elam and His angels. My priority was to save the Crown Prince of Malloria.

The mountains grew lower as I flew south, and the temperature dropped. Small valleys and canyons appeared, nestled between short mountain ranges, green and wonderfully pleasant. I saw caves upon occasion but none high enough to protect us from predators yet close enough to water and game for our survival. Our rucksacks and water skins carried only two day's survival rations and water for normal people. Shape-changing princesses and injured warriors needed more.

I backwinged when I found the perfect place. A north-facing cave yawned at me from above a ledge wide enough to berth a ship, its interior so deep it looked black in the evening light. A small waterfall cascaded from a cliff above its left side into a modest pool just below the ledge and then flowed into a creek further below that. It was bordered by tall shade trees and lush grasses.

I landed on the ledge and paused, using all my animal senses to search for danger inside the cave. Faint footprints, large, definitely feline and old, lay under a fine layer of dust. Other than that, nothing.

This amazing place had a high domed ceiling curved downward to the floor in ridges that looked like the ribs of a great beast. A dozen natural horizontal shelves connected a number of those "ribs." Some were at just about hip height, perfect for our bedding.

"Gore! Pardon me, Princess, but look at this place!" Zahra said, slipping from my back and steadying Gideon as I went through the arduous, painful task of changing shapes. "'Tis a perfect warren for our wounded warrior."

Gideon's fingernails dug into my skin, and I was grateful to have Zahra help me seat him on the nearest shelf. I turned and grabbed my sweetheart's shoulders.

"Gideon? How are you?"

His eyes squinted in confusion. "I never knew my horse could fly." He barked laughter. "I must be dreaming. Horses cannot fly." He seemed thoughtful for a bit then groaned. "It hurts, Theona. It hurts."

He was perspiring, feverish. He needed food and water—and a miracle. So did I. I was stretched thin.

"I know, my love," I said, rummaging through his rucksack. I pulled out his blanket and spread it behind him on the narrow ledge, and Zahra and I carefully laid him down. We had no pillows, so we emptied all three rucksacks onto another shelf and made a crude pillow by stuffing ours inside his.

"Rhesalus, Moriana, Terius, I need you!" I cried.

When they appeared, it shocked me to see their faces pinched with worry.

"Gore, my lady!" Zahra hissed. "Is it them?"

She could see them! They weren't delusions!

"Yes," I replied.

Ignoring Zahra, Moriana leaned over Gideon and looked at his wound.

"A poisoned javelin," I told her.

"Wish you hadn't taken it out," she muttered. "We cannot smell or taste. We rely on the injured one for that. The best I can do is tell you that the poison's laced with magic, like the arrow that hit you, only different. Give me your hand," she insisted. "I'll do the best I can through you to at least slow the poison's progress until we know what it is."

She took my hand, and I placed my other one near the wound, closing my eyes in concentration. The Language flowed effortlessly from her lips and drew my healing *parhelia* to the center of the wound, both our powers rushing into every millimeter of injured tissue, into every vein and nerve touched by the poison.

I felt weak, desperate, when not near enough happened. I could feel Moriana struggling, too, until, at last, she managed to fashion a buffer around the poisonous mass. It stalled, writhing angrily, hemmed in by the invisible boundary that at least slowed its progress but did not destroy it.

"What is it?" I demanded, so panicked I ripped my hands away. "Why didn't you remove it?"

Confused, she glanced at Terius. "You didn't say it would be like this."

You didn't say it would be like this? She knew this was going to happen? Terius knew it? If they'd been mortal, I'd have shape-changed and torn them to pieces.

Terius shot me a defiant glance. "This is not the way I saw it. *She* disobeyed."

"You had a premonition this would happen, and you didn't warn me," I accused.

"Theona," Rhesalus said, coming to place a hand as firmly as a shade could do on my shoulder. "Terius told you to stay away from the fray. All you needed to do was keep yourself safe."

"You mean sit back and let those monsters kill Gideon? If you'd prepared me, we could have defended ourselves."

"No!" Terius said between gritted teeth. "We can only interfere with the future to a point without making things worse. I saw him shot by an arrow, not the shaman's lance. Your Prince would have been injured, and you coming here would have remained the same, but you would have been able to heal him on your own."

I looked back and forth between all three of them, horrified at realizing what they were telling me. To Moriana, I said, "fix him."

"I can't. I don't know how."

Guilt and desperate anger suffused me. "Then what use are you?"

"Stop it, girl," Terius said, coming face to face with me. "We don't want him dead any more than you do. We need him."

That stopped me in my tracks. They did need him. He was a powerful man in the Eastern Realms, but he was also their alternative if anything happened to me—something I couldn't let happen.

"I'll need time to ponder a solution," Moriana insisted.

"Then go, ponder it," I snapped, waving my arm at her and locking all three of them behind my shields.

The silence felt hopeless. I met Zahra's gaze and realized she was shaking with fear. Poor woman had just suffered a brutally abrupt education on magical demons.

"I don't know if they can help him," I said, my chin quivering. "I just don't know."

I broke into tears, softened by Zahra daring to gather me into her arms. I clung tight, grateful for a shoulder to cry on.

She didn't give me long to get through it. "My lady," she said with caution, "you've been through too much. You need food, water, rest. And might I suggest old-fashioned herbal medicine for the prince. We do have our kits in our supplies, and the land around us likely produces plenty of herbs."

"First, we need to set up camp," I said, wiping my face with my sleeve. "I'll help you, Zahra, and don't try to coddle me. That won't help any of us. Tell me what to do."

She sighed. "If I can't talk you out of it, and considering 'tis best for the prince's sake, I welcome it."

A rag from Gideon's supplies soaked in the waterfall provided him with a cool compress. The water also refilled our waterskins and gave us delicious refreshment, but we needed a way to boil larger amounts of it.

Zahra insisted I eat what I needed from my provisions and rest briefly. I ate it all but couldn't rest. It at least gave me the strength to build a fire near the front of the cave, fashion magic-hewn cooking utensils and crude equipment from rocks, and devise a tripod on which to hang a magic-made stone pot over the fire.

"My lady," said Zahra at last, "either of us can care for the prince, but I've lost my bow, and with your magic you're the better hunter. Bring back anything you can find, game, herbs, fresh greens and fruit."

I nodded and knelt beside Gideon's stone bed, touching his fevered brow. Unbuttoning his shirt, I found the surface of the wound near-healed but somehow wrong. I rested my hand on it and sensed the poison tightly rooted inside him, a dark ichor that writhed the instant my magic touched it. My prince's eyes fluttered open, and he whispered for more water. Zahra helped me with sating his thirst and settling him again.

I sat on the floor with my back against Gideon's stone bed and rested my head in my hands, elbows perched on bent knees. I was too tired and discouraged even to cry. I'd call the sorcerers back, but Moriana needed time to consider what to do for the prince and I was too angry with them to think rationally.

Zahra's plain face was marred with worry, the wound on her cheek encrusted with dried blood. It took only a second to heal it, and then I laughed at the challenge I had set out before me. I needed to eat and rest so that I'd have enough strength to find game so that I could eat and rest—and I'd be sick if I didn't do either or both. It didn't seem I was destined to have a good evening at all.

Despair plagued me. I needed answers, but even the sorcerers didn't have them.

"Zahra, have you been able to Mind-Pair with Amari?" I asked. Perhaps she already knew the outcome of the battle.

Her eyes grew sad. "No, my lady. I've tried a dozen times since we crossed the chasm. I cannot reach him."

My heart sank. I knew she feared, as I did, that her brother, my brother, and Kendal—perhaps the entire army—was dead.

Zahra went to toss the contents of Gideon's and her rucksack's food into the water now boiling in the pot, and I knelt again to stroke Gideon's cheek. He grunted and turned his head away. Paired with him, I said, *"Please be strong, my love. I'll return as quickly as I can."*

I then Paired with Zahra and asked which healing herbs she'd like me to look for first. She ignored me. I tried again, and she never turned her head my way.

"Zahra, I just tried to Mind-Pair with you. Did you not hear me?"

Startled, my warrior-maid shook her head. "No, my lady. I sensed nothing. Try it again."

I repeated my request, and she still didn't hear me. A blend of confusion and relief swept over her face.

"Perhaps there's something about these mountains that prevents it," I suggested.

She swiped tears of hope from her eyes. "Maybe my brother's safe after all."

"I so hope so, Zahra. I hope they're all safe."

"I'm grateful we've hope, my lady, but since we can't Pair with each other, we can't share news or call for help. Please be careful."

She was right. Beyond needing to return often to assess Gideon's condition, we had to pray nothing would happen to any of us while we were separated.

Dusk hung outside the cave's mouth, and I had no idea what to expect from my brief hunting expedition. I longed to portal to the plains in Kildaria, or better yet, to my home in Mithradell, to Cook's kitchen. I could sneak off with a ham and vegetables, or perhaps a chicken or two. Medicines or healing tisanes. Pillows, blankets.... No. I couldn't portal that far, and what good would it do if I died trying?

I flew south, over more mountains, grateful we were free of the brick-oven-hot expanses of the Badlands. Our mountain stream joined a small river, which fed the light forest below. I glided over it, eagle eyes attuned for game. The further south I went, the greener the landscape grew, but strangely, the warm, fertile land seemed to offer everything except wildlife. Finding no larger creatures, I sought smaller ones but uncovered no evidence that animal life existed here!

I decided to concentrate on smaller areas than larger ones. I shifted from dragon to bird, and on the ground from horses to snakes of all sizes. I found nary a rabbit, a squirrel, a skunk or a worm. Not a peep or growl, not a single screech. No feathers, no footprints, not even spoor on the ground. The hush was omnipresent, as if this world held its breath, waiting for me to leave.

How bizarre.

Even stranger, I found wild berries, acres of watercress, tubers, and wild mushrooms—and some of the herbs Zahra wanted for Gideon. How could things grow so well without the presence of animal life?

After filling my own belly, I gathered all I could carry and returned it to Zahra then set out again. Sunset neared. I needed to hurry.

Soon, I found wild ramps and more herbs, but still no game. I returned when night descended and hurried to Gideon, asking, "Any improvement, Zahra?"

"No, my lady. He's hardly moved a finger, but his breathing's good and his fever's come down a bit."

I sighed. At least we had that good news.

She'd turned our simple rations into a watery vegetable stew that tasted amazing considering the few ingredients, but she was delighted to add some of what I'd brought to the concoction. She stirred and tested it as it cooked.

"I tried Searching for you while you were gone," she said. "It didn't work any better than Pairing."

"The same for me."

"This place is eerie."

"Beyond. Even at night, there should be forest sounds. Crickets or owls or wolves." It was as if all of Elam's creatures had gone into hiding.

"'Tis impossible," Zahra insisted. "Plants need dung to grow, don't they? Or at least earthworms. And birds and bees."

I shook my head in confusion. "I've done all I can tonight. We'll see what tomorrow brings."

Zahra took the first watch, knowing I'd done too much already. She kept the fire stoked, checked on Gideon, and supposedly protected our cave from predators. Truth to tell, I actually wished a predator would appear. It would prove something besides plants existed here.

Bone-tired, I didn't care about having to lie down on a thin blanket on cold, hard stone. I just wanted to sleep. Unfortunately, sleep gave me no respite. Instead, it tormented me with nightmares of the horrors of the battle. A sadistic shaman. Changelings. The lance slamming into Gideon, and the screams of injury and death, of thirty-five thousand warriors, some of the finest fighters in the world, who'd likely met their doom today.

Then came venomous snakes with wings. Horses with fangs. Dragons with eyes that glowed like molten lava, horns razor-edged blades adorning their heads, and snouts spouting volcanic flames that melted snow-topped mountains into blistering mounds of desert sand, and Gideon lay on top of it still as death, his violet eyes turned red with unholy fire. An armor-clad warrior stood over him with Slayer in his hands, and behind the two of them rose Mt. Draakheda in its magnificence.

I came awake trying not to scream. Terrified to close my eyes again, I took the watch from Zahra early. I needed to clear my head, and she desperately needed to sleep.

After stoking the fire, I wrapped my blanket around my shoulders and sat with my feet dangling over the cave's ledge, looking at nothing but the darkness. No moon yet, scattered clouds blocking the stars. The silence haunted me. Granted, a breeze whispered through the trees, the waterfall splashed, and the stream murmured below, but no sign or sound of wildlife—not even insects—punctuated the night.

Why? The need to know dug into me. What if Gideon's salvation depended on the answer?

In the early morning hours it rained, soft and light. Then the clouds cleared, revealing a full moon rising. The sorcerers had said I should be at my magical best right now, that I should be at my weakest during a new moon. Oddly enough, I'd never felt any change beyond that which came from exhaustion and starvation, but I did feel the magic differently with the full moon. It coiled more adamantly inside of me, craving freedom again. What would it want from me next?

CHAPTER 16

Dawn arrived in brilliant oranges, reds, and grays on a cloudy skyline, but a strong breeze quickly herded the clouds away. I was glad to find Gideon no worse than before; I was disappointed to see him not yet recovered.

"He's holding his own," my warrior-maid tried to encourage me.

The headache of hunger stalked me, and I nodded, not at all encouraged. "There's something strange about this place, Zahra. I have a feeling its secrets are as important to us as food."

Zahra sighed and handed me my rucksack for collecting whatever foodstuffs I found. She'd traded her folded blanket for it to pillow Gideon's head.

I flew high when I left the cave, my gaze drawn back toward the Badlands. I didn't realize until I heard the now-familiar crash of the surf that I was flying blindly. As before, the enormity of the Chasm overwhelmed me. I spiraled down into it, loving the sounds and smells of the sea.

Supposedly, a violent earthquake tore this arrowhead-shaped peninsula from the mainland hundreds of years ago. It was now an island, so they said, although our school tutors had taught us it was small. It didn't seem at all small, but no doubt the devastation had been cataclysmic.

A half-mile across, a half-mile deep, the abyss stretched from the horizons, east to west, bringing together the two sides of the same ocean. Named the Irenic Sea by my people on the west side, it was called The East Wind Sea by Gideon's people on the east, and the waves crashed into each other in a mighty struggle for dominion.

The scent of the sea and the thought of fresh fish made me salivate. I longed to dive into the dark, blue-green water beneath me. It likely harbored sea turtles, sharks, or even dolphins; crabs, mussels, clams, lobsters, a veritable king's feast. Any number of creatures, including human, could live on an herbivore's diet in the Lost Lands, but not a shapeshifter. Use of the *parhelia* placed too much strain on bones and sinews. I had no selfish need to shape-shift, but I did care about saving Gideon, and if carrying him away from here as a flying horse was the only way to do it, I had to be ready.

Still, the surf pounded, battered, and boomed, and I had no doubt riptides abounded in this relatively narrow area. I couldn't help Gideon if I drowned.

Instead, I chose to find answer and overflew the Badlands and the battle scene we'd survived. I did so, surprised at my findings. The cavalcade was gone! Not destroyed, just gone, meaning there were survivors! It left in its wake gouged earth, torn carcasses, broken weapons, and damaged wagons. The vast majority of the horses and an even larger proportion of the slain warriors were Hamar. I flew low enough to know I recognized none of the dead from the United Forces and that Ian and Kendal weren't among them. I swallowed hard. Hopefully they'd hadn't been taken prisoner.

Tracks leading eastward suggested the army had moved on. Not taking the time to bury the dead suggested they were in a hurry, and I followed the tracks briefly. Not far ahead, evidence of a sandstorm obliterated any further sign of the caravan's travels.

I needed to return to the Lost Lands and Gideon, but at least I had a few answers. Portalling would take me back faster, but I'd need sustenance to do so. I sought and found a shallow watering hole at the edge of the Nomad Margin, and a small herd of desert deer. Swiftly changing into a dragon, I feasted on all of one deer and most of another.

As an eagle, I portalled the remains back to our cave, and while Zahra made a face at the mangled rear-quarter I gave her, she also mewed in gratitude at its bounty. Even more wonderful was the news I relayed of what I'd discovered of the battlegrounds.

She began dressing the meat, and I set out again, in search of whatever mysteries the Lost Lands held. It was still devoid of animal creatures. Wildlife should abound here, but I found not so much as a spider's web. Even if man had never set foot here, nothing could stop birds from coming from the mainland, yet not one graced the skies. None of this made sense.

Whether flying or portalling to and from the cave, the demands on my energy and the time it took escalated my frustration. One of my attempts turned to near-disaster when I portalled too far while too tired. I stepped across the threshold from a field to our cave and found myself plunged into darkness thicker than the night! It turned up into down and spun me in circles. I floundered as I panicked, certain I was falling to my death, terrified I was lost in a void of darkness forever.

Suddenly thrown out into the light of day, my knapsack fell from my back as I crashed to my knees. A horrid headache and a gray haze all but blinded me as Zahra abandoned her place beside Gideon and ran to my side.

"Princess Theona!" she cried, dropping down beside me, and when I explained what happened, she said, "Mercy, my lady, I'm thinking you might not want to be doing that again."

I couldn't help barking cynical laughter. "I think I agree with you, Zahra."

"You look awful, my lady. Here drink this. I made more soup from the venison and vegetables. Already fed us, but there's plenty left."

And it tasted wonderful. I gulped most of it down, using the first half of the strength it gave me to heal my bruised knees. Then I finished the rest at leisure and curled up on my bedroll to sleep for an hour.

As always, I felt much better when I rose, but I was beyond thrilled to find Gideon awake and sitting upright on his bed, staring at me.

"Hello, love," I said, coming to my knees and touching his hands, nestled in his lap. He watched me, his violet eyes fixed on my dark brown ones. He hardly blinked. No smile touched his lips. No flicker of recognition warmed them. Where had my prince gone?

"His fever's down, my lady," Zahra said, coming to join me, "but it's not enough. We need to try different healing herbs if you can find them." She gave me the names and described them.

I found and delivered them twice but knew improvement would take time. We could do nothing more for now but wait, and the mystery of this place plagued me. I had to solve it.

"I have one more thing to do before night comes," I told Zahra. "Don't wait supper for me."

The tug drew me southward, but I took my time, flying toward the southern mountains in a zigzag fashion from southeast to southwest, trying to get a feel for this place. I landed to take water, but other than for cropping grass as a horse or consuming certain nectar, fruits or plant life as a bird, I found foraging difficult. The landscapes were spectacular but taking time to enjoy it vied with my fatigue. The sun's casual stroll across the sky marked the hours that passed.

When I found one of many lakes on my journey, I settled down to rest and to listen. The hush, beyond running water and a soft breeze, felt wrong. Where were all the animals?

"Perhaps you have answers," I said, calling out the dragons.

They'd barely responded to my call when they went off on one of their frenzied capers, flying all around me, racing as far from me as their connection would allow and back over and over again, screeching, bellowing, acting like something had lit them on fire. I waited with patience, knowing that I would get nothing out of them until they were ready to explain.

"Fly, Theona," Ramah said at last. *"We aren't close enough. Fly."*

Close enough to what? I didn't bother to ask. I knew they wouldn't answer me until they were ready. I took wing as a falcon, praying the sacrifice I made in not being able to find food yet would bring compensation somewhere.

They flew just ahead of me, urging me through several small valleys. I grew weak as a kitten.

"What's wrong with this place?" I asked, explaining the oddity of not finding animal life here.

Enya's head dipped toward me, her eyes whirling as if she thought I'd gone mad. "Game abounds here. If we could eat it, we would," she said.

"She's forbidden to see it," Ramah explained. Then to me, he said, "The Land wards itself until invaders prove they have good intentions."

"Wards?" I asked.

"A magical boundary that keeps beings from either going somewhere or seeing something. Some creatures of magic can fashion them, but others, like Elds and sorcerers can also place them on other beings or objects. Consider The Keeper. The Elds warded the object, preventing us from escaping. You broke the ward when you opened it. Here? The Land's refusal to sustain you was designed to test you. If you pass the test, you can stay. If not, the Land will either leave you to die or force you to leave."

I gulped. It wasn't my imagination. This place *had* played tricks on my senses. What would I have to do to pass the "test?"

Traveling was hard enough under the circumstances, but the longer I flew, the further I got from the cave and the more I worried about Gideon. How would my warrior-maid and my prince find a way off this island if I didn't make it back?

We came to a wide vale at the edge of a tall mountain range. It felt different here, cooler and moister. On the southern side, a thick forest, draped in mist, hugged the mountains. A forest? I did a double-take and wondered if this was real, or was I now hallucinating?

Dreamwood trees! They were Dreamwood trees, an entire forest of them! Gideon swore Malloria boasted a plethora of them, but I'd never seen a single living specimen in my life, only drawings, and paintings, and old articles made from Dreamwood like my bracelet— and The Keeper. A sculptured Dreamwood tree stood atop Mt. Draakheda, The Keeper's sculptured mountain, where I'd met and dreamwalked with Gideon. It looked just like these.

The dragons streaked into the forest ahead of me, disappearing into the mists. I supposed they were reveling in it, like they had at Lake Tralee in the Cleary Pass. I wondered if they would ever explain why they behaved this way.

I landed in the vale, my hunger momentarily forgotten. I had to bend over backwards to see the tops of the mighty giants that scraped the bright blue of the sky above. Bark deep red and spongy, dark-green needles on arms that stretched both wide and tall, their scent filled my nostrils, clean and light, almost cinnamon-y. Water from the morning's earlier rains still dripped from the thick canopy above. I could hardly believe what I was seeing.

My heart threatened to jump out of my chest when I thought I heard whispers emanating from within the undergrowth. I should run away, but my magic instead drove me into the forest and toward a group of six massive trees clustered together in a circle so tight their roots overlapped. It seemed like a living lacework of brotherhood.

The loamy forest floor and its thick layer of fallen needles cushioned my footsteps. Stepping into the center of the ring, I half expected to find fairies fluttering around inside it. Instead, the whispers grew louder. It reminded me too much of the sorcerers' whisperings when they'd first possessed me. I braced myself for the worst.

Nothing happened.

I examined the closest tree on my right. Its bark seemed fissured, like cracks on a red rock. I couldn't help touching it and found its surface—for a split second—squashy, almost like cork.

Then fire swept through me, light, not flames, as if I'd been illuminated by the glory of a hundred suns! I cried out in ecstasy, my voice echoing in the distance. Everything felt at once both completely upside down and completely perfect as faint music glided over my skin and the color of pleasure bathed my ears. Time seemed irrelevant; life as permanent as the throne of deity.

Then, a faint voice splintered the loud silence.

Find them, child of Elam.

What did that mean? *Find whom?* I managed to think. *Who are you?*

Do not turn back.

Why?

You will know when you find them.

The Voice faded into nothingness.

Them? Who? What am I looking for?

No answer.

I pulled my hand away from the tree, horrified when the bark snapped and a piece came off, stuck to my hand. I'd broken it? How? It tingled far more intensely than any piece of Dreamwood I'd ever touched, and feeling guilty, I tried to drop it. It wouldn't come off. I tried throwing it and then pulling it off, but it felt as if I'd rip off my skin. Frightened, I ran from the ring of trees and into the glade and then took flight as an eagle as fast as I could go, terrified by what I'd just witnessed. What would Gideon or Zahra think of this?

"Ramah? Enya?" I called for them in desperation.

They joined me, and at the same time wildlife appeared all around me! In the air, on the land, in the distant river. The dragons laughed their odd dragon laughter, taking to the river to frolic while I caught game of every kind and feasted as if as starved half to death—as I was. When I'd stuffed my belly so full I thought I'd pop, lethargy took hold of me and I found shade under a tree that wasn't a Dreamwood tree and gave in to healing sleep.

I awoke to Enya snuffling my face and jumped back from her in surprise.

"We must go, Theona. We're running out of time."

She was right. It was late afternoon now, and I had a long way to go to return to the cave.

"No, not that way," she corrected me, joining Ramah as he headed even further south.

"But I need to make sure Gideon is alright," I Paired.

"He is not, but he is alive," Ramah replied. *"What you must see next will help him, and it will prepare you for events yet to come."*

I attempted to Mind-Pair with Zahra, but that gift still refused to work. I sighed an eagle's sigh as I took flight. More riddles. More magical sparring.

However, when I crested a low mountain at the edge of the range, I found a large kidney-shaped lake in a small valley. I paused mid-air, shocked at recognizing this place. I'd been here before! Once upon a time, in what seemed more than a lifetime ago, I'd knelt as a prisoner before King Desmond Fitzpatrick and been taken away in a vision in the form of a horse, racing through a lush, grassy field. Then I'd turned into an eagle and soared over a large lake, beautiful and welcoming.

This was that lake. I hardly believed it. I didn't have a moment to make sense of it when more whispering startled me.

"Tarry not...seek them...you will know when you find them."

The faint susurration—and fear—nudged me on. I ignored the dragons, knowing they'd follow me, and as I'd seen myself do in the vision in King Desmond's court, I flew further into the valley. There I landed and turned back into a horse, so that I could gallop for a while. Breathing hard, I climbed a small hillock and paused at the crest.

"What is that?" I asked myself, not sure if what I saw was real. In the far distance, I spied a large herd of horses, the tallest horses I'd ever seen!

I looked up at the dragons—only to see them gone. Was this what they wanted me to discover? Why?

The horses were a mystery, no doubt. They had to have been here since before the great earthquake. Curious, I jogged toward the herd, but before I'd gone far, one of the creatures raised its head and fixed its gaze on me. Its clarion call brought the entire herd together. Their stallion.

As a body, they turned toward me, making the hide along my shoulders ripple with apprehension. Horses normally ran from strangers, not toward them. They thundered across the meadow, and when they drew close, I couldn't help the human response of dropping my jaw in shock. This couldn't be real! I could never have expected this, but the Voice had told me I'd know when I found them. One look and I knew.

Clods of grass and soil struck me as the herd surrounded me. Many reared and struck the air with their front hooves; others squealed and gnashed their teeth, but not one of them harmed me.

I tried not to let my fear show, but children's stories were often far-fetched and this one was nowhere near the mark. The adults were all a good eighteen hands tall, the older foals nearly as large as the Hamar ponies. The stallion was massive, with muscles that rippled under his glossy, black hide. His large, shockingly intelligent eyes were framed by a forelock and mane that hung nearly to the ground, although no goat beard adorned his chin. However, a single, frightening, cone-shaped, spiral horn the color of obsidian projected a foot from his forehead.

The creature was a unicorn.

He squealed, and the herd came to a standstill, except for two sorrel studs that leaped into place on either side of him. One had a white snip on his muzzle and a translucent horn the color of saffron. The other bore an opaque, ginger-colored horn and, on his left foreleg, a white stocking.

The black stallion leaned toward me, his nostrils quivering. "You are not," a voice said, and I jumped. Had he said that? Could unicorns talk?

"After a fashion," he said, his tail twitching.

And he could read my thoughts?

"Yes, and I know that you are not," he repeated.

"I don't know what you mean," I replied in my mind. After all, ordinary horses—I—couldn't speak.

The two red stallions grumbled in anger, and the black one laid back his ears.

"You are not a horse. You are an illusion. Who are you? What are you?"

Would they kill me when I told the truth? Surely, they would kill me if I didn't.

"I am human," I replied. *"And I have the power to shape-change. I mean you no harm."*

The creature gave a brief horse laugh. "Many of our kind were killed by humans who claimed they would not harm us. We are fortunate to have survived as a race."

Sadness enveloped me. Why would anyone want to hurt these incredible creatures? Before I could say so, he bowed, right knee on the ground, left foreleg stretched out in front of him. I watched, fascinated, as his horn lengthened, and he plunged it into the ground. I felt the magic before I saw it, but by then, it was too late.

"I would kill you if I had not seen you," he muttered.

Completely confused, I saw the grass at my feet sprout like the tentacles of a million octopi, and in a flash, they climbed over each other and snaked their way up my legs and around my body. I could barely see between the crushing strands of grass. I couldn't move a muscle. I could hardly breathe. Even worse, my magic was deaf to my commands, just as when I'd been struck by the bewitched arrow. I stood, quivering from muzzle to tail. Equine tears wetted my cheeks. Zahra would never know what happened to me. I'd never see Gideon again, and he would die.

The stallion came to his feet and bobbed his head, his arched neck and bunched muscles making him seem fierce. "What is a Gideon?"

"He is my mate," I replied. I closed my eyes and imagined my beloved. Gideon's devotion. Our wedding. Our recent travels. The attack by the barbarians, the Changelings and Gideon's injury.

Finally, I imagined him lying in a cave and dying from a magical poison.

"You are...Theona," the stallion said. "I am Siddarth. I am *hund-nayda*...herd leader."

He nodded at the sorrel with the stocking. "He is Naja, second to lead. The other is Anshu." The one with the snip. "We have lived long, woman of magic. Your essence is overshadowed by others, two that are not human."

He could see the sorcerers and the dragons? How? I saw neither *illumina* nor Insight inside him.

"We should destroy her," Anshu grumbled, glaring at me and pawing the ground with a sharp, black hoof.

My grassy bonds tightened. It hurt to stay on my feet, but I couldn't bend my legs enough to fall down. The strands were crushing me.

"Enough, Anshu," said Siddarth. "You must respect the *Telling*. I have seen it."

Anshu pinned his ears back in anger, but the grass loosened enough I could breathe again.

What in the world was a *Telling*?

"Until a few weeks ago, I didn't know unicorns even existed," I told Siddarth. *"You are a mythical creature to my people, as are winged horses or dragons or even magic itself. Even when I did learn of you, I was taught your kind was extinct. Believe me, I would never want to hurt you."*

"As I said, you're not the first to make that claim," he said with cynicism. He didn't believe me.

Naja and Siddarth grumbled at each other, I supposed speaking in whatever language unicorns spoke. I wished my magic would allow me to understand them. Siddarth eyed me with wariness but bent and touched his horn to the ground again. Immediately my fetters withdrew, leaving painful creases across my hide. Immediately I also saw all the unicorns' magical auras, their various talents, even their intentions.

None meant me any harm, but wisps of the unicorns' thoughts terrified me. Hundreds of years ago, needing to escape their old enemies—Rhesalus, Terius, Pythius and their dragons—they'd fought for freedom and found refuge here, in this isolated land on the south side of the Great Chasm. Rhesalus had told me that the unicorns had all died because they were "charmed and magical creatures…too gentle for their own good."

Gentle? I'd seen mountain sheep ramming their horned heads in a fight. I couldn't imagine the horrors of being impaled by an angry unicorn. Rhesalus had confused gentleness with kindness, but at this moment I felt little of either from these creatures.

I changed into myself, and, finally able to talk, thanked him. Disappointment hit when I realized the lump of Dreamwood was no longer stuck to my right hand. Where had it gone? Then I brushed my tunic pocket and felt it inside. How had it gotten there?

Siddarth eyed me, and my worries about the Dreamwood evaporated. I felt minuscule beside the unicorn's powerful frame.

"Sorcerers once hurt you," I said, a brief vision flashing through my head of the monsters taking the unicorns' handsome horns—even slaughtering them to get them.

"They lusted for what was not theirs," Naja sneered. "To use it for evil."

"I am not your enemy," I insisted. "I came looking for food and for herbs—for answers that would help heal my mate. I heard the Voice telling me to look for...*you*."

"A voice?" Siddarth's ears perked.

"Yes. Near a circle of six Dreamwood trees north of here. I've no idea why the Voice chose me; but it sent me to find something and said when I found it, I would know. Then I found you."

Anshu stomped a forefoot and sneered. "You lie. You want our magic, even if you have to steal it."

"I would never do such a thing."

"If you will not kill her, Siddarth, I will!"

"No! I told you I saw the *Telling!* She is the one."

The one? What did that mean?

"She bears the evil ones."

"Without her, the half-world is doomed! I have seen it!"

Half-world? On the edge of considering fleeing, I felt something grab hold of me. My mouth opened, and I heard the Voice force from me bits of what I'd heard from Eld Tully in the Elden Temple in Kildaria.

"'*Great will be the slaughter in the land of the evil rulers, and the sword of Elam shall be smeared with blood; yeah, the land shall be made a mire with rivers of blood.*

"'*And unicorns will come down with thee, and the children of the winged horse will be seen upon the earth again.*'"

The entire herd stood stock still, their eyes wide in astonishment. Would they listen? Or would they attack?

CHAPTER 17

*A*nd *unicorns will come down with thee.*
The words resounded in my mind and awe laced my thoughts as I considered them. I'd seen this lake and this valley in vision when kneeling before King Desmond. I'd heard these words from ancient writ spoken by Eld Tully in the temple. I'd felt something drawing me here, to this valley; and the dragons had hurried me to get here. Now Siddarth said he'd seen what he called the *Telling*—my gift of translating tongues clarified: a vision—of me.

And unicorns will come down with thee.

Within the herd arrayed around me stood a fair number of mares and their foals without horns. I'd just seen Siddarth lengthen his horn, and fables suggested they could hide them, too, but if the sorcerers had stolen the horns from some of these creatures, they'd inflicted the butchery a long time ago.

"The *Telling* gave those words of prophecy to me," Siddarth said with awe. "I see your *ilustre*. It shines true. Your magic is great and shall grow greater."

"*Ilustre?*"

"The light of many colors within your core."

"My *illumina.*"

He gave a nod of acknowledgment then turned to stare toward the tallest mountain behind him. I felt breathless at the strength of the power that drew me to it.

"The *Telling* shows me that you need your mate to help defeat both our mutual enemies and the evil ones hiding inside you. I give you an offering. Use it wisely."

He bent toward the earth again and my pulse resumed its earlier frenetic pace. If he restrained me again, I might never get free.

He pushed his horn against a patch of rocky ground at his feet. My eyes widened as the horn changed. It began to shine, like a flame inside a lantern with the glass tinted black. It brightened, gradually turning red, like a hot coal, until the tip blazed white.

Muscles bunched, Siddarth drove his horn into the largest rock and snapped off the tip, which rolled into the grass and singed it. The stallion squealed and staggered, his dark eyes filled with pain.

"Why did you do that?" I cried.

"Take it, Theona. It may help you heal your mate."

A unicorn's horn. Men had supposedly almost destroyed an entire species to get them. I only wished Siddarth hadn't said it *may* help heal Gideon. That meant it may not.

I dared tap it with a fingertip. Finding it not much more than warm, I picked it up and examined it. For all the world, it looked no different from obsidian, an almost glassy black rock. Near the size of a robin's egg, although cone-shaped, of course, and sharp, it felt light as a feather.

"Why did you do this?" I murmured.

"Because I must." Siddarth groaned as blood dripped from the tip of the horn.

"But you injured yourself doing it." I wanted to heal him, or at least to take away the pain.

He raised his head to sniff at me. His scent reminded me of Caspian, the earthy smell of grass and horsehide.

"Breaking the horn is painful," the creature admitted, "but as long as the *plith* remains, it will take care of itself. Watch."

My magic told me that the *plith* was the base of the horn, a smooth, finger-wide band between his brow and the horn itself.

Again, he dipped his head toward the ground, and before my eyes, the drop of blood at the horn's tip took on the shape of the original one and hardened, not so sharp or crystalline in appearance but whole again. Gradually, he shortened the horn to its original length.

"You must go," Siddarth said. "You will return if you learn the reason for our paths' crossing."

I slipped the horn fragment into my left pocket, gave him a respectful nod, bid him farewell, changed into a falcon, and soared toward the tallest mountain. The thought horrified me of what the sorcerers might do if they learned about the unicorns. I must never tell them.

Once I'd flown out of the valley and was headed toward the high mountain, the dragons came out again. Given the circumstances, I now knew why they'd avoided the unicorns.

"You've found two important parts of what you need from this place," Ramah said, his great wing-width sweeping the skies just below my much smaller bird-self. "But it is time for us to share another secret. Enchantment prevents us from explaining it until after you've seen it, but you will understand when you do."

"You've been here before," I dared say. "Before the quake tore the Lost Lands from the mainland."

"Yes. Hundreds of years ago, and it wasn't at all lost then."

I couldn't help wondering if he was able to tell convoluted and manipulative lies like the sorcerers did. Should I trust him? As it was, I wouldn't return to our cave until late this evening—or not at all if I drove myself too hard. Dear Elam, what should I do? Was I falling into some sort of trap?

A comforting warmth, much like what I'd felt in the ring of Dreamwood trees, seeped into my veins.

You will know.

I started. The Voice again. And its message was clear. I needed to follow the dragons.

Ramah must have sensed my misgivings. His gaze met mine, his yes softening to a gentle shade of daffodil yellow. "I do not mislead you," he said.

We headed to the summit of the mountain peak that stood high above the others, so high the trees all thinned to almost nothing near the top. My eyes widened when I saw a single, bedraggled, gnarled Dreamwood tree, hauntingly familiar, crowning the mountain's peak. Massive, it stood a good three hundred feet high with a trunk at least twenty feet wide at the base. It should perhaps have prepared me for what I found on the other side of the mountain, but it didn't.

At the distant horizon's feet rolled the southern sea, thunderous breakers crashing on the white sands of the nearer shore. Laced with the scent of saltwater, the wind tossed the surface of the water into whitecaps and caught my wings, thrusting me upward. Beneath me, several waterfalls cascaded off the mountain's west-side shoulder, crashing into one mighty river, which in turn rushed toward the ocean.

But between mountain and beach stood an abandoned village, and it took all the courage I could muster to swing around and look back at the mountain's face, the tall, flat, striated cliff of Mt. Draakheda! Mt. Draakheda was here! It was real!

My mind grappled with all this place had ever meant to me: Gideon, magic, mystery. The beautiful village, the welcoming people.

Yet, it was not that place, for the village had lain so long deserted that the little bit left of it looked old enough to have turned to stone. I'd never been here. I'd only dreamwalked in this place, and for some reason, dreamwalking didn't show things exactly as they were.

I swallowed a lump in my throat that seemed determined to choke me. This was proof that Gideon and Zahra and I hadn't come to the Lost Lands by accident. The sorcerers had likely manipulated it, but Eld Tully's words, the Voice, and Siddarth's *Telling* supported my belief that an even greater force than all of us had more say in this situation than evil mages.

Determined to avoid remaining in any one form too long, I changed from a falcon into an eagle and circled around to the cliff's small shelf on which I'd stood when dreamwalking, just below the cavern's hidden door. The dragons shrank to their bat-sized selves and landed on the craggy outcroppings on either side of me. Where they'd once looked eager, they now had dread in their eyes.

"The cavern holds the secrets?" I prompted.

"Several," Ramah replied, every inch of him wound tight with anticipation.

I could imagine why. This place held the laboratory where the sorcerers had conjured the Mother Dragon more than half a millennium ago, and a cave where generations of her offspring had been bound to the walls by magical chains.

Must I go inside it now? Or ever? The idea unnerved me. Beyond the distaste, I was worried sick about Gideon, and Zahra had to be worried about me. It wasn't fair to abandon them like this.

"The sorcerers will force you here before you can leave these lands," the drake said. "Knowing its truths beforehand will give you an advantage."

Heaving a sigh of submission, I climbed to the hidden place above the door, where I pressed my finger inside the depression. I felt the click and jumped down to avoid the door as it opened. Almost silently, it slid out of the way.

I stepped inside to the stench of stale air and mildew. The dragons joined me, crowding the huge entry as they expanded to dragons the size of horses. In the glow of mage light, I stared at the spikes of the stalactites and stalagmites scattered around us—larger but not nearly as many as I'd seen while dreamwalking—and mostly near the center of the cavern. Just as I'd envisioned it, a small stream trickled from someplace in the dark on my left and wound its way through the stalagmites toward the shadows on my right.

The dragons fidgeted beside me.

"Are you afraid?" I asked them. "Why? There's nothing here that can hurt you."

Enya turned on me, her eyes now shining an angry, dark red. "We do not fear this place, we detest it, and we dread seeing what we have only imagined for centuries."

"I'm sorry," I murmured, shrinking back. This place, during their mortality, had no doubt been a type of devil's inferno for dragonkind.

Enya and I followed Ramah to the back of the cavern and found what I'd expected. Fastened into the enormous back wall were gigantic ensorcelled pinions, the magical chains hanging from them encircling the bones of dragons long dead.

Ramah and Enya, anguish roiling in their eyes, keened so loudly it shook the cavern and rained shards of rock and dirt down on top of us.

"These were our mothers and fathers!" Ramah shouted. "Our brothers and sisters, and all our offspring. The sorcerers held them captive here. And so did that." He looked upward at the high ceiling, from which dangled thousands of roots, Dreamwood roots, some dripping water onto the stalagmites below.

Even then, hundreds of years ago, the roots had spread through this part of the cavern, and even without the shackles, the Dreamwood's magic had prevented the dragons from using their own magic to escape. Together, the tree, the chains, and the cavern's sealed door entombed them.

"I'm so sorry," I repeated, flinching when Ramah roared again.

Enya snarled. "When Cleary the Brave caught us, along with Rhesalus and Terius, he locked us in The Keeper. The rest of Dragonkind was trapped *here* and left to starve. I can still feel their pain and suffering. It bleeds from the walls."

"The starvation maddened them. Many of them ate each other. They were doomed, Theona. Doomed." Ramah keened again.

"It's a horrible way to die," I murmured.

"It was a horrible way to live! We did so for more than a century before Cleary conquered the sorcerers. The mages distrusted us, so they tested our kind, tortured us, experimented with ways to blend our breed with humans, to become sorcerers who could transform into dragons at will. Not just to look like one but to become one, while maintaining all the faculties of a human. Then they would no longer have needed us and would have destroyed us all."

"Those of us not used for the experiments," Enya interjected, "became mounts for the sorcerers and for the Changeling armies in the One Hundred Years War. Pythius claimed Ramah's brother, Murcod, as his mount, while Terius rode me, and Rhesalus took Ramah.

"It was a deadly campaign. Hundreds of dragons died, but we dared not disobey. Our children or our sires or dams were brought before us to be blinded or robbed of their wings. We all complied. It kept hope alive that we could someday get free and save our kind."

An odd concept: dragons entertaining hope. A stark contrast with the cruelty they'd endured. They were considered monsters, but monster was too kind a name for the sorcerers who possessed me.

Ramah looked west, toward the waterfall and the laboratory where Rhesalus and his comrades had conducted their experiments.

"They tried everything. Elixirs that contained unspeakable ingredients, including dragon parts. Incantations and enchantments. They nearly succeeded, but the process was excruciating. No dragon survived. If suffering reaches unbearable proportions, it is the nature of our kind to burst into flames."

Flames! I stood dazed by the reminder. The day I'd become possessed, I saw a vision of the duel in which the sorcerers faced Cleary the Brave on a battlefield.

In mortality, an unexpected magical connection between the dragons and the sorcerers made them nearly invincible—so long as they remained in physical contact with each other. Separated, either one was as vulnerable as any other living being. Rhesalus and Terius stayed onboard Ramah and Enya, knowing they were virtually indestructible. Pythius, however, wanted the glory of destroying Cleary. He failed. After Pythius's death, Cleary struck Murcod with Slayer, and the dragon burst into flames.

Rhesalus and Terius had not, however, anticipated The Keeper. Nor did they understand Slayer. Both were magical, and while they couldn't send the foursome to the Underworld, Slayer did destroy their mortal bodies and the magic of the Elds locked their souls inside

The Keeper. If not for that, they could have remained in the world by taking possession of anyone nearby—like me—and carried out their schemes to return to mortality.

I could only imagine that for the dragons, this half-death inside The Keeper—and now me—, the suffering of their kin, and the agony of those bursting into flames....

"It would truly be a devil's inferno," I murmured

"Yes. An inferno for dragons, worse than the inferno of Eblis's Underworld," Ramah snarled. "Suffering that never seemed to end. For Enya and me, if death meant we could sleep, it would be bliss. We have no sleep in this partial death. We are trapped inside you, along with the sorcerers who want to resume their experiments as soon as you return them to life—where they will stop at nothing to gain immortality."

I fought with tears for them, even as I wondered how these creatures could possibly offer me good will. They had to hate humanity as a whole. What would happen if they regained their bodies and their freedom? Would they desire peace with mankind, or would they seek revenge?

Enya muttered, "You must find the truths hidden here quickly and return to your prince. Do what you must and leave us to mourn in peace."

I flinched at the dismissal then called mage light and jogged toward the laboratory. The pull on my magic felt the strongest I'd experienced up to now. The doors I'd seen while dreamwalking stood exactly where I expected them, on the northwest corner of the cavern, on the other side of the stream. Gideon had supposedly knocked them down when we dreamwalked together, the night before we married. In real life, they stood untouched.

I crossed the stream and tested the handles. They were locked. The doors were cold, smooth, thick, solid. They were also ancient, most likely brittle and dry. Could I burn them down? I called on Fire, but the doors seemed to mock me, wooden soldiers that blocked the way and went unharmed. I tried again and again, but still, nothing happened—except for the hunger growling in my belly.

I sighed and instead probed the doors with my magic. They grew even more forbidding, roiling with enchantment.

"They are warded. You will recognize the truth when you open them."

My heart did cartwheels at hearing the Voice again. It frightened me, but it also proved this was my goal for the day. I needed to open these doors.

Considering the thick lintel above me and the broad frames on either side of the doors, I couldn't imagine anything short of a battering ram knocking them down. Maybe not even then because of the magic. How could one, small sixteen-year-old girl get them open?

A thought dawned. The Language! It could amplify my powers a hundred-fold or more. I tried speaking the commands, but it didn't work. Instead, it triggered a heightening of the magic inside the doors, as if invisible watchdogs now sensed my presence and were ready to attack. That did not bode well.

I doubted Water or Wind would work, and an earthquake would turn this place into my tomb. What more could I do?

I jumped the stream and turned to face the doors, my back pressed against the stone wall. My every sense alert to the dark forces inside those doors, I hissed the words *"Pateface foris."*

The doors jerked on their hinges, and I jumped. Repeating it a bit louder, I saw the doors bulge outward, crackling and straining, wood against wood and stone. They crashed back into place. The third time I shouted it, throwing every bit of my power into it.

A horrid shrieking filled the cavern, and I slapped my hands over my ears against the sound of wood and metal being tormented. Then, a thunderous blast disintegrated the doors and sent dust and fine wood chips, metal fragments and stone flying into the cavern, and I screamed when the wave from the force slammed me into the wall.

Deafened, I couldn't hear my own cry of pain. My scalp burned where I'd been smashed into jagged pieces of rock. When I touched it, I took my hand away smeared with blood. Warm wetness ran down my face from a multitude of cuts.

Shocked, I stared at the laboratory, now freed of its doors. I'd done it! But triumph withered in the light of the unbelievable mess I'd made. The dust billowing out of the laboratory made me cough. Ramah had said the sorcerers would bring me here. What would they do when they saw what I'd done?

Quickly! The Voice urged.

I followed my mage light inside, finding the laboratory much the same as it was in my dreamwalk. Two long tables stood end to end just inside the doorway. The equipment piled on them made my blood run cold. Among them, rows of lengthy, sharp, double-ended forks. Swords. Saws. Knives. Broad shears that looked big enough to decapitate a crocodile. I cringed at the horrible suffering these instruments must have caused.

Around the corner, I found the familiar bookcase. I also sensed my answers stood here.

Wonderful. There must be a hundred books. Many more than in my dreams. Which one did I need? They glared down at me, as if they resented my intrusion. I reached for a tome on a low shelf and recoiled from a bolt of electricity that struck my hand. Ah. Magic resided here, too—and would defend itself from me.

At least my ears had recovered, and I could hear the hum of cankered magic around me. The books talked to me!

The Language silenced their wicked murmurings, and my magic took over again as the appropriate words to banish the magical protection around the books formed themselves in my mind. *"Drachta tishin,"* I hissed.

It worked. The restraint left, and I was able to touch the books. Now, which one might help my prince?

They all had different characters. One book released impressions of music, another a throbbing beat like primitive drums. Large books, small books, some lovely, others plain and crudely made. I grasped one of the books, but its chant gave me an image of several shamans gathered around their cauldrons and casting dark enchantments. I let it go.

Coming across the two books I'd seen in vision prior to my marriage to Gideon, *Eblis's Finest Children* and *The Perfect Birthright*, I recoiled. They held unspeakable evil.

Their bindings seemed to blend together, mostly shades of brown and black and an occasional dark garnet-red. Two were dyed blue, one a dark navy, another the indigo of healing—

My thoughts floundered. A book on healing? Here? Among so many tomes dedicated to destruction and torment? My jaws clenched when I considering the reason. If the sorcerers had gotten injured during their experiments, it would have taught them how to heal themselves. But when the cruelest of all thoughts dawned, my gut sickened. Had these fiends healed injured dragons so that they could carry on with their experiments and injure them again? And again? If so, this was truly a hellish place. Despicable.

I went to pull the book from the shelf, but cries escaped it, and I nearly dropped it. It was as if the book was alive and suffering in this horrible cavern. Cradling it in my hands, I found it—like all the others and just like those I'd seen in my dreamwalking—magically devoid of dust, its cover and pages pristine, untouched by the ravages of time. But inside this one, I could feel the goodness in its magic. Magic? I thought again about what Eld York had told me after I'd become possessed. That there was no magic, either good or bad, only a higher power and the knowledge to use it. The power in all these books had been used for evil, but not this book. I felt its Elden might. Like The Keeper, the Elds had created it to do good.

I set it on one of the tables and turned page after page, skimming its contents, storing information for later use. I couldn't see anything specific to Gideon's needs and went to tuck it into my pocket, intending to take it to the cave where I could study it in detail.

"No," the Voice said, and I winced.

"Put it back," someone else said, and I turned to see Ramah, and behind him Enya, still in horse-sized forms, watching me from the doorway. "When the sorcerers bring you here, they'll expect to find it. It's enough the doors are broken. Don't give them more to question."

"Then what was the point of my coming here today?" I couldn't help feeling annoyed.

"You will know when it's time."

I bit my tongue to keep from snapping at him. I'd grown weary of those words.

The *parhelia* of prescience took hold of me, warning me that Ramah was right. I would return here. Soon. I supposed that meant my questions would be answered.

I needed to leave. I sent the dragons away and returned the book to its place, surveying the laboratory and the wreckage in and beyond it. The magical protection was gone from the books as surely as the doors were gone from the room, and I could do nothing about it. Only now did I notice the burning and throbbing on my head and face. Even after I healed myself and removed my trail of magic, the destruction would give me away. How to fix as much of it as I could?

I ruminated. Wood burned. Dust blew. Rock and metal would melt. Nodding at the idea, I healed myself first. Then, calling on Wind, I sent it howling from the laboratory and through the cavern, sweeping every inch of dust and debris out the door into the sunlight. There, I razed it with Fire and called upon Water to wash myself and to wash away any remnants. More Wind dried everything quickly.

It amazed me to see the bones of the dead dragons dusted clean but otherwise untouched, as were the chains draped around them. They were ensorcelled. It was sad to realize that my power could not free them, not even in death.

I needed to hurry back to Gideon and Zahra! Zahra must fear for my life, and I worried about Gideon's.

My magic demanded feeding, and I flew out over the sea and dived deep, where I fed well on perch and tuna as a leviathan. Then I headed "home" on the wings of a horse.

CHAPTER 18

The back side of the mountain felt strangely welcoming now that it was full of game. I supposed it meant that the Lost Lands had deemed me worthy of seeing it as it was. It also meant I could switch between portalling and flying, feeding and resting, cutting the distance and the time into faster but safer segments.

I pushed myself hard. Valley after valley came and went. Nothing stopped me but the driving needs of hunger and rest, but I took as little as I could tolerate. I returned to the cave at dusk as a pelican and tottered toward Zahra. She watched wide-eyed as I approached her, opened my bill, and then spit a gift out at her feet.

"Princess! It must be you!" She sounded both offended and thrilled. "Oh! My heavens!" Her voice rose a half-step, gladness and amazement in it. "Fish! Fish! We can have fish stew for supper. 'Twill be wonderful."

I struggled to regain my human form, swaying from the strain of having used more magic in one day than ever before. How could I be hungry again? How many creatures had I eaten today? Too many to count but apparently not enough.

I shed myself of my rucksack and the foodstuffs I'd managed to gather on my way back. All I cared about was Gideon. He looked worse. Frail. Skin grayish, hot to the touch. Zahra joined me, sadness pinching her face.

"His fever comes and goes, my lady. When he's hungry, he rouses, he eats and drinks, wakes enough to walk careful-like to the ledge to relieve himself. Otherwise, he mostly sleeps, but he's suffering bad dreams, probably from the pain."

"He's so hot." The compress had slipped from his forehead to his bed. I unbuttoned his shirt and flinched at seeing the ugly black triangle had grown larger. My hand laid against it, I felt its strange aura, as if it were watching me watch it. It made me shiver with revulsion.

Zahra soaked the compress again and laid it across Gideon's brow. She murmured something about making our stew, while I sat with my prince and whispered my love and encouragement. My heart throbbed with hope when he finally pried his eyes open and stared at me.

"Where have you been, my love?" he squawked between parched lips.

"Looking for food," I replied, and almost to myself added "and answers."

His brows pulled together. "Answers? To what?"

I stroked his cheek. "How to rid you of the poison from the lance."

He closed his eyes again and shook his head. "Poison? What lance? Where have you been?"

Now my heart sank. He was delirious, confused.

"All over the island."

Astonishment flew his eyes open. "Island? What island?" His husky voice broke, and he coughed. I gave him some cool water to drink.

"We're in a mountain cave to the south of the Badlands."

"There isn't anything south of the Badlands."

"We're on the other side of the Great Chasm. In the Lost Lands."

He blinked, taking in our spare surroundings as if seeing them for the first time. "How did we get here?"

"I brought you and Zahra here. Don't you remember? It's a beautiful place." And a lonely and frightening and magical place. A tiny tug at the corner of his mouth served as a smile, but nothing relieved the grimness caused by his constant pain.

I shared the best parts of my day with him, painting a picture of adventure and beauty. It helped to wipe the distress off his face and calm my aching heart.

Gideon's eyes drifted shut not long into my storytelling, but I carried on, needing to tell everything I'd discovered, no matter how mental it all sounded and no matter he wouldn't remember it. Who would ever believe a story of wildlife that appeared and disappeared; of finding a Dreamwood forest that, in its strange fashion, talked to me? Of meeting unicorns?

I said nothing about Mt. Draakheda. I couldn't take the risk the sorcerers might glean the information from Gideon if he remembered it.

After supping on our fish stew, Gideon slept again and Zahra and I sat on the floor, again leaning against the rock shelf that formed his bed. Thinking about my day, I pulled the Dreamwood chip from my pocket and examined it.

"Dreamwood!" Zahra mewed, her dark eyes wide with admiration. "My lady, that's fresh Dreamwood. The story you told your prince was fantastical. I'd not believe it if I didn't know you, hadn't seen a fair bit of oddities around you already, and if it weren't for this scrap of proof."

I couldn't help chuckling. "I wouldn't believe it even with this scrap of proof if I hadn't lived it." I pulled the unicorn horn from my other pocket and offered it to her. She held it gingerly, eyes wide with awe.

"Two of the most powerful tools for healing," she murmured. "Dreamwood and a unicorn horn. And given to you by a tree and a unicorn themselves."

"I only wish I knew how to use them," I said.

"I want to see them," a voice said.

I started, looking over my shoulder at Gideon. He was wide awake and intense. We moved aside as he swung his legs over the ledge and sat up. I knelt before him and offered him the Dreamwood.

He grunted when he touched it, startled as I'd been by the intense tingling. Pulling aside his partially unbuttoned shirt, he pressed the Dreamwood to the black scar on his shoulder. I bit my lip in anticipation. Would it heal him? The pensive look on his face told me it didn't, and disappointment drooped my shoulders.

Gideon took the unicorn horn from Zahra and examined both, turning them around and around and holding the horn up to the light of the fire. Dreamwood against his chest again, he touched the horn's tip to the wood. A loud pop and Gideon's screech of pain brought Zahra and me to our feet. Gideon dropped both items, slapping at himself and screaming.

"It burns! It burns!"

He batted my hands when I tried to look at the wound. Horror racked me when I saw the skin over the triangle now red and blistered. An edge of the wound had torn open, and a putrid mingling of blood and pus oozed from it that made us gag.

"Ach, 'tis infected," Zahra said, her hand pressed to her nose against the stench. She hurried off for hot water and bandages, while I tried to calm Gideon.

His silence came in an instant, him suddenly sitting there staring at nothing, but when I picked the horn up from the floor, he snatched it from me.

"Let me have it, Gideon," I begged. "I don't want it to hurt you again."

"Hurt me?" He stared at me as if I'd gone mad. "It didn't hurry me. I need to see it."

With the wonder of a small boy on his face, he rolled it between his fingers, his smile gentling the look of misery. He pulled it closer and closer as he examined it, the point, long and sharp, aimed toward him. His pale cheeks turned bright red and his hands started to shake with effort. It was as if he couldn't hang on to the horn!

In an incredible flash of whitest light, the shard flew from his fingers and buried itself in his shoulder. The pain and the shock had him screaming again, and Zahra and I screamed with him. He toppled backward, writhing and digging at the wound. We grabbed his hands, trying our best to stop him from tearing his skin off.

Without warning, he fainted, and the silence echoed inside the cave.

"Gideon," I said, shaking him. He lay deathly still. I could barely hear him breathing. Resting my hand on the wound, I reaped a magical vision of the unicorn horn lodged deep in his shoulder, as if it had been driven there with hammer and awl. It nosed its way deeper and deeper into the ghoulish matter that I guessed was both dying tissue and the enchanted poison. I feared it could pierce Gideon's lung and kill him. Oddly, I noted the muck that encircled the horn seemed stuck to it, like flies on flypaper.

Desperate for answers, I reached for the sorcerers. Surely, they would do something now.

Silence again met my summons.

Why? I wanted to scream with fury. Did Moriana not want to admit she had no cure? How dare they play games with Prince Gideon's life? If they needed Gideon, why would they do this?

"Princess," Zahra said, touching my arm. "We need to treat the wound." She had everything needed to clean it and make a poultice.

When she'd finished, she also needed help with tying the poultice to his shoulder. Gideon remained oblivious to our ministrations.

During the long night, my prince burned with fever, but he refused the herbal draughts we offered him. He needed sleep but moaned and tossed with pain. He needed food and water but wouldn't take them. Near dawn, his skin pale and dry and his eyes rheumy, he awakened with a grunt. I knelt beside him and kissed the palm of his hand. His eyes fluttered open, wretched with misery.

"I'm. I'm going to die, aren't I?" he whispered.

"No, Gideon! Of course not! You're ill, but you're going to get better."

He shook his head then took my hand and laid it on his shoulder again. I gasped at what I saw inside of him.

"What is it, my lady?" Zahra asked, sitting straight up on her pallet.

"The horn! It's turned around. It's moving slowly, but it's headed back out and the poison is coming with it!"

Gideon drifted back to sleep. I kissed his dry lips.

"Praises be," Zahra said. "Our prayers are answered."

"I'll sing praises when it succeeds," I murmured. "I don't trust any of this."

"Ah, but you trust Elam, Princess, and that's what matters," she reminded me.

I did, but I didn't believe for one minute that this was over. Gideon was too ill for that. Zahra and I made him comfortable again, and then I settled down for a couple hours of sleep.

Light blossomed above me, a familiar dark orange color.

I looked around to see who'd brought it. No one was here but me. I willed the light to douse, and it did. I called it again and it obeyed, proving it was mine.

I stood in Mt. Draakheda's laboratory staring at the tall, forbidding bookshelves. One book stood out. I leaped to the top—no, I flew. I was a bird. The instant I landed, I stretched into the form of a snake and stared at a hideously ugly brown cover. It was turned backward. This close to it, I sensed a strange pulse coming from it, a pit-a-pat that countered the beat of my heart.

I ran my snout along the book's cover, tasting it with my serpentine tongue, then I pulled back enough to read the title with my human mind.

The Recreation of Mortality. *What did that mean? Urged by some unseen force, I slithered to the brow of the book and across its many pages to the top of the next one, a book an even uglier butterscotch yellow, no thicker than a horseshoe. This one throbbed, too, a cadence that both offset and complemented the first one, not unpleasant but haunting. Hanging from the top of the books, I twisted around enough to see this book's title. The words, etched in gold, shimmered, daring me to read them.*

Two words. Linking Souls. *Those words meant far too much to me. Sinister. Of Linking dragons with snakes or eagles or horses so that the monsters could use their bodies as their own.* Linking Souls? *I loathed the book even without reading it.*

The laboratory dissolved, leaving me falling for an instant until I'd grown wings and flown beyond the Great Chasm as a Pegasus. Where had Gideon and Zahra gone? I flew faster, hoping to catch them.

Faster, faster, my heart raced with the effort, and my soul shuddered with fear.

Hurry! Hurry! *A voice cried.*

Frantically I swung eastward following the army's trail through the Badlands. Desert clay turned into hillocks of fine desert sand. The trail split in three directions, but the one to the right stood out. I sensed the United Forces had come this way. Were they truly alive? Were they safe?

Hurry! Hurry!

I breathed hard. My heart beat harder. I dug my wings into the hot wind pushing against me.

Their enemies are coming! They need you! Hurry!

I came awake to thick darkness, panting, my heart still pounding. We needed to heal Gideon and find the army as soon as possible.

But I'd learned something in the dream I had to test. If only I could remember what. My thoughts whirled as I drifted back to sleep watching three snakes try to eat a pile of books half-buried in the sand.

The startling sound of twittering birds announced the day's arrival. Zahra and I scrambled to our feet at the same time, gazes locked, and then we ran to the ledge to witness birds of every variety fluttering from trees to mountain tops to the stream below.

"Will you look at that," my warrior-maiden said with astonishment. "Birds. Real birds."

"Amazing." I looked. And looked. What a joy to see so common a thing. It seemed the Lost Lands had truly accepted us. I only prayed it would continue.

Even more amazing, Gideon's fever had broken, and he gave me a wan smile. Seeing him better, I felt a bit more comfortable with leaving to forage again. We were out of fresh greens, herbs and other ingredients Zahra needed for both our soups and stews and Gideon's poultices. When I kissed my prince farewell, he croaked a request for berries, and I laughed my promise that I would try. My delight became joy when, later, returning with handfuls of vegetables and wild strawberries and a wild boar haunch, I found my love sitting upright on his bed and sipping a mug of warm tea. Maybe we could head back to the mainland soon!

Then I offered him some of the berries and paused. His eyes looked wrong. Somber. Unfocused. He at least recognized me and let me examine his wound. The horn was closer to the surface, the horrid black ichor still attached to it. It was a writhing mass, like a cluster of parasites angry at being deterred from hurtling their way into Gideon's brain.

I frowned in concern. The horn seemed smaller now, as if it was grinding down. I feared that if it wore out before it reached the surface the poison would resume its progression. I wished I could return to Mt. Draakheda's laboratory for the book *Healing*. It might tell me what to do.

Once the idea took root, I couldn't let it go. Then I remembered my dream last night and wondered if this was my mission after all. To get the book. I couldn't count on the sorcerers, so that left it to me.

Of course, I couldn't tell Zahra about Mt. Draakheda for my own safety, but she understood the Voice and its mysterious promises. Answers were out there, and I had to find them.

"Do what you must, my lady. His Highness seems to be holding his own for the moment, but if he takes a turn for the worse, what you unearth may save him."

I planned to alternate portalling with flying on this dreadful trip, which I began with flying. I sighed with annoyance when I invited the dragons to join me, but they didn't come.

The day was crystal blue, quite warm but pleasant. With the wildlife now abundant, I wanted to explore everything. It was all magnificent. Some of the animals I'd never seen before: several varieties of birds, herds of strange deerlike beasts, different sorts of wildcats and canine-like creatures. To do as little damage as possible, I fed while shifted into a bird or a snake, mostly on fish or on insects and similar creatures.

When I saw the sun pressing toward its zenith, I was shocked I'd remained a dragon for so long. I felt fine, however, and decided to continue, giddy with the excitement of playing with my gifts, changing sizes and colors, and tasting different foods and, oddly enough, discovering that everything about being a dragon was coming easier. My eyesight, my strength, my cunning. It felt good to stretch my wings and fly at different altitudes, slow and fast, and to sometimes do aerial acrobatics.

When I grew thirsty, I discovered a wide, turbulent river. The waterway coursed around a small, grassy island that looked warm and inviting. Fresh fish and a swim sounded wonderful.

Not until I decided to shape-change into a leviathan as I dived into the river did it dawn on me that I'd been a dragon for hours. I'd never stayed in one form this long and struggled—and failed—to make the change. Slicking my wings against my sides, I prepared to slice into the water and—

Cold, suffocating water hit me. My wings foundered. Kicking, splashing, desperate for air, I roared in shock. Where was I? I was a dragon and dragons did not swim. How had I fallen into water?

The current dragged me downstream then pulled me under again. I lunged to the surface gasping and spreading my wings across the top of the water like a giant lily pad, but I weighed too much for them to keep me long. I looked for something to grab with my tail. It would give me purchase. Where was I? How could I get help? It was near midday, and I was hungry. Had I come here to fish? I couldn't remember.

Mental images haunted me of humans and unicorns and dozens of places, of whispered words and voices which ought to mean something but didn't. Ahead lay a small island not much bigger than a dragon. It seemed familiar. I paddled toward it, my front feet grabbing the water plants, my tail snaking around rocks at the bank, and my hind legs digging into the rocks beneath the water. Struggling, I managed to pull myself out and fall belly down onto the lush grass, lying there gasping for air.

It was warm here. Safe. Birds chirped and chipmunks chittered pleasantly in the distant woodlands bordering the river. A fish jumped out of the water and splashed as it fell back in.

Sounds.

Comforting sounds.

I dozed.

———+—

I awoke with the sun well past noon. Snuffing loudly, I shook sand from my wings as I rose to my feet. I needed my mate, but I didn't remember seeing another dragon here. I couldn't remember another dragon at all, only that I had a mate.

Hunger plagued me. Taking to the air, I glided silently over the lake southward towards sparsely wooded hills. I spied a herd of deer spread out under the shade of several oak trees. I also saw a cougar, crouched in a tree beneath which rested a doe and her twin fawns, poised to leap. Odd. Wildcats rarely hunted in midday. Odd that I knew that.

I spiraled around, pondering. The cat would choose one of the fawns for lunch, but I couldn't decide which I'd prefer to taste. The doe and both her young? Or the cat? For some reason, I thought I should pity the doe.

I also knew I'd eaten deer but never cougar, and it was easy to reach it in the tree. I plucked it from its branch, hissing and spitting, before it even knew I was there. Its claws scraped in vain against mine. I reached the foothills and dropped it, the fall breaking its back. I wasn't sure I liked cat as well as I did…moose, deer, elk…. I'd eaten many things. I'd eaten some of them here.

But where was here?

As I dug a small bone from between my teeth with a claw, a sharp pain shot through my head and made me wince. I shook my head and snorted. Again, came the pain, longer this time. I moaned at what seemed a narrow band of darkness somewhere inside my brain. It oughtn't to be there, I thought. Ideas—memories—assailed me: of a handsome creature with violet eyes waiting for me somewhere. Then came fear. Something felt terribly wrong.

A strange energy stole over me. Magic. Yes. I knew magic. I needed to go home, but how? Where was home? I was a dragon, but I wasn't. I needed to keep my being a dragon a secret. Why?

A vulture, coveting the remains of my meal, croaked at me as it flew overhead. I could become a bird! The vulture fled after I shifted into a condor of monstrous proportions. I laughed inside.

The pain in my head came again, driving me to the ground, my wings spread out on either side. Rather than fight it, I relaxed my mind, curious when that darkness inside began to leak out of me.

"I cannot believe it," a creature said, standing near my nose. Strange that it looked familiar. A head, two arms, two legs. A man.

"You've gone and gotten yourself into a mess, girl. Didn't we tell you not to remain in any one form for too long? Your mind has grown wild. You've nearly forgotten you're human."

Human? I raised my head to better see his dark gray eyes and handsome face. Or at least I thought humans would consider him so. He wore boots trimmed in rabbit's fur. I liked rabbit.

"Let me come a bit closer, Theona," the creature said. Theona? That too sounded familiar. His hands radiated light, a soft lavender blue. They were pretty. Like stars. I wondered how his hands would taste. He touched my snout and—

I shrieked, a dragon-sized condor cry that rattled the ground beneath us and made the human cover his ears.

Burning! Burning! Magical fire streaked up my face and down my back. My wings withered before my eyes, and I roared again in fury. Lurching to my feet, I snapped at the man, but he disappeared!

"Your magic is fighting me," he muttered, now standing to my right but far enough away I couldn't reach him. "You should be back to normal by now. You've remained shape-changed much too long. Please, let Terius out."

I had no idea what a Terius was. I only knew I was slowly shrinking, now smaller than the trees that surrounded me. I panicked. I wanted to escape, but without my wings, I'd have to travel on clumsy condor feet. Stumbling, I wondered when I'd forgotten how to walk. I fell, rolling down a small incline and coming face to face with the human again—now on my left side.

"Be still, dear. It's working, just slowly. But I really wish you'd let Terius out. Together, we could do this faster and with less pain."

Pain? It felt as if something was breaking every bone in my body. How could I find this Terius thing? The agony was unbearable.

Another dull headache stabbed me, and this time I let the darkness inside me dissipate quickly. Another human now stood by the first, and together they raised their hands, all four so bright it hurt to look at them. Words sprang from their mouths, and the shrinking and bone twisting got worse. I screeched in anger.

"It's still too slow," said the Terius creature. "Let Moriana out, Theona. She's better at this than both of us put together."

Then why hadn't the first human asked for that one instead? I squealed as the third headache culminated in the arrival of a beautiful woman clad in a low-cut dress not at all appropriate for castles and kings.

The three humans began to chant the strange words in unison, the woman leaning down to touch my cheek. The pain lanced through me, sharp and fast, and then it was gone. I was human! The Terius offered me a hand and helped me to my feet.

"Why did you fly so far? You're a good five hours away from your cave. And what possessed you to become a disgusting giant vulture?"

Five hours? Looking at the sun, shifted even further west, and the pile of bloody cat bones and fur at my feet, misgivings assailed me. I remembered setting out before dawn on an important errand and should have arrived…somewhere…too long ago.

My cave? I could imagine it, but did vultures live in caves? I looked at my hands. They were human hands with human fingers!

The man that apparently wasn't a Terius approached me, taking one of those hands. His touch felt strange, delicate and light, as if he wasn't really quite there. He raised my fingers to his lips and kissed them. It tickled and made me chuckle. He grinned and leaned into me, his gray eyes twinkling. I found his scent irresistible, a blend of cedar and sweet orange and rosewood. It lured me into his arms, my lips parting as he bent to press a kiss to them. I could hardly feel his gossamer touch, but it made my skin tingle. I wondered if I'd ever been kissed before. It left me breathless and wanting more.

CHAPTER 19

"You're not really going to take advantage of the situation, are you, Rhesalus?" the Moriana woman queried, her dark eyes narrowed.

"Why not? I mean, after all, there's only so much advantage I can take," the Rhesalus replied. "When we've succeeded in getting her to do what we need and I'm able to claim her as my mage partner, there will be no end to what we can accomplish."

The Terius said, "And when she comes back to herself and realizes what you've done to her, you could lose her completely."

The Rhesalus laughed. "There is that, isn't there? I suppose I need to put an end to the fun."

He muttered more of those strange words that now seemed cast in a profusion of winged colors. My mind felt ready to explode as my memories came flooding back.

"You kissed me!" I screamed at Rhesalus, wiping my mouth as if he'd poisoned me. He laughed.

"And it was wonderful. I look forward to more of it in the future."

"Never! Never, ever again!"

Terius snapped. "You've been away from your prince for a while. How was he when you left him?"

I raised my hands and without thinking, did as Moriana had done before. I turned my nails into claws, which I'd have gladly used on him had he been mortal.

"He's dying!" I shouted. "I've called for you and you didn't come! Why?"

An uneasy looked passed between them.

"You don't know how to heal him, do you?" I snapped. "You've avoided me because of it."

"We know what to do now," Moriana said, more calmly than I'd ever heard her speak. "Get us back to him and we'll discuss it after I've seen him again."

I thrust them behind my shields and hurtled back to the cave—becoming a number of winged creatures but not once a dragon. I stopped only when I had no choice, but I ended through a portal.

Zahra started when I arrived but quickly recovered. "Princess. I'm so glad you're back. The prince's fever returned just before lunch and hasn't given ground since."

No, no, no, don't let it be true!

My stomach dropped when I saw him drenched in sweat, struggling for breath, his face gaunt and scruffy under more than a day's growth of beard. I wrung out the compress and patted his face with it, calling his name. His eyes fluttered open, filled with intolerable pain. If nothing else took his life, this could. Opening his shirt, I recoiled from the blistered skin around the edges of the black triangle. It leaked infection and appeared and smelled even worse than before.

The unicorn horn had moved closer to the surface but had worn down enough I doubted it would make it out. In a near panic, I opened my shields and shouted for the sorcerers.

Chaos erupted the instant they arrived.

"He's in trouble," Moriana said without even touching him. Terius yelled at her. Rhesalus grabbed her arm and insisted she do something *now*.

She wrenched herself away and offered me her hand. We touched him together. Her face contorted with fear as she took stock of the prince's condition. Then her expression went from distressed to shocked, alerting Terius and Rhesalus that something was...*wrong?* Mind-Paired, I assumed, they shared their thoughts, and Terius's gaze snapped to mine, filled with the avarice of a hungry wolf.

"How did you do it?" he demanded of me.

"You do realize the significance of what you've found, don't you?" Rhesalus added.

I felt sick inside. He wasn't referring to Gideon's condition or the poison or the healing herbs or draughts or poultices.

"I found a Dreamwood forest. One of the trees...gave me a piece of bark," I admitted.

"That's not what I'm referring to, and you know it."

No, he meant the unicorn horn. Which I'd not likely found just lying around in the wilderness.

"A marvelous discovery," Moriana said. "You should have summoned us sooner. We'd have warned you not to use Dreamwood and the horn together. It caused your prince further damage. Now, even with the horn, I don't know if we can save him."

I screeched my fury at her. "I did call you! And you ignored me!"

"If you'd—"

"Leave it." Rhesalus waved Moriana off. "She's right. She did call for us, but only one of our ideas would work, which we didn't want to use, and you had none. How was Theona supposed to know that the power of the unicorn's barb and that of Dreamwood are direct opposites and will react? The damage isn't irreversible, and we cannot afford to lose him." He glanced at Terius. "We need to do what we'd already planned *now*."

Terius nodded. "Yes."

"You must trust us, Theona," Rhesalus said. "If you do everything that we ask, he still has a chance."

Their words threatened to stop my heart. I looked at Gideon, surrounded by my enemies but perhaps having no hope of survival without them, and knew that I had to do whatever they asked.

Still, I glared at Rhesalus. "Ask what you will, but if my husband dies, I won't cooperate with you anymore. I don't care if you kill me. I don't want to live without him." The seriousness on his face proved he believed me. Both Terius and Moriana looked equally grim.

Terius said, "You must portal him to the furthest valley to which you've traveled south of here. You'll do it in one step, no matter how far it is. As with other attempts, our magic will protect you."

I saw how weak Gideon was and the fear on Zahra's face and knew that she understood as well as I did that I needed her help. I insisted she go with us.

Terius ignored Zahra. "If you must. It's a bit riskier, but if you insist, it's on your head. When we arrive in the valley, you'll need to hunt and rest straightaway. Then I'll guide you to a special place where we need to take your prince."

A special place? We were likely bound for Mt. Draakheda, and special did not describe it. How I ached to spit the truth in his face. But I schooled myself so as not to give anything away.

Rhesalus told us to lay Gideon on the floor and for Zahra to kneel beside him to stay out of our way. The sorcerers and I made a tight ring around them, our hands joined. Vertigo gripped me the minute I touched Rhesalus. The energy of our foursome engulfed me, like none I'd ever felt before. A moment too late, I realized this was what it most likely meant to be a mage partner. I'd reject it if I could, but I couldn't.

I formed a portal to the valley, the one I'd seen in vision in King Desmond's court. Rhesalus the Horse-sorcerer sighed his pleasure at my success.

"You've journeyed further than we could have hoped," he said. "Excellent. Now, your servant must pull your prince through, and then the four of us must remain together as we pass through the portal. You must come last."

Everything went as he instructed, but when I crossed the threshold, everything went black. I floundered in the darkness for what seemed forever, and then I fell to the ground, paralyzed.

"My lady!" Zahra cried.

"She'll be fine," I heard Moriana say, though I couldn't turn my head to see her. I could barely see at all. She added: "It's portal-shock, which comes from traveling too far. Without our help it would have killed all of you or lost you forever in the void. Feed and water her enough she can rouse to hunt. Feed yourself and the prince as well, or you could fall into a deep sleep from which you'll never awaken."

Zahra did as bid, and desperate to eat, desperate to sleep, I swallowed what she gave me. Gaining my faculties enough to feed as a small snake, I then napped beside Gideon. It seemed to take forever but traveling through intermittent portals and flying would have taken far longer. I needed to endure this to save my prince.

When I'd recovered enough, Zahra helped me get both her and Gideon onto my winged-horse back. Terius took to the air as an eagle, while the others remained behind my partially open shields. As I'd expected, Terius headed toward Mt. Draakheda.

Rhesalus spoke inside my head. *"You'll fly beyond the highest peak in front of you. You'll know where you are when you arrive, and when you do, you'll need to take your passengers inside through another portal."*

If I hadn't known the truth, I couldn't have made any sense of what he'd just said; but I did and wished that, rather than portalling while flying, I could just portal directly to the cavern. It would save so much time. But I couldn't. I needed to pretend I'd never been there.

I didn't need to pretend amazement when I again laid eyes on my dreams-come-to-life mountain, the desolate village, and the ocean beyond it. Tears stung anew at the devastation that had happened here. In awe, Zahra—having observed The Keeper in our tent every night since leaving Kildaria—pointed out what she recognized of the area and voiced her disappointment at seeing the real village destroyed.

Fear of trying to portal while flying had Terius demanding I pay attention and follow his instructions carefully. Thankfully, it worked. I opened the portal in the middle of the bones of the dead dragons— in my opinion a fitting place considering this reunion between these monsters and the proof of the carnage they'd inflicted.

I summoned mage light, supposing they hoped to amaze me with the genuine cavern inside the real-life Mt. Draakheda. I wondered if they'd be amazed when they saw what I'd done to the genuine doors to their real-life laboratory.

Zahra blanched at her surroundings, the huge pinions scarring the wide wall to the north of us, the chains that hung down from them like vipers made of iron links. The bones that lay in heaps in some places, in others rising from the cavern floor like the bars of ossein cages.

"Your legacy," I said to the sorcerers with disgust when I set them free.

"Forget it," Terius said, waving a hand at the cavern's magical door. It slid open, allowing normal light and fresh air inside. Still, he summoned mage light and signaled me to follow him to the laboratory. Zahra gave me a nod of encouragement. She would take care of Gideon.

When the sorcerers saw the enchanted doors reduced to nothing but scarred rock, Rhesalus and Terius turned on me, accusation burning in their eyes. I realized I'd become too comfortable with lying when I played the innocent, asking them what was wrong, but at least they didn't destroy me on the spot.

Still, they whispered to each other, Moriana reminding them that she'd only visited the laboratory through dreamwalking before being imprisoned inside The Keeper. She couldn't possibly have destroyed the doors. But if I'd done it, how had I breached their wards?

Avoiding their glares, I pointed at the stream that trickled through the cavern. "I was a snake here. You made me into a snake," I accused Terius. "When I was held in King Desmond's tower, you brought me here and changed me into a snake. I climbed up that tunnel to the top of the mountain, where I found a rabbit."

Terius snarled at me, his features sharpened by the shadows so deep inside the cavern. "Where did those doors go? How did you break them?"

I snorted in disgust. "If I'm strong enough to break down doors, maybe I don't need you anymore, sorcerer. Or perhaps I do because enemies stronger than you have found your lair."

He reminded me of a hooded cobra, arched and on the verge of striking. Then Rhesalus spoke.

"I think she's telling the truth, Terius. This must have happened ages ago. There's no trail of magic and neither dust nor footprints on the floor."

Terius glared at me but abandoned his attack. "The minute we're free, we'll need to ward it better. Who else might find their way here and steal our work?"

"Perhaps you should see if anything's missing," Moriana prompted, and I remained behind in the dark as the threesome hurried into the laboratory, their mage light brightening the room. The clunking of books being tossed around punctuated their frustrated conversation.

"It's all here," I heard Terius say with amazed suspicion. "Why break in to take nothing?"

"How odd," Moriana said.

"Where did I put it?" Rhesalus muttered several times. Then "Ah. Here it is." His ball of light sailed ahead of him as he left the laboratory and hurried past me carrying the book *Healing*. Moriana and Terius followed.

Reaching Gideon and Zahra, Rhesalus stopped to thumb through the book, his compatriots hovering over his shoulders. Zahra scuttled away, her terrified gaze pinned on the sorcerers.

When it seemed Rhesalus had found the right page, he held his free hand above the book and spoke words in the Language. The book snapped shut and transformed into a small, shallow box. He opened the cover, and I gave a soft gasp as he removed something small, as white as snow, and pointed. I'd been holding a magical book that was more than a book. And it contained a shard of unicorn horn!

The shock and fury burst deep inside me. "You knew Moriana had no answer, and you already have a unicorn horn? If you thought it could help him, why did you leave my prince to suffer and maybe die? Tell me the truth, or I'll do as I threatened."

Rhesalus sighed. "She's still learning, Theona, just as you are. And as you may have noted, unicorn horns wear down with use. We hoped to not need it, because we *will* need it when we face the Alliance."

"But you ignored me when I called for help."

He nodded. "Yes. And I regret it. We all do. Moriana needed to try her hardest. If I could do it over...."

He shook his head and set the book on the floor; then he knelt beside Gideon, ripping Gideon's shirt from his shoulder, and let the Language roll from his lips with precision and authority. He then touched the very tip of the white horn against the angry, oozing wound.

I held my breath, both wondering what would happen and amazed I'd understood Rhesalus. I'd learned more of the Language than I'd realized.

Even unconscious, Gideon responded with rasping moans. Blood began seeping in narrow rivulets from the wound that had once been prematurely healed, opened again, and then partially cauterized by the electric shock between Siddarth's horn and the fresh Dreamwood.

In the center of the black triangle, the skin began to split, the translucent, shining tip of the black horn nosing its way outward, as if drawn to the white one like a magnet. It was only half the size it had been, seemingly fragile, like blown glass.

The moment I saw it, I felt an odd kinship with it—as if in having touched it I'd befriended it. I yearned to Call it. Why now? Why not before?

"Hold on, young man," Rhesalus mumbled to Gideon. "The poison's magic is powerful and it's fighting me."

The sorcerer pulled hard on the white horn, the black one attached to it, but it followed reluctantly. Gradually, the black shard edged most of the way out. Gideon shook, his fists clenched, his moans rising to cries. I could barely remain still. Rhesalus's arms bunched as he struggled. The look on his face told me that he hadn't expected such a fight. When both horn fragments began to glow, I blinked. Did Rhesalus not see it? Why did he hold only the white horn? He should be holding both pieces. Wait. Where had I gotten those thoughts?

Uninvited, words floated through my mind and seeped into my veins, and I raised my hands and whispered, barely noticing Rhesalus's sharp glance. For a brief second, the sorcerer lost his concentration, and the poison ichor took advantage of it, snatching the black horn back inside the wound—and the tip of the white one as well. Gideon shuddered and, without thinking, I shouldered Rhesalus aside and took hold of the white horn—although my magic was centered on the black one. When I Called it, it came so quickly and easily that it shoved the white fragment into my hand and made me stumble back. Suddenly, something popped, like a cork from a wine bottle, and Gideon cried out as the black horn burst from the wound. I gagged, first at the wretched stench and then by what followed, something like thick, dark smoke snagged between the horn and Gideon's wound, alive and thrashing.

The enchanted poison!

What should I do now? The strength I'd felt faded, and so did my hold.

Shouting a warning, Rhesalus snatched the horns from me and pulled them until the poisonous strand was stretched tight. Again chanting the Language, he pulled harder and harder. Gideon arched his back as if trying to break himself in half, but Rhesalus grabbed the shadow with one hand, like catching a fly, and jerked it hard. The poisonous mass broke off with a snap.

Gideon lurched then lay still. The shadow in Rhesalus's hand flailed like a suffocating animal, and then it went limp, like a dead rat hung by its tail. At last, it disintegrated into a fine mist and drifted away.

I dropped to my knees beside Gideon, relieved to see him breathing so easily. I stroked his stubbly cheek and found his fever gone, and then rested my hand on the wound and wept when I could see no trace of the poison inside him. Bowing my head in gratitude, I poured my powers into healing the wound. In minutes, nothing remained but new pink skin and a small scar.

"He'll live," Terius barked. "Let's go. We've more work to do."

"No," I snapped. "I need food and I won't do anything until Prince Gideon is conscious."

Terius made a face, but Rhesalus sighed in submission. "Moriana, feed them all. Theona does need the energy for what comes next."

Moriana narrowed her eyes in irritation but did as bid, conjuring an entire meal on chargers and cool water in silver goblets. My mouth watered at seeing and smelling it, and the scent seemed to rouse Gideon, too. He opened his eyes and looked around in confusion, sitting up slowly and touching his chest in amazement.

"Gideon!" I cried, tears in my eyes. I threw my arms around him, so very glad to see him already looking a thousand percent better. He pulled me tight and rocked me, prickling the curve of my neck with his coarse beard.

"Where are we?" he asked.

I opened my mouth to answer and then laughed. "It's a long story—"

"And one you don't have time to tell right now," Terius growled.

Gideon started. "Who are you?" he asked.

"Gideon," I warned him to silence. I shook my head and handed him one of the chargers, urging him to eat before hearing the explanations. All three of us dove into our meals, my body desperate to make up for the magic I'd used.

Gideon still looked gaunt, but his appetite was excellent. When he'd devoured enough to again care about our surroundings, he paused mid-chew.

"Are we...?" He swallowed. "Are we dreamwalking in The Keeper?"

"No. This is real."

"But—but this is the cave inside Mt. Draakheda, is it not?"

"Yes, but we're not dreamwalking. We're inside Mt. Draakheda. The real Mt. Draakheda."

His eyes rounded. "And where is Mt. Draakheda?"

"In the Lost Lands. On the south side of the Great Chasm."

He fished for a response, then shook his head in disbelief. "This feels too much like the nightmares I had after being struck by the lance." He touched his chest again. "I remember it hitting me and almost falling off Valere. Then...I remember flying." He tipped his head. "Flying somewhere on Valere's back."

"No, you were on mine."

"What?"

"I shape-changed into a winged horse that looked like Valere—to make you feel more comfortable. I wasn't sure you noticed."

"But that means...."

"Yes. We left the horses behind. Hamar warriors were chasing us, my prince. We'd have either been captured or killed." I hated seeing the sorrow in his eyes. "I'm so sorry, Gideon. If I could have done otherwise, I would."

"I understand. But why do I remember a smaller cave, with a fire near the mouth? And fish stew. And berries. My mind was heavy, as if I'd taken a sleeping draught and couldn't shake it off. The pain was unbearable."

He touched the fine, white scar again, amazed to see himself healed. "You did this."

I shook my head. "As much of it as I could. One of the sorcerers, Rhesalus, helped." I nodded toward him. Gideon stared in disbelief at all three of the sorcerers.

"This is them?"

"Yes."

He paused to consider what I'd said. "But what of the other cave?"

"Our camp. We'll return there to gather our things before joining the army."

"If any of them survived."

"I believe some did," I reassured him.

"Theona," Terius insisted.

"We'll talk later," I promised Gideon. "For now, I must do something else. Stay here and rest. You're healed, but the fatigue will last until your body has recovered from the shock."

"*Now*, Theona," Rhesalus said, reaching for my arm. "We've work to do."

Gideon glared at him, but I smiled at my prince. "The Lost Lands are a place of incredible power, Your Highness. Secrets have been concealed here for ages, like this cave. It truly is the birthplace of the dragons. I'll share more later, but trust me, nothing we've experienced all these years has happened by accident."

"What do you want with her?" Gideon demanded of Rhesalus.

I replied for the sorcerer, "I suspect they think I'm ready to learn how to restore their bodies and return them to mortality."

The Recreation of Mortality.

I flinched, disturbed by the memory of the title of a book, along with another: *Linking Souls*. They meant nothing to me in my dream, but now? The re-creation of their mortal bodies was exactly what the sorcerers wanted to accomplish, and that book likely contained the incantations for doing so. I supposed *Linking Souls* also bore the secret for binding their *rumorias* to those bodies.

Gideon's face crumpled in disapproval. "No, Theona, you can't. That's what the sorcerers wanted Moriana to do. The Elds forced her into The Keeper to stop her."

Moriana's mocking laughter sent chills down my spine. "That they did, Mallorian prince."

"I know," I said, "but in their own bodies, they'll no longer possess me, which frees all of us." I grabbed his hand and kissed it as I Mind-Paired, *"I've my own plans, Gideon. Please trust me."*

I only had varying suspicions and a meager gathering of details that hinted at what I might someday do to foil the sorcerers, but I had to keep them to myself for now.

Gideon responded, "The vision of us fighting together warns me the world we know depends upon us."

My eyesight abruptly faded as a scene unfolded, tinged with the dark orange of prophecy. The army! I could see it in an unfamiliar place with unseen spies not far from them.

"Hurry!" the Voice whispered in my mind. *"Their enemies hunt them! They need you!"*

"Has a ghost stepped o'er your grave, my lady?" Zahra asked. "You look dreadfully pale."

"I'm fine," I lied, shaking myself out of the fugue.

"And I'm out of patience," Terius snapped.

I glared at him.

"She's the key to everything we need to accomplish, old friend," Rhesalus told Terius. "Please don't drive my—" he paused on the edge of saying "mage partner" when I gave him a deadly look. Grinning, he said instead, "the girl too hard. She needs time to develop the mettle necessary for when things get...difficult."

Difficult? How much more difficult could things get than this?

"She's ready now or she isn't," Terius retorted. He snapped his fingers and two books appeared. He handed one to Rhesalus, and the two sorcerers grinned and opened them.

CHAPTER 20

I cringed at the sight of *The Recreation of Mortality's* ugly brown cover and *Linking Souls'* dirty yellow one, the books I'd seen in my dream. The male sorcerers spent several minutes pouring over them, then handed them to Moriana. Rhesalus grinned; Terius rubbed his hands together.

"Good to refresh the memory. Now, let our fun begin," he said with a grin, heading to the end of the cavern opposite the laboratory and beyond the stalagmites, where the rock floor lay barren.

Rhesalus waved a hand to encourage me to follow, but I swallowed a lump in my throat when Zahra helped a determined Gideon to his feet. Moriana's smile mocked me with its display of needle-fine teeth. If I resisted, she had claws to match the teeth—and she might not use them on me.

"It's time to Call a snake," Terius announced. "The largest one you can find."

My heart sank. Now? *Linking Souls.* My beloved prince and my warrior-maid would never look at me the same after today. *Linking Souls.*

"I'm so tired," I said, near tears. Maybe Rhesalus would have pity on me.

Rhesalus's hooded gaze disturbed me. He had no pity, but he was smart enough to compromise. "She's used a lot of power, my friend. You should bring the snake."

Terius made a face but turned toward the cavern's doorway, the Language flowing from his mouth in a hypnotic, measured intonation with practiced grace. I felt the ripple in the air and saw the brief flash of baby blue light that meant he'd created a Calling.

A long, shrill screech preceded an eagle sweeping into the cavern, carrying an enormous, reticulated serpent. Zahra moaned long and low and ducked behind the prince. Gideon's eyes, rounded with shock, caught mine. He couldn't believe what he was seeing. The bird dropped its catch to the floor, the snake snapping itself into a defensive coil, its tongue darting in and out in fear. The eagle screeched its fury and fled.

"'Twill eat us, my lady," Zahra whimpered.

"No, Zahra. It's not big enough for that, and it isn't hungry."

"Are you sure?"

"Absolutely."

He was, however, angry enough to bite. I kept that fact, and that of his gender, to myself. I still didn't want the sorcerers to know I understood the connection between the dragons and their victims. I prepared to call Ramah, but Terius put up a hand.

"No, no, dear. No dragons this time."

This caught me off-guard, and my surprise made all three sorcerers laugh.

Terius waved *Linking Souls* at me and said, "Now that Rhesalus and I have refreshed our memories, we're ready to practice Linking."

Beyond angry, I asked, "If you can Link the dragons, why do you need me?"

Again, they laughed.

"That's not what we meant," Rhesalus said. "You're going to Link *Terius* with the snake."

White-hot terror shot through me as everything suddenly snapped into place. If I could successfully Link Terius to this snake, then I was ready to Link him to his re-created form. All that was left was to unlock *The Recreation of Mortality's* secret of how to conjure bodies for these monsters.

As shameful as it was, I wished something would go wrong today and Terius would die with the snake.

"Don't worry, Theona," Rhesalus said, approaching me. He seemed taller, leaner, even younger than before, and, heaven forbid, even more attractive than ever. "Remember, the risk is to the snake, not to you or Terius. Not if you do it correctly."

And if I failed and anything happened to me, Gideon was here. I understood the threat too well.

I approached the huge constrictor in trepidation, Terius beside me. The snake's tongue flicked, and he tightened his coils at sensing my presence. He'd fed recently and was sleepy and frightened and angry at having his hibernation disturbed.

The hateful magical ring shocked my ring finger, and I jerked my Dreamwood bracelet off to see it. Two horseshoe-shaped lines coalesced on the ring's surface, making absolutely no sense. I struggled for meaning and failed. Then they turned into almond shapes—and blinked at me. Eyes! Then they closed, as if in sleep.

Sleep! My chest swelled with the sudden revelation. Why had I never considered it before? As I'd put numerous guards and Kendal Tavish to sleep, I could sedate this poor creature so it wouldn't fight us so much—if at all.

I utilized that pale silver *parhelia* connected to the power of sedation, and the snake's head lowered, his entire body relaxing. Easing closer, I reached for his *rumoria* and prepared to connect with Terius.

Terius gave me a wicked grin, turned a translucent white, and stormed through me like a gale-force wind. The pain staggered me, and I gasped. Arms enfolded me from behind—Gideon's—and he hugged me tight. Knowing what came next, I begged him to let go and stand with Zahra. I didn't want him hurt.

Linking a human to the serpent felt completely different. Harder in some ways, easier in others. Unlike the dragons, Terius could—and did—help with the Language, which strengthened my efforts and eased the burden. Rhesalus and Moriana stood fascinated, knowing this moment was a turning point.

Lethargy made the serpent's struggles against the invasion useless. It writhed and flipped over several times, grinding the back of its head into the cave floor, but it was brief. When it rested, I heard sighs of anticipation escape the sorcerers. Terius had taken over.

I felt numb inside. Why hadn't the sorcerers suggested sedating the animals from the beginning, especially the horses? Some of my unfortunate victims might have survived the exercise. The thought sickened me worse than before.

The snake's body shifted then shortened and thickened quickly. Buds became appendages, and its head began to change. I held my breath in horrified amazement as the snake absorbed its tail, rose on two legs, stretched out its growing arms, and became...*him*. A man. Terius, in the flesh, and garbed in the same clothes he always wore.

Moriana laughed and ran to wrap her arms around him. The sorcerer's eyes smoldered with triumph, and he crowed, "It worked!"

Rhesalus agreed, grinning at me. "Excellent, my dear. You did it."

Gideon stared at me as if he'd never seen me before and Zahra buried her face in her hands.

Moriana offered the sorcerer a kiss, but disappointment dampened their joy.

"I can hardly feel you," he murmured.

She nodded, admitting she couldn't feel him at all. Terius was now mortal, no matter how temporarily, and Moriana had no corporeal being and most of the senses that went with it. He let her go and focused on walking around the cavern, carefully at first; and then he began to cavort like a child, spinning, jumping, and laughing.

"Marvelous!" he cried to his companions. "No wonder the dragons don't want to come out. I feel so—at home! We must hurry to do this right."

I frowned hard at him. "Why can't you just keep this body?"

He grinned his wickedest grin. "A human *rumoria* isn't at home in a snake's body, dear girl. It's another type of possession. If I stayed, I'd struggle with the snake's temperament every day and could lose my humanity in the process. When you produce our human bodies, we'll be able to stay."

My heart shrank at this declaration. If I failed, I might never rid myself of these monsters, but I also wished I could avoid it forever. Who needed them loose in the world again?

"Come, come," Rhesalus told Terius. "We've more to do, and you mustn't tax Theona unnecessarily."

My opinion echoed his. Terius came out of the snake with ease, and this time Rhesalus snapped his fingers and provided me with another plate of food, which I bolted down.

"On to our next adventure," Rhesalus said, a gleam in his eye. "Theona, I want you to Link me with a horse."

I stared him in confusion. "There aren't any horses here. Leastways not that I've seen."

He smirked. "Ah, but you know what does live here, now don't you?"

My face went cold, and I nearly lost my lunch. No. Never. Not in a million years. Not if I had to die to prevent it.

"I will never Link you to a unicorn."

"You'll do as your told, my dear—"

"Let her be!" Gideon growled. I grabbed his hand, urging him to stay quiet.

"You have no say, princeling—" Moriana began.

"She's my wife and I do have a say. The evil all three of you have wrought in this world is infamous, and mark my words, I'll do all I can to help Theona destroy you."

Terius laughed. "Hmmm. Such brave words, Prince Gideon Seville. But rather than hurting us, I can see a future in which you'll help us."

"Never."

"Take us to the unicorns," Rhesalus insisted, his gaze hardening. "Now."

My legs shaking from anger and fear, I made my decision. Consequences be hanged. "No," I replied, and I glanced at Gideon as I sent the sorcerers away.

Gideon wrapped his arms around me to steady me. I could see the uneasiness in his eyes and knew he didn't like anything he'd just witnessed. For whatever reason, he kept it to himself and murmured, "You've circles under your eyes, Love. You need sleep."

"Soon, but I have to take care of a couple of things first."

I began with the snake. Shaking off its stupor, the creature began unwinding itself and sliding across the floor. Trembling, Zahra stared at it as if she could set it on fire with her eyes. I called the serpent and sent it away, praying it would find a good life elsewhere.

"Thank you, my lady," Zahra said, sagging as she let out the breath she'd been holding.

"Please wait here," I asked them. "I need to fetch a few things from the laboratory." I also felt they needed distance from me to absorb what they had just witnessed.

On the way, I collected *Healing* from the floor. It was still in box form, and I opened it. To my surprise, both unicorn horns sat inside! How had Rhesalus done that?

Now I remembered what Siddarth had told me. That I'd return to him as soon as I knew the reason for the crossing of our paths. I knew.

I gathered the shards, finding them so beautiful I could hardly imagine letting go of them. I slipped them into my tunic pocket, opposite the Dreamwood, and closed the book. It flattened in my hands, and peeking beneath the cover, I smiled at seeing the pages returned to their proper place.

Although I hated touching them, I also gathered *The Recreation of Mortality* and *Linking Souls* from where they'd fallen from Moriana's hands. Hurrying to the laboratory, I set all of them on one of the tables, beside *Eblis's Finest Children* and *The Perfect Birthright.* The hair raised on my neck at the sensation they were watching me. Considering the lot of them, I wished I could destroy all but *Healing.* I'd read bits of *Finest Children* and *Birthright* while dreamwalking but had, of course, never opened the other two. I couldn't help my curiosity.

I couldn't open *Mortality.* It reeked of arcane magic and was likely sealed with it. I had no idea how to create a human body, but given its title, I again supposed this book held such secrets. I had no desire to learn them. There could be nothing divine about them.

In contrast, *Linking,* which I imagined worked with *Mortality,* opened as if it welcomed me. I meant to read only a few pages, but there weren't more than twenty in the entire thing, and after I'd finished it, I tried to destroy it. I sought Fire, but it wouldn't burn. I called water and tried to ruin the ink that scarred the pages; it did no harm. I tried to tear it apart and found the pages impossibly strong.

I even dared grab the shears that had most likely cut monstrous things in half, but they could neither sever the cover nor cut even one of the pages. I threw it to the ground and stomped on it, but when I picked it up, it still looked newly bound.

"Theona, what are you doing?"

I jumped. Gideon stood in the doorway beside Zahra, shock on their faces. I huffed in surprise and pushed loose wisps of hair from my face.

"Wishing to destroy something that seems utterly indestructible."

Zahra came to look at the book. "It's magical?"

"Yes. And wicked. No one should ever use this book again." Again? Had it been used before? I feared my sorcerers couldn't take nearly as much credit for the evil they'd wrought as people gave them. This book and its companion had likely been written and used by sorcerers older and perhaps more wicked than they. "But I've no idea how to get rid of it."

"What's in it?" asked Gideon.

"I'll not speak of it. And no one should open it. Ever. It's enchanted." Not entirely true, but I'd rather frighten them than have them endure the revulsion and fear I felt at this moment. Gideon's scruffy cheeks lost most of their color. He remembered the other two books and the horrors they contained. No doubt he understood my agitation if this one was worse than those.

"Perhaps you should drop it in the ocean?" Zahra suggested.

I shook my head. "There are spells bound to it that I suspect would somehow bring it back to land. It mustn't fall into hands worse than my own."

"You're taking it with you?" Gideon asked.

"All of them. I have no choice. If I have them then no one else can get them." Besides, I believed the sorcerers would send me back for them if I didn't.

Without warning, a terrible pressure seized me, the flavor of magic enveloping me. I staggered against the table, and then the Voice touched my mind, bringing me an incredible sense of peace, a balm to my spirit.

"You must defend the defenders," it whispered.

"The defenders?" I thought. I had no notion what that meant, but I gave my solemn promise.

"Are you alright, Theona?" Gideon asked.

"Just a bit of a headache. Let's get out of this place," I said, grabbing the books and heading toward the cavern's mouth.

I was again amazed by the vista outside, looking just the same— and yet completely different. Gideon, seeing it for the first time in his right mind, uttered his shock. "What in the world? What happened to Draakheda Village?"

As expected, his response echoed mine. The mountain, the sea, and the surrounding terrain had changed little; but the fields and crops were as dead as the people in the village, and the village itself was little more than a sad reminder of a once lovely and joyful place.

"Theona, how could we dreamwalk through a town that doesn't exist anymore?"

Before I could answer, the Voice took hold of me again, and through me said, *"This, dear child, is where your sorcerers first gained control of mankind. It is also here that they became three of the most dangerous sorcerers of all time."*

Instantly, a scene came to life in the valley below. The village in its prime, just as I remembered it, blind to the arcane workings hidden in the mountain's cave and carrying on with everyday life. And then, one day, a mythical creature fractured reality and sprang from the mountain top, bearing the sorcerers—Terius, Rhesalus, and Pythius— on her back. I could hear the screams, see the people panicking.

The scene shifted. Was it months later? Perhaps years? Now there were dozens of dragons, and the populace stood in endless lines, their ankles and wrists chained together, trudging slowly up the mountain. Parts of the town were leveled, fires burned in various places, and wails of grief surrounded me.

"What happened?" I asked the Voice.

"Those without magic worked to feed everyone. Those unable or unwilling became fodder for the Mother dragon and her offspring. The people gifted with magic were apprenticed to the sorcerers and then became the test subjects used to attempt blending humankind and dragons."

None of them survived it, but the sorcerers believed success was near when Cleary put an end to their reign. As I'd seen before, prior to marrying Gideon, I envisioned a world in which Terius, Rhesalus, and now Moriana prepared to apply the process to each other. If they succeeded, they would rule the world in sorcerer-dragon terror, taking, using, and destroying whatever they wished.

Gideon leaned into me and moaned, his face marred with despair, which pulled me out of the vision.

"What a terrible hallucination I've just had. I saw the sorcerers enthralling Draakheda's population and experimenting on them."

"I saw it, too," Zahra added, a hand pressed to her head as if it hurt.

"As did I," I said, grateful to not have to bear this alone. "I know you're both leery of my association with the sorcerers and I don't blame you. I feel the same. Unfortunately, mages aligned with the Central Alliance are supporting the war, and we cannot beat them without my sorcerers' help. If we fail, yesterday's past could become our future."

"Then we must face the hard things so that we can do our best to save the world," Gideon said with solemnity. I touched his face in gratitude.

I offered a faint smile but added, "I'm afraid I have one more thing to do before we head to our cave. It's in a place not far from here. You'll understand when you see it." I flinched when those familiar words came out of my own mouth.

I entrusted the books to Gideon and assumed my winged-horse self. He and Zahra climbed aboard, and I launched out of the cavern headed northward. It was Gideon's first time to fly when fully aware, and I smiled inwardly his amazement.

———┼—

I stood on a low knoll in knee-high grass, Gideon and Zahra on either side of me. They gaped, awestruck, at the meadow in what I'd named the Valley of the Unicorns, filled with grazing unicorns.

"Please stay close to me," I whispered to my companions. "I've no idea how they'll receive you."

Siddarth's head sprang up in alarm when we came down the hill. With a snort and a soft whinny, he headed toward us, Naja and Anshu on either side of him. The mares and foals surrounded us as they had done to me before.

Gideon took my hand, no fear in his eyes, only amazement. Zahra murmured her disbelief, the light in her eyes bordering on reverence. I introduced my companions, and Siddarth dipped his head in greeting.

"Welcome, Theona and Theona's mate and her companion. It is good you saved your Gideon, Theona. I see he is troubled but his loyalty shines within him. Warrior Zahra, may the Great Skyllia strengthen you to guard your mistress against the darkest of arts." Then to me, he added, "Have you discovered the reason for the crossing of our paths?"

"Yes, I believe so," I replied. "For one thing, I need to thank you for saving Gideon."

He snorted. "Another helped you."

I nodded. "Yes, but I'll not speak of him." Rhesalus might have been indispensable, but I would give him no more credit than was necessary. "In gratitude, I've brought you something I think is important," I said.

I pulled the horns from my pocket and dropped to one knee, presenting them as one would to a king. Most appropriate since he was a king.

Siddarth's eyes widened in amazement, and he neighed over his right shoulder. A tall white mare not far behind him moved forward, a foal as black as Siddarth at her side. The foal, as hornless as his dam, peeked around her forequarters, his large, liquid brown eyes curious. Both animals were incredibly beautiful, but without horns, they looked…wrong.

At sight of the horns in my hand, the mare's legs nearly went out from under her. Siddarth leaned into her to hold her up.

"You've offered us an unparalleled gift," Siddarth said with huskiness. "I care not how you found it, but the horn is hers. I regret that this gift requires I ask for another."

"Anything that is in my power to grant."

Siddarth sniffed noses with the mare and then said, "This is Puritasia, the First Mate of my heart. Her horn was taken and broken into pieces, along with many other unicorns', by your sorcerers hundreds of years ago. She is the only survivor—a rarity—but a unicorn without a horn produces young whose horns cannot bud."

My sorcerers had done this? They truly were monsters. I thought Rhesalus callous when he said unicorns had vanished because they were overly gentle creatures—as if they were foolish. But this? I clenched my teeth against the outrage.

Siddarth continued. "This is a foaling year; it will be half a century before another one. All the unicorns you see here without horns are mine and Puritasia's. If her horn can be restored, the magical barrier against our offspring may be lifted, but rarely can the restoration happen. We have no way to hold the horn in place."

My spirits soared with excitement. "I can hold it for her," I said.

He nodded, and a solemn mood filled the meadow. Gideon, Zahra and I watched in fascination as every creature, even the foals, pushed a left foot forward and sank to the right knee, heads bowed and horn tips—those who had them—buried in the earth. As the stallion explained what to do, I pressed the wide end of the white horn fragment firmly against the scar on Puritasia's forehead.

The horn felt as cold and lifeless as stone. When I'd begun to fear nothing would happen, I felt something strange under my feet, an aura of strengthening that I supposed came from the herd—or perhaps from the very earth itself. The grass began to grow, the tentacles rising high enough to grasp my ankles but no further.

Light flickered inside the white horn, and its surface tingled. Puritasia grumbled and then squealed, her pale blue eyes squeezed tight with pain. Afraid for her, I sent my healing power to comfort her as the horn began to attach to her brow. It grew warmer and larger and longer, spiraling outward as it lengthened—and inward as it anchored itself. Blood, bright red, ran from beneath it and down her snow-white face. She trembled, sweat breaking out on her neck and shoulders and running in rivulets down her forelegs. Her nostrils flared and she grunted every time she took a breath, a testament to her suffering.

As I fought to help heal the wound and dampen her discomfort, a faint sheen of indigo light crept across her brow and down to the end of the horn. It seemed the process would never end, but finally, Puritasia calmed and chuffed in relief. She stepped back from me, the blue glow of healing fading. Her horn had reattached!

In a deep, pleasant voice, she said, "Thank you, human. My debt to you is *siderial.*"

Siderial? It meant…manifold, almost insurmountable, as lofty as the stars.

"You owe me nothing. I am indebted to you and Siddarth for my mate's life," I replied. "I'm grateful I could help you."

She gave me a low, half-whinny laced with humor. "Kindness from a human. Strange. You not only returned Siddarth's horn and mine, but you also helped restore mine. I owe you a personal debt, but you have excused it. Such a thing rarely happens. Never in my lifetime, which has been long—and will be longer still if Creation's Author so decrees it."

Puritasia raised her head proudly, and light flared from her horn so bright that even in late afternoon it hurt my eyes. The mare bugled loudly, and the others joined her, all rising to their hind legs and pawing the air. Siddarth squealed his joy to her, and the two stroked their horns against each other in a peculiar form of affection. Was it only my imagination, or did both creatures have tears in their eyes? Zahra looked frightened, Gideon amazed, but I wanted to cry with the unicorns.

CHAPTER 21

Hunger nipped at me. Moriana had fed us not long ago, but I'd used a great deal of magic since.

"We must go," I told both my two- and four-legged friends. "I pray your herd will remain safe here, Siddarth."

"I wish it were so," said Siddarth. "We did not meet by chance, and we shall meet again, because your undertaking is not yours alone. Allow your sorcerers their delusion that they brought you here for their own purposes. They didn't. The Great Skyllia, Creation's Author, sent you. Had the Author not wanted you here, you could not have come—especially along with your evil companions. Likewise, you could not leave until you'd discovered everything you needed to know, especially the depth of your sorcerers' evil. You cannot save everyone from the cataclysm soon to come, but you are now better prepared for it. Keep my horn. When you need our help, hold it between your hands and call my name. We will come."

"We?" I questioned, startled.

"Yes. Our entire herd."

"Why?"

"I have seen the *Telling*," he reminded me. "When the time is right, you will know. Woman of Magic, you cannot fight the enemy alone, and we owe you *guerdon*."

Guerdon was the payment of a debt.

"You owe me nothing," I insisted.

"You returned both Puritasia's horn and mine unrequested, which has not happened to our herd in my lifetime. You helped restore Puritasia's horn and relieved the pain that can kill. Puritasia's debt is personal. When she acknowledged that debt and you forgave it, *guerdon* became required from the entire clan. Thus, I make an oath that when the time comes, our clan, *cland sincerus raimum*, will stand with you against those who would destroy you and the entire world."

My feeble "Thank you" felt paltry. I offered it anyway as I tucked the horn fragment back into my pocket.

"This is such a strange place," I murmured to myself. "Mt. Draakheda and all its mysteries, unicorns, a Dreamwood forest."

If a unicorn—like a dragon—could be said to smile, he did. "The core of this land and the source of its magic is the Dreamwood forest. Its roots connect everyone and everything, even the land and our magic, to them, and us to each other. Few have come here over the centuries and the Land has allowed fewer past its wards until now."

"That's why I couldn't find game when we first came here."

"Yes. The Ring of Brothers drew you to them to gauge your magic. Along the way, they found you True, allowed you nourishment, and gave you the sliver of Dreamwood. Then the Author directed your path to the Great Mountain, knowing it was best for you to discover it on your own."

The Ring of Brothers? The circle of Dreamwood Trees I'd stepped inside? Amazing. Why had I been allowed this honor?

I gave him a deep bow, both in gratitude and farewell. "I am glad to have met you, Siddarth."

"As am I to have met you, Princess of Malloria. Until we meet again, may your meadows be sweet, your skies blue, and your heart full of hope."

I changed back into my Pegasus form and my companions climbed aboard, silent with amazement. I heard laughter in my mind and glanced at Siddarth.

"You will one day see them, too," the stallion whispered into my thoughts. *"The winged-horse will come again."*

I nodded, remembering the words Eld Tully had spoken in Kildaria's temple, and then I turned on my heels and cantered a short distance away before leaping into the sky and heading northward. Prince Gideon and Zahra remained pensive, no doubt trying to come to terms with everything they'd seen and heard.

Without the sorcerers' support, I would again need to alternate flying with portalling, but it came easier now, both from experience and without interference, and now that Gideon was safe.

I found myself in a predicament, however, when evening came and my companions needed food as much as I did. I'd reached a long, narrow valley filled with antelope and other game—but also many dangerous predators. Grazing would take too long and hunting in smaller forms put me at risk, even as a snake. Here, I would be safest as a dragon; but Gideon and Zahra would see me, and not only might it be too much for them, I risked the sorcerers learning of it through them.

An odd sense of guilt tightened my throat, a fleeting thought that spurred me to offer a prayer to Elam. What should I do, I asked? Not that I expected a quick answer. But the fluttering of impressions that danced through my mind warned me that it was another betrayal to hide the truth from Gideon. As for Zahra, she was a warrior. She would know to keep her tongue, but more than that, I had no right to expect them to risk their lives for me without knowing that truth.

I landed not far from the herd of antelope and let my riders alight.

"I'm afraid I must hunt again, but this place is different so I must hunt differently." I explained the risks I faced with each of the various shape-shifted forms I could take. "I can, however, shape-change into something that no normal predator can harm. No one knows about it, especially the sorcerers—and they must never learn of it. If they did, there would be terrible consequences. They can read your minds, so you must never think about it, especially in their presence."

"I've seen enough miracles today to trust whatever tell me, Theona," Gideon encouraged. "Do as you must."

I wanted to cry, but I had to remain strong. My beloved's support meant everything in the world to me, but he hadn't yet seen what I would show him. "I will, but I forewarn you that it may shock you, perhaps even offend you. I hope you'll understand the advantages soon enough."

I pointed at a nearby rock, flat and near hip height. "It's past suppertime. I'll do my best to leave you food to enjoy while I'm gone."

I'd never conjured a meal before but did well enough for them with fresh apples, spiced meat and onions, and boiled potatoes. Part of me wished the food would so engross them that they wouldn't watch me, but the additional power it took to provide the meal made me wild with hunger.

I overflew the antelope as a crow to avoid scaring them and, after choosing an older doe without a fawn, I summoned my magic and became what I needed to be. When satiated, I returned to Gideon and Zahra, hesitant at the shock on their faces. Gideon spoke first.

"That was almost as amazing as it was horrifying. You've been doing this all along, haven't you? Becoming a dragon and hunting for us, to keep us alive. I couldn't make sense of much while the poison held me captive, but I knew we always had food. I suppose I understood you could do it as both a person and an eagle but, in my wildest dreams, I could not have imagined you could do...this."

Zahra did nothing but stare at me.

Dread filled me, until a twinkle of mischief popped into Gideon's eyes. "I do have to admit I could almost feel sorry for your enemies."

Zahra laughed and I gave him a tight smile as he offered me a hug.

"I pray to never become your enemy, my lady," Zahra said with more hesitation.

"You are more than my maid, Zahra," I reassured her. "You are my friend."

She summoned a solemn smile, but the sparkle in her eyes reflected her pleasure. Hesitant but real.

From then on, I changed forms frequently from dragon to winged-horse, a much safer proposition for me. Portalling was easier and faster but required more rest afterward. Still, we reached our cave at dusk, all of us exhausted. A good night's rest would restore my magic and have us ready for tomorrow's search for our friends.

Gideon scratched his beard and sighed. "And maybe in the morning I can find my razor and rid myself of this itchy mess."

I laughed with him, kissing him and telling him I rather liked his manly scruffiness. We settled down to sleep, me cradled in Gideon's arms.

If only the evil books now sitting on the floor beside us hadn't whispered to me. I plugged my ears with my fingers, wishing I could burn all of them except for *Healing*. That one encouraged me. I reviewed some of what I'd already learned from it and in time drifted to sleep.

———

I slept well for the first time since Gideon's injury. We all did. A hearty breakfast used up a good part of the perishable foods I'd gathered that we couldn't take with us. We also took the time to bathe in the pond below the waterfall, which was a luxury, although Gideon's razor had been lost.

We filled our rucksacks, adding the remaining food. I even turned some of the boar into dried meat for them, to last until we found the army.

"Isn't this the shirt I was wearing when you removed the poison from me?" Gideon asked, ready to exchange it for a clean one after bathing.

"Yes. I repaired it."

He barked laughter. "Either you're an exceptional seamstress or you used magic. It looks good as new, despite the dirt. Why grow cotton fields or raise sheep if you can do this, my love?"

Incredulous, I said, "A population of a mere ten thousand would go naked for a while if I had to make one garment at a time by myself, and can you imagine the herds of sheep I'd have to eat to do it?"

He laughed again. "Good point! Better to sheer than to kill. Shall we go? I'm leery of the Voice's warning about the army. Today is the troops' sixth day in the Badlands, and if they're marching well, they should be on their way to the secret pass."

We needed to catch up with them before they entered the pass. Mallorian warriors would stay behind for several days to prevent anyone from following, and while they would welcome Gideon if they recognized him, they might attack us if they didn't.

Before leaving, we also discussed the dangers of using more magic than necessary while traveling near the Badlands. My shields remained locked against the sorcerers and would remain so until we'd left the Lost Lands and I no longer carried my precious cargo as a dragon—but that meant the mages couldn't protect me from other sorcerers, either.

"We still cannot Mind-Pair here," I said. "I suppose the Lost Lands prevent it. If the gift returns when we reach the mainland, I think we should use it sparingly and should likewise avoid contacting the army. If it's been captured by our enemies, we don't want to give ourselves away."

Agreed, Gideon and Zahra shouldered our sacks and climbed aboard my dragon neck. Securing them with magic, I sprang from the ledge.

I enjoyed Gideon and Zahra's excitement at soaring over the Great Chasm and seeing the crashing waves up close. The ability to Mind-Pair returned the moment we reached it, and I flinched when Zahra shrieked, *"Oh, my lady, the view from up here is brilliant!"*

"It is amazing," I replied, touched with a bit of homesickness for my seaside manor in Mithradell.

As I approached the northern cliff, however, something caught my eye and I gasped with excitement. Our saddles, blankets, and bridles! The Hamar warriors hadn't taken them!

I landed nearby, Gideon and Zahra crying out as well and jumping off so that I could shape-shift.

"Now all we need is our horses," Gideon said.

This all seemed too easy. Was this a trap of some sort? So many things I'd once considered coincidental or accidental now made me suspicious. If Siddarth were here, would he tell me that the Great Author had willed it? I didn't doubt Elam. Perhaps he was determined to guide me to wherever he needed me. A better thought than fearing the sorcerers were manipulating me, but did I dare trust any of this?

"The Hamars are a superstitious people, my lady," Zahra said. "Your transfiguration into a winged horse terrified them, and they likely considered our belongings cursed."

That made me chuckle. It made perfect sense. Scanning the horizon, I Searched for our horses but couldn't find them. Had our enemies captured them? Killed them? If, like most horses and dogs, they tried to run home, I doubted they'd survived.

Zahra and Gideon packed our bridles in our rucksacks, but what to do with the blankets and saddles? We tossed around ideas until Zahra suggested I shrink them small enough to saddle a rabbit. We laughed when it worked, and they stowed them as well.

We located the Badlands Route, hoping to find evidence of the army. From up high, it looked like a buff-colored ribbon laid across an endless sea of sand, but the faint stench of rotting carcasses turned us eastward. Of course, the road lay empty. Thankful for scales that protected me from the sun's sizzling rays, I flew lower and slowly enough to allow my companions to look for signs of the army.

"Some distance ahead, the road splits in three directions," Gideon Paired quickly. *"If the army survived the attack, Malloria would take the right-hand branch. If they were captured, we have no idea which way they went. Let's land at the fork to search for signs."*

A dust storm had indeed obliterated any proof the Forces had reached the fork, let alone which branch they might have taken or if they'd been captured. Gideon said that the two left-hand paths eventually cut northeast through the Badlands, one disappearing somewhere near southern Grimstaad, the other reaching southern Langala. The far righthand route continued eastward toward the

Beldames. In my dream, I'd felt prompted toward the right-hand branch, but knowing dreams were unpredictable, I dared not make assumptions. If the dream urging me to hurry meant our people were in dire circumstances, then wasted time might cost lives. Should I ask the sorcerers? They might answer, but they might also punish me for disobeying them. No. No sorcerers. Again I decided to zigzag over all three roads—as I'd done in the Lost Lands.

Flying further but making less forward progress, the stress of the heat, and the weight of my precious cargo required frequent rest and food, but finally, we caught sight of telltale wagon trails in patches of soft sand on the right-hand road. A large group had surely gone this way, but was it our people? Were they alone?

We combed the area for evidence of the United Forces. We found none, but my prince still felt certain we should travel only this road.

Sometime later, I saw a cluster of odd trees ahead and smelled water. It was a welcoming watering hole, couched behind scattered palms, sumac and mastic trees, and a variety of desert vegetation. Even better than that, just as I landed, Gideon saw something and jumped down to pick it up, a rectangular piece of green cloth. It was a flag that had torn loose and bore a blue star on a green background. Mithradell! It was from Father's troops. They'd come this way!

Ignoring the dirt, I buried my face in the flag and wept. It was like touching a piece of home and offered me hope. What a glorious thing was hope.

"Come, my sweet," he murmured. "Let's all rest in our little oasis for just a bit."

I checked the area for danger before allowing my companions to forge through the foliage. Finding it safe, I hunted as a small snake, and we relished the clean, fresh water and the shade. Then we rested beneath a sumac, and almost immediately I fell into a light sleep.

My adventures in the Lost Lands joined me there, followed by watching Gideon and myself dreamwalking in Draakheda. In the background, I heard Moriana's voice taunting me as she recited the unsettling words of the poem *"If wishes were horses, warriors would ride."*

How differently I saw that odd rhyme now.

At the very top of Mt. Draakheda, beside the sickly Dreamwood tree, Eld Tully appeared. His dark eyes pierced me as he repeated the words he'd announced to me—and only to me—in the temple before Gideon and I married.

"'Hearken ye people of Elam. Heed the prophecies of Elden kings. The day of reckoning shall be upon you when least expected; warlords and high magick will usher in the hour of mayhem and holy justice.

"'Great will be the slaughter in the land of the evil rulers, and the sword of Elam shall be smeared with blood; yeah, the land shall be made mire with rivers of blood.

"'And unicorns will come down with thee, and the children of the winged horse will be seen upon the earth again. Chariots shall be drawn by the fiery steeds of valiant rulers. The wild beasts and serpents of the land will gather to destroy the wicked.

"'Thorns shall come up in the palaces of the evil ones, nettles and brambles will choke their fortresses. Theirs shall be an habitation of dragons, and a court for owls.

"'Think not that Elam will side with thee blindly. The cowardly shall fail; the deaf ear shall fall to destruction. Only the work of the noble shall be sanctified, only the choices of the obedient servant. Hear oh beloved children, and Man shall rest in a place of virtuous habitation, and your kings and queens shall rule with honor.'"

With each line, I could almost—but not quite—see the prophetic visions behind them. I feared witnessing their fulfillment. Warlords? High magic? Herds of winged horses and unicorns ringing a killing field and ready to join the battle?

I couldn't have imagined either before. Now I could imagine them all too well. How could such creatures as wild beasts and serpents have the intelligence or the capacity for such a thing? How could briars destroy palaces and keeps? Why would dragons want to claim fortresses as their homes?

Siddarth's friend Anshu appeared in the dream and encased me in a grass-like spiderweb, a living tomb. Trembling in terror, I saw something gliding overhead and thought my heart would stop at seeing a ruby red dragon with someone on its back. I struggled but couldn't break free of my bonds.

The dragon landed. It was young and had eyes the color of fire. Its rider wore a conical helm and armor that seemed perfect for riding dragons. The warrior's gaze pierced me through the grating of his helm. He was a sorcerer! He, too, was young and powerful. Powerful enough to have recreated dragons?

Was this the future that awaited us? If so, we were doomed!

A voice whispered, but I didn't understand it, and the dragon disappeared. My grass-web receded, allowing me to breathe again. Then my angelic messenger, the man with the blue eyes I'd met in the temple, walked toward me, saying, "Never forget, Theona. Exoneration…is possible." He cast a hand behind himself, and grassy plains appeared.

He repeated the words he'd spoken in the temple.

"You will soon be confronted with innumerable tests, many of them perilous. Remember when you are faint-hearted that if your gifts are used for good, you may yet find peace in your quest. Heed well the words of the prophets of old you shall hear this day, daughter, the warnings from holy writ. Forget not that Elam is the Father of Light. And when given a choice, place others' needs above your own, even in the face of death."

I'd stolen my father's keys to his library. I'd opened The Keeper and violated Kildarian law. In doing so, I'd become possessed by evil spirits who manipulated me and my powers—and perhaps even some of the people around me. I'd lied and feared someday I might have to do worse. I'd been condemned to die. And yet there was still hope?

I felt something move beside me and came awake with a jerk—at least I thought I was awake. I sat up in bed, and a shadow in the night, something long and thin, rose up into the air above me. A gigantic snake? A thin man? I squinted, trying to make sense of it. It turned its head toward me, and its eyes began to glow, a golden glow that seemed more appropriate for a dragon's eyes than a human's. It whispered to me, a slow, dangerous hiss.

"I don't understand," I told the voice, then wondered why I'd spoken to it as if it was really here. Like it would understand. Like it could answer me.

Here? I looked around and found myself in a palatial bedchamber I'd never seen before. Where was I? I set my feet on the cold, smooth marble floors, rising and taking a step toward the foot of the bed. The creature followed me, step for step. It hissed again. This time I heard *"save them."*

"Who?" I asked.

"Set the prisoners free."

What prisoners? The army? Panic hit. Had they been captured?

I rounded the foot of the bed and came face to face with the wraith, or whatever it was. Darker shadows, spreading out from its shoulders, fluttered. Wings? They wreathed its head like the wings of a fabled Phoenix. My gaze trailed downward to its feet. Hooves. Equine. But the eyes drew me again. Draconian. Not Enya's, not Ramah's, but still a dragon's eyes.

The creature opened its mouth and out came a flame, gold entwined with black, and in the light that bore no heat, I saw—

I gasped and sat upright.

"Theona?" A hand touched my arm.

I looked up into Prince Gideon's worried gaze then took in our oasis and sighed in relief.

"You were having a bad dream."

One of too many. "Thank you for waking me," I said. And for driving the awful nightmare from my mind, in which the monster I saw was...me.

"You've slept for three hours," Gideon noted. I looked around in surprise. The afternoon was late.

"Are you rested enough to carry on?" he asked.

Three hours? Yes! We needed to fly!

We headed directly toward what I now could see were mountains. The Beldame Mountains! We were close! A mere ripple in the late afternoon heat, they accompanied the change in the landscape that soon greeted us. I wanted to fly higher to avoid being seen from the ground but could only go so high. The cold and the poor air were hard on my passengers, and it made the smaller details on the ground difficult to see.

Gradually the sands receded. Occasional hillocks, brush, and patches of wild grass turned into shrubbery, high prairie grasses and occasional trees and sporadic wildflowers. Considering I saw no sign of the army ahead of us, I rejoiced at the thought they'd made it through the Badlands. Now, had they done it alone? Or as prisoners?

Then Zahra shrieked, "Princess Theona! Prince Gideon! Look! I'm thinking that's the tail end of the army ahead of us!"

"I think she's right," Gideon said with excitement.

Yes! Despite a thin cloud of dust that hugged the feet of the mountains northward, my eye perceived the occasional glint of light reflecting off metal. Weapons? The tiny brown rectangular shapes must be wagons!

Not able to go further without the possibility of being seen, and worried that traveling at night risked overflying the army, I cupped my wings to rein in my flight and landed on the road.

"What's wrong?" Gideon asked, no doubt upset with the interruption in our journey.

"I'm sorry, Your Highness, but they'll see us." I explained my other fears, and Gideon groaned and pushed his fingers through his hair, both frustrated and disappointed. Ironically, the troops were at least a good three or four leagues ahead of us. Close enough they might see me in the air but impossible for us to catch up on foot—and they were still moving.

Gideon sighed then pointed ahead, just beyond a rocky prominence, where there was enough greenery to suggest it would make a good place to camp.

CHAPTER 22

The area around the low hill boasted a thin, shady woods, pleasant vegetation in almost every direction, and a most welcome spring. We could camp here and set out before dawn tomorrow. That way we could assess the army's condition without detection. If all was well, we'd land a fair distance away—for the same reason—and alternate traveling on foot or with me carrying them as an overly large horse. We hoped to catch up before the end of the day.

Again famished by the strain on my magic, I suggested eating lunch before making an early camp. Gideon agreed, and during our meal, I noted his color was better and he looked a bit fuller today— as was his beard. He also seemed stronger. He pushed my unruly hair out of my face and kissed me.

"You're quiet, my love. Is something wrong?"

I shrugged. "I'm just beginning to realize how close we are to getting answers, and it terrifies me."

His engaging grin tugged at my heart. "We'll be fine. I feel it." Then the grin faded. "I only wish we had our horses. It would make life so much simpler, wouldn't it?"

Zahra chuckled. Teasing, she said, "If I called for Chip and she was nearby, she'd come." Fingers to her lips, she created the most ear-piercing whistle I'd ever heard.

Nothing happened, of course. We hadn't expected otherwise, and Zahra laughed at our response. "Whistle's even better than calling a name, you see. Horses can hear it farther away."

I froze, shocked at feeling vibrations in the earth beneath me. Zahra's eyes rounded and she jumped to her feet as, from just around the hillock to the south of us, the sound of crashing foliage fractured the quiet. What in the world—?

A small cloud of dust proceeded Chip charging around the corner and sprinting toward Zahra.

"Impossible! I cannot believe it!" Zahra cried. "Chip! Chip!" She ran to greet her mare, the two of them clashing in the strangest tangle of arms and hooves and squeals and laughter I'd ever witnessed in my life.

"Oh, 'tis good to see you, lass," Zahra said, patting the horse vigorously, pulling foxtails from the mare's tangled mane, and wiping debris from her eyes. "Where've you been, you scalawag?"

"Not far from here," I replied, my mind turned the direction from which the mare had come. I'd Searched for Caspian…and found him!

"I'm a fool!" I shouted, laughing. "I can smell more water, farther away. Why didn't I notice it before? Why didn't I Search for the horses again?"

I grabbed Gideon's hand and we sprinted along the mare's path. It led us between briars and thick hedges to a shaded pond, surrounded by a good-sized meadow, and two horses grazing. Caspian and Valere!

"Val!" Gideon called. The stallion started, and flipping his tail, he bounded up to the prince, pressing his forehead into Gideon's chest and grumbling a fond welcome.

"Good heavens," Gideon murmured at seeing the scars that marked Valere's right shoulder and nostril. "My beautiful stallion. You're a true warhorse now, aren't you?"

"I did the best I could." I was sad that the injury had marred the beauty of the animal.

Gideon squeezed my shoulder in reassurance. "It looks bad enough I believe he'd have died if you hadn't healed him."

"I could have done it better with more time—"

"You saved him. I'm forever grateful. We all have our scars, Theona. We've more important things to fret about."

Caspian followed Valere, nickering to me with pleasure.

"You've no idea how glad I am to see you, boy," I said, scratching his throat latch. "We need the three of you more than you'll ever understand."

Zahra joined us on Chip bareback, bringing the rucksacks we'd left behind. She dropped them and herself to the ground grinning.

"I suppose we don't need to make camp after all, but while it was easy to bridle my four-legged friend, 'twas a bit of a challenge to saddle her."

She held up the toy-sized blanket and saddle. I released all three saddles from their magical spells and, laughing with joy, we set about wiping down and tacking our animals. It felt magical to have my beloved Caspian carry me rather than me carrying everyone and everything else.

We took it easy at first, to settle into the saddle and let the horses get re-accustomed to our weight. The afternoon was hot but so much nicer on horseback.

Dusk came, supper filled my belly, and I fell onto my bedroll beyond exhausted. Then Gideon tossed an arm over my shoulder and whispered, "Theona, do I have the gift for making portals?"

"What? Why do you ask?"

"If you could teach me to portal, we could take turns. It would relieve the stress on you."

My joy soared at his wanting to learn to use his gifts and wishing to spare me, but that joy deflated with the knowledge that it wouldn't work. I rolled to face him and brushed his cheek.

"Magic has a never-ending set of fantastical rules, Gideon. For one, I cannot portal anywhere I haven't been before, so I cannot portal us to either the army or Malloria. And taking too many people or portalling too far is deadly."

At first crestfallen, he rallied when he learned he did have the peppermint-scented, sienna-brown *parhelia* for portalling. I rested my hand over his heart and guided his awareness to it.

"Ah," he murmured when he sensed it. "Portalling could help us in other ways, though, couldn't it?"

"Of course. Our talents are meant to be used."

"Then I want to learn as soon as possible. It pains me to see you struggling with the weight of all you bear."

I loved his gentle compassion. He kissed me tenderly as my exhaustion all but dragged me into sleep. How would I ever manage…facing…the sorcerers…tonight?

Magic and sleep. One created miracles, and after only a few hours, the other healed. I came awake dreading facing the sorcerers, but with the army on tomorrow's horizon, I dared not put it off. The sorcerers' fury at my locking them up after my marriage was nothing compared to refusing to Link them with the unicorns. I wasn't sure I'd live through it.

I faced it a while time later, standing there and staring at Rhesalus with only my right eye. I couldn't see with the left one. Terius had beat me, and blood ran from nearly every part of my body from Moriana's feline bites and scratches. Now I faced my would-be mage partner and wondered what he would do to me?

At last, he said, "That's enough. She's taken her punishment. Theona, tell me you at least brought the books."

Finest Children. Birthright. Mortality. Linking. Healing. How I wished I hadn't had to. The first four were deposited in my rucksack, which sat on the ground beneath a nearby gnarled oak tree—which in turn stood a good mile from our campsite. *Healing* I'd left in camp, hoping to avoid confrontation over my returning the unicorn horns.

I pointed at the sack, and it flew into Moriana's outstretched hand with a whisper of the Language. She dug inside and brought them out, letting the bag fall into the dirt.

"You have them!" she said with awe. At Terius, she looked as if he'd given her gold.

His anger dissipated and a grin creased his face. "Yes, my love. We have them. Now, everything is in place."

"You lied to me," I said, matter-of-fact, hiding the anger. "You promised to teach me everything I needed to know to return you to mortality before we left Kildaria. But you couldn't. You had to have those books first."

Rhesalus chuckled. "Too bright for your own good," he said. "But we didn't lie. We just did what we needed to do to keep you motivated."

"Yes," I said. "I see that. Including holding threats against Prince Gideon over my head whenever I've balked. If you knew the Hamars were going to attack us, why didn't you stop it? What if the shaman had killed him? What if she had killed me?"

"Oh, it wouldn't have gone that far, would it, Terius?" Rhesalus said, his grey eyes turned toward the eagle-mage. His voice seemed calm; his expression bore a hint of animosity that I'd never seen before.

"Not likely." Terius stroked one of the book's covers in Moriana's arms. "You know the gift of prophetic foretelling gives me glimpses of future possibilities, but I cannot always separate what may happen from what will, or what consequences may come from intervention. I saw the tribe attacking the army and knew they wanted both Theona and the prince: the prince, to torture for information before killing him, and Theona to enslave her powers—which of course we will not allow.

"Another vision came to me of Seville in Mt. Draakheda—our ultimate destination—and where I saw Rhesalus heal him. He'd only need healing if he'd been injured. The consequences could have been worse if we interfered, and driving the prince and his horse toward the Lost Lands drew Theona after him. That in turn meant we could get her to the mountain, collect our books, refresh our memories regarding Linking, and get what we needed for..." His golden eyes blinked once as he added, "for getting our bodies. I didn't know about the poison, and *her* disobedience and her delay in bringing us out is what nearly killed the prince."

Moriana handed the books around, and the three read several pages from each one. Then Rhesalus handed them back to me.

"Guard them well, my sweet. Study *Healing* but leave the others alone, especially *Linking Souls*. You're not yet ready for them."

I struggled with my temper. He really wanted me to read *Linking Souls* and was trying to goad me into it. Seeing its ugly yellow cover again made me want to destroy it. I would never be ready for it. I would never follow its instructions. Not even if these demons killed me.

"You're upset, my dear, even if you're not showing it," Rhesalus said, his handsome mouth quirked up in mock sympathy. "Don't be. The Hamar shaman would have destroyed every single warrior in both armies to capture the two of you. As soon as you left, many of the Hamars fled. Their shaman made them appear more powerful than they really were, you know. She was most impressive. The Changelings did more damage than her warriors, but she was as afraid of them as your people. The moment you and your prince rode off, she sent them back to the Underworld and commanded her remaining warriors to retreat."

The hostility settled into my bruised bones. I kept my swollen, battered face still, but the venom dripped off my tongue.

"You let me think my brother, Kendal, and perhaps the army, may have died. You could have told me the truth and didn't! And you refused to come when I asked for help, even at risk of Gideon's life. You're monsters. All of you."

Terius just stared at me. Moriana tossed her hair behind her shoulders and grinned at me like a child who enjoyed torturing animals.

"You still have so much to learn," Rhesalus commented.

"And when I met you, you said I had little time to learn it, but you constantly leave me floundering. That wastes time, which makes no sense."

Terius growled, "Had you called us out when you reached the Lost Lands, we'd have taken you to Mt. Draakheda that day. It would have required all of us to heal your prince with only one unicorn horn, but we would still have healed him—and much sooner. And we'd have enjoyed this discussion yesterday, which means you'd already have met up with your army."

I wanted to scream, and each comment felt like nails being driven into me. I couldn't trust these monsters blindly, and Siddarth told me that Elam was the one who had brought me to the Lost Lands, not the sorcerers. I was glad I'd met the unicorns and found Mt. Draakheda on my own.

But I could never justify nearly killing Gideon and it would lie on my conscience for the rest of my life.

Moriana made the point: "You understand you have no choice about working with us tonight."

As much as I hated it, I did.

"I will, but I want you to teach me to make wards," I said, their startled looks proving I'd caught them off guard. "You said that you put wards on your laboratory doors. I suppose that means you have a magical way to protect them. I want to know how to protect whomever and whatever I choose to protect."

Terius snarled, "You have no rights—"

"*You* have no rights," I snapped. "You had no right to possess me and take everything you've taken from me. If I can't be rid of you, then sometimes I want to learn what I want to learn."

"And I want my body back. Now," Terius snapped.

Moriana laughed with contempt. I wanted to rip out her eyelashes.

"Stop!" Rhesalus snapped at them. "You're needling her, and that only makes things worse." To me, he said, "You're not ready to learn warding, Theona. You need better mastery of the Language. One slip and a ward could smother someone to death. Besides, we only have tonight to address more important lessons before you join the army."

Resentment held sway at first. No doubt he was lying for his own benefit, but I had no choice, and strangely enough, his chastisement felt sincere.

"Leave us," he told Terius and Moriana, and to my great relief, they disappeared.

"You've persisted in portalling without our guidance," the horse-mage accused me, but not unkindly. "Mistakes could kill you or your prince. We need to work on it tonight."

In the light of a gibbous moon, he summoned his lavender-blue mage light and with his index finger glowing the same shade began writing in the air.

The gleaming figures he scrawled became three columns of numbers. From left to right, he said, were distances traveled, the time it took to travel them, and the energy—measured in meals—required to go each distance.

"Here you see it takes but a second to travel twenty miles, and it requires the equivalent of half a meal. Seems simple enough, but were you to walk, fly or swim it, you would expend the energy along the way and stop as needed to address your fatigue and hunger.

"Not so with portalling. You'll hardly notice the effort of forming a portal, but the instant you pass through, the entire cost of the passage hits at once."

My eyes rounded at remembering the painful lessons I'd not understood while portalling. It may only take seconds to travel fifty miles, but the immediate price of two day's walk could kill.

Even shorter distances, he explained, disoriented the brain—the cause of my headaches and stomach aches.

"Two hundred miles, not quite as far as the distance between your cave and Mt. Draakheda, would take around ten seconds and cost nearly two days' food," he added, "and would likely send you into the abyss—the reason you needed us. The Elds recorded experiences long ago when some attempted such things and were never seen or heard from again."

"But I must have portalled a hundred miles from the Valdellian Warlords' camp to King Desmond's castle and had no such reaction," I insisted.

Again he laughed. "Fatigue and darkness skew the truth. It's nearer fifty miles, a little over one meal and less than four seconds worth, in theory. Our magic supported yours, just as it did with going to Mt. Draakheda. If not, you, your prince and your maid would not have survived it."

I suspected I had a taste of the abyss the time I'd portalled back to our cave as a pelican, plunged into terrifying darkness, and then coming into the light to land hard on my knees. I had no desire to ever do it again.

The last portal I'd just left open winked shut, proving Rhesalus right. When he sent me back to the oak tree, I felt the first grumblings of hunger but no headache. One meal? Somewhere around thirty to forty miles then. After I'd fed, Rhesalus answered more of my questions.

I could take numerous inanimate objects or one traveler with me with only slightly more energy use, but greater numbers of living beings and further distances affected me *and* my travelers. They could experience disorientation, for some amnesia—especially with considerable distances—and some might suffer insanity and may never recover.

I sighed at the meaning. Taking the United Forces anywhere through a portal was a deadly-dangerous proposition. Portalling to Malloria was out of the question.

Rhesalus also insisted I always keep food with me, adding, "Eat at least a little before and after each attempt."

I tried it, and the immediate feeding decreased the gut pain, while the shorter distances prevented most of the headache. Both lessened the fatigue.

"Why should I never close portals?" I thought of at least a half dozen reasons why I'd want to.

He chuckled. "'Never is a ridiculous absolute. Few things have no exceptions. In dangerous situations, it's the better choice. Just remember the cost. There is, however, one more thing that will help you when traveling farther is needful."

"And I'm not possessed by a sorcerer who can help me?" I replied with a touch of sarcasm.

"Yes, of course." He grinned wide. "Learn to couple portals. It's an invaluable tool. You break the longer distance into two or three shorter segments, opening all the portals at the same time, and then passing through them quickly. The distance between these magical doors is not more than a few steps, which gives you plenty of time to pass through, but it carries you many miles away."

Wonderful idea! If I could open three portals, one to the Lost Lands, one to the Badlands, and one to Kildaria, how would it feel to stand in each land for mere seconds and arrive home in just a few minutes?

Home and dead, of course. The three shorter segments were still hundreds of miles apart and likely to send me into the life-threatening void.

Rhesalus must have seen the longing on my face. "Theona, coupling has its own set of rules."

Of course, it did. Rules, rules, rules. He raised a brow at my petulance. "No one knows why it works, child, but it does. Pay strict heed. You mustn't couple more than three portals at a time, and *eating and sleeping* before making any more portals is *mandatory*. Listen to your body's needs. Do not shirk this advice, Theona, especially when needing to make more portals. It goes without saying that if you die, any passengers portalling with you are doomed. Do I make myself clear?"

"Perfectly. Why did you not teach me these things in the first place?"

"We told you not to portal until we had time to teach you, and you've had more important things to face since the moment you discovered the Valdellians were after your prince. And we'd have done so in the Lost Lands if you hadn't kept us behind your shields most of the time you were there."

I bit down on my anger. "But you didn't come when I summoned you."

"The first time. Our goal was to get you to Mt. Draakheda in the first place, and you know why, and when Moriana couldn't find a cure for this specific poison, we would have sent you there if you hadn't cut off our communication."

It was always my fault. And to some degree, he was right.

"The final warning, my dear...for now," Rhesalus said. "You portalled while flying into Mt. Draakheda's cavern. Don't try it without our help and until you've gained more experience. Also, you must *never* portal while warded. They are opposites in magical nature. You'll either be thrown back out of the portal...or incinerated."

I gulped at the thought. I saw the advantage of warding myself while portalling into unfamiliar territory—perhaps in the midst of enemies—but there was no advantage if I died doing it.

"Now. For what you seem to have the least aptitude for but which you must master, my dear. Let us work on the Language. And none of those irritated looks. It will lessen the work of wielding magic and open your mind to things you cannot imagine."

Most likely devilish things, I thought, but if I had no choice, there was no sense avoiding it, even if I preferred to call out the dragons tonight.

My reward? Gaining control over three new enchantments that I could use against other sorcerers. If only that power didn't beg me to fly off and punish all my enemies with it. I had to fight to tamp it down.

"Very good, dearest," Rhesalus said, his face softening with kindness. He pressed a hand to my cheek, and although I flinched at the sting of the wounds he touched, I was rewarded by him healing me of the beating I'd taken. "You're getting the idea, Theona. Hunt. Rest. Terius told me that tomorrow will demand much of you but will end with many of your questions answered. Call us out tomorrow night."

I found a late-night snack before calling the dragons. They growled at me for having kept them locked up as I had the sorcerers but calmed when I explained.

"Wild horses are nearby," Ramah noted, his nostrils turned northwest and flaring.

"Then let's find them," I said, only this time I flew as a winged horse. The dragons did the same, Enya soaring alongside me and Ramah just above us.

Linking came easier, but I wondered if I should celebrate it or regret it.

CHAPTER 23

A s we rode out the next morning, we discussed how to approach the army, discover whether it was free or captive, and if it was complete or split into separate groups.

I was grateful Gideon had followed the urgent request I'd made of him before we married. I'd seen a vision of enemy warriors who'd somehow scaled the hidden passes' high cliff walls and attacked the cavalcade as it passed through. He reassured me that he'd sent six Mallorian scouts out ahead of the army, hoping to find and kill them. Eld York had even provided Dreamwood bracelets for them to protect them from magic, but the terrain itself was perilous. If they failed, for whatever reason, we might find ourselves in even greater danger than with the Hamars.

And then, of course, there was Nevin Leath and possible traitors within the army itself—and my family among them—if they were still alive. My stomach hurt from facing so many worries at once.

We pushed the horses as hard as we dared in the heat. Armies move along at a swift walk paced by the condition of the wagon horses, but we needed to catch up before dark. When we were close, I planned to fly over them as a bird to surveil the cavalcade for signs of the enemy.

We crested a rise in the road late morning, and I took my first good look at the Beldame crags. They appeared close enough to touch, dwarfing the Carinors and even more formidable than those in the Lost Lands except for Mt. Draakheda. They sliced their way so high into the sky they looked more like sheer granite walls than mountains. Even now, several snowy summits pierced the few pale clouds that hovered low.

"I can't see the army anymore," Gideon said with excitement. He chuckled when I furrowed my brow. "It means the road has turned north! They're headed toward the pass."

Unbidden, a magical map unfolded in my mind. It was more like a picture painted from the back of dragon, and every detail spoke to me. The mountains formed an almost perfect north-south barrier between the western lands of both the Central Alliance and the Badlands and those of the Eastern Realms. All around were various bodies of water, grasslands, some forests and of course the mountains.

Pointing northward, Gideon said, "We're on the southern border of Langala. This part is a narrow wedge between the Badlands and the Beldames."

I could almost see the borders, as if drawn on a map.

"North of Langala are Ionish and then Gadish. The Great Northern Lake in Gadish empties into three rivers, the largest being the Varigo River. The Varigo runs southward along the Beldames until it reaches Ionish, where it turns southeast and cuts through a gorge in the mountains. When the river reaches Malloria, it continues southeast to our southern border, turns due south through Mandu, then empties into the East Wind Sea. You'll only catch a glimpse of the river, because we'll come to our secret passage long before reaching it."

We slowed our pace as the day grew warmer. The road that turned north rose and fell and became bumpy, pocked, and strewn with stones. Whoever took such meticulous care of the Badlands Route did not come here. Weeds and tumbleweeds sprouted from the dust in these southern parts, except for those flattened by the army's passing.

One rise offered us a view of Langala's grasslands to our left and the mountains, marching ever northward, on our right. My breath caught when what I thought was the ocean ahead of us turned out to be the magnificent Varigo River.

The heat was only slightly better here than the Badlands. We had the faintest of breezes, and later, lingering dust and evening sunlight, evidence of the army's movement, which cast everything ahead of us in a bronze-brown haze. The wagons still looked as small as a child's toys.

Gideon insisted on pushing the horses, repeatedly cantering until they were lathered then walking them until they'd dried. It was hard on them, and I felt Caspian's fatigue more than my own.

Finally, I reined in. "I should fly over the army to make sure—"

The loud clarion call of a bugle interrupted me and spooked our horses.

"Someone has seen us," Gideon said, reining Valere in. "I think the entire army has come to a halt."

"It has, my lord," Zahra agreed, her sharp eyes taking it in. "I'm thinking I see riders coming towards us."

She did. My own eagle-eyes watched four men—Mallorian by the uniforms!—headed toward us at a lazy lope, armed, and at this point not looking friendly. Good! Conquerors wouldn't send Mallorian warriors to investigate!

"Come," Gideon urged, pushing Valere into a tired jog.

We stopped a safe distance from them, but amazement brightened the warriors' faces. One of them cried out, plunged his sword back into its scabbard, and kicked his horse into a gallop. Nearly upon us, Sir Lance bolted off his horse and ran to Gideon, like a man whose lost brother had come home. Gideon dismounted and met him halfway, keeping Sir Lance from falling to his knees in reverence. They shouted and pounded each other's shoulders, Sir Lance demanding explanations but too excited to hear Gideon's replies.

Zahra and I dismounted as General Bellamy and two of Gideon's guards arrived, the general's face seamed and his beard appearing a bit grayer. He limped toward his prince and dropped to one knee, his shoulders shaking. It humbled me to see the tears that trailed the dust on the older man's cheeks.

The others joined him, equally joyous, but Gideon begged them to stand and clasped Bellamy's hand in earnest friendship.

"Seeing you alive has lifted the burden from my heart, Your Highness," Bellamy said in a voice that rasped. "I couldn't make peace with losing you, and try as I might, I couldn't imagine how I'd explain your demise to your esteemed father. I'm so glad I won't have to face that day."

"As am I, my general," Gideon said. "You're limping. The Hamars?"

Bellamy shrugged and backhanded the moisture from his face. "Some fared far worse. Please forgive me—us—for failing to protect you—"

Gideon raised a hand. "Warren, there are few good ways to stop arrows and javelins without a shield. I'm well. How goes the army? Why are you with the rearguard?"

"When we lost you, I split our division in half, with Captain Gerard in the vanguard, the rest with me in the rearguard. Kildaria and Gerard's group resumed the lead as soon as we left the Badlands.

That allowed my half to hold back and watch for you." He glanced at me. "And to assure your safety if—when—you did rejoin us."

"Especially since the army has at least one traitor," I said with empathy. "I'm grateful to you. We both are."

Bellamy nodded. "What happened, my lord? You had a spear the diameter of my thumb run through your shoulder."

The prince grinned, again scratching his beard. "We've a mighty tale to share and much of it you won't believe," he replied. "But we need to address it later. It's more important to join the army, but first I need to know the outcome of the battle."

The general sighed. "I've no sensible explanation. Not two minutes after your horse bolted, the shaman raised her fist and again screamed her horrid blood-curdling scream. A half-dozen Hamar warriors set out after you, but the others turned tail and ran. The shaman again tapped the ground with her staff and spoke some gibberish. The Changelings dissolved into the earth like melting snow and left the bodies behind, and then she rode off without another word."

Just as Rhesalus had described it last night. Chills ran over my skin.

"I ordered Lance and two dozen men to go to your aid, while the rest of us set about assessing the damage. Lance, you should tell your tale in your own words."

The knight did so. "We hadn't gone far before we ran into the band of Hamars who'd followed you—heading back to join their war party. I'll never forget the look on their faces, as if they'd seen ghosts. One of them, their leader I believe, had every hair on his head and his beard turned as white as snow."

Gideon's eyes locked with mine in private understanding. Along with Zahra, we fought laughter. We knew what had frightened them.

Sir Lance continued. "We followed your tracks and came to the cliff of the Great Chasm. What a shock. Our lore teaches that it's on the other side of the mountain range. Your horses' hoof prints disappeared there. I sent half the warriors to follow the chasm east and the other half west to find sign of you, while I remained behind to search for any evidence of where you'd gone."

My amusement turned to sorrow, but...hadn't they found the horses' tracks and followed them? Hadn't they seen our saddles and...? "Sir Lance—"

He carried on as if I'd not spoken. "When we found blood on the ground and no sign of you or your horses, we feared you'd all fallen to your deaths in the chasm." His voice cracked, and Gideon placed a hand on his shoulder, his face tight with compassion.

"Lance, you couldn't have found us had you tried."

"My lord?"

"Princess Theona found a hiding place for us. I'd been mortally wounded. Without her, I wouldn't have survived. Now, what about our losses?"

"Minimal for such a frenzied attack," Bellamy replied, bemused. "The vast majority were theirs. Of the three hundred dead, only twenty were ours, and oddly enough, fairly evenly distributed amongst the divisions. One Kalbarrian woman was captured. Three wagons were destroyed, and most of the bird cages were damaged, more than half the birds lost.

"Of the five hundred warriors seriously wounded, only thirty were ours. All survived, but the Hamars preferred to die than accept our aid. Only twenty of the at least four hundred horses that died or were put down from serious injuries belonged to our army. Since leaving Kildaria, we've lost a total of fifty-four warriors, twenty-six horses, and three wagons."

Gideon shook his head at this. "Incredible. Amazingly good news but also disturbing. We regret the fatalities, but things could have ended far worse. Unfortunately, the bird loss will greatly hamper our communication with Kildaria and Malloria."

Sir Lance agreed. "I find it strangest of all that only two of the warriors killed were Mallorian. It defies the odds. The heart of the assault seemed centered on us, particularly you and Princess Theona. They should have killed us all."

They should have, but certain evil sorcerers had controlled the events to send me to the Lost Lands and retrieve some horrid books for them. Gideon—and the army—was, in essence, collateral damage.

"My lady, I can't tell you how grateful I am that you saved our prince," Bellamy said with gravity.

I took his offered hand. "I did my best to save my husband, General," I replied. I then diverted his attention by asking about my brother and Miss Kendal as I healed him. Caught off guard, he flinched, and then he stammered a bit as he answered, "L-l-lord Ian was most stalwart, defending his lady with his life, Princess. Neither sustained serious injury. Councilman Leath was also unharmed. Not surprising, since I found him hiding under one of the wagons after the enemy departed."

He flexed his leg and murmured more thanks to me. "Er, our wounded could benefit from your kindness, Princess, if you're so inclined to offer and they aren't so foolish as to refuse."

Again regarding Gideon, he added, "Your Highness, I regret not taking the time to bury our dead. We feared the shaman would return with reinforcements. We took enough risk salvaging everything we could before fleeing."

"You did what you thought best, Warren," the prince reassured him with kindness. "Warren, Lance, we left Kildaria with the army earlier than the king planned but a week later than we'd hoped. We must set a strong pace to arrive home close to when the king expected us." He glanced toward the army, the sea of people watching us with uncertainty. "No doubt, they're wondering who we are. Shall we join them?"

"Of course, my lord."

As we mounted, I noticed Zahra's face, tight with worry.

"Zahra, search for Amari, please," I urged her, and an instant later, when I saw the brightness flower on her face, I knew he was well. At least this part of our journey had a happy ending.

Tonight's camp was already selected, a place familiar to Gideon and situated beside a small lake not far ahead. My prince reassured me that tonight we'd have a normal supper made of normal human food, three waterfalls and proper soap for bathing and laundry, and a clean change of clothes—plus a razor for the itchy beard that he dearly wanted to remove.

Gideon's men and the army's generals celebrated his return. For the most part, I was ignored—beyond the warriors I healed—and Ian and Kendal, of course. The healed ones were beyond grateful, and my brother and his fiancée near broke my ribs deluging me with their tearful hugs. Ian seemed changed now, grown up. He treated Kendal with the grace of a future duke, and their love radiated from them.

"Your Highness, I must insist that once we've reached Malloria," I said to Gideon, "that we arrange these two lovebirds' marriage as soon as possible. It might not be the ceremony they'd have enjoyed at home, but they need to be together."

Gideon laughed and Ian and Kendal flushed as red as lobsters.

I appreciated supper, as plain as army fare ever is but far better than watery soup, rats, or bugs. Good humor and joy led to a comparing of notes about our separate experiences after the attack— although Gideon, Zahra and I avoided much detail about our time in the Lost Lands. Later, Zahra asked for permission to seek her brother and returned with him just as Ian and Kendal excused themselves for an evening stroll. Zahra's brother was a tall, dark-skinned man likely in his thirties, his eyes bloodshot with fatigue and a jumble of emotions on his face. We stood. He kneeled.

"Corporal Amari Timbu," I said, knowing him immediately, even if we hadn't yet met. He could pass for Zahra's twin. "Thank you for coming. I'm so glad to make your acquaintance. Please rise." I offered a hand in friendship. "I'm grateful you weren't harmed in the attack."

"As I'm grateful for my sister's life, Your Highness," he said in a deep bass voice that bore Zahra's lilt. Her winsome smile also brightened his face. "'Tis so good to see her happy again, not like when she worked for Lady Kell."

"I'm glad to hear that." I chuckled. "We needed each other, corporal, and I'm blessed to have her companionship."

We visited for a bit, but I shooed them away to enjoy what little time they had together that night. That in turn bequeathed Gideon and me a rare bit of privacy on a clear, starry night, touched by a soft, comfortably warm breeze. The privacy was an illusion, of course. Although hovering at a distance, our guards never left us alone.

Then not an hour later, three men strolled in our direction, two wearing the colors of Kythos, the third shrouded in shadows. When the flicker of firelight finally caught his features, my stomach tightened into a hard knot. Nevin Leath.

His gaze sharpened the moment he saw us. Hands clasped behind his back, he offered a bow to us so minuscule it was more a slight than a salute.

"Prince Seville. Princess. Rumors do not disappoint. I saw the arrow you took, Seville, and your flight afterward with my own eyes. I'm surprised you survived your harrowing escapade."

Considering the lack of respect in his tone, his association with Darby Murdock, and his dislike for me, I'd sooner believe Leath was more disappointed than surprised by my prince's survival. Again, I wondered whether the councilman had anything to do with the attack on my family in Kildaria that took the lives of my old nurse and my sister. Was he also connected to the king's assassination attempt? Ian and Kendal's kidnapping?

And why was he here?

Gideon sat rigid beside me, his own expression impenetrable. "Congratulations on your own survival, Leath," he said. "It appears hiding under a wagon bed is a commendable defense."

I bit my lip against laughter. Leath bristled, which drew the four Mallorian guards into the light, two on either side of us. Gideon rose, pulling me against him.

"Since you denied me weapons, how could I defend myself at all?" Leath growled. "Perhaps I should have thrown sand at them? Now, if you'll excuse me, I'd like to finish stretching my legs before we all bed down for the night." He did not wait for Gideon to excuse him before striding off.

"Impudent man," Gideon Paired. His gaze, the stormy violet of anger, met mine. *"The weapons wagon wasn't far from where he was hiding. No one would have stopped him from swiping one. As much as I disliked Darby Murdock, my gut tells me Leath is more dangerous, but not necessarily in ways that involve weapons."*

My thoughts echoed his. Despite Leath's refusal to support Murdock's several schemes to attack us, I doubted it was because he had principles against the idea.

When it came time for all of us to retire, I looked forward to a tent and a soft cot rather than hard ground or a stone bed. However, as soon as I stepped inside, I came to a stop, my skin tingling with the power of magic. Gideon, Kendal, and Zahra didn't seem to notice it, but The Keeper and Slayer, sitting in their usual places, shimmered with an odd, mystical presence.

"You alright, Love?" Gideon asked, his brow creased.

I forced a smile. "I'm...I'm just tired." We were all tired, but all I wanted to do was escape.

The minute everyone went to sleep, I hurried off into the grasslands to summon the sorcerers. For the first time, I looked forward to working with Moriana, even if she did drive me hard with the Language. The men insisted I Link the dragons with snakes and eagles, then had me try one of the relief horses that had wandered from Segovia's herd.

Enya and Ramah delighted in the exercises, but the mare fought Enya hard that she died when I separated them.

I suppose I should have grieved more than I did, but my hunger outweighed everything. Later, I began to wonder if my heart had grown hard, because I worried more about having to share the tent with The Keeper and Slayer than I did about how anyone would feel when they found the dead horse.

The routines claimed us. Sunday morning, Dundee took the helm from Kalbarri, and the army finally spread out wide and traveled faster over the gently rolling plains as we forged northward. No one mentioned anything about a dead or missing horse.

Gideon asked Amari to join our group, an honor for both the warrior and Zahra. Unfortunately, we'd not gone more than half the day when a Dundeean wagon broke down. One of the wagon-masters whispered to my prince that he believed the damage was manmade.

Gideon halted the entire cavalcade and ordered the reassessment of every vehicle's condition while the wheel was repaired. Three more wagons had problems, all suspicious, and we took the rest of the day to address it, requiring us to set up camp early.

Thankfully, the next day went without incident. We headed out early and traveled until near-dark to make up for some of yesterday's lost time. That night's pleasant camp again allowed the animals to graze and warriors to their leisure. Sir Lance and General Bellamy helped Gideon regain his strength with his sword work, while Zahra and I found a private place to continue my nearly fruitless quest for competency with both hand combat, knife and sword.

Later, as warriors bedded down, Gideon and I took a stroll into the grasslands with Zahra so that we could work on their magic under the canopy of mage light. My delight soared when my prince gained enough control of his warlord *parhelia* to transform almost instantly into his powerful persona as a warrior imbued with roped muscles and incredible fighting speed and strength. He, in turn, expressed fascination with Zahra's budding ability to become her lovely swan-self, especially when she finally succeeded in learning to fly. She wasn't good at it yet but loved every minute of it.

Each morning, the divisions made their routine changes of position, Dundee replaced by Kythos, Kythos by Segovia, and then

Kildaria took over. Already a day behind, my prince's mood grew prickly when another wagon broke down midday on Tuesday.

This time a tongue worked its way loose, and the horses panicked and dragged it off. Outriders had to collect and calm them while the wagon was repaired. Again fearful this was engineered by our traitors, Gideon ordered another early camp to inspect every vehicle. Anger swept through the army when someone discovered another wagon with spokes partially sawed through. Gideon sent out death threats to anyone found perpetrating such acts in the future, but he admitted to me that traitors already knew the risk they were taking and wouldn't care.

We were now a second day behind our original objective. Gideon fretted at the impediments, worried about his country's safety, and while he'd sent messages by bird to his father-king with an estimate of when to expect us, too many delays might make King Olivier think we'd been taken over by the enemy. Gideon also muttered through clinched teeth that the longer we remained on Central Alliance soil, the greater the danger of their scouts catching us.

The wagons were finally deemed fit for travel by late afternoon, too late in the day to set out but also too early for supper, so Gideon again gave begrudging permission for personal pursuits. Zahra and I found a private place by a nearby cluster of trees surrounded by tall brush, where she continued her quest to improve my fighting skills. I worked hard but paused, sweating, when a dozen spectators, all female warriors, came across us. Some hard-faced and critical, others amused at my awkward attempts at swordplay, they no doubt itched to make quick work of me themselves.

"Always find it curious that those who can't do something right think they can teach others," one woman muttered, Kalbarrian by the accent and the looks of her: short but husky, tawny-skinned and dark-haired, almond-shaped eyes the color of amber.

Zahra never flinched, forcing me to concentrate on my footing a while longer and reminding me to pay attention to my balance, especially with prolonged swinging and thrusting.

"She'll get the devil killed," the woman muttered. "Couldn't fight off a mouse with moves like that. But then, mightn't be a bad idea if the monster ate a true warrior's blade anyway."

My cheeks heated in anger, but when we finished, I followed Zahra's Salute of Swords marking the end of our workout, raising my short sword's point heavenward, the grip clasped in both hands at my waist, and giving a small bow. Mind-Paired, my maid warned me not to sheath my sword and to walk slightly behind and to the left of her as we turned toward our campsite.

"Look, Bridget," a red-haired warrior with a Dundeean accent goaded. "You shamed them enough they're runnin' off."

"Cowards," the Kalbarrian taunted, tossing her dark, waist-length braid behind her shoulders.

I couldn't help smiling. Cowards? What I felt wasn't cowardice, it was dread. I certainly wouldn't relish facing this nasty-tempered witch in battle, but I had no doubt Zahra could turn her into mincemeat—and I doubted she'd like facing a dragon.

"What's so funny?" another Kalbarrian sneered, thrusting her shoulder into me and knocking me away from Zahra.

I paused, intimidated despite myself and nearly hypnotized by her yellow eyes, a curious contrast with her tawny skin.

"I said what's—"

"Watch your mouth, Kalbarrian," Zahra rebuked her. "She's Princess Theona to you."

"She's no princess to me. She's daughter to that usurper, Cedric McArthur."

Usurper? I couldn't help bristling. Of all the things of which she could accuse my father, being a usurper wasn't one of them.

"My lady," Zahra murmured, warning me against reacting. "We'd best—"

"Turn tail and run, cowards," the redhead sneered. I wanted so badly to sink fangs into her long, rather homely face.

"There's no need to prove anything to them," Zahra urged.

The woman Bridget laughed. "There's nothing to prove. I could pull every hair out of her head if I so chose," she jeered. Then, in an instant, the snick of metal announced the unsheathing of her sword.

CHAPTER 24

Zahra's sword whipped up into fighting position. "You'll not touch one of those hairs without going through me, traitor," she growled.

They set to, the clang of metal-on-metal jarring. I kept my eye on the others, lest someone tried to put a knife into either of our backs. Deep inside, the feral part of my magic fought to take control, to shape-shift me into something deadly ferocious. I would protect both of us with magic if I had to but feared I couldn't control it.

Zahra and her opponent appeared almost evenly matched, and my heart stepped up its nervous cadence. No doubt Bridget would come after me once she killed my warrior-maid—and I couldn't allow her to do that.

And then it was over, Zahra's feint to the right, a backslash to the left, a kick with her heel bringing Bridget to the ground, a deep gash gushing blood from her right arm.

Zahra neatly tucked her boot's toe under the woman's sword, flipped it into the air, caught its haft, stabbed it into the ground and leaned on it.

"You won't be wielding a weapon for a while, fool. Pray you're not ruined. If not, look for a better teacher. You were weak on the right side and too quick to rush your bloody assault."

Bridget clamped her hand on the wound and roared her anger. The redhead knelt beside her, tearing off a section of her shirt and binding the gash despite her friend trying to slap her away.

"Shush, Bridget. It was a good fight. You can't win them all."

Bridget's golden-eyed gaze drilled into mine, brimming with hatred—and with magic. I hadn't seen it until now. Had she been hiding her *illumina*? The implications weakened my knees.

Six major *parhelia* she had, and all of them roiled within her as if she knew their presence, knew their purpose, and could hardly hold them back! She could have won her fight with Zahra without even trying had she tapped into them in the beginning. Why hadn't she done so? Because of pride?

One of Bridget's talents granted her the power to heal, which she did instantly. The others watched her every move, ready to follow her lead as she came to her feet.

One glance at Zahra and I knew her surprise echoed mine. I Paired my vehement desire to her to leave now. Bridget wouldn't hold back this time. Zahra heartily agreed, but before we could walk away, three of the warriors drew their swords and shoved themselves between us.

"You don't want to do what you're thinking," I warned them.

"We'll do as we please," said an older woman whose entire shaved head was tattooed with narrow zebra-like stripes from her brows backward to the nape of her neck. Her deep voice resounded with power.

I looked at the others, seeing beyond the obvious: the uniforms of the Western League nations, the weapons, the hostility. The magic. Every one of them resonated with it, and many of their *parhelia* bore unfamiliar talents. The sorcerers' warnings that I needed to prepare for battle with other sorcerers suddenly made too much sense.

"Don't do anything rash, my lady. Follow my lead," Zahra Mind-Paired.

Panicked, I Paired briefly with Gideon, sending chaotic pleas for help.

Crouching down, I kept my sword raised and backed slowly away from my enemies. Bridget followed, her manner predatory. I swallowed hard when they all avoided Zahra and focused on me.

I'd grown used to the idea people wished me dead. I was corrupted, something both less than human and superhuman at once, something they could not abide. Still, no one had confronted me quite this way, and I felt clumsier with my sword than ever.

While I kept my gaze locked on the warriors—and theirs on me— Zahra sneaked into the bushes surrounding our small glade and made her way behind me. I ached to use magic to protect myself. I wouldn't stand a chance fighting as a mere mortal. But what if some got away and told the tale to others? What if I lost control and killed them all?

"Time to stop playing around," Bridget growled, glancing first at the redhead on her left and then the brunette on her right. The three women dropped their swords and raised their hands, muttering in the

Language of sorcerers! Shock turned my face cold. Ordinary people could not use the Language.

Their curled fingers shimmered with a pale blue luminescence, their eyes taking on a hypnotic hue. Magic begged me to shape-change and fight back. I struggled to keep it at bay.

Seemingly out of nowhere, Zahra jumped in front of me just as the threesome set loose bolts of mage-fire that had my hair literally standing on end. As she'd done when I was attacked in the courtyard, my warrior-maid roared, her arms spread wide, and turned into her mirror self.

The bolts struck her, blasting into her head, her chest, and her belly and instantly flashed back to their owners, striking all three in the chest.

Their screams of agony cut short when they burst into flames and shriveled like burned parchment. I felt bile rise into my throat and nearly dropped my sword. Cries of terror, mingled with outrage, came from the other warriors. Three raced towards us, swords raised; the others fled.

Zahra's form brightened. The colors of her skin and clothes bled through the black, the light flickering off her sword.

"Back-to-Back, my lady, as I taught you," she prompted in my mind. She faced a Kythosian and a Segovian; another Kalbarrian confronted me.

I cringed when the first strike against my sword jarred my arms painfully. The Kalbarrian rained a storm of strikes and thrusts on me, metal clanging and screeching and clanging again. I was tired and hadn't the strength or the wits to do more than hold the sword in front of me and parry her blows. How did Zahra do this?

Ignorant question. Zahra's lemon-yellow *parhelia* of stamina would sustain her beyond normal human capacity. I wanted to laugh as guilt fled. I possessed the same *parhelia* and I wasn't fighting ordinary mortals. I found it and put it into action.

I took what I hoped was the advantage of an opening, struck the sword from my opponent's hand and completely by accident laid her right arm open to the bone.

Her screams followed her as she staggered away from the fray, leaving me mourning for what I'd done.

I heard a thud and knew Zahra had dispatched one of her attackers. I turned to see the Kythosian lying dead at her feet. The continued ringing of steel with the other assailant grew labored, the Segovian's breaths coming in faltering gasps. Countless wounds leaked runnels of scarlet down the front of her tunic and her arms.

Zahra grunted as the Segovian's stroke nicked her left wrist but drove into the warrior, her swings so rapid the woman could do nothing but hold up her sword and hope for the best. The warrior stumbled and lost her footing, dropping her sword and then falling to her knees, bowing.

"I surrender!" she begged. "Have pity. Please."

"Pity?" Zahra spat. "You offered no pity to us, and considering you've got that pig-sticker in your right hand, I'm thinking you don't mean it. Drop it before I run you through."

I hadn't realized the warrior had pulled a slender dagger out of her boot. I almost admired her tenacity. Her and her friends' attack confirmed she was a traitor, of course—which seemed ironic, considering who I was and everything I'd done—but I hadn't chosen this attack. She had and she would pay for it.

The two women moved at the same instant, faster than I could blink, and it wasn't until I saw a severed hand flying across the glade that I realized what had happened.

Zahra's hand? Or the warrior's? I couldn't hold back the bile this time at the sight of the Segovian's gore of arterial spray. Her screams of agonized rage rent the air, and then suddenly the area was filled with people. Among them, my prince bristled with fury, his shoulders broadened and biceps bulging. He'd found us at last!

Zahra gave him an accounting with precision. I did nothing but wipe my mouth of vomit and shake like a leaf in an autumn gale.

"Bind that woman's arm and get her to the infirmary," Gideon commanded Amari, who stood beside Zahra. "I want her grilled for a list of her compatriots before trying her for treason."

Amari grabbed the woman, while Gideon sent others to follow them, receive the information, and apprehend the warriors who'd fled. I almost felt sorry for the Segovian, crying out in agony as someone wrapped her bleeding stump snuggly. Tears bathed her cheeks, but she likely grieved more about losing her sword-hand and having failed to rid the world of me than whether she would die because of it.

"Princess Theona," Gideon said, formality in place but terror on his face. "You're injured."

I met his solemn gaze, amazed at how mesmerized I'd become by the horrors that surrounded me. Letting go of my magic also made me aware of the wounds I'd sustained without realizing it. Dozens of them, on my arms, my left shoulder, and my right hip all blazed to life with pain. He slipped a hand under my elbow and led me toward our tent, my legs as limp as willow sticks.

Sucking in air, I straightened my back and squared my shoulders, determined to present a strength I did not feel. I needed nourishment to heal myself, but perversely, I also wanted to let the army see what the traitors had done. That if they could do it to me, they could do it to anyone.

My resolve wavered when I caught sight of Nevin Leath in the center of a collection of Kythosians, his eyes angry. Angry? Because of the attacked? Or because the attack had failed? The questions—and suspicions—multiplied like flies.

A chill rippled down my spine but not from anything sinister. The temperature had dropped, and thick clouds gathered overhead. I groaned when raindrops splashed my head and cheeks. We were in for a storm.

Dread filled me. Gideon had told me in confidence that tomorrow we'd reach the hidden pass and the ravine that would take us through the Beldame Mountains to Malloria. I'd once seen a vision of that very pass, cloaked in snow, with the cliffs above harboring enemies garbed in white, determined to kill every, last one of us. Rain could easily turn into snow.

———

Backlash. Punishment. Ultimatums.

Apparently, a soft shade of strawberry-red colored *parhelia* was connected to a picture-perfect memory. For Zahra, it was a minor *parhelia*. She wasn't perfect at it; but she was exceptional, and it allowed her to identify all of the warriors involved in the incident. I now understood why she'd recalled the words of the Language she'd heard me speak only once in my sleep in Kildaria. After she encountered something, she rarely forgot it.

A rusty orange *parhelia*, which seemed content to hide behind Gideon's dark-red-warlord *parhelia*, told a different story. It made him a diviner of truth. Gideon had never understood why truth shone so brightly for him but, when he could control the gift, it did. That night was a perfect example and opened my eyes to why my prince believed in me when ordinary men would not. He knew from the first moment we met, in both Draakheda and in real life, the truth of who I was, and he believed in his own manifestations of the future. He saw truth in me and believed we were meant to be together.

When Gideon and our friends and I discussed the attack later, we were disturbed that the warriors implicated in the attack hailed from every one of the Western League nations, even Kildaria, and knew each other. More important? Bridget and her friends had wielded the Language.

The woman who'd lost her hand, and all of the warriors with her and Bridget, were executed before supper. I had to eat, but the horrors made it hard to swallow.

Warriors disgruntled by the executions were also ferreted out and brought up for interrogation. Most were just resentful of the situation. Some lied but weren't guilty of treason. I supposed they'd take care with their alliances from now on. Considering, however, that Gideon couldn't very well interview more than thirty-five-thousand people, he had no way of knowing if all the defectors had been caught. He could only hope the executions would deter them.

A while later, in the soft drizzle of rain, Kendal gripped my hand as Prince Gideon Seville mounted a high, flat boulder to address the army as best he could. We stood with Ian, Zahra, the Elds, General Bellamy and Sir Arnoe at the base of the rise where the boulder sat, while all of the commanders gathered at his feet, bearing torches. The warriors spread out around us.

My prince outlined the attack and the executions, with long pauses to allow the criers to repeat it to the troops too far away to hear.

"Friends," he said pointedly. "We come now to the most important juncture in our venture. We shall soon take the hidden passage to Malloria. Mallorians have guarded its secret for generations and share it only because without your assistance, our kingdom's future is dim. You know that if you successfully help us fend off the alliance, you also protect your own lands.

"No one should be surprised by the price required of you for receiving such knowledge. Your generals have just received a copy of an oath that they will study with care. Before you bed down, they will explain it to you in detail. In the morning, every warrior will swear loyalty and silence regarding the location of the pass before being allowed anywhere near it. Make no mistake. Breaking the oath will bring punishment by death."

Grumbling swept through the crowd, some of the warriors not pleased by this.

"Malloria will gather here at dawn tomorrow to await word of your compliance. Your own generals will administer the oath to you. Mallorian warriors will witness and record every pledge.

"If you refuse the oath, you must leave. Go any time between now and sunrise tomorrow, but…. You. Will. Not. Follow us. If you do, you will be slain. You must make your own way home, and you may take your horses and any equipment that is yours, but you will not take army provisions. Game and water are plentiful here. Make use of them. Protection from enemies is your own concern.

"We believe your love of family and country will quell any reservations and solidify your commitment to the cause. Remember, if the Eastern Realms fall, it's only a matter of time before the Central Alliance comes for you. The enemy will seize everything you own, burn your homes, and steal your cattle. They will slay you, your fathers and your sons, rape your wives and mothers, and turn your daughters into slaves and concubines."

Grumbles rose again at Gideon's allegations.

"You are *warriors*. You've all known war, small or large, or you wouldn't be here. Conquerors will stop at nothing to make themselves rich at the expense of others. The Eastern Realms will fight alone if we must, but we cannot win alone. Neither can you. Together we are formidable, and I for one want to grind their hateful faces into the ground."

Shouts of agreement rose from the Mallorians, fists raised into the air.

"Honor!" one soldier cried.

"Valor!" a second added.

"Victory!" a third shouted, and throughout the Mallorian troops came a staccato repetition, a chant that raised the hairs on the back of my neck.

Honor, valor, victory, repeated three times, and then came a shout of exultation that ended in complete silence.

I waited, stock still, for the rest of the army's response. At last, a Kildarian soldier likewise raised his fist.

"For country, for home, for family!" he shouted the League Motto. Again, he said it, and half the Kildarians joined him. The third time, the rest joined in, clapping their hands together and stamping their feet.

A Segovian raised the chant again and Kythos and Kildaria united with them, then came Dundee and finally Kalbarri, again stamping feet and clapping hands and ending with the mantra "hurrah!"

A deafening silence floated over the campgrounds, despite the patter of rain. I wanted to cry at seeing eyes filled with the gleam of enthusiasm and faces reddened with excitement. Maybe there was hope for us after all.

Still, as the army disbanded to bed down, I wondered how many would desert us during the night.

The greetings I received from the sorcerers and dragons that night didn't help my turmoil over the day's events. The sorcerers stood rigid, looking into the distance as if they perceived something troubling. As for the dragons, they again appeared drawn, almost pale, as if they were ill.

Terius faced me first, devoid of his usual rancor. The urgency in his voice caught me off guard.

"Enemies are at work. You're only focus tonight is on learning to fight enemy sorcerers."

Shivering in the rain, I glanced at Rhesalus to see if he agreed. Both his and Moriana's faces were set in tight lines of concern. My pulse stepped up its pace. Would I actually face enemies tonight? No. But I must face the sorcerers as if they were the enemy.

"You ride Enya; I'll take Ramah," Rhesalus insisted, vaulting aboard the dragon. Enya bowed her head so that I could climb on. I still didn't understand how, as a mortal being, I could ride either of the dragons' shades.

Rhesalus added, "Terius will instruct you in your mind as we fly."

Everything else seemed unimportant as within my head Terius reviewed how to cast a sorcerer's spells on dragon back and how to either unseat Rhesalus or destroy him—which wouldn't work with a spirit but was fine practice all the same.

The challenge grew ten-fold when the dragons pitched mock battles with each other. I needed both hands to cast spells and could only rely on the strength of my legs and a touch of magic to keep me from falling off. Enya flying upside down had me screaming in terror.

It didn't take long to realize how little I knew and how poorly I used the Language. My only consolation was that I at least succeeded in casting the spells I remembered. I could take no more when we ended our session, but Terius pushed his face into mine and warned me, "Keep your eyes open, girl. The enemy is all around you in more ways than you can imagine, and you must be ready if and when they attack."

"Why can't you just tell me when and how?"

He glared at me. "Possibilities are not probabilities and knowing the future doesn't guarantee you can change it. Sometimes, interfering can have deadly consequences."

I glared back at him.

With his typically kinder voice, Rhesalus added, "What you now understand, Theona, is what we've been trying to teach you all along. Great and terrible things are coming, and if you are not prepared, everything you hold dear will be destroyed."

They disappeared before I could ask any more questions.

Dawn, soggy from the night's rain, brought the commanders back to the flat boulder where General Bellamy gave them the oath. I joined them, even if Gideon insisted I didn't need to. He knew my loyalties, but I was determined the army witness my sworn fealty.

Not all of the warriors took the oath. Amari told us that a good two dozen had disappeared during the night, taking stolen provisions with them. Four refused to take the oath and departed as we watched. Between the executions and these individuals, we'd now lost another forty warriors, twenty-eight horses, weapons, and food.

"Prince won't care, my lady," Zahra told me, a wry smile on her face. "They'd like as not die without them and their stealing means they dare not return. His Highness sent teams out early to hunt and gather whatever food and game they can find and as much firewood as possible to replenish our supplies before we enter the pass."

The plains offered much besides open spaces, particularly plentiful game. The hunter-warriors ventured every morning and every night anyway, and for my needs, the wild herds offset the grueling toil the sorcerers and dragons inflicted on me—something the army's victuals couldn't meet.

The clouds broke up briefly, and from our vantage point on the boulder and with my eagle-sight, I saw herds of antelope and thick-necked creatures I supposed from textbooks were buffalo grazing in the far distance. Perhaps we wouldn't march immediately if creatures that size were caught and first needed to be dressed. I could have sped their work up greatly if I'd hunted for the army, but ironically, they likely wouldn't appreciate buffalo carcasses being dropped at their feet by a gigantic raptor.

By the time we were ready to march, voices grumbled when the rain turned into a light snow, and the vision I'd had of the dangers in the passageway loomed too real.

"I don't like this," Gideon murmured, face turned upward.

"Nor do I."

His thoughts melded with mine. *"It rarely snows here this time of year. On our trip to Kildaria, it was splendidly warm and beautiful, and that was weeks ago. Obviously, foul weather will increase the dangers and slow us down. Even worse, the troops are muttering about its cause, even some of the generals."*

"Me?" I asked with resentment.

He made a face. *"They fear the sorcerers are making you do it. They're a superstitious lot."*

"Why would I want to make our trek harder? My life is in jeopardy, too. Do they think I nearly died trying to kill the king so that I could pretend to save him? Or called a shaman and his wild savages to attack us?"

Gideon took my hand in his. *"Some may, but I know the truth and so do my most trusted men. We must remain patient with the doubters."*

I sighed. *"Are you sure about the scouts you were to send out before we left Kildaria?"*

"A half-dozen, just as you instructed. Only a few days before we left Kildaria, of course, instead of the week you suggested, because of our hurried departure, but I sent them."

"We have a chance then."

His gaze snapped towards mine. "Only a chance?" He said aloud.

I regretted my wording. "I *meant*," I replied, "we've a chance your men will find our adversaries before they can engage us. If you'd not sent them...."

The vision unfolded in my mind again, as vivid as I'd first seen it. Magical enemies high above us; the ravine itself destroyed on both ends by something cataclysmic that would trap us there. Deep snows, dire cold, deadly starvation. The vision closed, leaving my mind numb.

Not knowing how long the inclement weather might last, the entire company donned winter outer clothing and I asked Sir Arnoe to bring Ian and Kendal to me for a discussion.

"It's so cold," Kendal moaned, her teeth chattering as snowflakes eddied around us.

Zahra had unearthed a jacket for her from my trunk, and a knitted cap, a thick woolen scarf, and mittens. Gideon handed Ian a set of his own winter wear.

Both expressed sincere gratitude, Kendal sighing in relief. "Oh, that's much better. Thank you, my lady."

"We must talk," I told them. I explained to them what Gideon had explained to me. "You need to understand the dangers of the pass. It's a deep ravine, wider in some areas than others, but you must imagine enduring sheer cliff walls on both sides of you, like a maze made of rock, and steep switchbacks that will take us over the mountains and most of the way to Malloria. If the snow continues, it will make it more hazardous, but our greatest danger is our enemies." I explained the vision I'd had in the king's garden prior to my marriage to Gideon.

"But we'll manage, won't we?" Kendal said, eyes wide and brimming with tears.

I did my best to encourage her, even while speaking to her as emphatically as I would to a servant.

"Kendal, to have the best chance of survival, you must agree to something you won't like. Please believe me, it's necessary. You two must travel beside me, where Gideon, his guards, Zahra and I can help protect you, which cannot happen with you riding a distance behind us in a wagon. Sir Lance has a horse for you." I raised my hand to stop her protest. She was terrified of horses, but it didn't matter. She *must* comply. "Ian will lead you. All you need do is sit in the saddle. I beg you to make this sacrifice, Kendal, even if you find it hard. If you don't care about your own safety, think about Ian's."

Anger flashed in her emerald-green eyes, the emotion surprising me. I'd seldom ever seen her upset with me.

Ian bent to whisper in her ear. She looked up, eyes leaking those tears, and nodded. Without a word, she turned her back on me and let him lead her to the saddle-trained dray horse the prince's knight now held for her. I hated seeing more proof that everything I'd ever known had changed because I'd opened The Keeper, including the trust of my dearest friend.

The Elds climbed the flat rock to give the morning's prayer and the day's blessings on the trek. Having the sensation of being watched, as I was by angels in Kildaria's temple, I looked around twice to find the source.

I saw nothing but warriors with their heads bowed.

CHAPTER 25

We traveled for an hour, Malloria's army now mingled with Kalbarri's vanguard and their wagons. A half dozen Mallorian scouts at the front finally turned the army toward a flat-faced cliff. Its base was as crowded by trees and scrub brush as the rest of the mountains, so nothing seemed distinctive about it. When I felt certain they'd run us into the cliff, the path took a sharp left turn and sloped downward behind the heavy brush.

The shadows created by the rough granite wall on the right and the undergrowth on the left hid the huge gash in the earth we entered. Dust, dead leaves, and a thin coating of snow muffled the sounds of our passing. I felt a touch of panic as the ravine descended deeply enough that we could no longer see out of it. How I hated tight, dark spaces!

The Beldames may have appeared to be one long, impenetrable mountain, but that was an illusion. Here, the edge of the peak's base on the left created a narrow wedge that overlapped the cliff on the right, leaving just enough room for us to pass between. No doubt such occurrences were repeated throughout the range and were indistinguishable from this one. We followed its righthand curve heading northeast, my heart thumping as we continued the downward slope. No doubt a flash flood could turn this pathway deadly.

The road finally leveled and continued for an hour. I'd have panicked if the snow had thickened or if the path hadn't led us into an amazing rectangular box canyon, but it did.

An incredibly wide waterfall cascaded from a deep overhang above the flat wall opposite us, a bright green carpet of vines hanging behind the waterfall. The vines were so thick I couldn't see the wall behind them. The water plunged into a small, turbulent lake, which hugged the north wall of the canyon. An unnerving vortex at its far end pulled the water underground and off to some unknown destination. When rain and melted snow swept this way, that vortex likely swallowed them and anything that they brought with them.

The wind blew high above us, a bedeviling, faint, shrill whistle. We halted near the falls, snow drifting downward and stippling the ground at our feet. My prince waited until the canyon held as many as it could before nodding his permission to the half-dozen Mallorian scouts waiting ahead of us. Two of them dismounted and pulled long, thin ropes from their rucksacks. I watched, puzzled, as they headed toward the right of the waterfall. The crag projected much further from the rock wall than I'd realized, and the scouts disappeared behind the waterfall.

Shortly, the men reappeared, one on either side of the falls, their ropes attached to the vines, parting them like curtains and tying them to a projection on the wall I couldn't see from this distance. A tunnel! Its mouth, dark as midnight and recessed behind the falls, was enormous but so craftily hidden by nature I doubted I'd ever have found it on my own.

Gideon rose in his stirrups to catch the troops' attention.

"Sentries will make sure everyone understands what comes next. This tunnel is forty feet wide and four miles long. Appointed warriors will carry torches to light our way, but beware. The cave is natural. No one has ever shored it. The noise and vibration of so many horses and heavy wagons create enough danger. We insist on no conversation or, if necessary, little above whispers for the duration."

He waited for the murmuring to stop before adding, "It takes about an hour to get through. There's another box canyon on the other end, big enough for everyone. The vanguard will rest until the rearguard scouts signal us that the entire army has cleared the tunnel, then they will rest while we proceed."

Three of the scouts continued to pilot us. The other three hung back. Gideon murmured to me that these would remain behind to repeat the instructions to those who followed and to help as needed. Six more scouts followed the rearguard. Not only would they erase our tracks from the trail and release the vines, they would also make sure none of those who'd deserted had followed us—and deal with anyone who might try to desert now. I refused to ask what that meant. Gideon was a prince and would do what he needed to do for his people, but I didn't want to know if he was sometimes forced into ruthlessness.

Hoping to decrease the shaking of the ground and the noise, each country's divisions alternated cavalry ranks with wagons. Our movement caused a constant rumble in the confined space, and only the torches kept me from panicking in the near-black darkness. Gideon and Zahra did their best to keep my mind off it by Mind-Pairing with me.

We arrived at the other end of the tunnel in the time promised. Similar foliage was tied back by the lead scouts, and another waterfall greeted us, the tunnel emptying into another box canyon three times the size of the one from which we'd come. I sucked in lungfuls of air in relief, praying I never had to do something like that again.

The waterfall fed a large pond, nearer the center of canyon, and had no vortex. We maneuvered around it and watered our animals then rested in groups as the others continued to stream in.

Ian helped Kendal dismount, holding her hand as she walked stiffly beside him. He pressed a kiss to her cheek and murmured something I couldn't hear.

"How are you faring?" I asked with concern.

She refused to meet my eye but replied curtly, "It wasn't nearly as terrible as I'd expected, but I do believe my legs will never be the same."

I laughed but cut it short when she didn't smile. She was still angry with me, but I could see Ian was proud of his future Duchess. She'd just proved she could and would do the hard things.

During our wait, the temperature dropped again, and the snow fell in earnest. General Bellamy sent out orders to don our light armor. It offered more protection in an emergency but would also hold in the warmth. The pass may offer seclusion, but with a swift escape impossible in an emergency, it was also a trap.

My apprehension deepened when I saw Nevin Leath climbing a pile of rocks on the south end of the canyon, his supposed custodians teasing him. Near the top of the pile, he stood with hands on hips and then turned around carefully to look over the army.

What was he looking for? Why was he here? Outcroppings that looked suspiciously like handholds on the cliff walls behind him might lead to the plateaus above us. Had Gideon's men climbed up those cliffs to search for the enemy? If the Central Alliance didn't know about this pass, then how would the enemy soldiers I'd seen in my vision get up there? If enemies had found their way here, then this route was no longer safe. Gideon had to know that.

Leath laughed and jumped down to join the others. More than ever, I needed to unearth this man's intentions.

Kalbarri continuing at the helm with the third and last part of our trek. We left the canyon behind us and set out through the deep ravine more than three-wagon-widths wide. We could possibly have driven them in fours, but the commanders kept the left side of the passageway free for the outriders, unexpected breakdowns, or reordering the company as needed.

Despite my reservations, I knew we'd arrived at a pivotal point in our journey. The longest portion of the trip was behind us, and it seemed safer here, even if it was only an illusion. We were at the mercy of those high cliffs and defenseless against attack, but at least we were long past the Badlands and safe from the Central Alliance scouts on the plains.

A good two hours later, the grade took us up a series of steep switchbacks. Still, the flat granite walls rose to more than ten feet above us on both sides. It seemed impossible for this pass to have come about naturally, but I couldn't imagine what sort of cataclysm had created it. Perhaps the earthquake that had torn the Lost Lands from the mainland? The cliffs also robbed us of the view of the terrain below. It certainly protected detection by anyone below us bearing a spyglass, but the thought offered me little comfort.

At first, the wind drove the snow into our faces in tiny, hard flakes of powder that made us hunch into our coats. As the clouds darkened, the snowfall increased, so thick it almost looked like fog in the near distance, and our breaths puffed like thousands of steaming kettles. Soon we trudged through snow a few inches deep that our horses churned into mud. It almost made me wish for the heat of the Badlands.

The steep climb required frequent rests for the horses. They huffed and grunted, dripping sweat and shivering in the cold. I patted Caspian, reassuring him as best I could that he was my hero. He nodded his head and snorted as if he understood.

We'd just stopped for the fourth time when Terius snarled in my mind, *"Heads up, girl. Evil comes."*

The blood drained from my ice-cold face when a horrid shriek echoed through the pass. Instantly, a brief flash of dark orange prescience slammed into me, followed by the sound of flapping wings and a faint stench.

"No, no, no," I muttered, examining the clouds and praying that whatever I'd just envisioned wasn't headed our way.

"Theona?" Gideon asked warily, knowing something was wrong.

Then it was there, in the clouds, a great, gray and brown, red-eyed monster, larger than I'd ever dreamed possible. It had the body of an eagle and a vulture-like head.

"A roc," Rhesalus answered the question I hadn't asked.

"A fable," I riposted.

"No. But few still live and none in this area. I doubt anything but sorcery could have lured it here."

"Archers!" I shouted. "Draw your weapons!"

The warriors who heard me cast me defiant looks. I had no authority to command them.

"Look!" I screamed, spearing a finger toward the sky.

"What are you waiting for, fools!" Gideon roared. "Archers! Prepare to shoot it! Sir Lance, Zahra! Get the princess, Lord Ian and Miss Kendal out of the way!"

Shouts of terror followed, and weapons rose, but not quickly enough. The roc raked the lines of men and horses near the top of the switchbacks with his claws. Screams of pain and shock echoed through the pass, and one unfortunate soul found himself unhorsed and carried by his chain mail above the army.

Sword in hand, he fought valiantly, swinging at the monster and slashing its belly. The bird responded with screams of its own, pausing mid-air. Then it reached down with its curved beak and tore the man's head from his shoulders.

Horrified, I leaned over Caspian and lost the contents of my stomach. Kendal began screaming and wouldn't stop. Zahra pushed Chip into me and urged us to the side of the road. Sir Lance grabbed Ian's and Kendal's reins and dragged their animals toward us. The hovering bird tore at the warrior's carcass but didn't understand the armor. Exasperated, the creature dropped its catch, the body fluttering downward to land somewhere out of sight.

Archers were ready when the beast came again, even angrier than before. It met a volley of arrows that peppered its underside and sent it floundering mid-air. Flying low over Kendal's head and then mine, splattering us with huge droplets of blood, it crashed into a wagon a distance behind us—the wagon in which Kendal had ridden—tossing it to one side like a toy and knocking the screaming horses, three warrior-washwomen and the driver to the ground. The creature bounced then landed with one wing broken and its wounded gut rammed against the cliff wall.

"I've never seen such a monster," a Kalbarrian warrior, just ahead of us, said to his companion.

"Aye. A devil, I think. Straight from Hell's Acres."

"Yeah, and *she* probably conjured it," the first warrior snarled, glaring at me.

Gideon straightened in the saddle and pointed his drawn sword at the man. "If she hadn't sounded the alarm the beast might have torn *your* head off," he snapped. "And if all of you had listened sooner, that warrior may not have needlessly died."

The arrows made the roc look like an overgrown pincushion. It writhed, its claws scouring the cliff walls, its good wing and feet sending showers of stone and snow flying. With its back to our party, however, it could do little damage. It died, leaving a silence that felt unearthly and abandoning us to wonder from where this dreadful creature had come.

"*Rhesalus?*" I asked. "*What does this mean?*"

"*The enemy is here and is prepared to test you.*"

"*Me? Or the army?*"

"*Both. And you must both pass succeed before you reach Malloria.*"

"The monster's blocking the path!" someone shouted, breaking the bewitchment that paralyzed all of us.

Commotion erupted. Warriors righted the wagon and assessed its occupants. The driver was bruised but otherwise alright, but two of the women had broken bones. The look on Kendal's face told me that she knew she'd have suffered the same or worse if she'd been onboard.

Gideon shouted orders in concert with other leaders. The Elds and a handful of healers ran to help up and down the line. Not a soul looked to me for assistance, and stunned, I found myself not inclined to offer. Not after so recently being attacked by the female warriors from our own army.

Troopers pulled the injured horses from the traces to be treated and replaced them with fresh ones, while another group dragged the roc's wings out of the main thoroughfare. No doubt rumor had spread like wildfire up and down the army, but many wouldn't believe it until they saw it themselves.

I huddled in my jacket, my hood pulled close to my ears, and shivered along with Caspian, while Zahra wiped the blood from my face and then Kendal's cheeks with her dampened kerchief. Kendal sat in silence, her face even paler with shock than Ian's. My brother's horse stood head to tail with hers, and Ian held her gloved hand in comfort.

My dear, sweet friend oughtn't to be here. She and my brother should be home, planning their wedding.

It seemed to take forever to put everything to rights, but finally our trek forged on. The snow stopped, but the thick cloud cover made it impossible to tell the hour. The trail narrowed slightly but continued its switchbacks upward.

Later, without warning, the walls disappeared, and we reached a huge, flat plateau, big enough to house a city. The summit! The glorious sight in all directions shook off the malaise that gripped me. The spires of the Beldames stretched out like fortress walls from north to south, cutting off the nations of the Central Alliance; to my left, the brownish-gray expanse of the Badlands melded with the green-gold of the open plains of Langala and Grimstaad's far-distant verdant fields. To the north shimmered the faint blue of the Varigo River. Behind us, eastward and in the mountains that the pass cut through, spring was in full bloom, trees, vegetation, and a riot of wildflowers cloaking the mountainsides and the small dales between them.

More mountains sat eastward, the nearer ones tall enough to block most of the view of the rest, but the enigma was seeing the pass and only a few miles on either side of it coated in a light blanket of snow. Could anything but magic channel a snowstorm on so narrow an area?

The sun broke through the clouds to reveal late afternoon, and Gideon sighed with disappointment. It had taken too long to get to this point. Again. In good weather, travelers could traverse the entire pass in no more than a week, but equipment purposely damaged had slowed us down two full days, and now unseasonable weather and a magical creature's attack had stolen half of another day.

When rested enough, the vanguard abandoned the plateau and left it for the troops following us. Each group would rest and then follow. Now, we faced the precarious descent. The switchbacks rose and fell, sometimes so steep the horses struggled, especially on the slick, wet road. Worse, Gideon warned that nearer the bottom, the road narrowed and the wall on the right side disappeared, leaving a two-hundred-foot cliff with jagged rocks below. I heard two wagon-masters say that anything less than meticulous negotiation could lead to disaster.

The pass narrowed a little more. Zahra and I let Ian and Kendal take the lead, my brother's fiancée still pale and red-eyed and avoiding me. Hours later and without warning, the company drew up. A scout rode back to talk to Gideon before hurrying on to update the commanders behind us.

"We've reached the steepest descent, the most dangerous part of the pass," Gideon explained, his face tense. "Everything should go well if we all do our part."

As with the cavern, we broke into sections, selected riders followed by clusters of wagons, followed by more riders, with the wagon-masters working their own special magic to brave this dangerous downgrade.

Zahra had me turn Caspian so that he tackled the descent at an oblique angle, but his heels still skidded on the wet road several times, planting my heart in my throat. How could heavy wagons manage this?

I was shaking when we finally made it down. Then we all watched the first wagon tackle the grade. Snow began falling again. At least it was powder, and the wind swept most of it off the cliff. My fingers tightened on my reins as Gideon explained the procedure.

Gravity, not the horses, would bring the wagons down. The teams' tasks were to hold them back. Horses from the third wagon were unhitched and harnessed to the back of the first wagon, putting four horses in front and four in back, the animals well-trained for the task. Even they seemed to understand that everyone's safety depended on maintaining control.

I heard the wagon-master's calls as the grueling descent began, and my respect grew for these people who knew their business. I sighed when the first vehicle made it down without incident. Our prayers were answered.

After the handlers returned both teams to the top and left them to rest, the process was repeated with the second wagon, borrowing its rear team from the fourth wagon. They, too, made it safely.

Now the first and third teams brought down the third wagon, and the fourth wagon repeated the process with their horses. Sixteen wagons in all completed the descent and now moved aside for the next group of riders. After the entire vanguard made it down, we would ride on to make room for the next division. Seeing the rest of the army on the treacherous trail above us and more wagons preparing to embark convinced me it was a miracle any of us had succeeded.

I'd just entertained these thoughts when Zahra gasped. "No! No! Look!" she said, pointing.

My hand flew to my mouth when I saw the second wagon poised at the top of the grade. It waited for the one before it to finish the trip, but one of the lead horses was throwing his head and champing at the bit. The wagon-master was doing his best to command the beast and a handler stood at the horse's mouth trying to calm him. They were losing the battle.

The plunging animal jerked the wagon forward enough that the horse next to him slipped. The wheel horses behind them panicked and began pulling in different directions. The handler had to jump out of the way to avoid being trampled.

The wagon-master shouted in terror as the wagon began sliding down the slope, out of control. The horses hitched to the rear were all but dragged off their feet, staggering and slipping on the slick rock and mud and terrified by the weight of the vehicle they could no longer curb. Screams came from all around me. All of us bit our fingernails against sure disaster. The wagon-master no doubt thought he looked death in the face. Whether his team ran into the horses and wagon ahead of him or the crazed animal leaped off the cliff, taking wagon, driver and horses with it, they could all be killed.

We could do nothing but pray. Even if someone else could manage the horse, there wasn't enough time—

Time? My thoughts screeched to a halt. Time! I had more time here than when the king was attacked. More than when Gideon was struck by a javelin. Instinctively, I seized the amber *parhelia* that stopped time.

Now everything around me stood still. Even small snowflakes hung in the air. I dropped Caspian's reins, vaulted into the sky as a swift, and sped toward the frenzied horse. What I saw up close filled me with grief. The animal hung in space near the edge of the cliff, front legs in the air. One more leap, and it and its companions were doomed.

How could I make the best of it? I flew around, considering every angle. The wagon-master sat firm, reins held tight. The animals to the rear nearly sat on their haunches, their last effort to fight the inevitable. The three other horses in front were tugging the wagon to the left, away from the cliff.

I could see only one answer. Stop the unruly horse. I landed on top of it, became myself, and drew my knife. Quickly, I cut the lines from the horse's bit and his harness from the wagon. He would die an awful death, but he wouldn't take the rest with him. I flew back to Caspian, reclaimed my seat, and gave a sigh of terrible sadness as I set time free.

Louder screams rent the air, but gasps rose when the wild horse plunged forward, spun to the right, and landed on nothing but air. Tears sprang to my eyes as the poor creature flipped off the edge of the cliff and fell into the rocks below. The other horses, freed of their teammate, pulled the wagon to the left and then obediently scrambled their way down the road.

At the bottom, both wagon-masters did a masterful job of avoiding a collision, but only when I saw both wagons safe could I breathe again.

"What...What just happened?" Ian asked, his knee bumping against mine. "I swear I saw something, a shadow of some sort, and when the horse jumped, I couldn't believe it didn't pull the wagon over with it."

"I saw it, too," Kendal said, her eyes wide with fright.

"'Tis a miracle, I'm thinking," Zahra replied, watching the wagon-masters.

"An incredible one," Gideon added, his gaze shifting to mine. "For which we must give our utmost gratitude to Elam."

I bowed my head, not wanting them to see me cry. Hadn't I shed enough tears in the last six weeks? Hadn't I seen enough death and suffering?

We marched on. The walls rose on both sides again, but I found I didn't mind it so much, compared to steep cliffs. Even better, the pass widened after a good hour, making it possible to return to our columns and hurry along.

Gossip flittered, mutterings of blame, superstition, evil spirits, witchcraft. And then there was me. The disaster was my fault. I itched to take wing and flee over the mountaintops, away from those who stared holes in my back. I wished I could snatch Gideon and fly him to Malloria. It would take no more than a day or two. I'd be exhausted. I mightn't be able to become human again. But I'd be away from those who'd like to burn me at the stake, and Gideon would know of Malloria's safety.

I couldn't do it, of course. I'd likely set in motion something even worse than what we already faced, but I wanted to.

I also wanted to hug Zahra when she Mind-Paired encouragement to relax my stiff fingers and let go of the tension in my legs. Could we practice our magical skills while we rode, she wondered? Could I talk to her about her other *parhelia*? She was eager to learn of them.

A soft smile relaxed my flattened lips. I didn't know nearly as much as she thought I did. I had too many *parhelia* of my own I still didn't understand. On the other hand, this might be the perfect time to test them.

Making any discoveries heightened our curiosity while it also entertained us. We giggled about talents with odd odors, strange flavors and varying sensations of texture or color. Among the several shades of green in both our *illuminas*? Sea green, blue-green, forest green, the color of the artichoke, the fern, and the olive.

Eld York was right. Each talent was so different that, in truth, being "green" meant nothing. I'd already learned, along with using the Language, to command objects to come to me or fly away. Now I noticed its connection to a lovely teal green *parhelia*.

To Zahra's tribute, she learned to use it faster than I did, and we had to stifle laughter when she accidentally snatched the cigar out of the mouth of one of the wagon-masters. It flew like an arrow, ricocheted off her chest, hit Ian's ear, and then dropped to the ground, spooking poor Chip and sending her bouncing into Caspian.

Ian frowned, touching his ear where I feared he'd been burned, and the wagon-master looked everywhere for his lost cheroot, his bewilderment sending us into gales of laughter.

It helped me let go of the day's solemnities. Despite the weather, I also enjoyed the strengthening of my abilities to both Mind-Pair and to teach. I had no idea how fortuitous that would become until we finally called a halt for the night.

The ravine had a slight cant downhill but remained near-level for the last few hours. We passed a few shallow caves the scouts pronounced safe, and two gaps in the south side of the pass that led to additional narrow box canyons. Neither were wide enough to ride a horse through. Seeing my concern, Gideon reached over to take my hand.

"Dead ends, I promise, and the scouts made sure they're empty."

I sighed and nodded, even if his reassurance was an admission that Malloria knew breaching the pass was possible.

CHAPTER 26

Setting up a comfortable camp at the end of the day came fairly easy on the near-level road. Supper came harder, the blowing wind and light but persistent snow making it difficult to cook.

A request from Sir Lance took Gideon away mid-meal, and he didn't return right away; but before I bedded down, Gideon startled me by Mind-Pairing a request to not change clothes. He arrived shortly with a half-dozen Mallorian warriors, which he waved inside our tent. All young and frightened, they were also red-faced and tense with excitement.

With a touch of formality, Gideon said, "Princess Theona, you and Eld Kane said our troops need to learn to use their magic. These men are loyal. I would trust them with our lives. They heard Eld Reagan's explanation of magic the day the snakes assailed us, and they want to learn. Will you teach them?"

I looked at them with amazement. The thrill of being treated with kindness—no, more than that, with respect and even a touch of admiration—had me near tears—again.

Gideon introduced them: Leo. Pierre and Avery. Morrell. Julian and Henri. Their *illuminas* were filled with a handsome array of *parhelia*. Even better, the men proved diligent.

Leo learned faster than the others, but all six went away having achieved some level of awareness of their powers and having put at least one *parhelia* to use. I offered prayers of gratitude to Elam. If only all of the United Forces' gifted warriors had the same attitude.

I found a small, wooded plateau above the sleeping army to meet with the sorcerers that night. Terius glared at me when I insisted it was time for me to learn to ward.

"If I can only ward my prince, I am satisfied," I said. "I'm not asking to ward the entire army. If you teach me, I'll cooperate with anything else you want me to learn tonight."

Moriana huffed and glared at me from under the hood of the most beautiful mink coat I'd ever seen. She didn't need the warmth of a coat. Shades did not get cold. Rhesalus and Terius wore what they always wore. She just loved appealing to her own vanity and the appearance of beautiful things.

Rhesalus went to reply, but Terius interrupted. "We've more important things to work on, girl."

I growled. "Not to me. Teach me what I want to learn first, or I'll send you away."

"Perhaps you'd like your prince turned into a salt pillar?" he said, his tone as cutting as the wind that swirled around us.

My teeth chattered, somehow ruining the look of defiance I shot him.

"Perhaps you'd prefer I flew back to Kildaria and refused to leave? Better yet, maybe I'll open a portal to my country and walk through it? I suspect at such a distance I'd risk getting lost somewhere in the dark space between here and there. Would that please you? Or would it destroy you? Shall I give it a try?"

"Oh, this is childish," Moriana sneered, planting her nose inches from mine. "You'll freeze to death before you learn anything." Turning to Rhesalus, she snapped, "Teach her, mage. She needs to know all of it anyway, and at least she's willing tonight. You're both foolish not to take advantage of it."

My eyes widened in surprise. I could never have imagined Moriana championing me for anything.

Terius snarled, "Letting her make demands sets a precedent—"

"Stop!" she shouted. "As you've said more than once, we're running out of time! Give her more of what she wants, and she'll *hunger* for the rest of it."

Rhesalus coughed laughter into his hand then cleared his throat. "Cannot underestimate the value of a mage partner, Terius. Moriana, I applaud your wisdom."

Terius growled his protest but otherwise held back.

Rhesalus turned his kind, gray-eyed gaze on me, putting me on my guard. His smile, however, was suggestive enough I wanted to throttle him.

"Let us take a journey," he said. As he'd done before, he pushed my awareness deep inside my *illumina,* drifting lower and lower past *parhelia* I'd never seen before. My fascination made him pause.

"You're aware of all of it," he whispered into my thoughts.

No use denying it. *"Yes. I feel them, and sometimes I can smell or taste them, and...I can see their beautiful colors."*

A pause was followed by a proud sigh of approval. *"Ah, "* he said. *"Which means you have Insight and are aware of it."* He offered a brief explanation, and when I acted properly schooled, he added, *"Have you found where it's placed?"*

"What?" Insight had a place? What did he mean by that?

"Let me show you." His magical power now shoved me the deepest inside my *illumina* I'd ever been, a place neither hot nor cold, neither light nor dark, and guided me between the hypnotic maze of clots of gathered *parhelia* and gaps of stark white nothingness until we arrived at my *illumina's* core. There, a small, dark rectangular shape caught my eye, one easily dismissed as a shadow. It bore the quiet color of brown sugar, and unlike the others, it neither sparkled nor shifted.

"This, my dear, is the gift of Insight. Yours is nearly dead-center and larger—and therefore more powerful—than any I've ever seen beyond Terius's and my own. It's even larger than Moriana's. Parhelia are rarely detectable by anyone until the talents mature in a child, around eight years of age or even older. People with Insight can detect Insight in newborns, but in today's world, most who possess Insight aren't aware of it, while those who are aware shun it."

"People with Insight can see Insight?" Eld York had told me it wasn't possible.

Rhesalus heaved my awareness from my *illumina*, leaving me feeling wrenched from a soft and lovely dream into the harshness of reality. I caught my breath and my footing, fighting both dizziness and the shock of the worsening cold and heavier snowfall. I wondered if my body could freeze to death while I enjoyed a mental journey within my *illumina*. Terrifying thought.

Rhesalus continued. "Those with Insight can see another's Insight, but it's a learned talent. You are one of the few born in recent times with Insight. Your maid is another, but she has little control over it. There are three steps to warding: mastery of your Insight, control of the *parhelia* of warding, and skillful use of the Language."

My shoulders drooped in disappointment. "Then I wonder if I'll ever be able to do it." I'd made good strides with the Language, but I was hardly skillful.

I stumbled back when Terius suddenly lurched into me shouting, "You have the gift of tongues, girl! If you were to meet someone from the other side of the world whose language you'd never heard, you know your magic would translate it. The Language is a language. It makes no sense you cannot master it, except that you have a mental resistance to it. I want you to pause for a moment and watch and feel as I place a simple ward around you."

Terius grabbed my hand, and the harsh, guttural words of the Language made my insides quiver, the incantation's power seeming to rise from my very soul. No, *his* soul. His spiritual aura dwelt inside me, and his power touched mine.

He repeated the words, now stroking the air with his hands to form something bubble-like. It grew larger and crystal clear but faintly blue, curved enough to catch the light and give the impression of thickness.

His hands spread the bubble longer and thinner, the recited words changing its character as it molded around and around both of us and seemed to disappear. When it settled, I felt as if I was enclosed inside a glass house and away from the storm.

Terius's golden-eagle eyes met mine, the challenge plain.

"I've never taken that long to form a ward in my existence," he said. "That was for your benefit. I also gave it a faint bluish tinge to allow you to see it. After you've learned how, you can do it instantly, and it will be completely invisible. Your problem isn't with the talent, it's the Language." He snapped his fingers and the bubble vanished.

Stunned, I realized every step of his creation felt burned into my brain, into my very bones. My *illumina's* surface and the Language melded together, the power rising up inside me. The breeze swirled before me, tiny particles too small for the naked eye to see, and yet I could. I raised my hands to feel the frozen air whisper across my palms and then, with care, murmured the words *"Palliam affectis templarim."* Veil of Sanctuary.

The air settled itself on my palms and stayed, an inexplicable weight that proved it existed. I repeated the litany and snow no longer fell on me. Once more, and I felt cradled inside an invisible cocoon. Inside it, my own mage light offered no reflection. My *parhelia* warmed the narrow space and my freezing hands.

"Ahhhh," Rhesalus said, pride shining in his eyes. "Superb. I couldn't have done it better."

He touched it with an index finger, and it popped. He laughed. "Well, perhaps I could. Practice will help, my dear."

Moriana began to clap, slow and loud. The men joined her.

"The only thing standing between you and your success is your stubbornness," Terius said. "When you put it aside, the world of magic will be at your fingertips."

Astonished by what I'd done and by the Language itself, I practiced a while longer. Of course, once I'd begun to make good headway, Rhesalus had to ruin it all by lecturing me about rules and consequences. Blast the confounded consequences!

"You cannot change them, Theona. You just need to know how to make wards without killing yourself or others and the appropriate times to use them. When you erase the trail of magic, you remove the visible proof you've used magic, but what about talents that have other characteristics? Scents, sounds, or even impressions cannot easily be erased. You wouldn't want enemies to find your location by the scent of any food you're cooking, but what about a *parhelia* that another sorcerer could detect?"

The *parhelia* of portalling smelled of peppermint. Could a sorcerer smell it? Could he or she smell it on either side of the portal?

"Yes, my dear," Rhesalus affirmed, warning me I'd allowed him into my thoughts. I tightened my shields as I sighed my understanding. An Eld might recognize and understand the scent of peppermint whenever I created a portal.

He continued. "Wards confine those attributes, and although you cannot portal while warded, you can make a ward on either side of a portal. You can ward inanimate objects almost indefinitely, but small wards hold breathable air for only twenty-four hours, larger ones for three days. Anyone warded too long will suffocate."

The laboratory's doors had been warded for centuries, keeping hidden the atrocities inside, but I knew the sorcerers' evil had tainted me when I realized wards could be used to capture, control, or even kill someone.

As if on cue, Rhesalus said, "Be warned. Any magical gift can be used for good or bad. In olden times, those who used magic to harm or destroy were detained with magical chains."

"Like the ones in Mt. Draakheda." The ones that hung from the walls. My stomach dipped at the thought of the suffering those chains had inflicted on hundreds of dragons.

"Yes. But gifted people could break free of them, so malefactors needed harsher restrictions and punishments. The Elds sedated them and bound their *illuminas*, which meant they warded the offender's talents from him- or herself and rendered their magic unobtainable."

"Didn't they do that to Moriana?" I asked. If so, how did she manage to escape prison?

Moriana's lips turned up into a smug grin. "Yes and no. Even then, the Elds had forgotten some of the old ways and didn't know the process had two parts. Binding the *illumina* works on a person *without* Insight, but if an offender has Insight, then his or her Insight must be bound *first*. The Elds' mistake allowed me to ward my Insight from *them*, and in time, my Insight set my *illumina* free. A matter of self-preservation, of course. Where you're concerned, Kildaria's Elds have lost most of the old ways and don't know how to bind you at all. But the Elds who travel with you will learn, Theona. The Elden tomes you gave them will teach them. You also have no idea what to expect from Malloria's Elds."

I remembered Enya warning me about the punishment of binding, but I had no idea what it meant then. Now, I had no desire to trick the Elds if I did something wrong, but I might be able to use it against the sorcerers. No wonder they had put off teaching me.

On the other hand, alarms went off inside my head as the temptation rooted itself in my soul. I didn't want to turn my magic evil.

"Do you still want to learn the magic of invisibility?"

My mental ears perked! He was offering?

"Rhesalus?" Terius's tone conveyed the same surprise.

The horse-mage held up a hand. "She's conquered worse tonight. Let's see if it's opened doors previously closed to us—to her."

I didn't like his quick correction and wanted to protest. Then I flinched as the cold bit into my hands.

"I must take care of myself first," I insisted, closing them off and fleeing into the mountains, away from the ravine. There, a warm night free of snow allowed me to heal fingers threatened with frostbite and stuff my stomach as a night hawk. I portalled back to the plateau, filled with even more anticipation, and recalled the sorcerers.

"You know where to find the *parhelia*," Rhesalus said, all but daring me.

I did, and I did.

"Splendid. By simply touching it, you'll find it shows you everything in all directions as if every inch of your body had eyes."

My breath caught when exactly that happened. Above and below, on all sides, I could "see" everything without turning around.

"How?" I managed to ask.

"It absorbs the light and passes that image through you to the opposite side. A hundred people in a circle around you or a bird flying overhead can only see what's on the other side of you. You see everything from the center, where the images cross."

"Amazing."

"And dangerous. It does not damper sounds or smells, and it can sap your strength without your realizing it. You know the ramifications. You mustn't use it for more than an hour, maybe two—and then it will *demand* sustenance and sleep."

"Not convenient if I'm in a hurry or in danger."

"No. But you can use all of your other talents with it, including portalling. If you must get away, open a portal no larger than the smallest creature you can become and immediately find shelter."

The thought fascinated me. But could I master it?

"Shall we?" He asked.

Again, he guided me, but I fell to my knees, my mind spinning and my stomach heaving, when I got a firm grip on the *parhelia*.

"Deep breaths, girl," he said. "There. Calm your heart and still your mind. Rise slowly and carefully. You're still visible but fading. Do as you're accustomed. Stroke the *parhelia* and demand its obedience."

The uneasiness on the three sorcerers' faces told me when I'd done it. I dared not giggle as I took careful steps away from them, hoping to hide. I couldn't go far—after all they were bound to me by possession—but I had to try. Their looking around askance proved I'd succeeded!

A branch just beneath the snow at my feet snapped, giving me away. I changed into my owl-form, hopefully still invisible, and glided to a small tree behind Rhesalus. When I hurled my mage light at Terius, I startled him, which made me laugh out loud.

"You've had enough fun, Theona," Rhesalus said with amusement. "You've done well, but how do you feel?"

Exhausted. I could have described it as feeling nearly invisible, which again made me want to laugh. I fluttered to the ground, became myself, and set the *parhelia* free.

Rhesalus's eyes widened in shock. "Go. Now. Eat, then hurry to your cot. You've done too much."

Everything seemed comical as I obeyed him, until I returned to my tent. There, I collapsed onto my cot, alarms going off in my head. Not only because I'd done too much, either. I'd once wondered what sort of person I could become if all I had to do was wish for something and it happened. Now that I could remove the trail of magic, portal, ward myself, and turn invisible, I'd become almost as close to invincible and undetectable as any mortal could get, and I feared I could become the worst of monsters.

Not a pleasant thought to take with me into my dreams.

"I'm guessing you've a headache, my lady," Zahra murmured as she roused me from my dead sleep. "You've been doing a fair bit of moaning for the last few hours. Understandable, considering you were again gone a good part of the night."

"I'm sorry I disturbed you, Zahra."

She gave me one of her cheekier grins. "'Tis the curse of being a light sleeper, but it means I can protect you better. At least from ordinary things. The sorcerers are another matter. My lady, Prince Gideon prefers to let you sleep as long as possible, but now he's sent for you."

I gave her a weak smile and sat up but cringed at the sound of the buglers' morning wake-up call. At least I wasn't as nauseated as usual, despite having used more magic in the last twenty-four hours than ever before.

We were alone. I supposed Kendal had gone off with Ian. Catching a glance at The Keeper and Slayer and suddenly feeling a pull toward them I could hardly resist, I hurried Zahra through dressing me. I wanted to get away from them even more than I wanted food to fill my again-starving belly.

I came up short when I stepped out of the tent and found myself knee deep in snow—and the snowfall unabated. The storm! I'd forgotten about it.

Gideon stood by our campfire alongside a group of concerned commanders and scouts. I followed their gazes, fixed on the scene of the pass smothered under two feet of snow—deeper in myriads of snowdrifts—as far as the eye could see.

I came to Gideon's side, and he gave me a wan look as he wrapped an arm around me. "Imagine trying to shovel our way through miles of that," he murmured.

"The wagons can't get through it?" I asked. The horses likely could.

"Where it isn't steep and the drifts aren't too deep, but look." He kicked the snow away with his boot, revealing a sheet of ice underneath it. "It's still falling, and the ice and any changes in the grade ahead will exhaust the horses and endanger the wagons. A secure camp we already have is better than moving through terrain that's too risky. Best to stay put, even if it puts us another day behind."

"Or two or three days or more." Sir Lance said with fatigue. "Hopefully we won't exhaust our provisions before we reach Malloria."

Eld Kane approached Gideon, his face drawn. "Your Highness, I bring more bad news. A Mallorian warrior has taken ill. The healers are concerned it could spread."

I felt the weight of Gideon's duties pressing down on him. I urged him to avoid touching the man as he turned to follow the Eld to the infirmary tent. He also promised to call for me if the warrior would accept my help.

Troubled by our predicament, I Paired with Zahra. *"I've an idea. Have two of the young Mallorian men I tutored last night sent to me. Leo, the tall redhead, and Pierre, the one with the shoulder-length black hair."* Of the six students, these two did best with the Elements. *"I've a lesson for them that might help us get back on the road."*

They came a short while later, their freshly filled rucksacks and water skins slung over their shoulders as I'd asked. Zahra and I drew them into the prince's tent to discuss my idea, which elated them. They were young, of course. Older than I was, but more naïve than I thought I'd ever been. They thought this would be fun.

On the right side of the pass behind Gideon's tent stood a rocky shelf a good ten feet above the road. Thick bushes and shrubs had taken root there, a perfect place to hide our deeds from curious eyes.

Zahra climbed to the shelf behind us to act as lookout, while we dusted off the ledge and sat down.

"Your goal is to learn better control of the Elements. You may not accomplish it now or even tomorrow, but when you do, the three of us might be able to clear the snow from the pass."

Pierre, the dark-haired warrior—more reserved than his companion—asked with hesitation, "Is it dangerous?"

"Magic is always dangerous, Pierre, especially Elemental magic. We could get hurt. We could hurt others. Displacing a storm here may send it elsewhere. It may dissipate along the way or strike farms, destroy crops, cause floods or hurricanes that sink ships—and we may never know."

He frowned in disapproval. "Malloria cannot afford to lose its farmlands."

"Who can? But will avoiding the risk to your crops today matter if the Central Alliance attacks your people next week and turns your farms into killing fields? I won't force you, of course. But if you follow my lead, you'll learn how to use your magic as safely as you can, and with practice you will become good at it." I hoped. I was hardly an experienced tutor. I only prayed he'd give it a try.

He nodded, despite his reluctance, and I explained the checks and balances we'd use, things the sorcerers had taught me...*after* I'd taken great risk with Elemental magic.

The redhead, Leo, grinned with excitement. "We have to give it a try, Pierre. I'm smelling our homeland and aching to put my feet on its soil once again. Just tell us what to do, my lady."

"We'll start small," I cautioned him, making sure they both understood that rushing the process was more dangerous than the magic itself.

For the next hour we experimented with Water, Fire, Earth, and Air. They did their best to wrestle with their *parhelia* which, like Zahra's, didn't yet know how to obey. In addition, Leo's exuberance and Pierre's reluctance made them unequally yoked partners. It took time to synchronize them, but when we did, Air—cloaked as Wind—became our best ally: first as strong gusts, then as dust devils and finally brief squalls. We were on the right track, but they quickly exhausted the food in their rucksacks—and themselves.

"Restock your sacks and get some rest. We'll try again later this afternoon."

Both swore their allegiance.

Gideon Mind-Paired a request for me to join him at the infirmary. He was still with the Elds, a healer, and the two ill warriors. I agreed with the healers. Nothing felt malevolent about the diseases, just ordinary colds. The weather was the likely culprit. Coming from warmer climes, the wind, snow and unseasonable cold invited illness. The dark, unwelcome looks the warriors cast me, however, repelled my desire to heal them. Eld Reagan whispered his disappointment.

The Eld quarantined his patients and then went out to warn everyone, especially their closest traveling companions. He also muttered something about not knowing if being stuck here was a blessing or a bane. The warriors could rest, but our camps' conditions were far from ideal. For one thing, horses didn't tolerate standing in snow for days at a time. Warriors could dig out areas where they could stand and could bind their hooves against freezing, but it still wasn't a good situation.

Darker clouds gathered, and by late afternoon the snow fell harder. An unnatural, oppressive weight bore down on my soul from the storm. If someone or something could trap us here this way, I wondered if sending Gideon's scouts from Kildaria to stop our enemies had accomplished anything or just sent them to early graves.

Leo and Pierre's second attempt went better but had to stop because of the cold. Thankfully, as cooks lit campfires and warriors shared supper, the snow tapered off, and although it was too cold and wet to bring out musical instruments, storytellers engaged warriors around many a campfire, while folk songs and shanties echoed up and down the ravine.

CHAPTER 27

The snow stopped; the temperatures fell. Terius taught me that warding myself against the cold used less energy in the long run. "This storm has a magical source, doesn't it?" I asked.

Rhesalus grinned. "You're growing more aware. It does, and it will take magic to overpower it. Let's work on perfecting your wards so that you can deal with such threats safely."

I agreed without realizing the cost of the work, but I did reap the rewards. In time, Rhesalus couldn't pop the bubble I created, and Moriana couldn't hit me with rocks—though she thoroughly enjoyed trying. Terius failed to strike me with tree branches, and Rhesalus unsuccessfully cast fire at me. I learned to ward only my hands from the cold, my eyes from sandstorms, or my lungs from drowning. I could ward anything or anyone, and if I warded an enemy before he attacked, I could in essence imprison him. I had no one on which to practice warding Insights, but Rhesalus assured me that I could do it.

Of course, he had to spoil my fun with even more rules: my wards were mine alone. In most cases, no one else could remove them, and unless I wanted to commit murder, I must remember to free any living creatures inside them within twenty-four hours. The Brotherhood of Trees had warded my senses so that I couldn't find food. What if they'd left me to die? I never wanted to do that to anyone.

Dismissed from my lessons, I fed and then called out the dragons. My jaw dropped and I took a step back at seeing them looking...*wrong*. Why? Spirits experienced neither hunger nor disease.

"What's wrong with you? Why do you look so frail?" I asked.

"We are far from home," Enya replied, distracted.

I made a face. "Dragons get homesick?"

Her gaze snapped to mine, the dragon suddenly on guard. Had she said something she'd shouldn't have? "Yes. We miss our home just as you do."

Ramah snorted. "There's a large herd of wild horses in a valley a short distance north of here, Theona. Let's practice Linking."

He wanted to distract me. Like the sorcerers too often did?

It irritated me, but we flew to the small valley where the horse herd slept. Wisps of mist hugged the foothills, but when we landed, agitation spilled out of the dragons. When Enya Linked, she screeched her joy and shut her mind off from me. She flew away, her soul tugging at mine but thankfully not far this time. When she returned, her jade hide glistened like polished stone, her eyes sparkling the most iridescent blue green I'd ever seen. Her transition out of the horse came almost without effort.

Ramah touched noses with her and then, snorting like an eager racehorse, Linked with the herd stallion like lightning, the brutality of it rocking me.

My anger spilled over when he returned from his flight every bit as refreshed. "Do not lie to me! Do not ignore me. What are you doing that rejuvenates you this way?"

He growled and hunched down before me.

"Ramah!" I snapped when he remained quiet.

"We've drawn strength from a Nexus not far from here," he grumbled.

Nexus? Irritation flared. Another unfamiliar word? Another secret? "You've drawn strength from a *what?* What is a Nexus?"

He narrowed his eyes at me. "The intersection of magical ley lines that encircle the entire world," he said. "Their power is a hundred-fold the sum of the ley lines involved, and that power invigorates our spirits. It did the same to our bodies when we had them—almost as if we were reborn. The main reason for our long lives. Mt. Draakheda is our hatching place and for us is the greatest Nexus in the world, but we can take energy from any of them. There were a few Nexuses along the road from Kildaria to the Badlands, but there have been none since we left Mt. Draakheda—until now."

I flushed with anger from head to toe. The sorcerers had lied once again. It did affect the dragons to leave their hatching grounds. Without Nexuses, they *could* sicken and die! And if they did, I supposed their souls, their *rumoria*, would be dragged into the Underworld. Along with the sorcerers? A nugget of truth to treasure.

The instructions in the book *Linking Souls* crashed into my thoughts, forming a knot in my belly. Now I understood its purpose in ways I couldn't even say out loud, and I despised it as much I loathed the fact that because of Nexuses, they and the sorcerers could become next to immortal.

I glared my resentment at them, and likely sensing it, Ramah again touched noses with Enya and they disappeared. I headed back to my prince-husband's arms praying for some hope that we could beat all of this.

———

Four feet of snow fell in Friday's wee hours. I saw worse than fear in many a warrior's eyes as they struggled from their tents, and even Gideon looked beyond crestfallen. I sent for my two students and placed a reassuring hand on Gideon's arm.

"Have patience, my love," I murmured to him. "Two of my warrior-students and I are working on a solution."

Suspicion arched one of his brows upward. "Which is?"

I shook my head. "Best you don't know until it's done."

My faithful warrior-maid and I then slipped off to join Pierre and Leo on the ledge. Faithful Zahra had had the young men collect twice the foodstuffs this time.

I pointed eastward. "We haven't the luxury of taking this easy," I said with apology. "This storm seems determined to trap us here forever. At this point, the pass looks straight as an arrow as far as we can see, a good sixty miles or more. We need to create winds strong enough to blow away the storm and push the snow through the pass. But," I emphasized, "we cannot lose control or it could destroy everything in its path—even us."

In my mind's eye, I recalled my first experience using the Elements with Moriana. I'd watched the sorceress turn rain into a flood, fire into something the size of a small sun, command winds that destroyed part of a forest, and shake the ground until it broke. Later, with Moriana gone and me not aware of the dangers, I'd done my best to rectify the damage she'd caused, coming close to destroying myself in the process.

"You think we're ready to rid the pass of the snow?" Leo asked, the thrill turning his cheeks redder than the cold. Pierre merely gulped.

"If all goes well, warrior. We'll at least try. Let's get started."

We clasped gloved hands, and I slipped inside my magical world and took them with me. As I'd done with the healers when I'd been wounded, I used their magic to amplify my strength while teaching them how to better control their own. Their combined power wasn't even half as strong as mine, but oddly enough, the synergism made us five times stronger together. Air churned into Wind pushed the clouds southward, but they resisted, billowing and flowing, crackling with electricity. I demanded more power. The warriors dug deep to give it.

We ramped Wind into a squall, sweeping it from the far west end of the pass eastward, stripping snow from the stone and sand floor and blowing faster and harder until it turned into a tempest. Soldiers cried out; horses neighed. Tents were blown over, a few blew away, and in the near-blizzard whiteness we could see nothing. Wind howled, clouds fractured, and people screamed in fear. I curbed my students, and the wind gradually dwindled to nothing.

Then, in the dawning sunlight and eerie silence, the pass lay bare as far as the eye could see. My students knew they'd done something extraordinary when shouts of exultation and praises to Elam erupted all up and down the cavalcade. The young men stood mesmerized, their magic still bound to mine but their hearts and minds following the storm.

I struggled to release them from their thrall, and when I succeeded, they went to the ground, Leo on his back, laughing hysterically, Pierre on his knees, retching. I sat down hard, my head spinning.

I glanced at Zahra, who flashed a wry smile and handed over our rucksacks. We bolted down every bite and gulped great mouthfuls of water from our skins.

"You know it's best you don't take credit for it right now. And don't fight sleeping today," I ordered them. "Tie yourselves to your saddles if you must, but sleep."

They nodded and stumbled back to their company. Zahra took my empty pack and smiled at me, knowing I needed to hunt. I'd used far more power than the men, but I couldn't take any more than the essentials from our army's limited stores.

I returned amazed to find the army feverishly breaking camp. The mood had altered completely, with frequent shouts of excitement and more smiles than I'd seen in days. Gideon greeted me with even more enthusiasm, adding that the ill warriors had simple colds and were deemed fit enough for travel.

"We owe you a debt of gratitude they don't even understand, my love," he murmured.

"Reaching Malloria quickly and safely will be gratitude enough," I replied. He squeezed my hand in appreciation.

Claiming our mounts, Gideon, Zahra, and I joined Kendal and Ian, already on horseback and talking with a handful of Kildarian warriors.

"Can't believe that tempest," Ian said, his gaze fixed on me. "Literally swept the snow off like a giant broom."

Kendal nodded. "And brought us fair weather. It's wonderfully warm now."

Of course, some of the warriors muttered even more superstitious nonsense, but they seemed the exception, and the bugle-call to prepare to ride stopped further discussion. Gideon winked at me as we set out again, so very grateful to move forward.

I happily dozed to Caspian's swaying gait a good part of the morning but roused when our path sloped downward. Uneasiness struck when I saw the walls rising again, the strip of sky like a narrow blue river overhead. Familiar with this place, Malloria's men seemed unfazed, but the rest moved uneasily, faces lined with worry. Tight spaces were one thing; the indefensible position was growing worse. Again, paths led at various angles from the main route on both sides, but they were supposedly blind paths and none much wider than a starving man turned sideways.

Trying to make up for another lost day, we carried on into dusk, though it came early with such high cliffs. When we bedded down, we were at least grateful that the hard, cold, rock floor was dry.

Tension draped the next morning's preparations. Sunnier day notwithstanding, the high cliffs created a gloom that increased the troops' restlessness. Murmured complaints included everything from feeling buried alive in a rock coffin to even more superstitions surrounding how the snow had been blown from the pass.

I sighed and shook my head. No one could reason with people who wanted to accuse me of everything malevolent.

As we set forth to the sound of canticles sung by the Elds and the echoing clatter of wagons and hooves, my heart fell when my skin began to crawl with unease.

No, no! Nothing good ever came from that harbinger of danger.

Ever vigilant, Zahra's gaze combed the ledges above and the occasional shallow caves on either side. We depended on the scouts, but she pointed out that no one could prepare for everything—and what about the traitors we feared?

For better or worse, nothing untoward happened and monotony came to roost. I wanted to sing when the road leveled and the walls suddenly dropped. They still held deep snow, but I could see green peeking out from under the blanket of white at the edges. Beyond that, the view of the surrounding mountains revealed their sides still clad in the splendor of spring. The day warmed and the mood lifted.

Gideon's mood, however, did not.

"What wrong, Love?" I asked him.

He glanced at the cliffs again, as he had so many times during this trip. "My scouts. They should have joined us by now—or at least left some sign they've come this way."

That awful feeling of dread tightened my stomach again, but before I could respond, one of Gideon's riders cantered up to us from the vanguard.

"Your Highness, good word," he said in Mallorian. "*Dernier Canyon* lies just ahead."

Last Canyon. What did that mean? Gideon sighed in relief.

"Finally. Thank you, warrior. Carry on."

The young man set his heels into his mount and continued down the line with his news.

To me, my prince said, "It's the largest canyon in the pass and the last one where we can all camp together. That will be good for everyone."

"Wonderful," I murmured, but my thoughts remained on his missing scouts. Where were they? Anything could have happened to them. Besides falling victim to our enemies, they could have been captured, attacked by beasts, starved or frozen to death, taken ill…or perhaps they just couldn't reach us.

When we arrived at the box canyon, I could have imagined it a small valley if not for the sheer cliffs surrounding it. Its spacious area contained three large ponds, grazing land, and an abundance of shade trees. Already in leaf and in bloom, some had taken a bit of damage from the cold, but for some reason not much snow had fallen here.

Camps sprang up, supper brought normalcy, and the requisite instruments and dancing followed. The army's noise made me uneasy, but Gideon's worry about his missing scouts made it worse. What if I'd sent good men to their graves?

"They're wearing the bracelets the Elds gave them," I reminded, trying to reassure us both. "They should be safe from any enemies bearing magic."

"There is that," he agreed, nodding.

"You know I look for them whenever I hunt. I've found no signs of human life anywhere outside the ravine."

He gathered me into his arms and buried his nose in my hair. "I know, my darling."

Then I saw Nevin Leath strolling through some of the campsites with his little entourage of guards and felt my anger rise. What was that man up to? He had no business here, but he behaved as if he were the main attraction in a very important gathering.

"We've done everything we can to prepare for this," my prince pointed out. "Elam will see us through."

I hugged him tight to calm both our fears. Danger lurked above us. And behind us. And ahead of us. Even within us. If only I knew where and what it was and how to stop it.

"I feel like going to bed early," I told Gideon, pulling away. I knew he wouldn't go to sleep until he was certain the camp was safe. I kissed him good night and purposely avoided Zahra and our guards as I slipped into the shadows.

"I need to practice becoming invisible," I told Rhesalus.

Disapproval muddied the amusement in his laughter. *"In a crowd?"*

"Especially in a crowd. I need to spy on Leath when he's talking to others."

He laughed again. *"Invisible? Clever girls can get more than they bargained for."*

"I'll take that chance."

"But you'd like my blessings."

"No. I'll do it anyway. But I don't mind a watchful eye or a word of advice if needed."

"Ah. Very well. But do not ignore me if I sound alarms."

I nodded then began the awkward process of donning a ward for protection before daring invisibility.

"Excellent," Rhesalus praised me. *"But you won't last long. You're already hungry."*

I laughed quietly. *"I'm always hungry. Now, for Leath."*

I knew the councilman was up to more than strutting about like a peacock when he took a lantern and excused himself to visit the latrines. No guards followed, and in the shadows between tents and flickering fires, he changed directions toward the far side of the canyon. Two shadows, men who whispered, met him with only a hint of camaraderie.

I circled the men to get a better look at them. Both had dark hair. The man on the right wore a Segovian uniform and a scruffy beard. The other, a Kythosian, had a hooked nose and an eye patch that made him look like a pirate.

Nearly elbow-to-elbow with Leath, I prayed my disguise held, only regretting I didn't have the strength to add Mind-Pairing to my magical escapade. I'd have loved to know what Leath was thinking rather than just hearing the carefully crafted words that would escape his mouth.

"Fin'ly caught ya alone, Leath—"

"No names, fool!" Leath hissed sharply at the Segovian. "The Mallorians may have no idea who I am, but the Western League does."

"The whole United Forces army's aware of your *kidnappin'* councilman," the man replied. "I'm guessin' your snarlin' will perk more ears than my greetin'."

Leath huffed but swallowed a reply.

"'Sides," the Kythosian added, "Handin' this over is more important to us than who you are." He handed Leath a bulky envelope.

"At last. I was worried I wouldn't get it before we...*arrived*."

"Same with us. We can't read, need you to do it for us."

Leath snorted in disgust as he handed the Kythosian the lantern and carefully opened the parcel. Glancing inside, he withdrew a bit of paper and unfolded it. Leaning toward the light, he whispered as he read.

"To W:

Seems you survived the delivery, hopefully before the 4th summit. Congratulations. Reminders/precautions: no conflict with princes or generals. Civility gathers information, i.e., about monsters. Friendship creates vulnerability on both sides. Beware. Safest position near the M's but not ahead. Welcoming committee within a few days of gaining access. Failure assumes an interruption, change of plans. Drive through. Amulets within. You know the assignment. Only work if touched.

Hawk"

The message made little sense. The delivery? The 4th summit? Perhaps the monster was me. Who were the "M's"? The welcoming committee might be King Olivier. If someone or something failed, what did "Hawk" mean by "driving through"? Amulets were magical. Who would get them? What did they do?

Leath's cohorts seemed equally mystified.

"A bit confusin', if you ask me," the Kythosian said, scratching his head.

"Because the note wasn't meant for you," Leath muttered. Did he understand it or was he bluffing? "Put these on. Keep them under your tunic."

"Alright," the Kythosian said, taking two objects and handing one to the Segovian. "Wha's it for?"

"Just put it on and keep it on," Leath hissed.

Both men did as instructed, slipping chains around their necks.

"You doing the same, Leath?" the Segovian asked, grinning. "Wouldn't disobey the master if I was you."

I watched as Leath examined a third chain. I only caught a glimpse of a large pendant dangling from it before he pulled it over his head and stuffed it under his own tunic. Then he responded, his voice dripping with venom. "Disobey? You err, my friend. Hawk and I are *partners*. Thwart *me*, and *you'll* regret it."

The two men's faces blanched, even in lamplight. Through my mind flashed hundreds of scenarios, memories of my last several weeks' association with Leath. His calming demeanor with Darby Murdock had kept Murdock in line. His quiet standoff with Egan Gilroy had drawn the line between them. The only one who seemed to unnerve him was Gideon, but was he truly intimidated by my prince? Or playing another one of his games?

The three men parted without any suggestion they would ever meet again. I opened a portal and returned to our camp, finding Zahra, who scurried frantically back and forth between the rows of tents, no doubt looking for me.

"Zahra," I called to her. She jumped, not expecting me to be where I'd not been just a second before. "I need your help."

We sequestered ourselves in our tent, where she brought me the food I needed. I apologized for abandoning her without warning but explained the reason.

"I was as safe as I could be," I reassured her. "But I now know that Leath is part of a plot, maybe the same band that attacked the king, maybe not. The letter proved it, even if it didn't make sense. On the other hand, I feel something bad is coming, with or without Leath. I can feel it in my bones."

"As I do in mine," Zahra agreed. "But you're looking frail, my lady. Your prince may join you late. You'd best take advantage and get some sleep. Maybe not visit with your evil magicians tonight."

I chuckled as I managed to pull up my blankets and collapsed into my pillow. "Sorcerers, Zahra. They're not magicians, they're…."

———┼———

Dundee took the leadership from Kalbarri on Sunday morning, the twenty-second day since leaving Kildaria. The ravine snaked slightly eastward, but the pass narrowed, and the walls rose to a good thirty feet, which renewed the army's edginess. The occasional openings we passed in the walls were still not likely to hide villains, but I also prayed that whatever cataclysm created this peculiar place didn't recur while we rode through it.

We marched doggedly from dawn until past dark. The itch on the back of my neck turned beastly, and neither my *parhelia* of prescience nor Moriana's ring cared to enlighten me. The sorcerers offered no comment.

Rain, feeling as unnatural as the previous day's snow, driving and cold, came as we set up camp. By the time I met with the sorcerers, I knew another bad storm had come. The sorcerers wouldn't address it, and I cut them off. Flying south, away from the pass, I quickly left both clouds and rain behind, more proof this storm was as magical as the last.

When I called out the dragons, Enya's first words stunned me. "You've learned a bit about fighting on dragon back, but now you must learn how to fight as a dragon."

Another secret. She didn't even have to explain. My heart sank.

"The enemy's truly near."

"Yes. And dragons are among them."

"*What?* But how can they have dragons? I thought you two were all that was left, and you're..."

"Dead. We don't know. We just know it's true."

I thought of the dream I'd had, of the young man on the red dragon.

"Theona, just learning to fight isn't enough. You must learn to fight as if your life depended upon it. Watch."

The pair then offered an exhibition that left me open-mouthed. Like puppies play-fighting, they demonstrated skirmishing on the ground and then battling in the air. Ramah was stronger, Enya faster. As the competition escalated, the violence seemed cataclysmic, a bewitching dance of bashing wings, entwined necks and tails, slashing claws and vicious fangs. They couldn't have given such a performance in mortal bodies without fatally wounding each other.

"You must try it," Enya said, urging me to don my dragon persona. "The sorcerers can kill you in their spirit form; we cannot, but you must practice warding yourself for your own good. First, we'll teach you self-defense. Let your dragon-self take over. Your instincts will banish your human fears."

She was right. Even when we played the game of changing sizes to trick each other, my magic seemed to know what to do. I managed to give her better competition than I'd ever given Zahra with a sword. I just knew I wouldn't survive a clash with a mortal dragon for a second.

Ramah then taught me specific maneuvers that he claimed might one day save my life. After I sent them away for the night, I flew high in a sky thick with clouds to try to sort out the emotions that bombarded me. I should feel safer knowing these things, but I feared placing my trust in creatures that might be manipulating me as much as the sorcerers. I could learn all sorts of fighting and portalling and making wards, and perhaps I could someday vanquish mortal enemies, but was I really learning anything that would protect me from *them*?

Flying lower, I found myself following the ravine. It took a slight southeastward bend, and I gawked when I saw a mountain of snow hiding there! No! The snow Leo, Pierre and I had sent off! It had landed here. The army couldn't get through it. Daytime heat had melted some of it, but the nights had turned it into a ten-foot wall of ice that stretched on for miles.

I landed in a nearby tree, wondering what to do. The solution that dawned on me would have thrilled Pierre and Leo if they were here— if it worked.

I dropped to the ravine's floor, became myself and called Fire. Remembering how Moriana had done it, I summoned flames on my fingertips, which I fit together into a small orb and swelled it larger and larger. When the heat stung my skin, I thrust it from me, daring to wield the words of the Language. Still growing, the orb rolled away, blazing like a small sun, its light and heat filling the ravine from wall to wall. Moisture sizzled and hissed as it near-instantly vaporized in the orb's path. Ahead of the orb, water boiled and shot toward the stars in narrow geysers that evaporated. I followed, first at a walk, and then a jog. Finally, I took wing and rolled it faster.

Moving so quickly, the heat turned the snow into a roiling river, crashing downhill. Miles later, the snow ended, and I doused the fire, grateful to let the river move forward on its own. Provided we had no more freezes, the river should be gone before we arrived.

I returned to Gideon, still in the midst of the rainstorm, and left the night to fend for itself.

Monday smothered us with frigid, pounding rain, but I feared manipulating the weather any further. We rode until near noon then took a break to rest the livestock and to let the army eat. I whispered a need to find game to Gideon and, sneaking off to don invisibility, I also went to search for evidence of the prince's lost scouts.

Winging southward, over the closest mountaintop, I shape-changed: eagle, Pegasus, dragon, I enjoyed becoming all of them as I hunted. Game was plentiful, but of Gideon's scouts I found no evidence. My nose wrinkled, however, when I caught a rank scent in the air. An instant later, something slammed into me and sent me spiraling to earth!

CHAPTER 28

M y head rang with the concussion, and my wings hung useless. What had I run into?

I fell toward the earth, but a second strike spun me around like a limp dishrag. On the last revolution, I saw a dark, feathered form nearby, four-legged like a horse but not any horse I'd ever seen. Likewise, it wasn't a roc.

Finding my wings again and frantically righting myself, I met the stinking creature's glaring eyes, red and angry, its *illumina* alive with a handful of colorful *parhelia*—which meant it was a shape-shifted human! I searched its Insight and saw none, but he—she?—could be warding it. The creature had an eagle's head with a huge beak. It also had avian front legs, pale gray and tapered to taloned feet, each claw as lethal as my prince's sword. Broad wings were covered with shimmering, dark blue feathers. Its torso and hindquarters, however, were equine, with dark gray muscular haunches and a flowing white tail.

Rhesalus said a person couldn't shape-shift into something that never existed—the reason he and his companions were determined to create dragons. Once created, they could be copied, but this obviously wasn't a winged horse.

The intelligence in this shape-shifted creature's eyes glittered with hatred.

These thoughts took only seconds. Fear clapped my wings to my sides, and I dived toward the earth again then leveled off just above the mountain tops. Heart pounding, I flew at breakneck speed north, across the ravine and away from the army, away from the bird-horse-monster that chased me. I didn't have time to eat. I couldn't stay shape-shifted too long. I had no idea how to fight it.

I recoiled as the creature streaked past me, uttering a spine-tingling screech. I summoned Rhesalus but reaped silence. No response from any of them came, not even the dragons, and I nearly panicked. I was on the verge of being slaughtered! I couldn't learn anything from this lesson if I died!

I backstroked, tail down and wings flapping. The monster soared past me then wheeled around and came at me, jaws gaping wide. I couldn't open and close a portal in time to escape it but realized the strategies Ramah had taught me might work. In times like this, I might either have to kill or be killed.

I escaped the stench by diving into the forest canopy as a swift. Weaving back and forth among the branches, I did my best to outfly the fiend. It seemed all but glued to my tail feathers.

Streaking as high as I could go into the atmosphere, I did a somersault and changed into a winged horse. This brought the creature as close to a halt as it could manage in midair. I'd surprised it! I'd found my advantage.

It circled me with a lazy flapping of its wings, while I glided on the stiff breeze flowing past us.

My eyes widened when the creature's eagle-face metamorphosed into an incredibly ugly, savage man's. Dark blue feathers receded, leaving greasy blue-black hair slicked back from his brow, skin so pale I imagined him the Grim Reaper, and dark circles around his loathsome red eyes.

He grinned at me, revealing teeth sharpened to arrow points. I felt him collecting himself, like a runner about to leap forward. I donned invisibility and dived toward the earth.

The creature roared in fury, flying back and forth looking frantically for me. I leveled off, coasting in silence.

Sniffing like a hound, he followed me as best he could. My *parhelia*? Could he smell them? Lightheadedness assailed me the moment I warded my Insight. Food! I needed food.

Again thwarted, the creature squawked repeatedly, sending an unseen something barreling into me. It bounced off me, and before I knew it, he was chasing me again. Somehow the creature had managed to use sound as a way to find me!

My magic began to fail. I couldn't remain shape-changed, warded and invisible at the same time, but if I changed anything, he'd gain the advantage.

I had no choice. My ward was the hardest to maintain so I dropped it. We resumed our meandering chase—up, around, and down, back and forth. I tried the sorcerers again with no response. Furious, and on the edge of hysteria, I barely remembered Enya's instruction to allow my magic to take control. When I did so, with my shields tight, I came to a near-halt and turned into a dragon. Hovering in the air, I dropped my invisibility and snatched the monster between my jaws.

His screams of terror and pain vibrated between my teeth. Gliding on dragon wings, I pulled him from my mouth with a dragon-fist to examine him. Now just an ugly man, his eyes bugged from his head in disbelief at what he saw, and I knew I couldn't allow him to share his tale about a shape-shifted dragon with anyone else.

I felt his magic die as I chomped down on him and split him in half, and then I swallowed him. An instant later, the thought of what I'd done made me retch him back up. Streaking toward a large lake nestled in a crook of the Beldames, I changed into a sea monster and dived deep. No matter how much water I drank, I was sure I'd never get the taste out of my mouth: human blood, not my own. I'd killed and eaten a man! The horror made me wish to die myself. What sort of creature was I now? Not just a sorceress. Something worse. Far worse. I floated in the water, weeping monster tears.

Then horror hit me when I realized I could no longer shape-shift. I needed food. I dived deep and ate more than I needed, to compensate for the magic I would use to get out of this mess. When I breached the water, I shapeshifted from behemoth to blackbird and flew to the banks. There, I rested briefly in the sunshine as a snake before I risked opening a portal to the rain-drenched meadows above the pass. I'd made it! I was hungry again, but I was alive. I fed once more before searching out the vanguard and Gideon.

Zahra saw me first when I sneaked back into our group. *"Good heavens, my lady, you look pale,"* she paired.

Gideon's alarm matched hers when he glanced at me.

To both, I responded that I'd talk about it later. Of course, I needed time to manufacture a plausible lie. I'd never tell anyone what I'd done to the winged monster. If it weren't for the awful taste lingering in my mouth, I'd have thought it another nightmare.

"Did you see my scouts?" Gideon asked, fear echoing in his mind. He must think I'd found them torn apart.

I shook my head. *"Not a whisker,"* I replied, bolting down more food from my pack. As in the Lost Lands, it didn't matter that I'd eaten dozens of creatures today, possibly half a lake full of fish. I needed more. I glanced at the darkened sky.

"I'm sick of the rain," I muttered. "These storms are magical. Something evil is hampering our progress. It's warm and sunny away from the ravine. I wish I knew how to stop it."

I'd hoped the eagle-horse-monster was responsible for this storm, but if so, the rain would have ended with his death.

The caravan chose to set up camp early again, miserably cold, unable to start fires, forced to eat a cold supper, and settling down with nothing to comfort them but prayers to stay dry and to rise to a better tomorrow. I had no comfort, remembering first Leath reading the note to his fellow conspirators, and then me, killing a man with my teeth.

———†———

I stood almost toe to toe with the sorcerers, furious at their amusement at my expense.

"Whatever has your spine so bent?" Moriana said, looking back and forth with confusion.

"As if you don't know."

"I don't!"

I growled at her then turned on Rhesalus. "What sort of creature attacked me this morning?" For the third time, I described the man-eagle-horse creature in detail. My skin crawled at the thought.

"A hippogryph," Terius mused.

"A hippo what?"

"Another blended creature made of horse and eagle, like the winged horse, but the eagle dominates. It's a vicious creature. You're lucky you survived it."

I turned on him like a virago, teeth bared and fire in my eyes. "Yes, I am, sorcerer. And you owe me an explanation!"

Rhesalus said, "Now, now, be civil, my dear. I was concerned, but you cut us off just as we went to respond."

"Another lie!" I snapped. "I cried for help multiple times and you know it." I then explained every detail of what happened—except for killing the monster as a dragon, of course. Lies did propagate like flies. "What would you have done had I failed?"

Terius smiled for the first time in a long time. "I knew you wouldn't."

I gritted my teeth in anger. Again, he'd seen enough of the future to feel confident I'd beat the hippogryph. And if I asked why, he'd claim that meddling with the future was dangerous.

I wanted revenge but couldn't get it. Instead, I closed my eyes, bowed my head, and forced myself to let go of the anger and collect my thoughts. Praying to The Creator helped, and I felt a warmth surround me, like loving arms. It startled me but brought me focus and calmed my pounding heart. Enya was right, just as was Rhesalus. I shouldn't lean on these evil creatures if I didn't need to. If nothing else, it might prevent me from becoming like them.

Then the warmth blossomed into a tiny ray of hope. I might feel like I was about to fall off the edge of the world, but whether I fought poisonous serpents, rocs or hippogriffs, wild barbarians or sorcerers, what mattered was the task that Elam had given me, to help my beloved prince and the Eastern Realms destroy the Central Alliance's plot.

"I'm fed up with your manipulations," I warned them. "Go do whatever it is you do when I don't let you out." I locked my shields and again swore I'd ignore them for a day or two. Longer than that, and they might destroy me and take Gideon instead; but I was determined to make them regret how they treated me.

The dragons came quickly, and their meager draconian concern gave a bit of comfort. However, Ramah granted me more lessons in dragon-fighting I'd never forget.

The next day brought neither rain nor difficulties, and we moved forward with haste. I searched for Gideon's scouts several times, but not finding them wasn't what disturbed me. What did was finding a new storm ahead of us, angry black clouds already smothering the pass with another snowstorm. The hostile chill and the blinding white were even worse than the last storm, without a doubt magical.

Wednesday morning, we awakened to two inches of snow on the ground and flakes still falling, but the real storm lay a good distance ahead of us. This was slushy snow and melting, so the commanders agreed with Gideon to travel until we couldn't.

Gideon and a group of Kildarian warriors stood beside our morning fire with Eld Reagan. The cooks weren't around, but a plate of biscuits sat at the edge of our fire, and I took one and waved it at the Eld. I went to take a bite when he leaped toward me and knocked the biscuit into the fire.

"NO!" he shouted.

"Eld Reagan!" Gideon cried, indignant.

"Forgive me, Your Highnesses. 'Tis poisoned!" He gasped, bending over to rest shaking hands on his frail knees. "Wash your hands, my lady. 'Twas tappas leaf. It causes seizures and few survive it. I'm sorry for frightening you. I caught the scent of it just before you bit into it. Did anyone else touch them?"

No one had. Why hadn't my own prophetic talent warned me? Maybe I shouldn't have locked the sorcerers behind my shields.

"Where did they come from?" Reagan asked, gray brows beetled together in exasperation.

When silence met his question, Gideon called for the Mallorian warriors assigned to cook for us today. They came quickly from the main cook-fire a short distance away, one carrying a tin platter filled with biscuits, the other crisp bacon. Their jaws dropped when they heard the news.

"Just finished your breakfast," the first one said, nodding at the biscuits. "We didn't make those."

Gideon gathered all the nearby warriors and questioned them. All disavowed seeing anyone deliver the biscuits to our campsite. Eld Regan tossed the rest of the tainted biscuits into the fire and the two of us scrubbed our hands.

At least Eld Reagan pronounced the food Gideon's warriors delivered safe. I declined, however, my appetite ruined by the thought of almost eating poison. Poisoned drinks, poisoned food, poisoned arrows and lances. Would there never be an end to it? I could feel Gideon beside me, tense with rage. Who'd committed the treason this time?

I at least found a moment to again don invisibility and search for safe provender outside the ravine—grateful no hostile creatures tried to eat me.

We set forth afterward, slogging through snow turned to slush turned to mud, with nothing to see but gray skies, thirty-foot-high gray granite walls on either side, and a dirty gray road that stretched before us forever. It stopped snowing in late morning; but it was still freezing cold, and we all hunched into our coats. It worried me that Caspian seemed fidgety, flicking his ears, snorting, dancing at the simplest sounds. I patted his neck several times but failed to sooth him.

Leath and his guards rode ahead of us. The councilman looked nervous, too. More nervous than I felt. He kept playing with the chain round his neck and glancing at the right-hand cliff, the very one that chafed at my magic. What had him worried?

"Commanders!" Gideon called out. "Tighten your ranks. They're getting sloppy."

He was right. The columns had turned into random clusters. He insisted that while camaraderie was good, too much left us inattentive. Even Kendal and I were guilty of chatting too much. At least Zahra and Ian remained vigilant.

Caspian shied into Valere, then turned, snorting, to eye the top edge of the southward cliff. Wind flung snow at the company from it in fine particles that stung our faces and dusted our clothes. Horrid dread coursed through me. Something was wrong.

Ian pulled up, staring at that same cliff, and I gasped when I saw what my brother saw. People! Dressed in white bearskins and camouflaged by the backdrop of snow and cloud cover, two of them huddled behind huge boulders that lined the clifftops.

"Gideon!" I Mind-Paired in a shout. He flinched, but his eyes followed my gesture, and his entire demeanor changed instantly, his warlord mantle bulking his muscular physique.

"Assailants above right!" he shouted. "Company move to the left and face right! Archers, ready."

I froze, torn between wanting to stay close to defend Gideon and attacking our enemies myself. Where were Gideon's scouts? Why hadn't they stopped them? The archers moved with enviable precision, but I doubted arrows could hit anything with accuracy from this position. And what about Dundee's wagons, just ahead of us? They couldn't easily escape the knot of men and horses around them. Zahra joined the prince's guards in shoving our horses against the opposite cliff wall.

Then the world erupted.

What sounded like an explosion roared in the far distance behind us and a second later an even worse blast came just ahead of us. Bedlam broke loose, screams of terror echoing through the pass. We were under siege, and we were trapped.

Just ahead, where the enemies had been, I saw a huge plume of light and smoke and felt the percussion of a third explosion. In horror I saw three of the boulders and the edge of the cliff in front of the vanguard blasted apart, the debris avalanching into the ravine.

Two more explosions sounded, one still a long distance behind and another ahead of us. Men and horses bolted, charging back into us, terrified by the devastation. Leath's horse crashed into another as he made a desperate attempt to escape, knocking it and its rider to the ground. His animal leaped over it and dashed onward.

Many made it out of the mayhem. Some, especially the wagons, did not.

I sat there horrified, in shock. The shattered rock had crushed innocent people and horses, provisions and wagons. Blood seeped into the muddy snow from under the edges of the pile that spanned the road—and trapped us in the pass, as I'd seen it in my vision. We were going to die here after all.

"Rhesalus! What just happened!"

No response. I supposed that meant he wouldn't do anything for me that I could do for myself, but I didn't care about myself. I wanted to protect everyone. Desperation whipped through me, and I cast a warning glance at Gideon and Zahra. I didn't have the luxury of caring about whether others knew I had magic or how I used it—except the sorcerers, whom I shielded. I had to stop the slaughter. I tossed Caspian's reins to Zahra, Paired my love to my sweetheart, and shifted swiftly into a peregrine falcon.

Warded, I hurtled upward, catching our enemies lumbering through the snow to another series of boulders a distance behind us. No! They'd set explosives all along the ridge, determined to kill or maim as many of us as possible and leave the survivors to freeze or starve to death!

My dragon-self—bent on avenging my people—flew into them roaring, fangs bared, and claws outstretched. They jerked around, and one man's mouth gaped wide in a terrified scream. The rest windmilled backward from the horror that I knew I must appear.

The carnage I inflicted stunned even me. I snapped the first man in half with my jaws and impaled four others with my claws. It was hard to remember the guilt I'd felt at eating a man just two days ago. These were the enemy, they'd attacked us, and they would pay for it.

I flung them aside and chased the sixth man. Hatred gleamed brightly in his eyes. He had a firebrand in his hand and ran to push it toward the base of another boulder. A fuse!

I crashed into him, knocking him over the ledge into the pass—and changed into an eagle as I fell with him. I snagged his coat, sparing him from death but landing him hard enough on the muddy ravine floor to knock him senseless.

Western League warriors recoiled from me, and as I flew off, a Kythosian archer sent an arrow after me. It bounced off my ward and fell to the ground harmless, but I committed his face to memory.

Dropping my ward and coupling three portals, I shifted into a horse and prayed I wasn't traveling too far. When I arrived at the cliff above the rear of the army, I arrived in time to stop a second group of a half-dozen attackers, including two women, from exploding another volley of boulders. The pain of portalling fanned my fury, and I barreled into them, breaking bones on two and knocking three of them to their deaths in the ravine. Summoning wings and swinging around to the last warrior standing, I saw the woman crouch down in shock when I came at her as a Pegasus. Her face turned white when I shifted again into an eagle. I grabbed the hood of her coat, yanked her over the cliff screaming, and dropped her on her backside beside the still-unconscious man below.

Mind-Pairing, I told Gideon my story then became myself and waited for him, my sword at the woman's throat. Gideon ran to me with guards, warriors, and two United Forces generals in tow. Relinquishing my captives, I nodded to Gideon before melting into the shadows and then portalling back to the mountainside above.

Rhesalus's warning flittered through my mind. I'd coupled portals and needed to eat and rest. Food I found, but rest had to wait. High in the clouds as a dragon, I searched both sides of the ravine for more assailants. To my surprise, I blundered upon a campsite not a quarter of a mile southward, nestled in thick, snowy woods. How had I missed them before? The macabre scene there puzzled me. Four men in white wolfskins tended a small fire, but a good twenty yards downwind from them were the bodies of twelve men and women laid out in blood-stained snow—wait. In white *bearskins.*

Bearskins. Wolfskins. The enemies wore bearskins! The wolfskin-warriors must be Gideon's scouts! They'd caught a dozen of our assailants! Half of the total that had bombarded us. It was good to see the scouts had followed their orders and taken no prisoners, but where were the other two Mallorians?

Flying low over the ravine's cliff, I scanned the area, finally spying two men wearing white wolfskins struggling through knee-deep snow to reach the cliff. Gideon's other two scouts! The explosions likely had them frantic for their prince and the army.

As I flew close, I realized why I'd never found these men—or our enemies. Not only were they wearing clothing that camouflaged them in the snow and were trained to hide, but even now I could hardly sense their *rumorias*. The Dreamwood bracelets the Elds had given them almost completely shielded them from my magic! Our assailants had similar clothing and likely had similar magical defenses.

I Mind-Paired what I'd found to Gideon and smiled at his relief. I met him near our horses and portalled him to a place not far from the two Mallorian warriors. Their heads jerked up when they heard the crunching of our boots in the snow, their jaws dropping at seeing us approach.

"Prince Seville!" one cried in Mallorian, both men falling to their knees.

"Your Highness!" the second man said. "We feared the explosions had killed all of you. How did you find us? How did you get up here—"

Gideon held a hand up to stop him. "A long story, Lieutenant Lionel, but first tell me what happened here."

Lionel bowed his head in shame. "We searched for them for weeks, Your Highness. We stayed as close to the ravine as we dared but found no sign of them. Just two days west of here, when we made camp, we finally saw you and the army when you arrived. We couldn't risk approaching the cliff, but we continued to hope we'd catch the enemy before they could attack." He pointed at the other man. "Captain Joshua and I were shocked to stumble across their camp last night, *east* of us. We have no idea how they got past us, a dozen of them, well-armed and well-guarded." His voice caught and he shook his head in frustration. "We caught them by surprise and took no prisoners, as you ordered, but we had no idea there were others, my lord. No clue they'd placed charges all along the ravine. How did they do it if we supposedly followed them every step of the way?"

The captain pulled his hood further over his head to block the cold wind. "We imagine the second group was alerted when the explosions didn't happen, came to see why. The minute we heard the first explosion, we came running. Did they do their worst, my lord?"

"Bad enough, Captain, but you did what you could. They'd have done much worse had you not stopped the ones you did. For now, we need to hurry back and help save those we can."

Captain Joshua's brows bunched. "Pardon me for asking, but how did *you* reach us, Prince Gideon? Those cliffs are impossible to scale except on either end of the ravine."

Gideon's violet eyes met mine. "We'll talk, but I need your fealty, even if what you hear sounds either preposterous or objectionable."

A vastly abbreviated version of our trek from Kildaria and through the Lost Lands came out, Gideon promising he'd give more details later, but for now they must understand my magical talents had helped the army. They didn't like his tale—or me—any more now than they had in Kildaria, but Gideon insisted they understand their mission was based on my ability to see the future—even if the gift wasn't perfect. The Dreamwood bracelets I'd made sure they received had likely protected their lives, and their efforts at least stopped half our enemies. It appeared the scouts revered Gideon and his father enough to both champion them and tolerate me.

I rued the misfortunes of war requiring Gideon to leave the dead unburied, but we still had scouts to retrieve and injured troops to succor. I opened a portal to the scouts' camp, and while I did my best to ignore the throbbing headache and gut pain that now assailed me, Gideon repeated our story to them. They liked it even less than Lionel and Joshua, but personal experience with the portal had at least made Lionel and his companion believers.

The scouts recounted their own story since leaving Kildaria. They'd ridden to the pass, hidden their tack, and set their horses loose on the plains. From there, they'd walked to the box canyon where Nevin Leath had climbed the rocks and had, indeed, scrambled up those very rocks and scaled the cliff to the top. They should have been in place to catch our enemies. Why, then, had their mission failed?

CHAPTER 29

I Paired with Zahra to prepare her for our arrival.
If the scouts hadn't believed what I could do before, stepping through the portal into the pass convinced them. Jaws slack, they took it all in with amazement, but the shock of this final portal hit me hard.

Zahra held onto me and pressed food into my hands. I hardly chewed before swallowing, afterward gulping huge mouthfuls of water. It almost didn't stay down, but when it did, it barely calmed the raging wrongness inside me.

"Go, my lady," she whispered. "You're far from helpful to anyone in this condition."

Rhesalus's warning clanged inside my head again. She was right. I could pay a terrible price for not taking care of myself after portalling—especially with coupling portals and traveling with others.

I flew to the higher reaches to the south, where the sun shone bright, and fed then curled up in a warm meadow to nap. When I returned, the dark clouds and the horrors still awaited me, the cries of the maimed and dying floating through the smoke-stained air. Broken bones and crushed bodies, seared flesh, severed limbs. Any of the healers could bind wounds or set bones, so I turned to those with little hope of survival.

I felt Siddarth's horn, still tucked into my trouser pocket. After dozens of healings, I wished I dared use it; but I had no idea if healing ordinary injuries would affect it, and I couldn't risk it. Siddarth's promise to come to our aid could only happen if I didn't use it up.

On the day my family and I were poisoned in Kildaria, I'd barely learned to heal and didn't have enough strength to save my sister. These people, some writhing in pain, others unconscious, had families who loved them, too. I had to do everything I could not to fail them as I had Edana.

The destruction was mind-numbing. No one could be spared from addressing it. The hundreds of healers—those not injured—

welcomed those who could help, even Gideon and me, the generals and other commanders, Zahra, Ian and Kendal. Even Nevin Leath, his face paled by the shock of blood and gore, lent a hand. At one point, he seemed tearful, leaving me wondering how he could have been a part of this while being left to die with us.

Teams of warriors coordinated the efforts, receiving and noting reports, making sure the able-bodied were fed, bringing water and supplies to care for the wounded, setting up tents to move the worst-injured out of the mud and cold. A Segovian commander emptied the goods from one of his wagons to make a conveyance for the dead.

I moved through the pass from one group to another of severely wounded and dying. Some of the warriors shrank from me, and I ignored them. I could heal damaged bodies, but I could do nothing for closed minds.

"Princess?"

I turned toward a familiar voice. Julian. Pierre and Leo's friend. One of those I'd begun training a week ago. He had a gash down his left cheek to his chin crusted with blood and his pale blue eyes were filled with sadness and pain.

"You said I possess the gift of healing, but I don't know how to use it. I feel useless. How can I help?"

I wanted to cry. He wasn't asking for himself but for others. I smiled, took his hand, sought out his *parhelia*, and helped him identify it. Bidding him to close his eyes and follow my lead, I helped him heal his own wound. Shocked, he touched his face, amazed to find the damage gone. By the looks of him—a handsome young man—he also likely dared believe he wouldn't scar so badly. I made sure he wouldn't scar at all.

"You'll learn as we work," I promised.

"Morrell and Henri want to help, too!"

My other students. When he called them over, both gasped at their friend's healing and clamored to follow his lead.

Hours later, I wondered if they regretted their involvement. The effort sapped their energy, and rest and food were far between. Still, they did well enough I left them to carry on while I again addressed my own needs then flew to the rear of the army. They had more healers but likewise more injuries and many far worse. Some of the rearguard troops were trapped on the other side of the final avalanche—too many to move by portal, and some were wounded. They had few provisions and only two healers.

I treated the gravest wounds on both sides of the avalanche then Mind-Paired to Gideon for more help. I needed healers to come by portal. A short while later, he responded that Eld Kane and several healers were willing and ready.

But was I ready? I was so exhausted! My back to the cliff, I slid to the ground, buried my pounding head in my hands and wept. Eld Kane's willingness answered my prayers, but how could I portal them without killing myself?

Rhesalus's lessons on portalling kicked into mind. I struggled to my feet and shoved down food I snatched from a plate near an open fire, food the cooks kept ready for anyone who needed it, then marched to a spot with the least traffic. Searching for Gideon, rather than flying back to the meet him, I coupled three portals to him but did not step through. Gideon stood with Kane and the others, all of them pale-faced and drawn.

"Are you comfortable doing this?" I asked the Eld. I didn't want anyone panicking—or being brought against their will.

I could almost hear the wry smile in the Eld's reply. "Portals are recorded in the Elden history books, Princess. Past generations just concluded we'd lost the talent. Magic should never be taken lightly, but before we left Kildaria, Eld Tully urged Eld Reagan and me to trust you so long as you serve Elam. Helping those in need is our greatest sacrifice and Elam's finest service. Beyond that, we fear the army may have no hope of surviving without you."

Eld Tully told them this? I couldn't imagine The Prime Advocate trusting me that much. I couldn't believe Eld Reagan and Eld Kane had such faith in me. My heart swelled with emotion.

Still, I feared I would fail him. After all, villains like Rhesalus, Terius, and Moriana had their own plans for me, and monsters roamed the earth.

Reagan led the group, all bearing supplies, all worn ragged and terrified, through the portal. Zahra came last, her dark eyes meeting mine filled with sympathy.

I smiled at the gasps of awe from my travelers as they arrived, but an instant later, I felt the same awe for a different reason. Bringing them to me through the portals caused me little hunger, far less pain and the barest increase in my headache. What a marvelous discovery! I still needed recovery time, but I'd not likely die.

The work consumed us into the early hours of the following morning. Over time, the cries of the suffering dwindled. At last, I collapsed onto my cot, set up sometime during the night in Gideon's tent, unable to heal one more time.

———

"Theona?"

I sat up and drew a deep breath. What a joy to have had a brief rest. It was brief, wasn't it? Gideon knelt beside me.

"What's wrong?" I asked.

"Sorry to wake you, but Eld Kane's on a crusade. Your warrior-healers' success has him determined to make every healer and every warrior who has the *parhelia* learn to use it well. He wants them to learn by healing every wounded warrior completely, even from scrapes and bruises. He wants your assistance."

I snorted. "And then he'll want to coerce every warrior with any talents to learn to use them as well."

"Perhaps, but that isn't my greatest concern."

Eld Kane was normally a practical sort, although he also had too kind a heart. No doubt he wanted both the givers and the receivers to see the good that came from magic's healing. The ramifications were the problem.

"We cannot afford to feed dozens of would-be healers while they learn," I said. "The vanguard alone lost five wagons full of supplies. Besides, no one should be forced to embrace anything they doubt or fear."

"Agreed. Eld Reagan thinks we should wait but likes the idea when the time is right. Gifted warriors will learn something about their magic whether they like it or not."

I sighed and closed my eyes in thought. The realities of the vision I'd had of the dangers in the pass haunted me. If only I could take the army to Malloria through a portal.

"I must decline, my prince. I'm sure he'll see reason," I said.

"I agree, but I couldn't speak for you." He kissed me and left the tent just as Zahra announced herself outside it. She had my breakfast, and afterward, it was glorious to have my warrior-maid rid me of the worst of the dirt, blood, and grime.

"You don't look anything like a proper princess, pardon me for saying," she said when finished, "but at least you don't look like a starving waif."

"No, just a starving improper princess," I said, giggling with her.

I stepped outside, relieved to see it had stopped snowing, but a funereal quiet gripped the army, despite the salvaging that carried on. Hundreds were healed enough to survive, but too many had died and too many were wounded in the soul more than in the flesh. Some sat with their backs against the cliff walls, a look of hopelessness in their eyes, in shock, grieving, trapped. Most of them were gifted. If only they appreciated the assistance they could lend themselves and each other if they learned to use their talents.

The full extent of the damage to the pass on both ends left me speechless. To the front, the wall of debris blasted from the high cliff stood at least a good fifteen or more feet high, a massive jumble of boulders, rocks, sand and dirt, melting snow and mud, and smoldering trees and bushes. Under it: crushed wood, wheels; even the leg of an unfortunate horse stuck out. Blood, now dried and nearly black in the drying mud, pooled around the edges of some of the stones.

How many had been crushed to death under the weight of the falling debris? How many burned alive? The stench of ashes mixed with charred hair and flesh nauseated me.

My hand covering my mouth and nose, I stepped closer, reaching out for any evidence of life within the wreckage. I was grateful to find none. The thought of anyone buried alive under the tons of wreckage appalled me. No one should have to endure that, and it would have been a nightmare to dig frantically through the ruins trying to save survivors who would likely die before we reached them anyway.

Now. How to move the rubble out of our way? I considered the possibilities but pulling it apart one rock at a time would take days— and with limited supplies and unpredictable weather, some could starve or freeze to death before we accomplished it. And even if we did get through, would we reach Malloria before the Alliance attacked it or King Olivier decided we'd been taken over by the enemy and attack us?

I scanned the clouds roiling above us, the weather cold and windy. Another storm would soon wreak even more havoc.

Gideon's anxiety tightened his shoulders as he recounted our losses, which included all the birds, some released from broken cages, others crushed. We could contact neither Kildaria nor Malloria.

"It's a lot of earth to move," I said. "Burning it won't solve anything except to destroy the bodies and any goods that might have withstood the avalanche. Water might wash the worst away but still destroy the goods. I have no idea what it would take to blow it down the ravine." I sighed and shook my head. I had the feeling I couldn't do this alone.

Movement in the corner of my eye caught my attention. The two combatants I'd captured were tied to a broken wagon on one side of the pass. Warriors continued to question them while they sat mute.

"What will you do with them?" I asked Gideon.

"We'll execute them. Sooner and kinder if they cooperate with us." He saw the dread on my face and added, "The damage they caused us means we cannot afford to feed them, Theona, and if they escape, they could take more lives and perhaps bear tales to enemies far more dangerous. It's worth it to keep them alive a little longer if they tell us what we need to know but no longer than that."

I did not know this side of my husband. I hated cruelty, even if these scoundrels deserved it. I also understood it completely.

Thunder rumbled in the distance. I shivered from the cold, but I dared not meddle with the weather. I needed strength to address the wreckage.

"This pile and the one at the rear of the army are the only ones spread across the entire pass."

"Designed to trap us?" Gideon said.

I nodded. "I have to look at it from above," I murmured before taking wing.

Here, my raven's eye saw that the ravine wasn't more than thirty feet wide. The pile filled it, a veritable wall. At least fifteen feet high or in some places higher, it was as deep as it was high. How could I move it? How could I move it without destroying what was salvageable beneath it?

Rain sprinkled from the sky, but as I flew further eastward, I found more snow. Winter didn't belong here, but the freezing wind ripped at my feathers, and dark clouds like rumpled metal thwarted the sun. They were natural enemies wielded by something unnatural, but what else waited for us? I hated the idea of getting us free only to find worse dangers ahead.

I sped above the chasm toward Malloria, looking for signs of enemy soldiers or shamans wielding magic. I saw none. As with the day before, however, spring lay green and beautiful on either side of the pass, and wildlife of all kinds proliferated there.

I fed, took extra food with me, became myself, and portalled back to the other side of wreckage. I stared at it as I chewed, letting my mental wheels turn. Every potential solution had a drawback I didn't like.

"Quite the conundrum," Rhesalus replied.

I looked over my shoulder at him, surprised he'd finally accepted my summons. I hated asking for help, but I needed his experience.

He gave me a droll smile. "The dead are already buried. You'd serve the army better if you opened a crater in the earth and let everything fall into it, then closed it up."

I'd even considered that. We could march out of here the minute I was done.

"No. We need whatever equipment and supplies survived the blast," I said. "And I will disrespect neither the living nor the dead."

Solemnly he said, "Theona, we told you serious conspiracy is shaping things faster than we'd anticipated before leaving Kildaria. You'll waste time and energy with the dead that would better serve the living."

He was right, but I had to fight to remain human. If Gideon were under that rubble, I'd want his body recovered. The men and women whose countrymen had died in this formidable place deserved no less.

He sighed. "Then let us move the rubble for you. It would be faster and safer."

They wanted to help me? They wanted to protect me? What did they not want me to learn from doing this?

"No. I'll learn better by doing things myself. I need ideas, and something you said has inspired me."

"Then do as you please," he said with annoyance.

I shook my head and pushed aside my childish need for approval. Terius and Moriana joined us, all three offering suggestions and warnings.

The project was dangerous. I must move carefully. I should ward myself. Mind-Pairing with Gideon, I warned him how I planned to proceed and urged the army to stand clear of the heap. My prince's gentle reassurance pushed aside my worries, and I turned to the Elements.

Calling on Earth, I sought to dig a crater at the foot of the cliff to my right, not under the rubble. I felt the magic inside me grow eager, hot and powerful, and the Language flowed from my mouth, commanding the earth to break apart. It heaved and bucked beneath me, almost knocking me off my feet, and the cries from the horses and warriors on the other side of the barrier were nearly drowned out by the sound of the ground's cracking. When I caught my balance and the dust cleared, I gaped at the crater that stretched from west to east, a good ten yards long and five feet wide—and who knew how deep.

I caught my breath and summoned Wind, thrusting it at the top of the pile of rocks, directing the debris into the chasm. Bits and pieces responded but not as quickly as I'd expected. I doubled the power but felt resistance. I multiplied it until a gale whistled with anger and the snow fled through the ravine in a tempest. Sand and rocks crashed into the hole, but Wind fought me, twisting and bending, snapping with energy. Lightning struck the cliff to my left and showered me with rubble.

I shook my head to clear it and carried on. Gradually, I pared down the top layer of the pile, but the lower it dropped, the harder it grew. The pull on my magic all but consumed me, and I struggled to control it as much as I did the wind. Gradually, several layers fell, but fear and weariness filled me with despair. I'd never worked so hard for so little. Despite the wind, the clouds remained fastened to the sky.

"What am I doing wrong?" I begged Rhesalus.

"Nothing, dear girl. You're fantastic. But you're not just fighting the Elements. This storm, just like the last one, is mage born, and whoever sent it is powerful. We cannot find him—or her—but whoever shaped it is challenging you from the other side of the storm."

I stared at him, not sure I'd heard him right.

He gave me a faint smile. "You've maintained superior control the entire time, Theona, but your magic's flagging. You need our help, or you'll lose the battle, and I fear the storm-mage will undo whatever good you've done."

Storm-mage? What was a storm-mage?

The pain in my gut and head felt too much like portalling too far. "Then help," I begged.

The three sorcerers' powers clamped onto mine, raising my hair on end with static electricity, and together we seized the Elements trapped within the storm.

Wind howled, thunder boomed, and the wall of debris gave way. Fire burned trees, bushes, and grass; Wind blew the smoke and ashes away and hurtled the last of the boulders and rocks into the ditch. I did reserve a mountain of dirt and sand beside the trench for filling it later, but at last nothing remained but the unfortunate warriors, dead horses, and broken wagons spread across the width of the ravine.

Mind-numbed, I felt my strength ebb. The army stood a hundred yards back on the other side of the devastation, packed together in fear. Why? I hadn't hurt them. I only did what I needed to do, to save them.

"Theona, you're too weak. Don't close us off—"

I did it anyway. I didn't feel right. I feared leaving my shields open if I fainted.

My stomach and head raged. Reeling to one side, I fell, my head spinning. I lay there, gulping air. The immensity of what I—we—had just done stunned me.

"Gideon?" I Paired, trembling. *"I can't see. I can't...I think I've gone blind!"*

Panic grabbed hold of me. If I lost consciousness....

————+——

"Awake, child."

"What?"

"Open your eyes."

I do as she says.

A woman kneels beside me, slender, lithe, her cinnamon-brown skin shining in the flickering flame of an ornate lamp burning beside me. Her gown is white as snow, her long, red hair hanging over her shoulders and down her back. She offers her hand and brings me to my feet. I'm also dressed in white.

"Where am I?" I ask.

The woman smiles, a sad but wise smile. "Where do you think?"

"I don't know."

"It is the Corridor between life and the eternities."

My heart shrinks. "I'm dead," I say.

Her round, lovely cheeks brighten when she smiles wider. "No. Death happens in the place of mortality and cannot come here. This is the Corridor of Waiting. If you choose to live, you will return to mortality. If you do not, then you will walk the Corridor through that veil into the eternities."

I see it then, at the end of a luminescent hallway, a curtain of shimmering beauty, the whitest white, made up of all the colors of the rainbow.

"Have I done something wrong?"

"It is the purpose of mortality to make mistakes. To learn. To grow. To hopefully make choices that raise us above the worst of what we are to become the best."

"Then why am I here?"

"If mortality's laws cannot be met, then life cannot continue."

"What laws?" Sadness makes my voice shake.

"Breath. Water. Food. Light. Shelter. Clothing. Love. Remove enough of them, and death prevails."

"Then...I am dead."

"No. You are between."

"Why?"

"Because your quest remains unfinished."

"But if death should prevail, how can I live?"

"If you decide to carry on, that the pains of mortality are worth fulfilling the quest, your wish shall be granted, and Elam shall spare your life."

"If they are not worth it?"

"Then Elam will give the burden to someone else, and you will find peace."

"But what will happen to my prince and to the others if I don't carry on?"

"Many will die, including freedom."

I frown. "Freedom cannot die."

"It always dies when hope dies. When heroes refuse to act as heroes, then those they were meant to save are often doomed."

"But I'm no hero."

"You are modest, which is to your credit. But few have ever been blessed with the power you have, and it could tip the balance in the battle against evil."

"Then I am forced to return to the pains of mortality regardless of how I feel."

She shakes her head, her dark eyes glittering with the flame of fire. *"Never. Elam forces no one to make such choices. But He does know the souls of true heroes burn brightest when they do what they were meant to do."*

Grief overwhelms me. I'm so tired, so frightened, so filled with sadness I cannot imagine going on. Then, in a moment of clarity, I see Gideon as he was when we first met dreamwalking and imagine losing him. All the tomorrows in eternity would mean nothing without him.

"Does that mean that if I choose mortality, death will lose?"

"For now. Death comes to all, but hopefully in its proper time."

"I'm afraid."

"You will not be left alone," the woman says.

Her voice drifts away from me as she glides toward the veil, her gown fluttering around her like wings in a breeze. *"Few are lone heroes. If you choose to return, others are waiting there for you."*

"Is Gideon a hero?" I ask.

"If he so chooses," she whispers. *"But he must make his own choice, just as you did."*

CHAPTER 30

"**O**bey my command!"
Torn from the incredible dream into the shock of real life, I struggled to open my eyes but failed. General Bellamy? He sounded so angry.

"Prepare the noonday meal *now*. And you *will* send a portion of it for Princess Theona. I'll *not* tell you again!"

Footsteps scurried away.

Noon? Then it was only hours since I'd cleared the pass. My head spun, but I heard warriors squabbling with each other in the distance. Someone—several someones—didn't want to give me so much as a drop of water. Even after everything I'd done for the army, they nursed their fear, hatred with some. It seemed turning into a bird and fighting attackers wasn't a popular thing to do. In the near distance, I heard Gideon's voice but couldn't understand him.

I swallowed, tasting the remnants of herbs and venison on my tongue. Someone had fed me broth?

I slept again, pleasantly this time, and then awakened to Zahra lifting my head and resting a spoon against my lips.

"Here, my lady, take more. You're gaining strength now. When you're ready, I've weightier food for you."

"She looks better," someone remarked. Kendal! My eyelids fluttered but still wouldn't stay open.

"Anything's better than how she did look," Ian said, and I realized my brother was holding my hand. My *brother*? Where was I? In a tent? Sounds seemed muted; furs beneath me softened the ground; furs on top kept me warm.

"She fainted because she used too much magic trying to get us out of this mess," Zahra snapped. "She does that too often, trying to save that lot of fools out there what would rather burn her at the stake than thank her."

"They don't understand," Kendal said. When my eyelids finally parted, I saw shame on her face. "Give them—all of us—time.

Besides, those who gripe the loudest are not the opinion of the majority. Many have whispered to me that they not only value what Princess Theona has done, they admire her tenacity despite being maligned."

"They'd best speak louder," Zahra persisted. "Forgive my saying it, but evil wins when good people do nothing to stop it. We don't speak up, bullies think they've won, and by and by, Eblis will grind us down 'til we've lost the right to speak out at all."

Kendal laughed. "Zahra, I'm beginning to think you'd make a fine stateswoman."

Zahra snorted. "Not likely, Miss Kendal. I'm likely not a particular good servant, let alone a stateswoman. I'm too quick to speak my peace."

"Rhesalus? What happened to me?" I asked the sorcerer.

"You are a hero, my dear," he responded, admiration in his voice. *"Your people will live another day because of it."*

"Another day, metaphorically speaking? Or only another day in the literal sense?"

His laughter rumbled through me. *"Metaphorically, my dear. The army will live to fight. Wake up, Theona. You need...."*

"Ah! My lady. You've decided to join us," Zahra said with pleasure.

Kendal and Ian gasped their relief as I sat up. They all looked wonderful to me: Zahra as zealous as ever, my brother happy to see me alive and well, and Kendal stronger, more self-assured than I'd ever seen her.

As for me, I now felt hale enough to gorge myself on "weightier food." I also drank enough water Ian complained the army's horses were likely to die of thirst. It amazed me to feel so good despite fearing I'd truly stood at death's doors only moments before.

"Need to set you to rights, my lady," Zahra said, shooing the others away. This time I needed more than a cursory scrubbing.

We'd lost water barrels with the crushed wagons, and our drinking water was now rationed; but in my near-death sleep, my warrior-maid had melted a bucket's-worth of snow on the nearby fire. She stripped me of my clothes and washed as much of me as she could before I froze to death, redressed me, and then brushed as much dirt out of my hair as possible. After she re-braided it, she tugged a warm knitted cap over my head, and while I couldn't say I felt good as new, I certainly felt better.

When we left our tent, my prince's joy at seeing me offset any of the disparagement I'd overheard from the others. He snapped orders at men around him and then wrapped me in his arms and held me tight.

"You're the best thing I've seen for two days."

"Even though I still smell like a rubbish heap?"

"More like a dustbin, but you're alive, my love. That's all that matters." We laughed together. I so loved my prince.

Then he added with gravity, "We thought we'd lost you."

"I think my magic did something…strange…to protect me." Or perhaps I'd truly chosen not to take the walk through the veil. I leaned back to meet his gaze, suspecting my dream hadn't been a dream, but I didn't want to think about angels and heroes' quests right now.

"I spent the entire day with you yesterday," he said. "Nothing I did—that anyone did—roused you. When the Elds tried to heal you, your magic resisted them."

My eyes flew wide in shock. "What? I was unconscious for an entire day?"

His nod had my mental wheels spinning. It was Friday, the twenty-fifth of May? We were another day behind. And why would my magic refuse Elden healing?

I searched for an explanation. Perhaps my magic wanted to defend me? Or take care of me in its own way? Perhaps that was part of its "learning process".

Noise from the busyness around us drew my attention. Everything had changed while I slept. The warriors had cleared the ravine of the broken wagons and gathered the equipment and the dead. Only two scars were left behind: the splintered cliff on the south side of the pass and the pit that awaited the deceased on the north side. Many were grooming horses and loading wagons, but Gideon grew solemn when I asked when we would leave.

"We can't, Theona. Another wagon collected the dead from the rear and brought them forward last night, but we cannot desert the warriors on the far side of the last explosion or those under it."

I felt punched in the gut. I hadn't removed the second pile of rubble! If only I'd been able to portal the warriors on the far side of the avalanche to the main body yesterday. I wondered what they would have done had I never awakened—or had I died.

Overhead, the clouds now free of their vitriol, were breaking up and drifting away. Relief hit me when I realized the unknown sorcerer must have abandoned the storm!

"I'll take care of it, Gideon."

"I'm terrified for you, Theona. Teams have been working non-stop to pull the wreckage down by hand enough to bring the rear troops through. It will take time, but I don't want to risk your life again."

"I know now what made it so difficult the first time. It won't happen again. I'll explain why later."

He rubbed his forehead. "General McBane would love your help. He believes in you, you know."

He was the commander who'd ordered his Kildarian warrior to abandon his stallion when it charged into the white sand spider nest in the Badlands. A stocky, graying redhead, he stood with one of Kalbarri's generals, overwhelmed and teary-eyed, when I arrived through a portal. He seemed as prepared for me as he could be when he welcomed me with grace and a plate of food. It saddened me to learn McBane's nephew was among those crushed beneath the debris.

"Princess, I'm grateful you're able to help," he said. He'd already ordered any family and close friends of the dead, along with some of the leaders, to escort the funeral wagon to the services the Elds would conduct at the east end's trench when it was ready. A good part of the rearguard was set to march; but a team of warriors worked feverishly to tear down the blockage, both to free the warriors trapped on the other side and to collect the dead. I sighed at so much grief and loss.

Any doubt I had that magic taught itself was banished that day. Granted, I wasn't impeded by the anonymous storm-mage, but my ease at opening a second pit and marshaling the Elements to remove the pile of rubble astonished even me. Rumors had abounded about me, and the warriors witnessing my handiwork stood more amazed than frightened—especially when the troops stranded on the other side, mostly Kalbarrians, rushed through to greet their comrades and receive badly needed sustenance.

I ate again as warriors gathered the bodies of the deceased and while I explained my plans to McBane about using portals to hasten the wagon to the front of the army—which in turn would hasten our departure.

"It would be a miracle, my lady," McBane said, the unease on his face from my use of magic offset by his gratitude.

I Mind-Paired with Gideon to warn him of the wagon's arrival then coupled three portals from one end of the army to the other, praying I could move the entourage that far safely. As they headed through, I flew at breakneck speed to join Gideon and found the group still enthralled when I arrived, amazed at having stepped from one place to another, near twenty miles apart, in a heartbeat. For me, not portalling with them gave me the boon of less fatigue and nausea, although Gideon leaned into me and whispered his encouragement to find rest as soon as possible.

"I suppose that means I look unappealing," I Paired. "It wasn't nearly so bad this time."

"You'll never look anything less than beautiful to me, but 'pale' does not suit you, Love."

He extended a hand to McBane. "General. I'm sorry about your nephew." He gripped the man's hand in solace.

"Everyone regrets every loss," said McBane.

My prince nodded. He'd lost one of his best scouts, two of his finest warriors, and an outrider in the mêlée. He understood war's casualties, even if his men weren't family members.

"What is our final accounting of the damage?" McBane asked.

"In all, two hundred twenty dead—a good portion from Dundee and Kalbarri, of course. They were the vanguard and rearguard divisions. We'd have lost many more if the rest of the thirty charges along the cliff had been lit—and if our diligent healers hadn't worked miracles. Eleven wagons were destroyed, and seventy horses, including two relief animals. Which means since leaving Kildaria, along with those who deserted, we've lost a total of three hundred thirteen warriors, ninety-three horses—dead, taken, or lost—fourteen wagons and, of course, all the birds. Our injured were one hundred seventy-five, but all were healed." He squeezed my shoulder in gratitude.

"Praise to Elam for that much. It could have been so much worse. I hear your end also recovered a respectable quantity of supplies, wood, wagon wheels, food and horse fodder, equipment, weapons and such," McBane said, his eyes again red-rimmed and his voice tight as he added, "and I see the vanguard is in place and the Elds ready to conduct the service."

"They are. The companions of the dead are welcome to remain for a while, but the rest will pay their respects as they ride by. Those who stay will rejoin their divisions after we make camp tonight. We won't go far but leaving this place will lift morale."

The outriders carried word it was time to finish loading and mount up. The troops responded with vigor. Zahra, astride Chip, waited for me with Caspian. I climbed aboard and devoured the food she offered while I Paired explanations to her. I looked forward to an afternoon napping on horseback.

After Gideon joined us, we met with Ian and Kendal and moved to the front of the army. There, I peeled the last of the clouds from the heavens and sent them scuttling northward, far away from us. The sun, now unhampered, sent bright, warm relief over the entire company.

The funeral wagons led the way to the trench, the softly grieving throng surrounding it as best they could to watch as warriors lowered the bodies into the pit with ropes. One of Dundee's generals read the names of the dead, a Segovian lieutenant gave a eulogy honoring their sacrifice, and the Elds sanctified the mass grave as a resting place for them for the remainder of time.

"Warriors, mount!" Gideon ordered at last. "Princess Theona will fill in the grave."

When all were ready, he nodded at me. Palms poised, I grasped Wind, which today felt like a friend, and like an artist hand-painting a scene, I used it to fill the trench with the dust and gravel I'd previously piled beside it. Gasps of amazement flittered around me, despite some persisting with their superstitions.

Eld Kane remained to offer comfort to those who needed it, but Eld Reagan traveled with me. Our ring of guards surrounded us as we again turned our faces toward Malloria, Dundee remaining at the grave and Kythos taking the lead.

We rode past Gideon's wagons to join the vanguard, and I saw the two prisoners riding in one of them, bound and gagged, bruised and beaten. Gideon's patience had run its course. They'd not live another night.

As we journeyed, I embraced boredom with gratitude. It was far better than the wrong kind of excitement. Then, unexpected changes took place. The cliffs dropped and the grade sloped downward, and in the near distance we could see the ravine carving its way through a wooded valley. A strange sense of peace touched my heart, and then came whispering from others who felt the same sensation.

"I cannot believe this," Ian said, admiring the lovely forest that surrounded us: pines and cedar trees, beech and oak, ash trees and even dogwood. But they were an afterthought compared to the endless miles of Dreamwood trees!

Gideon had said they were common here, but thousands upon thousands of them carpeted the mountains and spread out over most of the valley, their massive arms raised to the sky. Their height and breadth dwarfed everything but the mountains, and at their feet burgeoned tall shrubs, rhododendrons, ferns the size of sheep, bluebells, oxlip, trillium, and primrose.

The peace was the same I'd felt in the Lost Lands! Siddarth told me the Dreamwood Forest melded magic to the earth and tied the magical creatures to it. Was that what felt so wonderful here?

"Welcome to Malloria, my dear," Gideon said, smiling with pride. We'd crossed his country's border!

"Kildaria's beauty is famed," Zahra said, "but without question it's trumped by a Dreamwood Forest." She chuckled. "Imagine, my lady. The three of us are among very few people who've ever seen two of them in a lifetime."

"I'm all but speechless," Ian said with awe, adding, "especially since you'll be the queen of it someday, sister."

Would I? The doubt huddled inside me, waiting to disappoint me. I wanted to believe in better times, especially if—when—we conquered the Central Alliance, but did I dare?

Hope captured my soul when the ravine widened, not as a canyon but a generous pass, and a river full of the freshest water ran through it. Filling water barrels and watering horses and then moving on allowed the cavalcade to replenish its needs as we passed through.

Word had spread of my ability to portal, and that evening as the army made camp, I soared over the southern side of the ravine and found a small herd of deer. Mind-Pairing Zahra to collect my students and a wagon, I dispatched a good portion of the herd, which my crowing, laughing warriors returned to the army. Fresh meat would relieve some of the stress the attack had caused.

"I'm staying in camp tonight," I warned the sorcerers after I'd bedded down. *"I need a decent night's sleep before meeting my father-in-law."*

I felt Rhesalus's laughter in my mind. *"It won't matter my dear."*

"What? What do you mean?"

"Rhesalus." Terius sounded uneasy. Warning him to silence?

"Not to worry, Terius. Theona's beauty and her reputation will impress the man."

Then they shut themselves off from me.

Glad to be rid of them, I turned over—and felt my face go cold. The gems in Slayer's grip began to glow, jeweled eyes that stared back at me. I slammed my eyes shut and swallowed hard, certain I had to be imagining things and just needed to get some rest.

Saturday morning's sunrise felt dazzling. Gideon encouraged me to take my time readying myself. He and the commanders had last-minute preparations for our upcoming meeting with Malloria.

Kendal left our tent with Ian, and my warrior-maid went in search of Eld Reagan and my breakfast. I remained seated cross-legged on my cot, musing, and suddenly missing home. Father and Mother and the Tavishes must be frantic about Ian and Kendal—about all of us. Was Lon preparing to take Ian's place as future Duke of Mithradell? How were my father and King Desmond? Was Father already training as king-in-waiting to Kildaria's throne? I couldn't even picture it.

Something made me shiver, and again I turned my gaze to The Keeper and its small table. Slayer leaned against the table, encased in its dark, weathered scabbard, which was so old I had no idea how it remained intact. Perhaps through magic? Like the books in Mt. Draakheda's laboratory? The Elds had, after all, forged the sword with magic.

I'd never seen the blade out of its sheath, but someone had wrapped a narrow strip of light brown leather around the grip. Again, the precious jewels decorating the pommel seemed to wink at me. I could almost swear I heard the weapon whispering, which frightened me more. The sorcerers had lured me with such whisperings and tricked me into opening The Keeper. Now, I felt an enormous attraction to the sword, but I dared not respond. Did I?

I strained to hear the faint whispering, imagining someone—
several someones?—far away trying to tell me something. I didn't
realize I'd come to my feet until I watched with trepidation as, of their
own accord, my fingers wrapped themselves around Slayer's grip.
The surface was cool but something strange lay underneath that
coolness. It throbbed. Like some of the books in Mt. Draakheda's
library. Like a pulse? I gauged my own. It was the same. How bizarre.

An even stranger tingling wound its way up my fingertips to my
hand and to my wrist and warmed my Dreamwood bracelet. A soft
"pop" sounded, which made me jump, and then the tingling stopped.
It didn't hurt me, so I gave my racing heart leave to relax. The jewels
twinkled, as if the weapon was amused. What a bizarre trick of the
imagination.

Slayer was huge: a man's longsword, far too long and too heavy
for me. My short sword, the one the blacksmith had fitted to me, lay
in its scabbard on my trunk, along with my knife. But the beauty of
this piece—and having been the renowned Cleary the Brave's
weapon—fascinated me.

I sighed as I lifted it, marveling at its feather-light weight. It fit
me perfectly! How had Cleary fought so many vicious beings—even
killed dragons—with so light a blade? His reputation had always
seemed immense, but maybe he'd been small for a man.

I went to remove the ancient scabbard and nearly dropped the
sword when the sheath slid to the floor like silk. I gasped in
appreciation. The blade was beautiful! The fuller was shallower than
my sword's fuller, but the edges were razor-sharp, and the faces were
both polished to a mirror-like shine. The blade's tip came to a point
so craftily planed into varying surfaces it reflected light like a
diamond prism.

How could such a brutal weapon seem so delicate? How could so
ornate a creation be a useful weapon? It was at least twice the size of
my short sword, but it felt perfect. Neither too heavy nor too light.
Not too long or too short, as if it were made for me.

For generations, old wives' tales had frightened children about
Slayer, including me. The blade belonged to the McArthurs and
anyone trying to steal it would be slain by it. If it became separated,
it would return to its owner on its own. No one could lift it who wasn't
a McArthur.

Much of it wasn't true. After all, our porters delivered it from wagon to tent every night and from tent to wagon every morning, and it hadn't as of yet returned to my father. Still, I'd seen too many unbelievable things happen in the last few weeks to dismiss all of it.

I couldn't resist swinging it, just to see how it felt. Glorious! Before I knew it, I was doing a review of Zahra's lessons, one hand and both, lunges and stabs, back swings and slashes. Wind and Moon, Ascension, Shoulder Strike. Blood Pillar, Dancing in the Sky. Crouch, strike, step back, parry, spin, swing. I stopped, the silence around me unearthly. I'd never felt such fluidity, such grace.

It wasn't me; it was the sword. I'd worked hard for weeks to do nothing but prove I was no swordswoman. I was a sixteen-year-old girl whose body appeared years older but still didn't fit. Be that as it may, on this early May morning, I felt elevated. Superhuman. Gifted. The sense of power frightened me as much as anything I'd experienced with the use of magic.

I executed the Salute of Swords because I felt I should and laid the weapon on my cot. Wiping the sweat from my face with my sleeves, I grimaced at the evidence I needed a *real* bath.

I retrieved the scabbard from the floor and went to grab Slayer.

It was gone.

My heart froze in place. The empty sheath, soft as lambskin, now felt heavy in my hands. Slowly I looked down to see the sword nestled back inside the scabbard.

I hurried to The Keeper and set it against the table, vowing never to touch it again. Grabbing my jacket, I went to reach for my short sword.

Slayer lay in its place.

I gulped. I preferred carrying my sword on my belt than in the baldric when riding horseback, and Slayer's scabbard was now threaded onto the belt as if it were waiting for me.

I spun around to see my sword leaning against The Keeper's table. I went to collect it, but in the blink of an eye, I found Slayer, belt and all, where my sword had just been.

Fear hummed. Dread seeped through my veins. Could a magical sword insist upon claiming its master—or mistress? Did I dare suggest any such thing?

I gasped when Slayer, sheath and all, flew through the air and landed with a thump in the palm of my hand. My short sword again leaned against the table, and I now thought my heart would fail.

My legs felt like jelly, but it seemed I had no choice.

My shaking hands fastened Slayer in place, but how would I explain this to Gideon? Did I have a right to the fabled sword of the Elds? He'd think I'd gone insane at last. Even if he didn't, the rest of the company might, and some might want to rebel because of it.

Making sure my tunic covered the hilt, I headed outside to find Gideon. The glory of the morning at least calmed some of my unease, despite Zahra bringing me a plate bearing one small biscuit and a piece of half-burnt bacon.

"Seems our warriors gorged on venison last night rather than salting some to take with us. Now we're on tighter rations," she said.

I sighed and gave her my portion. I'd find a better breakfast elsewhere as soon as I could. Gideon stood on the far side of our fire with several generals and appeared far too busy for me. Thus, I found myself muttering my crazy story about Slayer to Zahra, shifting my tunic to show her the jeweled haft. The shock had her mouth hanging open.

"What oddities will happen next?" she muttered with dry amusement.

I coughed laughter. I couldn't imagine there were any oddities left in the world. They'd already tossed themselves at my feet.

Zahra at least had the foresight to lock my short sword in my trunk and tell the warriors who packed our tent that the prince had decided to keep Slayer there. I disliked her decision to fib for me but understood her reasoning. It put off having to explain what had happened to the famous sword. Even better, the warriors expressed their relief at not having to handle it.

Before we headed to our horses, I finally found a moment to tell Gideon about my adventure with Slayer. His shock turned his face pale.

"Please don't be angry—"

"Never." He placated me with a squeeze on my wrist. "I'm just reeling from the idea. The army barely tolerates you having any weapon. How will they react if they see you've taken Slayer?"

"I didn't take Slayer; it took me. Let them argue with that."

He grunted, not completely appeased, but he knew I had no choice.

I fed in the higher reaches then joined the army just as it set out. The warriors seemed lighthearted this morning, which cheered me greatly, despite my peculiar morning. Before long, the ravine widened enough to become a valley within a valley, and the cliffs lowered such that a person could climb them with ease. Wagons and horses couldn't go along, of course, so none would do it, but everyone stared with awe at the miles of Dreamwoods that seemed to march alongside us for the entire day and into Saturday. Barely beyond dawn, the cliffs disappeared, the forest receded to the hilltops, and the rolling countryside boasted every possibility: lakes, rivers, streams, and in time, a few farms with lowing cattle and bleating sheep.

Suspicion plucked at me "Gideon, are we...?"

He chuckled. "Yes, my love, we're nearly at the meeting point. We're a few days later than I told my father to expect us with my last missive, of course, but we'll be there soon."

Thrill skittered its way up my spine but was suddenly shattered by that awful uncanny apprehension that something bad was about to happen. Oh, no! Not again.

"Rhesalus?"

"We warned you."

"What is it?"

Silence greeted my comment. Then he said, *"You know I don't like meddling with the future. Just be on guard."*

"You're always meddling with the future. You're plotting to own it."

His laughter rankled. *"But some meddling would get you killed, and we cannot have that. Be on your guard, my dear. Things are not always as they may appear."*

CHAPTER 31

"Theona?"

Gideon leaned over to touch my arm. I jerked my gaze toward his, his worry reminding me that talking to sorcerers inside my head might frighten the troops around me.

"What's wrong?" he urged.

"I don't know, but I have an idea how I—how *we*—can find out." I promised him we'd discuss it in private as soon as we stopped to rest and water the horses.

Two hours later we claimed a shaded creek where the army could do just that and where Gideon and I excused ourselves to walk alone toward a thicket downstream. I remembered the desire I'd once had to turn into a dragon and take Gideon flying with me. Since then, we'd flown together more than I'd ever dreamed possible, but it hadn't been for fun. It wouldn't be for a lark now.

I told him my plans and asked him, "Trust me?" At his nod, I leaned over the bank and saw our reflection in the water. Gideon looked puzzled. I touched him as I donned invisibility and grinned wide at seeing both our images disappear. He gasped and pulled away, his reflection reappearing in the water.

I dropped my invisibility and said again, "Trust me." He took a deep breath to steady his nerves and nodded once more. I donned my horse persona and he jumped aboard, then I turned us invisible and cantered through the thicket into an open area. Vaulting into the sky, I also warded us and prayed we'd find an explanation for my ominous feelings, which for whatever reason drew me eastward.

The road meandered now, through rich farmlands and watercourses. The beauty threatened to distract me, but the moment I caught a brief glimpse of the Varigo River, my stomach clinched and Gideon Mind-Paired horror.

"Theona? Is that…?"

"We need to find out."

I flew low, praying my protections worked. Unseen, warded, quiet, I felt certain we could get the information we needed and return to the army unscathed.

"Should there be that many?" I asked.

"No. And I cannot imagine why there are."

Mallorian troops stood at the ready, every one of them horsed, every one of them dressed for war. Hundreds, maybe thousands.

"They look more likely to slay us than to greet us," I muttered. Had we just survived nearly four weeks and hundreds of dangerous miles only to run headlong into a deathtrap?

At the front stood dozens of horses and horsemen dressed in regal livery and equipment. On either side of a tall, dark-haired man on a red stallion, flag bearers held banners, the standards of Malloria and the Seville family crest. I'd never seen anyone presented this way but King Desmond.

"My father!" Gideon said. *"He never rides with the army except with serious conflicts, and then he never rides at the front. What's going on?"*

I had no answer, of course. *"Do we have any choice but to meet with them?"*

"No. The only other way out of the pass is to go back, but we haven't the provisions. If their plan is to attack, they'll follow us, and we'd be at an even further disadvantage."

I left the Mallorians behind and set Gideon down in a fallow field. As a bird, I fed quickly, then returned to embrace him. He held on tight, but I knew he was shaking inside. Afraid? Angry? I didn't ask.

"Come," I said, opening a portal to the very thicket we'd so recently left. Our stepping through together taxed me enough I had to feed again before strolling with him back to the army.

"It all feels like a dream," he said. He referred to the magic I'd just used, but I knew he meant it felt like a nightmare.

"It does," I replied, having had that perspective since the day I opened The Keeper.

He paused and squeezed my hand when we found the troops getting ready to mount up. "I think *I* have an idea." He outlined his suggestion, and I grinned my support.

"Much better than walking into it blind," I said.

Crown Prince Gideon Seville rose to the occasion, calling on his closest leaders and discussing his plan, then ordering the troops to don their armor. When asked for an explanation, my prince expressed his desire to impress Malloria with our strength, despite the trials we'd endured. Word spread quickly and outriders took the information to the divisions that followed. Zahra and I helped each other with putting ours on as I Paired an explanation to her. Zahra made sure it all fit well and pulled an edge of my tunic over Slayer's haft to hide it as best she could. Gideon then ordered his Mallorian troops to the forefront. They would take the brunt if things went bad.

Morning ripened. A soft breeze, birds, and butterflies celebrated its beauty as we rode. An hour later, Gideon stopped the cavalcade to take the next step in his plan. A few of the generals expressed displeasure but no one disobeyed. Perhaps leaving the Elds with them, along with Leath, Ian, and Kendal—who had no armor to wear— reassured them that there was no plot against them.

Zahra went with me as Gideon and his One Hundred warriors set out at a swift posting jog. Two corners in the road later and surprise pulled shouts from his men, some of joy, others of disbelief at seeing the king and Malloria's army waiting for them. General Bellamy and Sir Lance riding with us glanced at Gideon and gave deep sighs. They saw what Gideon did and didn't like it, either.

We'd cantered to within fifty feet of King Olivier when Gideon signaled a halt. Silence reigned for far too long. Then a half dozen of Malloria's men rode forward at a sedate walk. We rode to meet them. I remained warded, wishing I could do the same for Gideon but not sure if I should.

I'd have known the man on the red stallion anywhere. Dressed in light mail, with a crimson cape fastened to his cuirass, he could have passed for my prince's older brother—if he'd had one. Strikingly handsome and lean but muscular, King Olivier Seville's dark shoulder-length hair was held in place by a narrow gold circlet; his short, near-black beard was flecked with gray; and his violet eyes were so dark they seemed nearly black.

"We are heartened to see you alive and well," the king said, his gaze riveted on Gideon. Even his voice sounded like Gideon's, if a bit fuller and older—and not nearly as friendly.

"Thank you, Sire. We faced grim odds and grimmer enemies, but despite the delays, we've arrived with fewer than expected casualties."

The king's eyes glittered with wry amusement. "We see faces we don't recognize but, beyond our own warriors, no army."

Gideon chuckled. "We rode ahead to appraise the situation." His smile faded. "Why so many, my father? And why did *you* come? You taught me that kings protected their kingdoms by remaining safe and letting their men-at-arms fight the battles."

King Olivier nodded. "Very true. But difficult situations often call for difficult measures. Your last message-bird arrived early Wednesday morning. We were gratified to learn you'd made it most of the way through the pass, but later, when your flock of birds arrived *en masse* without messages, we feared you'd been attacked and that your enemies would arrive in your stead. We've been camped here since Thursday morning."

A most plausible explanation, but anger flared up inside me. Gideon's king—Gideon's *father*—feared we'd been set upon by enemies but didn't come to help us? I wondered if Gideon felt the same when he proceeded to describe the attack against us in enough detail his sire should have been chagrined.

"A terrible ordeal, indeed," the man said with the deepest sympathy. "I'm grateful you survived it." He then spoke to one of those I suspected was a general. That man in turn called to their troops to stand down, that the prince was safe, and the army Malloria had asked for was on its way. The message was quickly handed on.

Gideon signaled to one of his guards, who drew a horn from his pack. He trumpeted a signal that would bring the United Forces forward.

The king settled his gaze on me but said nothing, not even a welcome. Malloria's monarch disliked magic, so why did I feel something magical about the man? I saw no *illumina*, no *parhelia*, no Insight to prove it, but that only led to the unsettling conundrum as to whether he truly had no magic or was warding it. If that was true, suppressing magic among his people was hypocrisy—and what did that say about him or his kingdom?

While we waited, Gideon asked about his homeland. All was well, the king reassured him, except that Gideon's queen-mother had not felt well the last few weeks. According to the healers it was just a passing vapor. Gideon and General Bellamy then gave a summary of the losses as well as the final figures of those who'd made it to Malloria. King Olivier's gaze brightened at hearing the numbers. Any monarch would be impressed by receiving near thirty-five thousand mounted warriors, but added to that were the healers, the wagons, the dray horses and equipment, and the armor and weapons. Then he heard that my brother, his fianceé, a Kildarian councilman, and two Elds were in the mix, and a handsome grin split his face.

"Excellent. Not part of the original plan but ever so welcome."

The sound of the arriving troops silenced further discussion, and I watched with pride as Kildaria led the cavalcade in perfect formation, Elds Reagan and Kane, Ian and Kendal, and Nevin Leath near the front. Whispered reactions from my country's people upon seeing the Mallorian army echoed my own concerns. They feared we were about to be attacked.

When the troops came to a halt behind us, King Olivier stood in his stirrups to survey them. The quiet that fell allowed him to shout a hearty welcome. It bordered on a brief speech which should have encouraged me. I saw many a smile and warriors bumping their fists or slapping backs, yet that awful premonition still put goosebumps on my arms.

"Glad we are to see Crown Prince Gideon Seville return home safely. Thanks to all of you for making the dangerous journey here. Our enemies are likely quaking in their boots."

Laughter drifted over the company. Then the king whispered to a servant, who helped him dismount. Gideon did the same. They met in the space between the two armies, where my prince dropped to one knee and bowed his head in formal obeisance. King Olivier rested a hand on Gideon's dark head, sadness flashing across his face.

Sadness? Why?

In Mallorian, he said in a normal voice, "Arise, my son." When my prince did, they grasped right arms, hands on elbows, and hung on for a moment. Then the king said something so quietly I couldn't hear it. Gideon turned and beckoned the Elds and our kidnapped "guests", who dismounted and greeted King Olivier with deference. Gideon spoke Kildarian, so it wasn't a surprise that the king could, too, although with a stronger accent. The introductions and conversation were pleasant, and although King Olivier showed concern at how Ian, Kendal, and Leath had become a part of our party, he gave them a special welcome and returned them to their horses wearing happy smiles.

Now, King Olivier's gaze locked with mine and he lifted his voice. "My eldest son and heir sent a message-bird weeks ago about the advent of his marriage. Prince Gideon, Malloria has waited with bated breath to meet your bride."

My heart took off racing when Sir Lance came to help me dismount and escorted me to Gideon's side. Slayer bumped against my knee as I strode forward, reminding me of its presence.

Gideon took my hand as I dropped to one knee, my next wish being for the normalcy of skirts. They would have cloaked my trembling legs, and perhaps Slayer wouldn't be painfully digging into my ribs as if trying to hide. I wished *I* could hide, perhaps under the nearest rock.

In a strong voice, Gideon announced, "Your Majesty, King Olivier Seville, I present to you Theona Janae Nuala McArthur Seville, the daughter of Cedric McArthur, Duke of Mithradell and Kildaria's king-in-waiting, and the Princess of Malloria."

"King-in-waiting, hmmm?" King Olivier said, his brows rising. "Impressive." To me, in Kildarian he said, "Princess Theona. We've never heard that name before. It is…a rare beauty, just like you."

He sounded sincere enough I blushed. "Th-thank you, Your Majesty," I replied in Mallorian—glad my timorous voice at least didn't squeak—and watched the tiny tipping of his brows in response. Was he glad I spoke his language? Or just surprised? "Your country is lovely," I added, "and Prince Gideon is the finest man I've ever met."

In Mallorian, he replied, "Of which we are proud. We'd begun to wonder if he would ever find his future queen."

He encouraged me to my feet, and I felt the overwhelming magnificence of the man. He was Gideon at his finest, in every way a king, not just handsome but statuesque, powerful. If I'd never met Gideon, I could have fallen in love with this man in an instant.

A horrid thought I banished immediately. It reminded me too much of Rhesalus's manipulation of my feelings. I dared ease my shields just enough to sense the sorcerers, but they remained silent. That meant I had to manage this on my own.

As if in jest, the king grinned and took my hand and pressed my gloved fingers to his lips. Wanting to snatch them away, I was ever so grateful the gloves kept him from touching my skin.

"Come. Let us head home." He clapped Gideon on the shoulder and then returned to his horse. After we'd remounted, the king requested Gideon ride alongside him. I was relegated to a position behind Valere, which suited me fine, and Zahra joined me with General Bellamy and Sir Lance on either side of us. The wariness on Zahra's face mirrored my own feelings.

Ian and Kendal followed with Gideon's guards, and behind them came Leath with his personal entourage. They all chatted as if on holiday.

"How far to the palace?" I asked General Bellamy.

"Two hours after we cross the bridge" came his quiet reply. "The king has likely sent runners ahead to announce our coming. The servants will have a fine meal waiting for you in your rooms, if I know our king."

I wished I could question Bellamy, but he seemed to forget me, intent instead on my prince's conversation with King Olivier.

The king's army led the way, a sea of horses and armor and flags held high as we jogged our way to the shores of the Varigo River. I managed to relax after a time and allowed myself to appreciate the magnificence of the riverscape that greeted us. The Varigo was so wide it was hard to see the opposite shore and so blue it seemed made of liquid sky. An amazing suspension bridge spanned it, but the beauty was diminished by the tide of Mallorian warriors that streamed over it, taking a northward road that supposedly led to the palace.

The bridge was narrower than the road we followed, and we had to form smaller groups to cross it. Gideon purposely dropped back to join me, and I stopped breathing when his gaze caught mine.

"Mind Pair?" I asked.

He nodded.

"What's wrong?"

"My parhelia of truth burns inside me," he began with what felt like dread. *"I fear something terrible happened after I left Malloria. There's a malevolence here, an evil presence. It's like we've…stepped into a spider's web."*

I felt the emotions roiling in his thoughts as he added, *"I feel an even worse malevolence in the king."*

"What do you mean?"

He paused, as if afraid to say it out loud. *"Theona, the man you just met looks like my father, but I believe he's an imposter, a fraud. That man is not my father."*

I thought I would fall off my horse. This was worse than anything I could have imagined.

"But, if that's true, then...."

"What's happened to my father?" His gaze was filled with anguish. *"I'm not sure I want to know the answer."*

I took a dozen deep breaths to steady my nerves. Crown Prince Gideon Seville had never lied to me, and if he believed this then it was likely true.

"We need to find out," I said at last. *"If he's held captive somewhere, we need to find and free him."*

"A million scenarios of a king dethroned by a near-perfect look-alike do not have fairy tale endings."

He feared his father was already dead. It was all I could do not to break into tears. Then the Voice whispered in my ear and dizziness had me hanging onto Caspian's mane to stay in my saddle.

"Save them," it hissed.

"Who?" I asked.

"Set the prisoners free."

Panic hit. *"What prisoners?"*

"Loook...." The Voice drifted away. In the deepest part of my mind, I saw the rustling of dragon wings.

"Theona?" Gideon reached out and clutched my arm. "You look pale."

"I've—I've just heard...."

"What?"

I Mind-Paired my answer, and he replied, *"Prisoners? I'll visit the dungeon immediately."*

"No," I insisted. *"You're in deadly danger. Charlatans guard their secrets well. Let me go. Tell me where, and I'll make my way when it's safe."*

"After we arrive and we're all safe."

When we stepped off the bridge, the king waited for us, trapping me between himself and Gideon. Guards closed in around us, pushing Zahra, Bellamy and Arnoe far behind us.

"Eager to show your bride the beauty of Malloria's palace?" King Olivier asked.

"Yes, Your Majesty," the prince said with appropriate respect. He smiled at me, a forced smile in my eyes but not so the world would know. "My glorious diamond will sparkle inside it."

King Olivier gave me a hard look that made my legs shake. "That she is, my son." But that look hardened more as he met Gideon's gaze. "But she's also dangerous. She opened The Keeper. As you requested, we must free her of the sorcerers' possession, no matter the cost."

Terror in all its purity engulfed me. His message seemed clear. King Olivier planned to exorcise my demons, even if he had to kill me to do it.

He jogged off, our escorts forcing us along in his wake.

Gideon Paired, *"Get out of here, Theona. The moment you see an opportunity, you fly off and stay safe. I'll deal with—"*

"No. Remember the visions we had of fighting together, and the Elds' warning that we'll fail if we don't."

He gave a soft sigh. *"Then may Elam strengthen us for what is to come."*

"He will, Gideon. I believe it. He will give us everything we need to fulfill our quest. Perhaps if we walk carefully, go along with the king, we can get the measure of things at the palace and figure out what to do."

He thought long and hard, and then nodded. *"You're right. Exorcising you is exactly what we want and cooperating with him will get us more than fighting him."*

I nodded my agreement but didn't tell Gideon everything that I'd gathered from that brief eye contact with his father. Exorcising evil spirits was only a part of his plan. By whatever means, King Olivier knew everything he needed to know about me, perhaps even the strength of my magic, and he knew exactly how to destroy me.

I would enlighten Gideon later, but for now I summoned my courage and straightened my spine, vowing to Elam that I wouldn't let the man do it without a fight.

Writings preserved along with the Historical Records of Princess Theona McArthur Seville

I am five-hundred-sixteen-years-old, but I don't look a day over twenty-two. I was a prisoner of my own country, but I could have escaped at any time. I have dreams for the future but fear nightmares could destroy me first. I am the princess of a people I've never met and pray I will have the opportunity to meet them. I am a child. I am a woman. I am a sorceress.

I am a dragon.

I made a horrible mistake, and now I pay the price. I hunger for the power of magic even while I despise the day I discovered I could wield it. Angels have visited me, but I am forced to walk dangerous roads with devils.

War lies in wait for my people and my beloved prince. I did not cause it, but I may be able to help stop it if I can find the answers I need in time. In the distance, I hear an odd limerick that reminds me I am but a cinch pin in a monstrous machine of destiny. Duty calls, and I prepare to answer. I will go to my death protecting those I love, but I cannot help wondering if the ultimate sacrifice may not be my own life but those of the very ones I fight to protect.

I am a dragon. I am a sorceress. I am a woman. I am a child. I am only sixteen years old. How did all of this happen? How will it all end?

ABOUT THE AUTHOR

Susan Tietjen was born and raised a Southern California girl but is grateful to have lived on the Oregon coast and in the Rocky Mountains of northern Utah. She's now enjoying living with her husband in the incomparable beauty of the Redwood Forest, nestled against the rugged coast of Northern California.

She's raised a tribe of children, making ends meet as a registered nurse and lactation consultant, and is delighted that her tribe members now have tribes of their own. She loves to travel to see the grandchildren or the world and is thrilled with a good movie or a great book, but writing is her passion. She swears she has more stories inside her than she'll live to tell. *Dragon's Inferno* is the second book in the Dragon Unchained Trilogy. She hopes you'll enjoy it.

You can find Susan's other books on Amazon. Just type in her name. Have a question? Contact her at stietjen.author@gmail.com and take a peek at her website: https://susantietjen.blogspot.com. Want to leave a review? Please do so at your favorite retailer and/or Goodreads.

BOOKS BY SUSAN, AVAILABLE ON AMAZON:

The first in the Dragon Unchained trilogy. An epic fantasy unlike any other. Magic that will leave you breathless. A romance that will touch your heart.

Dragon Unchained

The long-awaited sequel to *Dragon Unchained, Dragon's Inferno,* propels Theona and Gideon across a continent and into deeper, darker mysteries and even greater danger.

Dragons' Inferno

A historical romance that will sweep you away into the hidden perils of Regency England and an arranged marriage that neither of them want.

Saving Lord Whitton's Daughter

One clumsy girl, a young man's betrayal, and what it takes to mend broken fences.

Grace Without Grace Stumbling into Romance